The Requiem Shark

The Requiem Shark

Nicholas Griffin

W F HOWES LTD

This large print edition published in 2002 by
W F Howes Ltd
Units 6/7, Victoria Mills, Fowke Street
Rothley, Leicester LE7 7PJ

1 3 5 7 9 10 8 6 4 2

First published by Little, Brown and Company
in 1999

A CIP catalogue record for this book is available
from the British Library

ISBN 1 84197 548 6

Typeset by Palimpsest Book Production Limited,
Polmont, Stirlingshire
Printed and bound in Great Britain
by Antony Rowe Ltd, Chippenham, Wilts.

To my family

CHAPTER 1

November 1719 – Coast of Guinea, West Africa

Williams refolded his journal and pushed it deep within his coat pocket. He wore no shirt, and as he laid his head back against the deck, his belly rose to keep watch while he rested. It was an empty night, with neither wind nor stars. The ocean, solid as a sea-chest, ran level from the *Success* to meet the shores of Guinea, three leagues distant. Listening to the treacly drippings of tar falling from the shrouds, he thought only of the surfeit of African heat. Even the mutterings of the slaves shackled tight in pairs could not distract Williams. He ignored the dialects of the different tribes assembled beneath as they gathered in chants and faded in murmurs like pleading breezes tugging them shoreward. Williams's eyes fluttered with sleep until his jellied middle shivered from a sharp kick.

He sat upright.

'Twice now,' said the bosun, 'you've shunned your watch.'

'What,' asked Williams, 'is the point of holding

1

watch in calm seas and a black night where I cannot see a foot before my face?'

'Below with you,' answered the bosun. 'Captain shall hear.'

Williams hoisted himself to his feet, retied the rope belt about his ducks and, ignoring his bosun, headed below to the fo'c'sle. The captain had forgiven him before, taken him aside, thanked him for his fine efforts pursing for the ship and then threatened him with a whipping should he fail at his duties again. Both men knew that Williams was not a sailor, that he had been seized and pressed into service near Plymouth. Yet Williams understood the captain's leaning. A slaver does not carry passengers, and though he might purse the ship and entertain the crew with a fiddle, there were no kind words for poor sailors. Few on board did more than nod in his direction. Even the cabin boy, Phineas Bunch, a pock-faced child from Clerkenwell, reserved the worst of his words for Williams. His heaviness, youth and education were marks against him and he knew that he dwelled in a liminal land between crew, slaves and captain. Williams was valued only by himself.

As always, Williams breathed through his mouth for his first minutes in the fo'c'sle. The stink of the unwashed crew and the heavy smell of bodies seemed to have been absorbed by the planking. Even the timbers of the ship sweated in the heat, reeking of the bilge water below that gurgled and frothed in the gentlest of swells. Williams rolled his heavy frame into his canvas hammock, and though he would not be able to confide in his journal until light, he composed tomorrow's entry in his head:

The captain remains upriver for the fourth day, disappeared with his cask of silks and India wipes, and shall return with negroes. Enough, I hope, so that we may sail again. What could I do, but resign myself to this journey, pretend it a chosen adventure, when Africa lay before me? I am now within sight of her, can smell the coast, and yet no liberty is granted to those who were pressed aboard. They fear I might run, but where to? There is much I would run from, not officers, but the crew. Not the bosun, but the boys, such as Bunch. They are shameless, pushing laughter on me when most would let me be. I have five years on them, though you might suppose it reversed. They have sailed before. It is all that counts aboard the Success.

Williams opened his eyes in the gloom of the fo'c'sle and stared. The middle watch was above, just four men, yet the padding of many feet sounded through the planking. He pushed himself upright. Across from him he could see Bunch, Smith and Wallis sitting in similar positions, all staring upward, their eyes tracing the sound of the steps.

'We're boarded,' hissed Wallis.

The sharp crack of metals meeting rang once.

Then many voices erupted. Williams could only distinguish the tones of his bosun, speaking loudly, calling for calm. He wrestled out of his canvas hammock and stood upright.

'Stay,' ordered Wallis in a whisper.

Ignoring his fellow deckhand, Williams wrapped his journal in oil skins and slid it within his coat, then left the fo'c'sle with no greater defense than gritted fists and headed for the weather deck. He heard the voices grow louder, but his frayed mind could not figure them apart as they rose together like garbled thunder. Putting one foot ahead of another, blood pounding and sweat greasing his palms, he climbed toward the night, only to be relieved of consciousness by the blow of a marlinespike to his head. It sent him backwards, his hands losing their grip, his body banging and turning against wooden struts, falling back to the gun deck.

From the hold, slaves were shouting upwards in Babel tongues for attention, not knowing who stood above them, buoyed by the hope that they were to be raised and returned to the coast. A pair of lanterns fought to light the weather deck, but their auras were weak and shadowed both the crew and the uninvited. Williams brought his hand to his egg-shell head and was relieved to find no blood, nor indentation. He felt the rain spit in his eyes, sat upright and opened them to the sight of his own crew facing him. Their faces betrayed shock, as if they were witnessing a resurrection.

4

His smile at their confoundment was short lived. Looking to his left and right, he saw the dead: one on either side of him, their stomachs down, toes against the deck, palms open, upturned, unmoving. Williams could not keep his eyes from them, trying to figure if they were his shipmates. Their stillness awed him. He studied them, expecting a shimmer of movement to betray them, like actors rising from their roles upon a stage. Through his throbbing head, Williams could hear his bosun calling him. Slowly, he crawled away from the dead.

The men of the *Success* were kept upon their deck throughout the night, save for their bosun who was ferried in his own gig into the darkness, along with the pittance of gold dust their captain had trusted to his ship. The wind gathered and pushed a heavy rain from the clouds above. It came at the huddled crew, so that they bowed their heads and closed their eyes, soaking them into shivers. None were permitted to speak and the night was endured in silence.

Williams cradled his head in his hands. All who looked upon him presumed that his skull must be sharp and swollen with pain. Yet he did not think of his fall, only of the taking of the *Success*. He could not answer the questions he asked himself. The ship had not been taken on his watch, but had it been approached through his sleep? Might he have heard the creak of sweep in oarlock if he had stayed awake, and prevented the loss of goods and life?

Questions haunted him until dawn brought an end to the rain. A three-masted ship lay anchored to the east and in first light, the crew of the *Success* watched with relief as their bosun was returned to them. He was accompanied by a man so finely dressed that Williams believed he would not have been conspicuous in King George's Court. A suit of black silks, buckled shoes that bore the polish of another man's hand, a fine lawn shirt with a clean linen stock. Williams had not seen any so well rigged since he had left his father's house.

The bosun levelled a finger and pointed at the cabin boy, Phineas Bunch. Then it curled in for a moment, before extending itself in Williams's direction. He muttered quietly to the gentleman and was dismissed towards his own men with a shrug of a silken shoulder. The bosun gathered Bunch and Williams on either side of him. 'You are to go when you are called.'

'Why?' whispered Bunch

'Who is he?' enquired Williams, rubbing his head.

'Captain Roberts of the *Rover*,' said the bosun. 'He wishes a cabin boy and a music. The investors, captain and admiralty shall know you were forced. I wish you good fortune. If you are taken by His Majesty you shall not be hanged; boys and music are excused.'

'We are to be traded?' asked Williams incredulously.

'Given,' corrected the bosun.

The *Rover* and the *Success* sat together for the remainder of the day. Since both Bunch and Williams held their tongues, it occurred to no one that they seemed curiously accepting of their fate. He could not speak for the younger cabin boy, but Williams would have admitted relief at the thought of distancing himself from the *Success* and her bosun. Though Williams had decided he bore only a featherweight responsibility for the neglect of his watch, he knew that the captain of the *Success* would not share the levity of his assessment. He believed the bosun shared the thought and released him for the good of all.

At nightfall, echoes of drum and fife carried across to the *Success* as Bunch and Williams, with their pair of sea-chests, bobbed in the gig between the ships amid the ocean swells. Captain Roberts sat across from them. Beneath the tricorn hat, pricked by a peacock's feather, was a steady pair of eyes, buried brown and heavy lidded, rising from darkened skin. They were bolstered by wrinkles that unfurled upwards, etched wings. He was old for the sea, thought Williams, perhaps close to forty. Williams tried to match the Captain's stare but soon looked down.

'You,' spoke Roberts to Williams in his native tongue of Welsh, 'where did you learn your music?' The voice was lower than his own, none of his teenage wavering, but seemed to possess its own echo. Williams could not contain a smile to hear his own language spoke, and smiled

7

even wider when Bunch looked about him in confusion.

'By Caernarfon,' blurted the young man. 'My father was—'

'What do you know?' asked Roberts, returning to English.

'Flute, fiddle, horn and—'

'Show me your daddles.' Williams lifted his hands. 'Either your music is so fine that you're spared aloft, or *Success* is your first.'

'He's a poor hand,' interrupted Bunch.

'Quiet,' ordered Roberts sharply.

'My father—' said Williams. 'I wandered among a parcel of squawkers, then was crimped.'

'What else? Your name?'

'William Williams. I read—'

'Do you write?' asked Roberts.

'With a fine hand.'

'He can't stop it,' said Bunch. 'Bosun's going to whip him, can't hear the call when his hands in ink.'

'Enough,' barked Roberts, and they settled into silence as they approached the side of the *Rover*, the cacophony rising from above.

When the pair arrived on the *Rover* they discovered that the kegs of the *Success* had already been tapped and that the crew were spread in drunken disorder. Music was forthcoming from the quarterdeck: the banging of drums, the fiddle and the splutter of a reeling flautist. Williams stared hard at the scene. He had never seen any man other than an officer stretch upon the quarterdeck, and never would a man have approached it wearing anything save his Sundays. Roberts strode between his men, eyes weighing and surveying.

Amid calls Bunch and Williams staggered below to the fo'c'sle with their sea-chests. The quartermaster, Sympson, accompanied them. He was a thin man, scrawny in sunlight and lean in shade. His brow was marked by three firm lines of worry.

'Mr Sympson?' asked Williams in the fo'c'sle.

'Lord Sympson,' corrected the quartermaster.

'Are there many Lords on the *Rover*?' asked Williams, while Bunch stood by in silence.

'A few.'

'Any commoners?' enquired Williams.

'You two for a start,' said Sympson, with a smile notable for the manner in which all his teeth leaned towards his right ear, like trees bending in a gale. He waved them back on deck, so that they might celebrate their freedom with a cup.

A stranger approached the two recruits by the mizzen mast. He paused beside the sorry figure of the bloated Williams and pushed a finger into his gut.

'Who articled lard?' asked the man.

''Tis a Welsh fiddler, Lord Kennedy,' said Roberts from the quarterdeck. He tipped his tricorn before heading below.

'What use is a man like this?' called Kennedy after his captain had disappeared, pointing at

Williams as if he were a dumb beast. He spoke not six inches from Williams's face, so that the Welshman might have guessed his last three drinks. 'Fat puppies can break royals, slow down ships in the chase. Explain the shape.'

'I'm the size of Wales,' grinned Williams, taking a small step back.

'And half its size,' said Kennedy and pushed at his gut again. 'Now don't offend me, fiddler, but make my friend and play a tune.'

'What shall I play?'

'The fiddle, you gundiguts,' said Kennedy and Williams was doused in laughter. He wanted to break a joint for every rum-soaked chuckle. A cannikin came flying over from the main deck and caught him square on the chest. It was thought hilarious.

Williams was handed fiddle and bow and he began in the middle of a jig where the notes moved so fast that they were barely sounded before the fingers had leapt to another string and then to another, and so on until it seemed as if there were a brother echo who matched his moves. The pounding ache of his head was supplanted by anger. Laughter died under his fury and Roberts's crew, who had suffered under drums and horns and piccolos, were held silent for almost a minute by the dance of a bow and a set of cheap strings. And then, as suddenly as it had started, Williams's fiddle began to imitate a chanty and the chorus went up and drink was poured into his mouth, seeping over his instrument as he played. Every seaman relied on his hands, and hands relied on fingers, and for a man to play a fiddle like Williams it meant that he knew how to use both thumbs and eights, and the speed indicated that not one was broken. To most it meant that, besides the music, even if he wasn't a good seaman he had been a lucky one.

On the *Rover*, there were variations of light but no day or night, no correlation between sleep and darkness. Time was kept with the turning of sand within a glass on the half hour, and the accompaniment of a ringing bell. But when hammocks are strung as close as sheaves in a wheat field, and when gun ports are latched and the sun barred, and lanterns are the sole source of illumination, then gloom is permanent. Add a hold filled with more liquor than water, and a crew that doubled the ship's design, then wooziness overtakes alacrity. All were above, all drunk, some stupefied, leaving Roberts in peace to visit the fo'c'sle. He held a bull's-eye lantern ahead, taking little time to locate the sea-chests of the forced recruits.

Both locks were open. The contents of neither sea-chest surprised him. Bunch's, merely clothes for a youth bridging the years between child and man and a small pouch of silver coin. Williams's chest contained two books, a bottle of ink and an oilskin, within which a small wad of papers was tightly rolled. Roberts plucked an early page and held it before the lantern.

I have two brothers in the church, two in King George's pay and three dead sisters buried under our great oak at home. My father did not mourn our mother, but sent his children unto the world, dissolving his family with a sprinkle of gold. I was given a letter of introduction to a man of some note down Grub Street, fifty guineas, and was pointed east. I was content. I slept in a meadow near a village called Fulham, close on London, and woke with neither money, letter nor coat. To my surprise, I remained content. Did I not think of my brothers, you ask? Had you begged them for my description, they would have looked at one another till one spoke, saying, 'Why, William is the youngest.' And one would nod, and then all would nod like merry milch cows. You will call my disdain pride, but to me, tis a mingling of patience and fervour. Have not men gone before me? Have they not risen on adventure and merit? Do they not return from journeys, and shine all the greater for their change in fortune? It is an honest intent, I think, to wish to return and cite, 'Presume not that I am the thing I was.'

Roberts understood little; used only to the names of stars and seas, the study of books had escaped him. Instead, he stared at the shape of the words, the way they leaned and held their lines in a regimented fashion. Though he could not grasp a single phrase, he believed he had learned much of Williams. From the fact that he wrote, he deduced him a learned man. From the manner in which he had grasped his papers aboard the *Success*, Roberts knew the value the youth placed upon his own words. The order of the characters showed a precise and careful man. He folded the sheet along its well-worn crease and slid the papers back into the oilskin.

CHAPTER 2

At sunrise, Williams and Bunch were ordered from the fo'c'sle and handed the stinking rags of the crew to wash. They were given no soap, since there was little fresh water to be spared. Instead they were told to wash the rags in chamberlye, a bucketful of piss and a gallon of ocean, more alcohol than ammonia. The morning sky was bright even before the full rise of the sun, but the sea still pitched her grim swells against the *Rover*. By ten, all the clothes were as dry as if they had been placed in an oasthouse.

The new recruits were intrigued their first morning at sea. A crew that operated under a system as free as a ship could bear, seemed strangely effective under sail. There was a semblance of order, gatherings of foremastermen, younger men working in the topgallants, others weaving cordage on the main deck. The hierarchy of the Lords had melted on a day of sailing, strong winds and clear sky and one couldn't tell the quartermaster from a deckhand. The *Rover* was uncommonly fast – a Jamaican built sloop hewn of red cedar, with a steeply raked mast and a freeboard much lower than her rivals.

Though Bunch and Williams had no kind words for the other, indeed they had no words at all, they were content in each other's company amid the sea of strangers. Better to share a manageable dose of mutual dislike than to face the unknown. Sympson relieved them of their companionship by interrupting their idling and committing them to different watches. The captain had ordered for Williams to be sent below, to make his introductions to Doctor Scudamore, who he would serve as surgeon's mate, when the need arose.

There was no surgery, merely a surgeon's case and three blankets drawn about gun number twelve. Sitting within the cloth walls sat Scudamore, a man of dignified deportment, stiff-backed, full-stomached, head bright, balding and red from sun. Though he had the stature of a gentleman, the noble suggestion was undone by a too-ready smile that shook your hand and clapped your back yards ahead of meeting. On seeing Williams's dizzy nest of sanded hair and freckled skin poking between the blankets, Scudamore closed his book and stood.

He pulled the portly fiddler in and shook him by the hand. The action made a considerable impression on Williams, for he had had no contact with another for some months now and was tempted to see this simple act of politeness as an invitation to friendship.

'You are the Welshman?' inquired the Doctor.

'Aye,' said Williams, and looked down at the

15

book that Scudamore had closed. 'Vesalius?' he asked.

The Doctor pinched his nose between a pair of fingers, as if he might hone his vision for an intense and sanguine examination of the fiddler. Like his hands, long and thin, and thoroughly incongruous aboard ship, his eyes were so peculiarly sharp that it was as if he had been born for the profession of surgeon. They coordinated, not in the rough chanty rhythm of the sea haul, but in tiny, precise movements – the machinations of a delicate time-piece.

He looked at Williams's fleshy face, his sunken eyes and thick neck, and asked, 'And what do you know of Vesalius?'

'My father owns it,' said Williams, nodding his head to one side.

'Does he now?' inquired the Doctor. 'Your age?'

'Nineteen.'

'And are you familiar with the Latin tongue?'

'I am.'

'How curious,' said the Doctor, 'to have found you.'

'No stranger,' replied Williams, 'than to have found you.' He gave Scudamore a small bow.

'Sit,' ordered the Doctor, and though there was no chair, or ledge, Williams put his bulky body down against the side of the cannon.

'Were you forced,' asked Williams, 'the same as I?'

16

Scudamore shook his head. 'It matters not for surgeons or musics, we are not considered in league with piracy. It was, in my case, a voluntary commission.'

'You have been long at sea?'

Scudamore shook his head. 'I was on the *Bleacher* captured off the Verdes, she was my first.'

'You were surgeon?' persisted Williams.

'I was a passenger . . . and I took to surgeon's mate, after we lost the true to fevers. Mainly I pulled teeth and sheared the men.'

'You were a surgeon afore?'

'Well . . .' said Scudamore.

'Can you heal a man?'

'Oh no, sir,' said the doctor, unruffled by the constant questions. 'I rarely intend to heal a man. I ease anguish. Rub oil on burns. Meet the eyes of the dying. Close the eyes of the dead.' Scudamore ran a hand over the remnants of his hair. 'There is a great difference between the surgeon, the doctor and the physician, as it were. You might say I practiced at all three. I was persuaded from the profession, by a series of unfortunate accidents.'

Williams nodded.

'Are you a Lord, sir?' asked Williams.

Scudamore smiled. 'The Lords are elected. The crew chooses its officers and our course. Even the captain is only captain in the chase. His cabin is his from the crew's good will. Lords may take it back.'

'He looks like a captain.'

17

'He dresses like a captain,' corrected Scudamore. 'Almost as fresh as you.'

'Not so,' said Williams, 'ne'er seen an older man at sea.'

'Save myself?' smiled the surgeon. Williams grinned and nodded his head. 'There are older aboard. Aged Q must have ten years on the captain. By freshness, I did not mean age. I refer to experience. Our captain was but a mate aboard a slaver not two moons ago.'

'And your old captain?'

'Captain Davis was shot, Roberts elected in his place. I am, I regret to say, unfamiliar with the world of waters, but I have heard that he is uncommonly knowledgeable as to the . . . charts and other matters. Winds and waves and all that threatens to sink us. Was why he was taken in the first place.'

'He too was forced?'

'Indeed,' said Scudamore, 'one of the few.'

'Well then,' replied Williams, 'there is no shame in it. If Roberts may rise to captain, perhaps I shall rise to Lord.'

'Unlikely,' shrugged Scudamore. 'It is drunken governing, rule by whimsy and affection. You might be a fiddler, scholar, perhaps surgeon's mate, but you do not look a Lord nor a sailor.'

Williams nodded his head.

'There is little difference in the share,' continued the Doctor. 'Captain two shares, crew one, Lord's between.'

'And what need I do as a surgeon's mate?' asked Williams.

'On the *Rover*?' questioned Scudamore. 'Nothing. If we are engaged, I shall call for you. Otherwise, you may continue your duties as a member of your watch.' The doctor rose to his feet. 'Away with you now.'

Williams spent the next two days in a lazy state of fiddle-playing, making the acquaintance of his watch. Most regarded him with the usual suspicion that had dogged him aboard the *Success*. They had only to witness his attempt to stow a sail to know that he was raw to the trade. Hardy, the bosun, a broad-shouldered Cornishman, treated the entire watch alike. Williams was not singled out, as he had been aboard the *Success*, but nor did he speak back to Hardy, as did those whose tongues had been loosened by drink. It would take a rare amount of rum to answer a man like Hardy, thought Williams, with his grizzled week's growth upon his face, nose broken and flattened. His left ear was torn and roughly stitched, ripped by dog or man.

Of his watch, only Aged Q the oldest hand aboard the *Rover*, showed him any kindness. Through thirty years of sailing he had retained his good nature and, by the look of it, the same dirty louse bag that held his hair together at the back of his neck. His skin was puckered like a burned raisin. He did not act as Williams's sea daddy, but had patience with the fiddler, as if

19

a little learning might transform the Welshman into a more likely tar. They were sitting together two days later, picking oakum, when the cry of 'sail ho' brought the crew to the deck. It took the *Rover* a short day to gain on her prey's leaden performance. It was a large ship, three-masted and low in the water, which on seeing the black flag raised, yawed and made to run aground.

'*Juliette*,' cried Bunch, causing laughter to ripple through the gathered crew. Williams smiled, but turned to Aged Q and confessed his ignorance in a whisper.

The old hand shook his head. 'Do you not speak to another soul?'

Williams shrugged.

'Tis what we seek,' continued Aged Q. 'A Dutch prize, the *Juliette*. Tis Roberts as has seen her. She rounds 'tween Accra and the Americas. Now a ship like that would force the thickest of heads to leave our trade. She could turn every deckhand to a duke.'

'Where is she now?'

'She steers by the same stars, but alters her course every year, so great is the weight of her gold.'

Williams narrowed his eyes on the approaching sail and wondered at her riches.

'What kind of a ship is the *Juliette*?' asked the fiddler.

'As big as a fifth rate, but her hold is finely

caulked to take her heft. Tower above us, darken us in shadow with her jibs'I.'

Williams digested the image. He stared at his calloused heel, and picked a piece of dead skin, rolling it in his fingers. The *Rover* groaned beneath them, its timbers adjusting to a warming sea. Always contracting, subsiding, complaining and sighing to the ocean below. Williams looked beneath his feet. The sounds were still strange to him. The *Rover* was a much more garrulous ship than the *Success* had ever been.

Watching the pursuit and capture of the ship, Williams felt a vague queasiness that he associated with sympathy for their intended victims. His only true surprise was in the bloodlessness of the affair. Their prey was, after all, merely a store ship, stocked with grains and livestock. Roberts had even insisted on paying for his acquisitions, albeit with gold dust taken from the *Success*. Among the goods brought aboard the *Rover* were two large chests of French silks. While the majority of the crew were concentrating on dividing a large cask of beryl, Williams stood on the quarterdeck hoisting himself in and out of various garments. He pulled a pale lawn shirt over his head, then sought to cover it in a black frock coat lined with a silver boulevard of buttons, braid loops and galloon. It split loudly down his back. He cursed to himself, then heard laughter. Looking up, he saw Sympson, the quartermaster, and Roberts facing him. Reddening to the accompaniment of their merriment, he removed the ruined garments and placed them back in the chest. Wearing only his ducks, his corpulent paunch lapping over his roped belt, he chose not to meet their eyes, but descended to the fo'c'sle.

Bunch, on his way on deck, passed by Williams in the tight confinement of the passage and asked him plainly, 'Mr Williams, did you not murder a baboon to steal his face?'

'Dear Mr Bunch,' said the fiddler from a wide smile of sarcasm, 'we are shipmates, and our watches will now keep us apart, so let us both praise God that we shall have no further cause to speak.'

Bunch nodded in agreement and they passed in their opposing directions. In the fo'c'sle, Williams opened his seachest, slung his hammock near the brightest of the lanterns, and with great difficulty arranged his bulk into a position to write.

It is a strange position I find myself in, and have Roberts to curse or thank for my discomfort. But did I believe that I might return home without pain? A man may change his ship but his character remains. Still there is a difference between the Success *and the* Rover *and it is the difference between melancholy and half a smile. As I have been told, a forced music retains his innocence, so it matters not which crew I play for.*

And yet, if we were to find the Juliette, *the music may profit the same as a deckhand. It is not the* gold itself that a ship might bring. But is it not a fine sight to think on? A ship that outshines the sun in gold? It is the fulfilment of character that such wealth might effect. The riches that allow a man to stretch into the life that he believes himself capable of. The Juliette seems no more solid than a vision, and yet it is made of cedar and pitch and canvas the same as any other. God grant us fair wind, full holds, the wealth of the unfortunate and stay the hands of men such as Kennedy.

Lord keep me from Kennedy, that stunted Irishman. He has no feet, just two pair of hands that let him crawl the rigging like a monkey. He drinks rum like beer, and beer like water, and he said he would rather be dead than drink water. Every cannikin of rum he consumed altered the shade of his countenance, from pink, to red, to scarlet, till at the end of the evening I believed I mistook him for another lantern.

If I have but one worry, it is that the oceans are too vast, too powerful to find fault with. Any blame, all blame can only be laid at the Captain's door. I am the Captain's recruit and it is the door that I sleep at. Still, the Rover sails well, a fine crew, save for the presence of our friend Bunch. I am sure there shall be others aboard, who do not take to an education better than their own, but I do regret the boy's presence, as he surely regrets mine. In some manner; I consider it reassuring to be despised for no reason. It can only stem from jealousy, or a lack of understanding. Or, in Mr Bunch's case, a

23

fierce combination of the two. But the Rover *is a village, where tongues wag between the decks, and I would not want my shipmates to hold the wisdom of Bunch against me. So, perhaps I am too quiet, too used to mine own company. But I have the ties of homeland that have brought me to the attention of Roberts. I conclude, it is not yet friendship, as perhaps it is with the doctor or Aged Q but neither is it the curse of family. I expect my own actions to determine my judgement among these men, and not the undeserved disdain that lies at home.*

When he had dried the last *e* with his breath, he wrapped the papers carefully in oil skin and returned them to his seachest.

The foredeck of the *Rover* quickly became an uneasy, filthy, and cacophonous blend of man and animal. Man, with the aid of fiddle and drum, was consistently the louder, but would retire to the heads to empty his bowels. The animals had a more uncertain aim, which brought ceaseless joy to Bunch and Coffin, the cabin boys, who moulded the piles of shit into dirty snowballs, moistened them with seawater and dropped them from the gear.

Williams slept only fitfully over the days of drunkeness. He was inclined to drink in the same manner as his fellows, but one or other would always withhold the final cup that would bring the relief of inaction. Though the crew was always anxious for a song, Williams was not accepted into any enclaves. He was long accustomed to solitude among company, and survived on the conversation of Aged Q the Doctor and the odd nod of recognition from Roberts. On the *Success*, Williams had been granted Sundays to himself, and would never consider raising his fiddle, but now all days were the same.

Williams watched as his Captain worked the quadrant and scratched the figures of observation on the rail with a knuckle-length piece of chalk. Roberts hauled and counted the knot line, using left thumb and elbow as crooks, and wound the wet rope in a tight and well managed coil. He was stripped to the waist, a solid frame, with thick dark rattlesnakes of hair on his forearms and chest. The white reeds of forgotten scars knit his back, and a tattooed cross of India ink followed the undulations of the spine. There was always a quiet deliberation about the captain, thought Williams. Perhaps even a reined-in arrogance and a self-reliance that seemed to suggest that the Lords and the Commons were extraneous, or at best, expendable.

CHAPTER 3

Williams did not know their destination, for the vote had been conducted before his arrival. Yet he was as relieved as any man to set foot on sand, to have at least the vaguest taste of a land apart from those he knew. At Annabon, two hundred miles from the African coast of Cape Lopez, their stay was brief. They traded for meats, keeping six cows in the longboat, and staying long enough so the carpenter could knock together a coop on deck for the chickens. Unearthing a rat-eaten sail from the hold, they laid it upon the beach, like a picnic cloth for the peerage. The cow was led to the centre of the canvas and Hardy, wielding the native machete with both hands, brought it down across the neck of the beast. The cow wobbled, the front legs buckled and the beast collapsed to the sand.

Roberts and the quartermaster, Sympson, joined in the stripping of the beef. Both had done similar work before. Decapitate the carcass, remove the entrails, carve the strips of flesh from the beast, rub them in salt and leave them to dry in between clean cloth in the sun.

26

'Look in its peepers,' spat Kennedy. ''Tis like nigger eyes. Big, dark and dumb.'

'N'really,' said Williams, carving a strip of flesh from the haunch of the cow. 'Not like a nigger at all. Nigger eyes have thoughts inside 'em. Now a cow, a cow is called *vache* in French, and in Spain it's known as a *vaca*, and it's reminding me of the English *vacuous*. Meaning that what's inside a cow is naught, no intelligence to speak of, no understanding.'

Kennedy stared at him, unprepared for a personal interpretation of etymology. 'Are you sayin' that I'm as thick-headed as a negress cow?'

Williams looked over his shoulder at Kennedy as he walked towards the ocean to wash himself of the blood. 'Not at all, Lord Kennedy,' he shouted. 'I was comparing a cow to a blackamoor, same as you were, and reached a conclusion that was other than yours.'

'You watch it boy,' said Kennedy, ''clusions or none.'

'Stop your brayin',' said Sympson, who then began to irritate Kennedy with other knowledge that he did not have, talk of how they would divide the cow by hocks and shanks, withers and chines, briskets and dewlaps and other particulars that might escape the notice of a seafaring man.

When Aged Q arrived to relieve the Captain, Roberts walked a few yards and pounded the sand into a slight bank as a rough support for his neck. He lay prone on the beach with a wet strip of canvas draped over his smiling eyes. They were creased with the pleasure of Kennedy's newfound silence. Not that Roberts was proud of his own learning; it was why he regarded Williams so highly. He respected a man who could converse in other tongues and hold forth on paper.

In Barbados he had seen a slave's skin reduced to flaps of lady's lace for practising words upon a dirt floor. Niggers, explained the overseer, believed that there was magic in ink and paper, in the bills that were passed only between white men, bills that could move a nigger, sell a nigger, kill and bury a nigger. They thought that a man who might learn the secrets of these letters might transcend the bonds of slavery. It had made Roberts consider his place in the world. Worse than that, he believed he could now see how he was viewed by those about him. He knew the negroes to be right. There were bonds and shackles throughout his world. Slaves were bound by iron, his chains were obscure. Perhaps, he thought, sitting under his sail cloth, cold under the damp canvas, that was where the seeds of his conversion were planted.

Where was the future for a limited man, who left schooling before the end of his eleventh year, who was a thirty-eight-year-old mate, and could not hope for a ship of his own? He had tried to improve himself, had learned navigation and the name of stars by rote, but never had a captain or an officer encouraged him to learn more. A man who was not born a gentleman had no word to give. Men like Williams could pick up a book and see another man's life, absorb in hours what had taken a lifetime to learn. While this reflection may have caused bitterness as a mate, as a captain it was merely a question of delegation. If a man could write but had little time on his hands – say a general, a king – would he not have a man who could read and write *on his behalf*?

Bunch, along with his fellow cabin boy Michael Coffin, had planted four stakes deep in the soft sand of the beach and, taking lanyards, had bound torches to the heads of the posts. The men gathered in between the flames, and divided into their customary groups, hushing at their captain's voice. Roberts talked of the *Juliette*. Of her beauty and wealth, making her seem so pregnant with gold that she might be spied at a hundred miles and caught in a day. The murmurs of those who had not heard of her were soon converted by the mutters of those who thought they had. Roberts spun the dream about them, weaved it in silver threads so that each could feel silk between their fingers, their own land beneath their feet. The *Juliette* was transformed by graceful speech into a floating purse that sent bursts of gold that would sink to the ocean's floor, should the *Rover* not intervene.

Their vote was still new to many of the men. The lands from which they came, the ships from which they had been taken, were hierarchical. On nights such as this, they could, for a moment, believe that the choice of a cabin boy weighed the same

29

as the captain's. Even the differences between the mock Lords and Commons were forgotten as the men moved at once to deposit their pebbles in the sand. To a man, they elected to follow the arc of the *Juliette* as she sailed westward.

The next morning there was a great optimism about the crew. Kennedy leaped from the arm of the main yard, arching his squat body into a graceful line, and dived into the water, under the hull and up again the other side. He rose smiling, pleased with the number of eyes that had followed his path, and confirmed that the *Rover*'s hull and keel were smooth enough for the ocean's crossing, and then added his opinion that they should run before the wind as soon as possible.

Sails were set and dampened with salt water to catch the wind, and men vied for the right to go aloft to set them. The *Rover* was not a large ship and could have been manned in comfort by less than twenty. There being sixty-two all told, enthusiasm was not something that Roberts actively encouraged on as fine a sailing day as this. Those who did not crawl aloft set themselves around the capstan and put up a fine cry as the anchor was weighed.

To their delight, to their dishonest surprise, three days out of Annabon they fell in with the *Experiment*, sailing out of Plymouth for Sierra Leone. She was a lightly armed vessel and struck as soon as the plain black flag of piracy was raised.

The first man to spy the sail, the Master Gunner, Wilson's honour on this day, was rewarded with the finest pair of pistols aboard.

Thirty-five volunteers were marched past Roberts. All of them boarded the *Rover* with admirable ease, despite the rise and fall of the pinnace against the ship's side.

'Village recruitment,' he said to Hardy, 'you whip 'em?'

'Nary said a word,' spoke the large man. 'They came at me, and asked a chance to prove 'emselves.'

'And the captain?' asked Roberts.

'Don't see him worse than others. Five faithful to him.'

'He keeps his ship. See how far he sails.'

The surgeon was climbing back aboard the *Rover*, instructing two from the *Experiment* to be careful with her medicine chest.

'The surgeon is pleased?' called Roberts.

'The surgeon has rarely seen a chest so stocked,' Scudamore answered.

'Did you leave her surgeon with a thing?'

'A bruise, my captain, for trying to cache the tincture of iodine,' said Scudamore, stepping on to the deck, 'but no blood today. I think we can agree that peaceful gain is preferable to unpaid pain?'

Roberts nodded in deference to Scudamore.

The spirit of the ship remained relaxed despite the presence of the thirty-five extra hands to feed. Roberts, confident behind a sure and steady wind, strode the deck under clear skies, assured that his hourly reckonings were accurate and that their course had been kept. Cliques were formed after the influx from the *Experiment*. Many of the new arrivals had been kept at arm's length for their first week on the *Rover*. They were treated equally, that is to say they were given fair measures of their own vittles and beer, but a little distance was maintained, to let them know that they had joined a crew of brisk hands who would not bear fools lightly. Kennedy was the first to cross the line, and could be found reaching out to the Experiments when all else held back, telling them tales of looting and murder and proving what a likely lad he was. Williams noted with great disdain the strict attention paid by Bunch to the Irishman's enclave.

CHAPTER 4

A ship sailing before a fair wind is like a saddled horse set at a gallop; she will run happily and smoothly by herself and will not call for reining. There are crossings whose logs reveal not a single sail reefed or doused in a month of sailing, and as the *Rover* continued west across the Atlantic, it looked to be such a crossing. In heavy seas, or shifting winds, work for a full crew might be found. Ideal conditions left many idle hands. On a merchant ship, a captain might tack unnecessarily or busy his hands with the tedium of picking oakum, or shining metals polished by the previous watch, but life aboard the *Rover* was relaxed when the sea was in a similar mind. The greatest problem was one of space, and Roberts was relieved that fair weather ruled, and that the crew were not forced below decks.

The fo'c'sle was slung with canvas hammocks and, if a man were to stretch to the left or the right, he would be close enough to scratch another fellow's head. In fine weather and calm seas the hatches would be opened, but even the ordinary swells of the Atlantic were too great. The fo'c'sle, positioned directly under the bowsprit, would be the first part of the ship to break through the oncoming waves, so hatches would remain closed, for a seaman rising from his watch would always prefer dry clothes to light. Instead, dull lanterns were hung from centre beams, casting pale light over sleeping men, and illuminating sea-chests stowed beneath them.

Within a fortnight, the stink of unwashed bodies began to take hold of the fo'c'sle. Williams had slung his hammock fore, close to the bowsprit, but the caulking of the bow must have loosened, for there was a slow and slight leak. Only Williams noticed. The water gathered on his stays and seeped down the twine and sat in the sack of his canvas swing. Once an article in the fo'c'sle was wet, it stayed wet. If it had been a scud-soaked shirt then Williams would have brought it at eight bells to the cook and had him find room for it in the galley. Though his watch would bring their hammocks to the deck, they were rolled tight above the pinrail, and only the fairest of winds and strongest of suns would every dry such tightly bound cloth.

It was deep in the night and a restless Williams took his pipe and passed by the galley to ask the cook for a light. Like many ships' cooks, the *Rover*'s was a disabled seaman, without the knowledge to carry him to further than the galley. He had only a thumb and a forefinger on his left hand, and was known as Pinch – the only culinary measure that

34

he could take. The rest of his fingers had been left off the Island of Nevis, carried away by a Spanish cannonball. He had received a hundred moidores for his loss, and gained the unexpected ability of being able to place the injured hand in a pot of boiling water without flinching.

Pinch snapped his left hand around the stem of Williams's pipe and, holding an ember to the tobacco, drew the first breath of the pipe.

'What kind of smoke is this?' he asked.

'A span of Orinoco off the *Experiment*,' said the young Welshman.

'Thought so much. Had to be English ship. Virginia smoke.'

'Hand it me then,' said Williams.

'One more,' said Pinch and sucked hard enough to drag the bowl down the stem. He palmed it back. 'Same as Bart's smoking tonight,' said the cook, exhaling.

'He not abed, either?'

'Never abed that one, like meself. On top, talking with Lords. None of you leek-eaters catch doze do you?'

'Fiddler's like a captain like a cook, always someone callin' for your service,' smiled Williams as he left the galley.

The wind was still favourable, and such was sailing as Williams had never seen. He looked up, sails turned to a cream in the kindness of moonlight, and saw three silhouettes astride the main yard. The *Rover* swayed gracefully over the waters, seeming a slight and dainty vessel under so much canvas, as if she might take off from the top of a wave, and fly for a fathom like a winged fish. There is magic to the sea, thought Williams, standing alone. A sharp wind stirred the belly of his pipe, then beat against the jib and topsails, ship timbers creaking with pleasure. Stars to where ocean and sky met all placed in the firmament, sailor's friends. It was as close to home as the deep sea would let him be.

Roberts was walking softly down the larboard side, picking his way through sleeping bodies, passing the longboats, hearing the heavy bovine breaths and the scratchings of chickens against their cage. He too had a pipe in hand, and turned to greet his countryman as he neared.

'Still in luck,' said Roberts, pointing his pipe outward towards the serene horizon.

Williams sucked on the stem. 'No finer night.'

'Too many men,' breathed Roberts quietly. 'Nary enow to keep 'em busy.'

'Don't think there are any so hard to this business as don't appreciate rest.'

'Ship gets smaller on the ocean. E'ry day. Lest she moves like this.'

'Then save your worries, Captain.'

'You're learning boy.' Williams could see him smiling in the dark. 'Tell me something, Williams. I need your vardy.'

Williams let his pipe rest by his side. He had yet to be asked an opinion, save to vote, since being

36

at sea. He was the rawest, pink and unproven to the rest.

'Would you consider yourself a reading man?' asked Roberts.

'A reading man?' replied Williams, surprised. 'I had learnin', I told you before.'

'And you write?'

'I've a good hand. What do you ask for?'

'I've a thought that might do good for two. Walk with me.'

Both Michael Coffin and Phineas Bunch had curled themselves into balls outside the captain's cabin. Cabin boys are like dogs, thought Roberts, better for the conscience to keep a pair over one. But two were a gang, and a mischievous pair at that, loosening the ties of a man's hammock, gathering dung from the animals and pushing it into the legs of empty ducks. They seemed to return naturally to his doorway, as if the shade of uncertain authority might ward off any repercussions. Williams and Roberts stepped over the sleeping boys, shutting the door softly behind them.

'I have Madeira if you want a pull,' suggested the captain.

'You wouldn't join me if I did?'

'I would not.'

'Then I'll drink what you do.'

'Very well,' said Roberts, and poured two cups of a brackish liquid from a kettle that sat on top of the desk. Williams gulped and spat the mouthful back into the cup.

'Cold tea,' explained Roberts to the fiddler. 'Think tis what keeps me from rest.'

'Are you sure tis safe?'

'Sure enow, Pinch boiled it 'fore the middle watch.'

'Why don't you take a stronger pull?'

'Must keep myself to myself. Not safe for all to drink.'

'With respect, Captain. I don't believe you. Did you ever drink?'

Roberts smiled. 'You've sharpness Williams. Try and keep it to yourself, sooner than not someone'll cuff you rather than return banter.'

'Ceased drinkin' for a woman?'

'Mr Williams, I am not some forlorn fellow as went to sea to stitch a breaking heart. I were aboard same age as boys at door. Ne'er seen a girl more than a month.'

'Then tell me,' insisted the fiddler.

'It was a promise.'

'Between?'

'The Lord and me.'

Williams threw his eyes up in disbelief. 'I spent the mornings of eight years in my father's church, and God ne'er stepped 'tween me and bottle. Even the Good Lord drank at Cana.'

Roberts laughed at him. 'Not so long ago, I suppose seven years, I was anchored in a square rigger, few cables out of Lucea, in Jamaica. Was a three hundred tonner, and we were tradin' with a Bajan sloop. They got harbour walls in Lucea, low tide as tall as five men. Drunk as the Devil, going about my captain's business, toting pig iron over plankin', 'tween ship and shore. I stumble and fall, plunge into water not to deep, ten feet, twelve, but I hang on to iron, like riding an anchor, and don't let go till I hit sands. I float to the surface, natural, but I'm no fish like Kennedy. The plank I was treadin' followed me down i' th' water, but I'm trapped 'tween my ship and coral wall.'

'You shout?' asked Williams.

'I screamed like a birthing. But they'd fiddle and drum and singing and drunks. First land in two months' sailing, and the stars in the sky are disappearing o'er my head with e'ry grain in the glass.' He leaned in towards Williams, and crashed his hands palm against palm. 'It was a pair of hands that were going to clap me 'tween them. I look up and I say God save me, the ship is nudging me towards coral. Splash beside me, bit of a line, and I clutch it like I've cat's claws, and climb it even as they're hauling me in.'

Roberts swigged his tea, and ran his tongue over his top lip. 'You must ha' seen ere now,' he continued, 'you make light at sea. A man loses balance aloft and falls grabbing for a line and catches. Eyes on his business, maybe a fellow or two'll joke him on it, but means nothing to none but him. But I saw that ship coming softly at me with the tide and I could get no purchase on the coral wall, took skin off my hands, bloody as could be, and I made a promise as I could keep and I did.'

'I see.'

Roberts offered the bottle of liquor to the younger man.

'No, I'll stay drinking with you.'

'Press peepers,' he pushed some cloth-covered books at Williams.

Williams read the authors' names aloud, 'Dampier, Exquemelin, Ringrose.'

'You've read them before?'

'Dampier yes, the rest not as yet, but if you'd be so kind as to lend them to me then I'd gladly read them.'

'At your leisure.'

'That's kind, Captain. You've read them yourself?'

Roberts looked up at him, was flattered by the presumption behind the innocent words, and said, 'In part.'

Williams nodded.

'None of us on this ship have learning,' said the captain. 'None know how to write and none know how to think like them that does write. We feel something for ourselves but you, you see, you're the only one can translate it for others.'

'Pursers?'

'No pursers on the ship. No clerks, no customs men, no accountants, no sons of privilege, no men who could do anything else that'd keep 'em from the sea, except perhaps the surgeon. You're on the deep sea, boy, but these are the men who came to the end of land and were pushed to water.'

'So I'm an oddity? An exception?'

'Oh, I expect that you're as bad as the others, just greener for now, but the rest is deckhands and ordinary seamen, means that this ship can sail like no other, but none have your talents.'

'With all this learning I should understand what you're about, but I don't,' admitted Williams.

'I would like you to write for me. You see these books – how many of them would you guess are about?'

'Thousands, I expect. Editions too.'

'And they make money?'

'Undoubtedly.'

'It would be your money.'

'Captain Roberts?'

'You would keep an account of the *Rover*, of her travels, of her exploits, her crew, her captain. When the *Juliette* is taken, you will have an end to your tale, return to England, find yourself a printing house and drive yourself a deal.'

'If we do not find her?'

'I have only one desire,' said Roberts, 'so who is to keep me from it?'

'And what would my journal hold for you?'

'I would be a patron of the arts,' Roberts smiled, unclenching his hands in innocence. 'Come Williams, I would be like Dampier, or like Morgan in Exquemelin, dead but alive. I would live through you and after you, that's the rub.'

Williams sat back and laughed at him. 'You're taking me for a fool.'

'At first you keep the log, a line or so, as is usual, then you turn to your own writings, course there'd be days like this, where there'd be little for a man of learning to talk about.'

'And,' said Williams, smiling, 'this piece of work of mine would be read like a fairy tale or a letter to the crew each night?'

'Course not, 'tween you and me. None else would know.'

'And say that we did this, it would be an account of our villainy.'

Roberts nodded.

'Or,' considered Williams, 't'would be set in opposition to the common opinion. But if we're taken they'd try us by it, line by line, act by act, would be a confession as would hang every man aboard.'

'Mr Williams, you speak in many tongues, do you not?'

Williams shrugged uncomfortably as if it were an accusation. 'My tutor was a Spaniard. I have Latin and French as well.'

'English, Welsh,' added Roberts. 'If a man knows five, then what to a sixth?'

'I would write in code? Like runes, or hiero-glyphs, so as only we could understand?'

'As only you would understand. I will be captain,

I would trust your tongue. I am not asking for myth-making or tale-telling. You are keeping your own log, and you report plainly what it is you see. You would have my trust in that.'

'This seems strange to me, coming from a seafaring man.'

'Williams, if you were a seafarin' man I would not ask it of you, but you're a scholar, and a fiddler, long fore you're sailor or natty lad.'

The bell tolled from the weather deck, and Roberts rose to his feet.

'Read if you like.' The captain pointed at Davis's books that lined a varnished shelf over the desk, and then stepped out of his own cabin, closing the door softly behind him.

Williams pushed back the lid of the desk, unfolded maps on the table, and removed reams of documents from the shelves. Untying the black ribbons that bound them, he surveyed the lists of names, figures and verbiage in which they were decorated. He pulled a book from atop the burry – the second volume of Dampier's voyages – and turned its pages, stopping now and then to absorb the odd paragraph of hydrography. Within minutes he had replaced the books and pulled his own pages from his coat to add:

A rare state of luxury and loneliness. A room to myself. And why not? One turn of the glass ago my presence aboard was ephemeral. Now I am charged with branding one man's name in paper, and so perhaps may preserve my own. Neither he nor I are men of means, those who are granted a name, a date, a carving upon their tombs. Sailors, such as Roberts, might be wrapped in cloth and cast into the sea, but my words shall be a compromise, an epitaph that shall be read by hundreds – whether the body is lost or not. He the sailor, I the writer, and I am recognized for the very things that keep me apart from this crew. Erudition, perhaps a certain lack of seamanship. And yet it is Roberts who faces judgement, and all I am asked to do is what I ever wished to do – to scribble, scratch and darken my hands with ink. I cannot explain my sudden buoyancy and am overcome with joy, as if I wished to gamble and had been gifted another man's banknotes. If previously I had resigned myself to the mere obtainment of riches, I am now reawakened to the possibility of repute. Upon my return, I shall have my coach and six, and an authorship as well. Praise God in His wisdom and Roberts for his purity of sight. Let my journal be faithful to my eyes, and let the understanding of others slow before the pages, for what shall be written will be the truth, even should it condemn every name it contains.

CHAPTER 5

It was the twenty-third day out of Annabon, and Williams had kept busy playing fiddle, making reports for Roberts as to the state of the crew, and inventing a code simple enough that he may learn it quickly, reproduce it fast and teach it if necessary. Most of the Experiments were picking oakum, others were sewing sails and clothes and Wilson, the gunner, was cleaning the whites of his nails with his dirk. The surgeon was on the deck with a pair of shears from some abandoned hedgerow, offering to cut beards and hair. It was an easy time, backed by a steady south-westerly wind.

Williams was sitting alone on the steps to the quarterdeck, running through his system of codes in his mind. He separated the alphabet into two vertical lists of thirteen letters, the left column running from the letter *A* down to *M*, and alongside it the letters *N* to *Z*. Every letter now had a partner. *A* had *N*, *B* had *O* and so forth. His own name, according to the code, was now *Jvyyvnzf*.

He further complicated matters by opting to introduce a rota of language into his code. English, Welsh and Spanish were used in sequence, with the exception of Sunday, when he planned to rest his pen. In addition, he created two symbols, § and ڗ, which were intended as the red herrings of the code, symbols that were both striking and meaningless. He began to run the code through simple tests, seeing how quickly he could encode certain words, such as *the*, and *and*, in all of the languages. At first it seemed tiresome and dull, but even within his first half hour of practice his coded table began to engrain itself in his mind, and the letters found their pairings with increasing agility. Always short words, then phrases, until he could string three words together. 'And the men' – *Naq gur zra*. The wind that blew steadily in his ears blocked all other sounds of the ship and he began to admire the workings of his own mind.

Aged Q was crouched like a monkey ten feet ahead of Williams. He had removed his shirt and had spread it flat over the deck. Pounding the shirt with a belaying pin, he crushed the parasitic inhabitants of the calico cloth by the hundreds. Intent on his work, Aged Q was grinding the life from a mite when a knife fell to the deck. The old man looked up and grunted, raising Williams out of his alphabetic reverie. He in turn looked upwards.

Thirty heads turned in time to see two men, ninety feet above, poised in the quarters of the main topsail yard, one struggling to keep his balance. A flattened palm buffeted the sailor from his precarious position, sending him flailing downwards.

Paralysed from his loss of balance, he fell in silence, arms ahead to soften the blow, but they broke like match-heads not ten yards from Williams's perch, and his head followed at a similar pace, forced back against the neck until the shoulders hit the deck. He seemed to bounce once and stay there still.

'Does he breathe?' came the cry from above.

'Come down,' cried the quartermaster, Sympson from the deck.

'Does he breathe?' he repeated.

'No.'

'Ain't coming down,' he stated and refused to answer another question.

Hardy walked over the fallen body towards Kennedy and a group of Experiments.

'Yours?' he asked.

'Aye.'

'And him?' Hardy pointed skyward until all the heads nodded in agreement. The chief mate moved off at his own long-legged pace, heading to the quarterdeck to meet Roberts who had been summoned from below. Williams was called from the steps and talked at quietly, instructed to head aloft and persuade this man, called Larkin, down to the deck.

The fiddler, who had spent the better part of his initial voyage to the African coast avoiding going aloft, took a first ponderous step on the timberhead and then reached for the shroud. He climbed slowly, a golden-haired sloth that argued its way upwards towards Larkin, who was hanging nonchalantly from the footropes of the topgallants, reefknife in hand.

When Williams was better than halfway up the main top-gallant mast, Larkin called down to him. 'Stay put, y'shaver, or I'll have you down too.'

Nevertheless Williams tried taking a step up, but the *Rover* skirted from the crest of one wave and pitched directly into another. The shudder of the ship caused the young man to swing outwards, one hand gripping at wind for a moment before it shot back to the gear.

'Careful,' advised Larkin, swaying comfortably above.

'The captain wishes all hands on deck,' said Williams. His voice seemed shrill, even to his own ears. He looked at the tarred rig to which his hands were attached and wondered just what sort of weight they were built to withstand. It would be so easy to let yourself drop, to succumb to the wind and throw yourself outwards against your own fear.

'I ain't going down.'

'But the captain . . .'

'The captain'll have me lambed or buckl'd or hung from the arm.'

'I'm sure he won't,' said Williams, staring beneath his legs, one hundred-odd feet to the deck. He could see that no one had moved the body from where it had fallen. A rotting sheet of canvas had been unearthed in the fo'c'sle and tucked over and under the corpse. He returned his gaze to the seaman above.

'Green, aintcha?' smiled Larkin.

'Very . . . I'm not to come down without you, or else I'll take a beating,' improvised Williams. 'Mate said that he'd hand Kennedy the lash for me.'

'What Roberts say he'd do with me?' asked Larkin.

'It's no man-o'-war,' said Williams. 'He wishes an understanding of the matter. The "why" of the thing, that's all. Thinks that the crew might hold you as Jonah and that you're to take leave at our next port with thirty pieces. It's the last he wants to see of you.'

'Thieving bastard,' said Larkin.

Williams swung gently from the topgallant shrouds, beginning to acclimatize to the heights. The wind caught the curls of his hair and spiralled into his ears.

'Baker,' Larkin pointed to the deck, 'he thieved. Knew it before like, and we was friends but then he's thieved from *me*. Whoreson.'

'There you go,' sang Williams, 'the man was a thief and has an end to him, and now let's down with us.'

'You're sweet with Roberts, aren't ya?'

Williams stared upwards, considering the question a moment. 'Aye.'

'You'd call the man a friend?' repeated Larkin. 'So's you can vouch one word for another, and a promise of yours is as good as the captain's hand?'

'My word,' said Williams.

'Well,' said Larkin, and wrapped the lanyard of his reefknife over a stitched loop in his ducks. 'Let's get you down, lad.' Larkin scaled the underside of the rig and passed beneath Williams on the weather side.

'Left foot, right foot,' said Larkin. 'Trust your ratlines, and the hands know themselves. Keep peepers on hands.'

The pair descended at Williams's slower rate. The crew was supposedly concentrating on their work parties, whipping and tarring, splicing and painting, but all watched the duo's progress with one eye or two. Roberts was perched on the steps to his own quarterdeck, making no disguise of his interest in their descent.

Larkin left the shrouds at six feet and used the halyard to swing to the deck. Williams clambered awkwardly over the pinrail as if he would have been much happier with four hands.

Roberts rose and walked the five steps between him and the topsman.

'Captain,' said Larkin, 'as I's explaining to your fellow here . . .' He turned his head to indicate Williams, who was rearranging himself around the port side timberhead. 'I says . . .'

Larkin's nose split under the swing of the belaying pin. As his feet staggered backwards, he bent forwards, head meeting hands in mutual sympathy about three feet from the deck. Roberts's second blow was aimed for the back of Larkin's head, but the slumping topsman rocked forwards and exposed his thin neck to the swing of the pin. Either way, the blow brought him down to the deck. Roberts pushed one foot into the small of his back and reached for Larkin's arms, pulling them behind him, and then trussed his wrists together with a thin lanyard. The captain sweated the rope twice until he could see it bite the skin. Standing on each of Larkin's legs, he repeated the procedure with his ankles.

Holding himself upright for the moment, Roberts ran his forefinger across his brow and flicked the sweat to his side. He coughed and arched his back, then walked to the spoiled canvas and ripped it back, exposing the body. Taking another pair of lines from his pockets, he lashed the corpse's broken limbs together in an identical fashion to Larkin's bonds. Roberts grabbed the dead man by his bloody queue and dragged the body six feet towards Larkin, who was moaning through a mouthful of blood. The more incomprehensible the rambling, the more effort Larkin expended to be heard, and the louder the garbled cries became. He began to writhe like an upturned beetle.

'Hardy?' called Roberts, his hand pressed against the small of his back so that his elbows seemed like wing tips. The mate emerged from a cluster gathered on the bow of the ship, and walked to join the captain. They passed a thicker line around the bodies, ignoring both the bloody dribbles from the dead man's neck and the outpouring of whines from Larkin. Hardy used an anchor bend to attach the sections of chain to the bitter ends, and together they dragged their burden to the starboard side of the waist, and shunted the bodies overboard.

Roberts leaned out over the chainwales, watching the colour of flesh being absorbed by the darkness of the Atlantic. By the time the two men were four feet deep they were invisible to their captain. All resumed their tasks, save for Williams, who peered into the water. The entire incident had passed within five minutes and he had been mesmerized by the swiftness of the events, only now ruffled by his own usage.

CHAPTER 6

In the two days since Larkin's execution, Williams had neither visited the captain nor dipped his quill in the inkwell. Instead he had retreated to his fiddle, and sidled into the midst of the crew. Their progress across the Atlantic had continued at a satisfactory rate. Some days they were seen to average eight knots or more, and the sea miles that separated them from Brazil began to evaporate through the sustained energy of the wind. Even on a ship with unlimited alcohol rations and an excess of crew, a vague order was kept according to the watches. Without a watch a sailor would begin to feel apart from his ship. On a three-watch system, where a man might draw two four-hour spells every day, there were included two tricks at the helm where the *Rover* soothed and straightened the drunk, the low, the discontented.

The quarterdeck, according to the navies and the merchants of the world, was a place reserved for officers. Even on Roberts's ship, where boundaries had supposedly melted, there was a quiet continued respect for order and space. So as Williams shared the helm with Johnson, it was to his chagrin that he saw Bunch mount the steps and signal for his attention.

'The captain,' sneered the boy, 'requests your immediate company.' Williams could guess from the snide enjoyment with which Bunch had delivered his message that the captain was in a state to be reckoned with.

'South-south-east,' said Williams to Johnson.

'South-south-east,' repeated Johnson, and laid his hand upon the wheel.

Williams made to pull out his usual chair by the captain's map table.

'You will stand,' said Roberts, and he was a shade darker, or perhaps it was just the shadows cast by the pair of lanterns that were positioned either end of the table. 'Mr Williams, I have the wrinkle that you have been judging me.'

'No, sir.'

'Yes, sir,' said Roberts. 'Judging me, avoiding me, shirking duty. It has been three days since you have kept your journal. If you are so eager to bear witness against me, then why not commit the crime to paper?'

'That, Captain,' said Williams, 'is what I sought to avoid.'

Roberts stared at him, wishing more.

'If I were to write when I was in anger,' began Williams, 'then would I represent the truth? I thought it best to simmer, then cool.'

'Williams,' said the captain coldly, 'you remain

a scrub. And shall be for a time to come. If you judge me, then you are an arrogant mopus. You put yourself above me. You have only the scent of what a sailor is, and you *choose* to misunderstand.'

'Captain . . . I am not . . .'

'A landsman is judged at his final hour,' said Roberts. 'Tars are judged in tempest and in calm. A wave the size of ten men is magistrate and hangman. Understand that sailors aren't one with the living, nor with the dead. If the *Rover* was thrown against a reef, and ten men drown where one survives, is that not a judgement? Is it not?'

'Aye,' said Williams quietly.

'All you can wish for is a fine ship and a worthy captain. Tis little to hold to, so do not take your stakes for granted. Now, sit down.'

Williams pulled his chair out, deposited his weight and continued to listen.

'I will kill a man who kills a man on board my ship. If one man wishes be at cuffs with another, he will do so on land, not some sly boots shabbing in Brazil.' Roberts rose, and his tone of voice shifted, as if the necessities that he had prepared to impart had all been declared. 'I expect you'd have need of a drink.'

'Yes, sir,' said Williams.

Roberts gripped a crystal decanter of Madeira, and half filled a pewter tankard. Williams took a large swig, and then another, before resting his tankard on the table. For the first time since he had entered the cabin, his eyes rose to meet Roberts's.

'I did not mean to offend you in any way,' began Williams. 'I . . . I coaxed him down . . . but I did not know his fate.'

''Twas why you were sent aloft,' said Roberts. Williams nodded, bowing to the exploitation. 'You are different lad, you have learning. At times these men will regard you with more suspicion than you deserve and at times, they will see fit to trust you.'

'And that is when I am of most use to you,' said Williams, with an open smile.

'You are not a man with many skills useful to the position in which you find yourself, and yet I believed that we had carved you a moment in the day. You are not "of use" to me, William Williams, you are invaluable.'

Williams sipped at his wine, and was warmed by the praise. Without a family, without touch for the better part of a year, these last words shone, regardless of calculation and intent.

'In Caernarfon,' began Roberts, '. . . a scholar?'

Williams nodded quickly, as if he would spill reams of words in return for more praise. 'My tutor wore me down with foreign tongues, while my father,' he added, 'buried me under manuscripts and clergymen.'

'Tis a quiet life you've led, is it not?'

'Captain, I've almost twenty years but I learned much between church and sea. I travelled down Pembrokeshire, oldest among chits, buggers and dippers. Turned from towns till I was pressed west of Portsmouth, and I seen men done down, and I seen death afore, but I never seen dying . . . so close, to be exact. I will admit some surprise.'

Roberts grunted, and sipped at his cold tea.

'I think it right,' said the captain, 'for young men to have some fear.' He reached out for his pipe and began to clean it with a thin, frayed line of cotton.

'Hardy was telling me,' said Williams, with the smallest of smiles, 'that the closest a hand will ever get to heaven is furlin' a royal.'

Roberts shrugged and then grinned. 'Good man, Hardy, but only godly under a wave. Sailors are closer to God than the rest, special to him.'

'Closer to the Devil too, then,' reasoned Williams.

'To the scholar,' relented Roberts, banging cups with his countryman.

When Roberts removed himself from the cabin, with pipe in hand and without another word, it was obvious to Williams that he was not expected to rejoin Johnson on the helm. Below, Williams slept in the fo'c'sle with fifty others. He shared his mess with twenty-odd, and the heads, though shielded somewhat, usually provided a partner to shit with. Williams could hear steps on the quarterdeck above, the sound of metal against metal from the galley. He stood for a moment, curled his fingers against his palm, and stretched them outwards and breathed a moment of pure liberty. Then he sat, raised the quill, dipped it in the black bottled ink, and began to dryly note Larkin's execution, omitting his own involvement, into a page of coded Welsh. After which he concluded:

The captain wishes me to note him as the dispenser of justice. He thinks his actions make me afeard or stricken to my Christian soul. What am I fearful of? I fear the sea. I am nervous of great heights, of never returning home. I have disdain for the roughest of the crew, yet perhaps Roberts still believes me to be too much of what I was. I am at the age of change. I gather layers of skin, deep calluses of experience that were not there a sixmonth ago.

I am not of the crew, yet we are all in common. We all wish home, though few have one. We all wish gold, with which to make our home. I have not seen a horse in six months, and think peculiarly of their smell. I will have me a horse, an equipage with a dozen black horses when I return. For I have a home. I do not talk of father and brothers. I have a home of brick and mortar, and it holds my memories within. I shall reclaim it, purchase it outright and fill it with the stink of horses. For now I would settle for the sight of any country and postpone my reveries.

CHAPTER 7

March 1720 – The South American Coast and the Caribbean

The anticipation of land after weeks at sea was tangible. Well beyond the line, where only a handful of British warships patrolled thousands of square miles of sea, coastal shipping was no longer about the fear of the press but fantasy of liberty. And this was not to be liberty meted out by a worried captain, fearful of runners and skivers. Land revealed itself through draped clouds, modesty raising its veil. Those holding bow watch strained to see more. They stared and sniffed at the solid horizon. The sea doesn't smell at all. When landsmen smell the sea it is only the coast, where the ocean's dead are brought to rot, where tides expose mud, and where the cities spill their filth. Now came the shadow of land, her shores and inlets, her birds that swung above in a curious welcome and, finally, when her coast was naked to the eyes, came the canoes. The competing pilots questioned their destination, men hawking fish, selling fruit, all surrounding the ship.

The island of Fernando de Noronha, a verdant

outburst off the Brazilian coast, sat four degrees south of the equator: a twenty-three-hundred-mile journey from Annabon, achieved in the remarkable time of twenty-eight days. The north-east trades had held steady, as Roberts had expected, but he considered himself fortunate, as nature was unconcerned with the expectations of man. Indeed, Roberts believed that the rapidity at which they had split the North and South Atlantics was an excess of good fortune and, as a man who throws eyes at dice and confounds the crowd, he began to suspect that he was owed a dismal turn in luck.

The crew of the *Rover* could not have been in higher spirits, informed that the *Juliette* had shared their harbour only a month or two before. After their initial successes they were eager for more prey, and those who were recruited from the *Experiment* were hungry for an opportunity to impress their veteran comrades. They secured a Portuguese pilot, a man whose efforts increased greatly once shown the shine of gold, who led the pair of ships into a windless bay on the leeward side of the island. The *Rover* had fallen victim to the toredo worm since they had entered the warm waters of Brazil. Thousands studded the hull, growing strong and fleshy off the ship's wood, their heads buried in the planking. A careen was now essential if they were to maintain the speed with which they cut the water.

The pilot led them through a narrow inlet into a

cove that proved to be, after many repeated soundings from the tender, approximately eighteen feet deep, a mere five feet beneath the *Rover*'s draught. Entering the cove, they lowered the pinnace into the water to join the tender, and began to kedge their way across the last league to a narrow strip of white sand beach. The sun had reached the tip of the dial and, with the ship under bare poles, there was nowhere for a man to hide, save beneath decks, where the planks themselves had begun to sweat.

The hands who did not man the pinnace were peering out over the chainwales staring at the sandy bottom of the cove, straight through her crystal waters. Even Pinch had emerged from his galley, and balanced his hands on the taffrail, peering into the waters with a fisherman's eye. The first mate nodded to acknowledge his presence.

'I's on the *Xanthes*,' said Hardy to the cook. 'Captain had us lost between Calais and Thames, and this prancer's gone taken one month and point to point, Guinea to Brazil.'

'Not hard when the winds astern,' said Pinch, dismissively.

'You whoreson,' laughed Wilson from behind the pair of them. 'You couldn't cross the mallybrook without a captain's hand.'

'I reckon I could h'a done the same, seein' as the wind and all,' said Pinch, waving his hand at the masts. He was smiling now, and the other two saw that he was teasing. 'Reckon a fish could do the same, and they's got smaller smarts than Roberts.'

They watched as schools of fish approached the ship under a midday sun. A thousand veered away as one, like the tail of a snapping whip. A devilfish swept under the hull, its shadow coasting the sands. Nothing seemed solid or supportive about the water that the *Rover* rested on. She was suspended in reflections, a fallen cloud poised above the ocean's bed.

The *Rover* slid with an audible hiss into a sand bank a hundred yards from the shoreline, and despite Hardy's foul-mouthed encouragements, the pair of tenders could not move her another inch forwards. The bosun was already balanced on the footropes of the *Rover*, attaching taglines and whips in preparation to lower the topmasts. He knew that they had to move as rapidly as possible to alter the leverage of the ship before the receding tide made her topple any further than she needed. The tenders returned to the *Rover*, and were tied quickly to her side.

As the tide receded, the *Rover* was slowly dis-assembled to a long-haul chanty. First the pair of topgallant masts and the trio of topmasts, then her yards, and by the time the ship lay naked and exposed in the low waters, her web of lines had been reduced to heaped coils. Roberts had the men hold their watches throughout the night, dividing the three parties into loading, manning the boats and unloading. After sunset, cannon by cannon and barrel by barrel, the ship grew lighter. When the sun rose, the *Rover* had been relieved of over half her weight.

Using the halyard lines, they positioned the cannon on the crest of the beach, on both the larboard and starboard sides of the ship, protecting her from any encroaching craft. A group of idlers, headed by the ship's carpenter and his mate, began a rough construction of lean-tos, made from palm branches and ship's sail. By the end of the second day, when there was little left to take from the *Rover*, the carpenter fitted the pettiauger with her mast and sail and set her out with twelve men and supplies to spend a pair of days surveying the island and the horizon for signs of prey.

The men were dressed in their shortest ducks for tarring and all, save the surgeon, worked bare-chested. In fact, all save the surgeon worked. He sat against a thick palm on the edge of the forest, reading Vesalius and repeating aloud various Latin phrases in an attempt to strengthen the crew's belief in his future diagnoses. Pinch was nearby, his duties never ceasing, standing at an enormous pitch kettle that he tended to with more care than he gave to vittles, keeping the viscous substance at a low bubble. The smell of hot tar was so thick that it seemed as if every sinus had been dipped in pitch.

It may have been the sounds of singing, or the rowdy drunken stories that seemed to echo around the cove for hours at a time, or perhaps even the simple motion of news as it ran from mouth to mouth but, by the end of the first week, a small village of traders had sprung up not half a mile north, on the banks of a thin river.

Populated by a clouded combination of Indian, Spanish and negro, it was not an island of any wealth, or even a single fixed town. The Fernandans could only trade in the natural produce of the island, namely, fruit, meat and themselves. Business was conducted only between men, and the islanders, despite their inexperience as traders, preferred to conduct business on an individual level, one buyer to one seller. The Rovers found it entertaining to fend for themselves in these merchant trades, and began to compete against one another to see who among them could drive the hardest bargains. Most days the discrepancy that arose proved to be too vast for the quicker tempers and fights would erupt, often between the men of the *Experiment* and the *Rover*'s older hands.

If the captain's ascendancy was hard to define at sea, it was indistinguishable on land. Roberts justified the lack of order by seeing the second week as a form of demi-liberty. None seemed in a rush to take leave of the island and when the pettiauger returned on the end of the sun of the second day with no word of the *Juliette* nor any prey there was never a whisper of disappointment as to the blank horizons. Instead her crew were given a warm welcome as if Fernando de Noronha held the streets of a hometown and was filled with family, and it was the sea that had become the stranger. It was as if none were eager to approach the dream of the *Juliette*, fearful of what such scrutiny might bring.

Occasionally the Fernandans would parade their few women through the makeshift shanty town of the *Rover* established on the crescent of the cove. There would be hooting and name-calling and, no matter how broad or old the woman in question, there would be a few less mouths for dinner, and an extra tale or two by morning.

In the softer environs of the island, Williams's role had changed, and he was less the captain's lackey and more the necessary friend to the crew. His skill at the fiddle had long since been noted, and was appreciated to the extent that he had few nights of peaceful sleep. Almost always, he was awakened by a nudge or kick of a mate and encouraged to join the men, who were all anxious for a tune. He saw little of Roberts, who kept mostly to himself or the company of Hardy and Sympson. Though Williams committed several small incidents to memory, nothing was noted on paper.

The work rate of the cleaning of the *Rover* had slowed considerably. Roberts and the lords had voted to establish a lenient pace, providing beer breaks and a large enough ration of rum to result in a hazy but satisfied crew. The *Rover*, at low tide, sat uncomfortably upon her bed of sand, a discarded ark. The first week she had commanded attention and been smothered by the eagerness of a crew determined to scrape her to a worthy sleekness. At sunset on the third day, when the light was deemed suitable for the task, all hatches had been battened tight and brush fires of dried palm had been lit in her hold. The bosun, carpenter and captain had surveyed the ship, marking the areas where smoke leaked from cracks in her planking in white chalk.

The next morning the crew drew lots to see who would be responsible for the cleaning of the hold. With uncanny coincidence, seeing as it was Kennedy who conducted the draw, it fell to Williams, the younger cabin boy Coffin, Aged Q and the quietest of the Experiments to take brooms below. Even after opening hatches and gun ports, the *Rover* was still unbearably smoky, especially in the fo'c'sle and the hold, the darkest and most inaccessible of places.

'At least,' coughed Aged Q leaning on his broom in the hold, 'the palm's done away with the stink of the bilge.'

'Look,' said Williams through a kerchief wrapped around the lower part of his face as he pulled a dead rat from among the stones of ballast.

'Aye,' moaned Aged Q. 'What we're below for.'

'Smoked to death,' mused Williams, as he dangled the dead rodent by its pink tail.

'Always a couple who plead their bellies. A month and the ship'll be crawling again.'

The pair began to sweep the sides of the hold,

every now and then stopping to pull the stiff corpses of rodents from the rocks. Under the lantern light Williams scraped his broom, collecting small piles of upturned roaches, their legs raised to the air in final surrender. Aged Q began to cough – could not stop – and waved an arm at Williams to signal his return to the weather deck. It took the young Welshman another ten minutes to ensure that he had collected the rodent dead from among the ballast, but in the darkest corners he could still hear the scampering of successful resistance. Through his watery eyes, he spied something decidedly out of place. He threw a dead rat at it, then raised a rock and knocked it square on the head. The snake could not respond. With great care, Williams draped five feet of dead serpent across his shoulders and then, hoisting his bucketful of rats, began to climb upwards.

Aged Q was stretched under the bright sunshine in the waist of the ship, slurping at water from the scuttle. He raised his eyes when Williams emerged into the sun, and nodded gratefully in his direction. Williams threw the dead snake at Aged Q's feet.

'Dead as mutton,' said Aged Q poking at the snake with his toe. 'Was bought in the Bight of Benin. Should have cured the ship of rats, but never an appetite.' He coughed hard. 'Take her to Pinch. I'll dig hole for vermin.'

The serpent was absorbed into a mixture of salmagundi, and seemed to have little effect on the men the next day as the *Rover* was boot-topped, first to the starboard side and then reversed by a system of heavy cables that the bosun had run around a string of thick-set palms. Fifty men rubbed her down with wax then tallow and tar and brushed her with a special mixture of sulphur and arsenic that the captain and cook had devised. Every fingernail and the sole of every foot had been blackened by tar.

When, at the end of the third week, Roberts declared that the *Rover* was in a seaworthy condition, he handed the empty ship to the surgeon, who had remained a pale character thanks to the shade of his favourite palm and his myopic habit of holding his book close to his face. He and the gunner, Wilson, were responsible for making sure that the ship was free from disease. Williams and Coffin were ordered to assist as caulked fires were lit in the hold and trains of gunpowder were flashed from the forepeak to the fo'c'sle. Finally, they washed the deck down with gallons of warm vinegar and scrubbed her with holy stones and sand, until the stains of salt and sweat, paint, wines, and blood were expunged.

Between the abundance of fresh meats and vegetables provided for Pinch every day, and his subsequent confusion with the changing numbers of the crew, three consecutive meals appeared at which there was an embarrassing excess of food. Williams, in his kindness, sought to share his portions with one of the scrawnier Fernandans, a boy of twelve or so with a brow concealed by a thatch of slick, black hair. He was dressed in a tattered Spanish frock coat, more holes than cloth, and covered himself with a piece of cow's hide that he had stitched across his middle.

They made one another understand, through an abomination of pidgin Spanish and vigorous movements of the head, that a deal could be forged. The youth signalled that if he might share Williams's food and drink for seven suns, and if Williams would give him his tarred and battered ducks, then he would, in return, give Williams a great prize that very night, the secrecy of which was emphasized by the low tones and stretched smile assuring Williams that he was getting the better end of the deal.

Williams thought for a moment of what surprise might await him. The crew had often told tales of the coastal tribes of Africa who swapped diamonds for leather boots and hunted with spear tips of gold. Whether or not the youth's gift was of use, Williams was not greatly concerned with the loss of food, drink and a ruined pair of ducks. And though the youth seemed fascinated by the crew and their customs, Williams's curiosity over the gift was tenfold.

CHAPTER 8

The moon was a sharp scimitar smiling upon Williams as he followed his charge along the banks of the skinny river. A canopy of elephant ferns crossed their leaves above his head. The boy paused once during the mile, and pointed to a large spider crawling up the river bank. It was close to five inches across its spotted belly, and moved slightly from the probing of a stick, as if it might challenge the two. Williams, in an awful moment of disappointment, mistook this creature for his great prize. He nodded in appropriate awe, and soon they were under way again, footsteps hushed by the sounds of the running river.

Williams almost walked straight into the palm-knit wall of the hut at the edge of the encampment, so concentrated was he on watching his footsteps in the darkness, hoping to avoid any cousins of the bristled spider. The boy pointed at the opening of the hut, then moved quietly off into the shadows of neighbouring structures, leaving Williams alone.

'In here?' whispered Williams to the darkness, but the boy had long gone.

Inside, under the weak yellow light of a tallow

candle, was a woman wrapped in a dark blanket.

'Hello,' said Williams in amazement. He wasn't sure what to do until the woman raised a hand to her hair and smiled at him, revealing her breasts unbashedly.

'Dear God,' thought Williams, 'a whore.' He stood there a little while, even though she was signalling him to join her. She lay on a bed of dried palm leaves, roughly shaped into a semi-circle that covered half of the small enclosure. There was little else to be seen in the hut: pewter jars and bowl, a couple of sticks fashioned like crutches propped close to the opening, and a cat, its paws crossed under its chin in sleep.

Williams wished he was drunk. She pushed the blanket from the top of her body, and beckoned him again. Finally, prompted by an uninterpretable murmur, he moved towards her and knelt beside her. She was a union of Indian and negro blood and, though the fiddler's body cast her face in shadows, she appeared to age as he neared her. Less likely the boy's sister, more likely the mother. Still, she smiled sweetly as if she were a maiden, even as her hand stroked Williams's belly in gentle circles.

Williams was naked, erect in her hands. He reached for the blanket, tugged it away, and held his breath. Where one leg was soft and shapely, smooth and dark, the other was withered and dis-coloured by a pale hue. She gripped the base of his cock with one hand, holding the blood inside, while

71

the other hand positioned the blanket carefully over her withered leg. '*Mi*,' she said. When he looked up she made him hold her gaze and then pushed him quickly inside her.

The young man quickly forgot about the hidden leg. He concentrated his gaze on her face, her breasts, the sight of his cock easing in and out of her. He could feel eyes on his back, but they were not against him, he was not in danger. There were eyes that smiled, small eyes, inquisitive and paired with giggles. She pushed him off her, and then turned over on her knees, repositioning the blanket around her leg, and raised herself to Williams as she rested her head on the palm fronds on the floor. He thrust, pushing himself deep into her liquids inside. Wilson had told him that black whores had teeth beneath, but she felt like a fabric of great softness.

This was what they called fucking on the *Rover*. Having the whole of a woman, not the bits of experience he had procured in his travels. He had been touched, had touched girls beneath. He had sniffed at his fingers, and smelled the strong scent of women, but this is what he had dreamed of. Moving inside an upturned whore, his flesh guided by hers, Williams pushed deep inside her. She cried out a little, just a touch of pain, but he increased his motion and looked down to see his white stomach slap against the crest of her buttocks. He held his breath and pushed her down, still thrusting, but now spent, nuzzling the back of her head.

She pushed him away and rolled back over, covering herself with the blanket but still smiling for his sake. She climbed to her feet and limped to a bowl in the corner, where she squatted, rubbing herself with leaves and water. It seemed a clinical and thorough rinse, and it disappointed Williams. It made him feel dirty, as if he had been the one used, and that his efforts had meant nothing but another routine fulfilled. Pulling up his ducks, he tucked his limp penis inside them.

Before Williams could put his shirt back on, her hands had grasped his and, looking in his eyes, she pointed at the shirt and pleaded, '*Mi, mi*.' It seemed only right for a gentleman, as Williams presumed himself, to give the lady a little something extra for her effort, to rise above his discontent and view the matter, as she did, as business. He released his hold on his shirt, and smiled kindly, then stood, managed a stiff, 'Thank you' and stepped back into the night.

He had not taken three steps when the youth reappeared in his frock coat and loin cloth, smiling at Williams with raised eyebrows.

'You like? You like?'

'Si,' said Williams.

'*Mi*,' said the boy, and pointed at his ducks.

Williams looked a trifle confused, so the boy took a step forward and pressed his fingers against the cloth of the ducks. The fiddler pointed to where the sun would rise, and moved his finger in a small circle. The boy shook his head and pointed at the ground.

'I can't give you my damn ducks now, I'll be bare to the night,' said Williams aloud. Though the boy could not understand such a trail of English, he had already unhooked the side of his loincloth and now held it out for Williams. The Welshman suddenly felt very foolish, standing there across from this naked boy. Short of knocking him down and causing a host of trouble with the Fernandans, he saw no other recourse but to fulfil the bargain immediately.

Naturally, the hide that was cut for the waist of a boy would not fit around a man of William's girth. He had lost much of his weight since signing on with the crew of the *Rover*, mainly because of an increase in work rate rather than any abstention at mealtimes, but still, even as he sucked in his breath in the darkness, the hide fell short, and the boy had disappeared once more. Clutching the cloth in one hand, Williams followed the course of the river back towards the cove, until the moonlit *Rover* emerged through the edges of the elephant ferns. Williams padded his way across the sand, one hand holding the hide to his front, making straight for his sea-chest.

Sympson, perched on his own chest, watched William's approach with interest. It was deep into the night, perhaps an hour or two before sunrise, but Sympson sat there peaceably, smoking on his pipe.

74

'That not the cloth of your young friend?' asked the head of his watch.

'Aye,' said Williams.

'Not been buggering, have you?' he asked suspiciously, but with a faint smile as if he really didn't suspect Williams of such a thing.

'No,' said Williams, and suddenly thought that he'd better add to the denial, before it seemed weak in the morning's rumours. 'Was trading for his sister.'

'The one-legged callet?' enquired Sympson.

'Aye,' said Williams, mildly surprised.

'D'ya not find her like dead sheep?' He sucked on his pipe. 'Surely, she was dead sheep to me. None too clean either. Go 'nd wash yourself down in the salt.'

Williams followed his advice. Standing naked in thigh-deep water, staring at his penis, he rubbed it red with sand and water.

CHAPTER 9

Within forty-eight hours the arduous process of reloading the *Rover* had begun. Water barrels were refilled well upstream from the Fernandan encampment, and the quartermaster set about seeing that the salted cod was crammed and stowed. Enough vegetables were brought to ensure a pleasant variation from dried fish, meat and biscuit for at least the first week or two at sea.

At high tide the *Rover* groaned and cursed her way from her sandy wedge. Sailing in slow circles along Brazil, out of the sight of her coast, there was nothing to disturb the blank horizons, save for the odd frigate bird that trailed their lazy progress with effortless sweeps of its wings. Early every morning, before the sun woke, the gunner would have the decks cleared for action and the sunrise watch would strain their eyes at first light, hoping for some small point of movement.

A small buzzing began in the fo'c'sle towards the end of the fourth week of sail, a controlled whine, much like a mosquito's pitch as it hovers in darkness. It was hard to say where the sound originated but it was insidious and directed first from Commons to Lords, and then from the Lords to the captain, and finally to Williams's journal in coded Spanish:

I confess a certain anxiety, though it does not seem to have brushed the captain. The lack of prey is not mentioned, but it is obvious enough that the good humour found and stored since our careen is now long gone. Seven weeks and now not even firing practice can alleviate the black mood of the crew. Few talk to me directly, knowing me as fiddler and conduit to the captain, but even the deaf and dumb might sense the discontentment. It is all this sailing without a destination – it is not port nor isle but sail we seek upon a thousand miles of ocean. None care if the Juliette *is the next sail that we see, but a sail is necessary, lest the discontent deepen. Roberts has steered our course westwards, to Bahia and fresh water. Then to the Indies where our luck must change. Roberts's eyes are dark but even. I am glad that our fates are cleaved if this rumbling crew rises. Or rather, I hope our fates are cleaved. But I do not think the crew's thoughts are so far from my own. To a man, we are more bored than angered. As you will note, my journal suffers – this, my first entry in a week.*

The fiddler had divided his time among his favoured messmates. He was most comfortable in the presence of Aged Q Coffin and one Christopher

Moody, a quiet but foolish soul who had sailed with the *Rover* since before Roberts's captaincy and yet had always avoided Lordship. Moody could not have been much above twenty-five, and though his slate-coloured hair grew thick upon his jawline, it refused to take hold above his top lip, making his face seem rounder than it fairly was. They were an odd collection of friends for the *Rover*, seeing as their group included both the oldest and the youngest aboard. The remainder of the crew looked upon the gathering as a convenient clumping of refuse, but thanks largely to Williams's fiddle and the melodious baritones of Aged Q and Moody, they were seen, as the surgeon was heard to say, as 'four notes of the same octave'.

In the first days asea from Fernando de Noronha, the surgeon and the Welsh deckhand had made a secure friendship of their own when Williams assisted Scudamore in several translations of medical Latin, so it was with great embarrassment that Williams reported to the sick bay. As yet the *Rover* had remained an outstandingly healthy ship, with no more to busy her surgeon than the odd crushed finger from overeagerness in the shot locker, or a bruised rib or three from a buffet against the main yard. Behind the curtain of the sick bay (which had been established by hanging three large blankets around gun number twelve and placing the surgeon's chest inside) Williams dropped his ducks and revealed his penis to the surgeon.

'Gleet,' said the surgeon, holding the deckhand's member in a gloved hand.

'For certain?'

'Or, as you and I would say, *Neisseria gonorrhea*. And yes, I am certain. Of course I am certain.' He squeezed the tip of Williams's penis and the young man yelped involuntarily.

'Note,' said the surgeon. 'A pale putrid discharge, an extravagant soreness, an exquisite pain upon visiting the heads?'

'Aye,' mumbled Williams, nodding vigorously, 'and what do we do?'

'We?' smiled the surgeon.

'Stop the pain, but save it . . .' pleaded Williams.

'On a naval frigate you might be fined for this.' Scudamore began to burrow in his medicine chest and then turned back towards the sorry-looking Welshman. 'Cover yourself, my boy,' he said. 'It is an easy prescription, one even I can remember seeing as I prescribed it to myself. Here we are . . . white powder for the white fluid.'

'What is it?' asked Williams in a high whine.

'Calomel,' said Scudamore, holding it to the light of the gun port. 'A tasteless purgative you will take for some time yet. Tis best we bleed you as well.'

Williams had obediently pulled up his ducks, and now reluctantly pulled off his shirt and waited for the garrulous surgeon to make his incision.

'Before I departed from my dear master,' Scudamore began, 'he taught me the odd thing or two about the doctoring of sailors.' The cut came quickly, and Williams's eyelids fluttered above the flow of his blood. 'He was neither a man who believed entirely in the four humours, and yet he remained unconvinced by the theory of solids. Fevers are indeed conceived in heat, and a man may well be cooled by bleeding. So I suggest a douse in cold salt water and an absence of meat from your meals for one week to start. Then we shall have another look at you. Not that bad, now, was it?'

'I feel,' started Williams, 'a sudden weakness.'

'Sail ho,' came the cry from the fore top. Though a man may not hear the bosun's whistle at twenty yards, and though the roar of practice gun will not wake a sailor from due sleep, the faint whisper of 'Sail ho' off the coast of Bahia was enough to have every hand on deck in under the minute. Even Williams, miraculously re-energized, burst on to deck with the other hands. Of course, there was nothing to be seen. A swarm, lacking Williams, headed for the shrouds, and climbed, hoping to see the shine of the *Juliette*, and then entered into a lengthy dispute until at last it was decided. It was not one, but two sails, standing close by land.

By three bells Roberts had fixed their position at the Bay of Los Todos os Santos and the sails counted had increased from two to eight. This did not slow the approach of the *Rover*, who, backed by a generous wind, slowly bore down on her potential prey. Every man became head of his own watch, and cried for yards to be braced and reef tackles sweated until they were silenced for their captain by a great cry from the bosun. Roberts spoke firmly, in low tones, and brought every sailor to his sense, and therefore to his station. The flurry of excitement was so contagious that even the ill-tempered Pinch was seen to be grinning in his galley. By six bells, when the estimate of the awaiting sails had been altered from eight to forty-two, the happy anticipation had been dampened by a hollow expectancy. They were sailing directly into what could only be a Portuguese fleet.

Roberts ordered the majority of the crew below and had the twenty who remained on deck dress in a vague uniform of dark britches and wide-cuffed shirts, while he himself emerged in the gaudy apparel of a bejewelled merchant captain. If the crew had not been so concentrated on the flock of sails ahead, and if they had not been so nervous for their approaching rendezvous, they might have found some humour in Roberts's dress. He sported a damask waistcoat of kelly green, and britches of similar brightness, a red feather jutting from his black tricorn hat and a thin river of gold chains wrapped around his neck. The clothes, at close distance, were even more absurd than their colours promised. Their previous owner had been both a smaller and slighter man than Roberts. The captain resembled nothing so much as a monkey dressed for a fairground's amusement.

The Portuguese flag was raised, and the thickest

of the anchor cables were secured to the aft timberheads, trailing in the square rigger's wake, both slowing the *Rover*'s approach and dragging her down in the water, making her sit heavily, a laden merchant. Most of the forty-two were under bare poles, attended by ketches and barques that billowed between the ships like leaves under winter trees. The *Rover*'s approach was ignored. The considerable armada had assumed a sense of security under such a busy horizon, and a forty-third ship did not raise a single eyeglass – not until the *Rover* bore down on the *Enero*.

The *Rover* struck her sails, and sat with her gun ports closed, with every gun crew prepared and at their stations. Though little enough air moved through the gun deck, it seemed as if few men remembered to breathe. Gun captains blew gently on the matches of their burning linstocks, so that the ends glowed a fierce orange.

From the leverage of the quarterdeck Williams used a bronze hailer, settling on Spanish as their common language before turning to his captain for orders.

'Any signal raised to alert her fellow merchant-men will result in the sinking of the *Enero* with all hands,' said Roberts to Williams. 'Tell him that he has a pretty little ship, but too small for my tastes. I wish his presence on the quarterdeck of the *Rover*, and a minute of his time.'

Williams hailed the captain of the *Enero* over the skinny stretch of water that separated the two ships. Roberts stared at the fiddler when the reply was shouted across the expanse.

'Think he is demanding some proof,' said Williams. 'He maintains you're a hedge whore – a thieving hedge whore – whom he condescends to obey because he is in a fine mood this particular day. Said he will see for himself whether you're a mountebank or fraud.'

'The rub?' asked Roberts.

'He will soon be with us.'

Roberts smiled, and took a seat on the steps of the quarterdeck.

'He apologizes for his words across the water.' The *Enero*'s captain stood on the *Rover*'s quarterdeck in stockinged feet, looking slightly worn and especially dingy compared to Roberts's excess of finery. His feet were splayed with toes pointing away from his body, as if he were a seagull. 'He explains,' continued Williams, 'that they were not intended for your abuse, but for the ears of his crew so that they might have a continued respect for him.'

Roberts seemed to give him a wink, then offered him an arm and escorted him down the main hatchway, along the gun deck, where the smells of sweat and the stares of over a hundred scapegallows were more convincing than any verbal explanations.

'Tell him I have a . . .'

'Language,' interrupted the Portuguese commander in Castilian, 'is unnecessary.'

'What's that?' asked Roberts.

'He says that language is unnecessary. Whatever you wish, I think he is predisposed to give you.'

'I wish him to direct us to the richest ship in the fleet. Either that or the end of his own command.'

Williams translated, the Portuguese nodded, grinned, and spoke.

'He agrees to the bargain,' began Williams. 'The *Sagrada Familia*, three ships leeward, has forty guns, one hundred and fifty men and a commander who is rival to him. A ballast of gold, a hold of hides and sugar. He says that your fight will be long and hard, that there are two warships stationed at Salvador, and that this *Rover* will sink with all hands.'

'Thank him for his kindness. Inform him that he will remain our guest until the *Familia* is taken, and that then he shall be restored unharmed to his *Enero*.'

Upon Roberts's insistence, as the *Rover* prepared to level her starboard side towards the *Sagrada Familia*, the Portuguese captain called over to his rival and invited him on board the *Rover*. There was a moment's hesitation, and then a formal reply that the captain gladly accepted the invitation and would be over directly. The captain of the *Enero* smiled, and nodded knowingly at Roberts, as if it was a ruse that the two had plotted together. He also edged forwards slightly until he was obscured from the line of fire by the mizzen mast. Roberts had not moved, but had his eyes trained carefully on the waist and gundeck of the *Familia*. She was hardly a fine sailor, with a poop deck that rose like an awkward tower and so wide abeam that she could only bully herself through water. Her graceful figurehead, a Man of God whose hands were crossed over the hilt of a long sword, only emphasized the crudity of her construction and vast tonnage.

'Lord Sympson?' questioned Roberts.

'Don't know, Bart,' said the quartermaster, rubbing his hand over his ribcage.

'No tender,' said Roberts. 'Look,' he pointed towards the gundeck. The heads of men running while bent over could be clearly seen. 'Mr Wilson, larboard guns fire at will.'

Williams was halfway up the main hatchway when the first cannon fired. It sounded unlike any practice round he had ever heard, seeming twice as loud, and was followed by the unmistakable sound of splintering wood. By the time he had reached the quarterdeck the entire starboard side had unleashed their first broadside, and there was little to see except the thick clouds of smoke that lay between the two foes. As the second broadside began, less than two minutes later, the impact of the shot on wood seemed more scattered, and it occurred to Williams that Lord Wilson had switched to grapeshot, hoping to clear the deck before boarding.

In between the bursts of the cannon, he could

hear the incongruous sounds of horns and drum coming from the bow of the ship. Williams grabbed his fiddle and joined three of the Experiments, who were busy creating an unholy cacophony to accompany the cannon fire. The only obvious thing to Williams was that fire had not been returned. He could no longer hear the report of the *Rover*'s guns or the squeal of carriages being dragged back to their ports.

The remainder of the smoke was driven by the wind, and the sides of the Portuguese vessel lay twenty yards and closing. The first of the grapnels went soaring into the air, biting into the Portuguese's pinrail. More lines were cast, and the crew heaved on them, causing both ships to shudder at their union. The deck of the *Sagrada Familia* was a scattered serpents' nest of loose and shredded lines, a fallen main yard and slivers of her bulwarks, ripped from her side by the opening broadside.

There was not a musketshot of resistance from the Portuguese – she had not even managed to clear her gun deck – and the Rovers streamed over her side in an expectant tide, shouting their fear from their bodies. The initial broadside had inflicted structural damage. Grapeshot had caught a portion of the *Familia*'s crew as they had emerged on deck to resist the boarding of the ship, and bodies had been shredded. The Rovers had succeeded merely by stepping on to the main deck. Williams could see Scudamore, moving across the waist of the ship, now kneeling beside a man whose left thigh had been removed close to the pelvis. He fumbled with a tourniquet, then obviously judged the case hopeless, and moved on to a sailor clutching one fingerless hand in another. The drummer nudged Williams, and he realized that he still held his fiddle to his ear.

Williams put his instrument down and leaped from the timberhead of one ship to the other. Sympson was shouting instructions, trying to organize a prize crew despite the screams of the injured and dying. For one turn of the glass the *Sagrada Familia* was a place of unrestrained chaos. There was the sound of scuffles from below, and those who had stayed on deck and surrendered looked stupidly about as if to convince one another that they had merely recognized the sole option first. The carpenter had taken a party into the hold to survey the damage, but was already suspected of having engineered an opportunity to take first stock of the prize.

The bosun was trailing through the strange rigging, avoiding torn and aged ratlines, and picking his way among the yards. Roberts had returned to his own quarterdeck and was staring upwards, to the mizzen top, where he had positioned Coffin as soon as he had been relieved of his duties as powder monkey. There was the distant echo of fire from all points and a slow procession of the setting of topgallants as the rest of the merchantmen squealed their signals of distress. Williams watched as the captain's curiosity overcame him. Stripping himself of his shoes, Roberts scaled the mizzen and joined the cabin boy as he observed the reaction of the surrounding ships and eyed the bay for the expected warships.

CHAPTER 10

The soles of Williams's feet were sticky and discoloured from the blood that ran between the struts of the *Familia*'s capstan. There was too much to be done for a bell to be rung, but the Welshman reckoned that two full hours had passed since the brief battle had erupted. They had suffered merely two casualties, Experiments who had been driven through by an eager young midshipman, who was, in turn, set upon by a vengeful mob and pulverized with the stocks of muskets and the hilts of cutlasses. All bodies were slid overboard. They seemed surprisingly few in number to the young fiddler. He had been mopping at blood on the main deck of the *Familia* and could not conceive how ten men (and only eight of them dead) could contain so much colour.

Williams knew his own mind well enough to realize that what had been fear was now excitement. Disgust was perverted to fascination. He raised buckets of sea water and watched as the water ran from red to pink and clear again, and then joined Christopher Moody on the chain wales as he shot at sharks and watched as they turned on one another.

Their play was disturbed by Sympson's angry voice and they were bullied back aboard the *Rover* and immediately sent aloft to set her topsails. From his perch above, Williams failed to understand what all the hurry was about. They had scattered the merchant armada with their first broadside and prepared themselves for the brace of warships, but still they did not come. The *Rover* had been disentangled from the *Sagrada Familia* with little damage to either vessel and the prize crew, captained by Sympson, had lowered both of the ships' boats and filled them with the Portuguese crew. Even though the Portuguese sailors sat worryingly low in the water, and the mildest of swells had them frantically bailing, the Rovers lowered the commander of the *Enero* into the second boat by way of the bosun's chair, his ship having sailed for the coast. Sympson wished him well and, according to Roberts's wishes, threw a small pouch of gold dust at their informant as the tender pushed off.

The *Rover* and the *Sagrada Familia* sailed from the Bay of Los Todos os Santos without further delay or interruption. Though Roberts spent the following days scanning the horizon, the Portuguese warships were never seen to appear. If they had, the crew would have been too drunk to notice. It was, without doubt, a mighty haul, somewhere between expectation and fantasy.

'I can't give the exact sum of all,' said Sympson,

addressing a remarkably attentive crew at eight bells the following day, 'as there are works of gold and jewels that have value that made even our surgeon havy cavy. And then hides, and sugar enough for a thousand days of punch. Tis best then, if we merely reckon in exact measures, and that would be to say that there are sitting in *Familia*'s hold some forty thousand moidores. Better known as seventy thousand pounds.'

It was, by any reckoning, a usurious amount of money, and the pronouncement silenced the crew. They had feared disappointment, nurtured hope, and were almost in shock that such a reward might be the result of a one-sided engagement. The sharing began immediately. Captain – two shares – presented in front of the crew to a wild cheer, that Roberts, still dressed in his peacock foppery, responded to with a low bow and a rare, wide smile. The Lords – a share and one half. The crew – one share, and half share for the cabin boys and music makers, but even this half share was a fortune to a working man.

Gold outweighed the importance of drink. By the end of the day sober and earnest calculations had begun. There were several differing versions of the exact amount that a share was worth. Eventually all bowed to the combined erudition of the surgeon and Williams, and the shares were valued at four hundred and sixty pounds and ten shillings. The decision was accepted until the early morning when an ecstatic Phineas Bunch alerted the crew to the fact that they had not reckoned in the demise of Bowman and Croft into the calculation. This set off a new round of debate and a gentle disappointment when it was learned that this only increased a man's share by another seven pounds or so. When the sum was finally settled during the following day (in a north-easterly direction, though few but the helmsman had any interest) all hours – whether on watch or idling – were spent translating four hundred and seventy-six pounds and twelve shillings into moidores, and out again, then into Pembrokeshire land, various estates of Ireland, London houses and coastal taverns.

Roberts's announcement on the fourth day out of Los Todos os Santos that their destination would be Devil's Island caused a change in calculations. Landed investments were suddenly commuted into alcohol and flesh. The bolder asserted that they would simply purchase taverns and bawdy houses and remain drunken in the arms of fleshy-breasted callets until they were swept from their seats by wind and wave.

The remaining days between the *Rover* and Devil's Island were a strange mixture of fulfilment and anticipation. Roberts had eventually removed his waistcoat and tricorn hat (the feather had long since been blown overboard). Of his original dress only the green britches remained. He seemed almost to have forgotten his captaincy, and was twice noted sleeping on deck among the commoners. Williams took advantage of his captain's wanderings and worked quietly in the cabin. Having secured three large bottles of black India ink from the stateroom of the *Sagrada Familia*, Williams's prose was loosened by punch. He could barely contain his good humour:

A day has brought a new world. If yesterday was salt beef and biscuit, tomorrow is oyster loaves, cold goose and jugged pigeons. Tomorrow is a pyramid of sweetmeats. You have never seen such happiness, and yes, I will track this joy to our captain, who smiled and bowed before the crew. May God bless him for his decisiveness and for his divine patience. And may we bless God for leading us to a foreign fleet.

He grinned then continued.

When the fortune of the Sagrada Familia *is combined with that of the* Juliette, *I shall buy an estate neighbouring to my father's. The very land that he wishes shall be mine. And with it, two carriages, twelve horses – no, twenty. One team shall be sent for my father, the other to the coast for the captain and Scudamore. We shall all sit down for dinner together, and it will be my father who shall feel awkward and unknown.*

'Is there much humour in your words?' asked Roberts in Welsh from the darkned corner of the room. Williams sat upright, upsetting the small ink pot and blurring his second paragraph of self-description.

'Damn your eyes,' cried Williams. He promptly apologized as he used his shirt tails and sand to blot the patch of ink.

'Never seen a man as rapt,' smiled the captain, easing himself into his bunk. 'Could have plucked hair from your knowledge box and you'd ne'er have missed a whisker.'

Williams shrugged, ''Tis bad?'

''Tis good for both of us, I trust. What you're writing on?' asked the captain. 'Come, show me.'

Williams approached the bed with a single page of manuscript and handed it to Roberts, and then carried a candle over from the table. Roberts rolled his fingers across the unintelligible lines that described the perfection of the fiddler's calves.

'I tell of the peace that fortune brings,' lied Williams. 'Ne'er seen men smile wide as now.'

'And will last as long as the gold.' Roberts looked up from the measured lines of script.

'Each has enow to turn gentlemanly pursuits.'

'You've ne'er seen a sailor reach port fore now?' asked Roberts.

'No sir.'

'I seen a brandy face offer a lady of easy virtue fifty pound just to bare her breasts. Would agree that a man of sense, or a brother of the quill such as yourself, might feel inclined to settle a while, but not these.'

'Well sir,' said Williams, 'then I cannot see the point in this.'

'In what?'

'In our pursuit. To gain riches makes little sense if they are not to be apportioned and then invested in the correct manner. Then a man might leave the sea behind.'

'Mr Williams, you came to sea late enough to trust the land. Most of these fellows ne'er make it past coast, town or village. They're cheated by presses, by whores, hostlers, tailors and urchins. Tis hard to know the value of a coin when its worth is changed ten times a day and the coves are too drunk to give notice.'

'But if a man could just remain on land a little while.'

'None would wish it. All belong to the sea. You can play a game and win still to desire another turn.'

Williams looked as if he was filled with words and that he might explode from the illogic of Roberts's conceit.

'But then,' started Williams, 'there can be no end to this.'

'Most likely not,' said Roberts. 'Except with the *Juliette*. We have wealth, but opulence lies ahead. You and I, we are patient men, but the rest shall look upon their pelf as coinage. Soon they shall strain again. After the *Juliette* there shall be no captain aboard this ship. Then they will consider.'

CHAPTER 11

Though both ships' companies had been raised by the cry of land ahoy over a day ago, the coast of Devil's Island, with its mighty cliffs and deep sea swells, teased them from afar. The wind had died when they were not more than four leagues from her shores, and they sat on the water, with courses and topsails slack.

It was testament to the crew's eagerness to reach land that there was a grand meeting called on the second day's calm, and a preponderance of volunteers stepped forward with the suggestion that the tenders should be manned and the *Rover* and the *Sagrada Familia* should both be towed into port. Volunteering was seen as as a strict measure of manhood, as if those who held back were considered effeminate and foppish and would not deserve first choice of the local goods upon arrival. They crammed twenty in the first tender launched, two men to a sweep. Williams was proud to have stood his ground against harder men and secured a pew next to Christopher Moody. Sympson sat in the bow of the tender calling gentle time.

The fiddler could feel them influence the inertia

of the *Rover* and was thrilled by the laws of the ocean that let a single-ton tender shift five hundred tons through the water. He let the rhythm of the stroke ease up his legs, then course through his arms, until he exhaled the beat in dirty breath. He could smell Kennedy's whisky breath behind him. Williams was generally as indisposed towards the English as Kennedy could ever be and considered the Irishmen compatriots under King George's shadow, but he reckoned Kennedy a teague and a bog-trotter. He pulled hard and ignored the occasional and deliberate nudge that Kennedy and his associate would give Moody and himself as they leaned into the end of their stroke.

The toll of four bells rang over the water from the *Rover*, echoed back from the *Sagrada Familia*, and the men passed up kerchiefs to Bunch who soaked them in the scuttle and returned them to grateful hands. Each man received a cup of water and they leaned back or bent over their oar locks, stretching to relax their muscles, and began to talk among themselves.

'Me,' said Kennedy, 'I'm going to find meself a bushel babby negress, blacker than coal.'

'What other colour negress would there be?' asked Christopher Moody, smiling. Williams laughed loudly; indeed, he crowed, and clapped his friend on the back.

'Laugh,' said Kennedy. 'Laugh away, young Richard Snary.'

This brought a snicker from most of the crew.

Though proud of Williams's learning, they were still closer to Kennedy and could appreciate a man lowered to their level.

'Why a negress?' asked Sympson, squeezing the water from a piece of canvas over his face.

'So I cannae see the dirt,' explained Kennedy. 'I tell you, the bigger the smile of a girl, the better the need of the bath. Even the rummiest of the birdies here ha' been mowed by a hundred French and a troop of Spanish, so tis safer to take them up the arse.'

'You do what?' roared Sympson with laughter from the bow. 'You're a bugger.'

Many heads turned towards Kennedy. He looked uncomfortably around himself.

'Sodomy's a sin,' said a poxed runt from the stern of the tender.

'So's bigamy,' answered Kennedy quickly, 'so's spilling your own seed, but if you don't sin, then how can man repent?'

Sympson tipped an imaginary hat in his direction.

'Besides,' said Kennedy, enjoying the role of teacher, 'ask the surgeon.'

'Ask the surgeon what?' asked Sympson.

'I say, take a whore up the arse, and you've less chance of catchin' bube. You see, an arse is like a warm cave, musty and dry, like. Now a quim is fetid and rotten as swampland – that being where you'll find your fevers. Keep to arses, same as I, and you won't be pissing peppers again.'

He leaned back considering himself thoroughly justified, but couldn't help poking Williams in the back with his heel and adding, 'Do you good, Richard Snary – priggin' others. Make change from spending the day with the captain's prick up your arse.'

'Up your arse,' tittered Bunch.

It was supposed to be a coda to the explanation, a humorous aside by Kennedy before the resumption of rowing, but Williams swivelled to face him.

'What you say, teague bastard?' said Williams, locking eyes with Kennedy. 'What you say?'

'Oh, come now,' answered Kennedy. 'Known for months you're used as his left-handed wife. Full of prittle prattle, you are, and a fine disguise, but you're all petticoats.'

'Petticoats,' chimed Bunch.

'All petticoats, ain't he?' continued Kennedy.

Nobody in the small boat had a chance to either agree or disagree, as Williams had leveraged one foot beneath the other on the narrow plank that served as his seat and leaped at Kennedy, using his head to ram the Irishman's gut. There was a brief scuffle, a frantic blow or two, and then, as the boat ceased rocking, Kennedy emerged with a wicked smile on top of the young man. The blade of a reefknife was pressed against the Welshman's throat.

'Easy,' said Kennedy. Williams ceased struggling, confining the hatred to his eyes. 'Won't be taking lives asea. Not under your master's orders. Wouldn't want to sink together now, would we? Shhhh, lad, shhh, little girl, fore I give you second smile.'

'Lord Kennedy,' said Sympson. 'Lord Kennedy?'

The Irishman looked up from his seat on William's chest.

'Don't worry, Davey,' he said to the quartermaster. 'No blood, today, ay lad,' he pinched at Williams's cheek.

'I can tell you,' said Sympson from the bow, 'the lad's no bugger. Saw him myself playing bread and butter with a Fernandan bitch.'

'Still Roberts's boy,' said Kennedy, and removed himself from the Welshman, spitting a string of saliva in his face.

Williams quietly took his place, vowing in silence a cold revenge.

'Which whore you have, Fernando?' asked the poxed man from abaft.

'Withered leg,' said Williams.

'As well?' cried three men at once. A thunderous laughter enveloped the tender, levelling all and causing Williams's tear-filled eyes to drain as he was once more enveloped into the goodwill of the crew.

CHAPTER 12

On the third day of the calm, with the strength of the current carrying them slowly towards the island, a boat was sighted. As she bore closer it seemed as if she were under sail and was receiving the cooperation of a wind that would not blow near the *Rover*. When dawn came on the fourth morning they could see that she was powered by eight sweeps. By mid-afternoon she finally drew alongside the *Rover*, responding to her flagship signal and ignoring the *Sagrada Familia*. She was manned by sixteen Spaniards, all thankful for a swallow of water. The smallest of them, a stunted fellow who had hoped to hide the missing tip of his nose with a vast and busy beard, offered gifts to the crew.

Perfumed undergarments were pawed and inhaled by the crew, as the Spaniard went to great lengths to describe the virtues of the owner; namely that she was a lady who had none. With merely a promise that they would patronize his nanny house, he further offered to act as their pilot. The Spanish pinnace was tied to the *Rover*'s bowsprit and the strange squadron altered course, pulling due east.

The following day they met with a soft breeze and were ushered slowly into the lee of Devil's Island.

At a glance, the island looked to be a cold and desolate place. The coastline was steep and harsh and the wind so steady that no plant could take hold. No seed had time to drop. And yet the wind ran from the surface of the water and warmed itself against the dark rocks as it rushed to the top of the cliffs, where it cuffed a man's cheek like the slap of a hot hand. And how could an island be called desolate, when her harbour hid a town of chandlers and hostlers, traders and innkeepers, and no less than three nanny houses? A sailor could easily forget the resemblance to hell, and presume that he had arrived in paradise.

The dock was deep and let a man step off the lower shrouds and set his feet on dry land. It was not a busy harbour, and the *Rover* and the *Sagrada Familia* were easily the two largest ships present. Clouds had been forced down over the harbour until they touched the truck of the topgallant mast, where they spilled a misty rain over the crews. There was no unloading of hides nor sugars until the governor had been met with the following day, but their bearded Spaniard remained anxious to accommodate his guests and departed to arrange a consignment of whores.

It was often said that upon first seizing a colony, the Spanish would build a church, the Dutch a fort, and the English a tavern. Devil's Island, though governed by Spain, had its own set of priorities. Far enough from land to discourage visits from the grandees of the Spanish main, and inhospitable enough to ensure a transience among her inhabitants, the island survived solely through merchantmen. Trade was indiscriminate, a stable, but not flourishing business, where all were dealt with, and never was there a man turned from her shores. The governor catered for the taste of seamen, and kept his island supplied first with liquor and then with whores. As a result she bulged with news, the debris of loose tongues that could not be relied upon.

The *Rover* was abustle with the sound of work songs, and the splash of men washing themselves down on deck: the cascade of fresh water, so precious at sea, now no more than a disinfectant. The strong odour of vinegar oozed from the fo'c'sle as even the hardest of the men lent the cabin boys a hand, scrubbing down the sides of their private cavern. The surgeon treated them to powders to perfume their hammocks and finest clothes.

Aged Q had taken the surgeon's powder and applied it to the remainders of his wet hair, hoping to give the impression of a wigged notable. It was aped by one and then another, until the fo'c'sle was choked with puffs of powder. Williams crept from the cloying smells and headed for the captain's cabin, where he hoped to borrow some piece of apparel that might distance himself from his fellow suitors.

'Williams, would you care accompany me?'

asked the captain. He was dressed in a pair of rum kicks, maroon britches lined in gold brocade and a cream linen shirt that billowed from the neck and sleeves. The captain of the *Sagrada Familia* had obviously been of a similar build.

'To be forthright,' said Williams, 'I thought that I'd stay put and wait upon the ladies.'

'According to the surgeon, you're not of health.'

''Tis healthy enough now. Where do you head?'

'No secret to those who follow,' said Roberts.

The fiddler thought hard of joining him on his venture, but to walk through the ship's company and take leave with Roberts when all on board were jousting like rutting deer would be to confirm the suspicion that Kennedy had cast. Better to stay and prove his manhood. ''Tis kind, Captain, but I would be missed as music.'

'I shall send your regards to the governor.'

'Aye,' said Williams with regret, 'would be kind.'

His spirits were considerably brightened by the reappearance of the bearded Spaniard, who held, upon each arm, a lady draped in blue silks. Both women had their faces powdered white according to the fashions of the French court, and their feet, noticed by all as they stepped aboard, were crushed into slim shoes the colour of bright sky. They were greeted by a welcoming chorus, and a small scuffle broke out as twelve men offered their arms to the ladies.

The surgeon, perched next to Williams, on the

main fiferail, pointed at the whore who first stepped aboard.

'Poxed,' he advised.

'Should we turn her away?' questioned the fiddler.

'Lose your life should you try.'

Williams smiled broadly to see that it was Kennedy who had bullied his way to her attention.

There was a cry from the upper shrouds, from where Bunch and Coffin had been trying to obtain favourable angles for inspecting lacy bodices. Bunch began to count off heads and a flock of women appeared by the waist of the ship. More than one of their number seemed to have begun the evening before their hosts, but their merriness seemed false to Williams. He may have lain with a woman who was no different from a whore, but it had been a spontaneous lapse. This was predetermined and well-organized sin.

'I wish I were not quite so old,' said the surgeon wistfully as he surveyed the long line of women being helped on to the deck of the *Rover*. By the time all were aboard there was little room on deck. None of the new arrivals were dressed in the hoop-skirted finery of the first two, though Williams spotted a couple he deemed far more attractive. Most were dressed simply, without stomachers, so that their natural figures were open for the eye to inspect. There were two men for every woman and the diverse whores seemed

105

to have been ferried from the coasts of Europe, Africa and the Americas, though the favoured tongue remained Spanish. Williams, accosted as he crept from the main deck, was forced into the role of both seducer and arbitrator as terms were set. As time passed and bowl after bowl of punch was drained, prices were negotiated by nods, head shakes or laughter, and Williams was called upon as fiddler.

Sitting on the top step of the quarterdeck, he started up the ballad of 'Jack West', but soon the sweetness of his tune was obscured by a chorus of drunks. While his fiddle sang away, Williams sat back in his perch and looked out across the flesh that filled the *Rover*. Most of the men and a number of women had shed their top garments, leaving the bodies of their dresses flapping around their ankles. In the darkness, touched by the soft orange hues of the lantern, the bodies took on a look of warmth and animation. All twirled in dance and their laughter, that might have seemed strained when sober, now rang in happy peals.

What was pleasure to the men was business to the women. Where the sailors did little to disguise their looks or intentions, several of the whores not only employed the pretensions of the coquette but were also decorated with face patches. It was the aura of artifice – whether the patch hid pox scar or mole – that saddened Williams as he continued to play. He saw couples pair off, disappear and then return, and others go willingly with women who had barely had time to straighten their skirts.

Aged Q took note of his dour expression and ferried cannikins of punch to Williams, until he forced a smile from his friend. 'Come now, taffy,' said the old man. 'You can't stay as misery guts when you make the ladies smile so.'

'Get lad,' ordered Wilson, sitting down next to Williams. He raised his fife to his lips and began his own tune, and Williams realized that he had been relieved of his duty. He lowered the fiddle, looked around the main deck and felt uneasy, unsure of where it was right for a man to place his eyes. Though many had gone below, some had stayed where they were on deck. Hardy's immense and naked frame was open to view as he lay on his back by the starboard pinrail. A woman was bending over his cock, her skirts gathered up in one hand, the other propped against his chest. She remained in her shoes. The ship had grown hotter. Against the taffrail Williams could see a girl milking two men at once, spitting on her hands then tugging at them as if she were pulling at a cow's udders.

Moody appeared alone in the aft hatchway.

'Was looking for you, brother,' he said. 'Was concerned on your behalf.' He steadied himself against the frame. 'Saved her for you. Tried her out and saved her and paid her for you and me both. So don't go throwing your coins at her. When you're done, don't let her go anyways, but do as I done, and get me straight after.'

'You're a firm friend, Christopher Moody.'

'All's sharing tonight, as good as with a friend as not.'

'Where?' asked Williams.

'To the hold. You'll see Sympson wapping a sporting blubber. Go past them to where the sugar's at. Young girl with roan hair. Call for her in your native tongue.'

'She's Welsh?'

'Aye, lad, I found a taffy lass for you.'

Williams's interest peaked considerably. He filled his cannikin, put biscuit and cheese inside his pockets, and nipped quickly down the main companionway before any could call for the fiddler.

CHAPTER 13

I t was pitch dark as he lowered himself into the hold. By the light of a small lantern perched upon the topmost water barrel, Williams could make out Sympson's skeletal form. He was so involved in his own fulfilment that he paid no heed to the Welshman as he crept past.

'*Noswaith*,' whispered Williams in Welsh to the darkness. '*Noswaith?*' Further down, there was the flicker of a candle. 'Lady,' he said in Welsh to a small shadow that sat upon a sugar sack, 'an open flame will have us in hell all the quicker.'

'Would you prefer it were it snuffed?' asked a delicate voice in his own tongue.

'Well,' said Williams.

'Do you not want to see me?'

'I . . .'

'What did Mr Moody tell you that would make you want to only fumble in the darkness?' she asked. 'Do you not find me a pretty face?'

Williams came close to her and could smell that she had doused herself in lavender oils. She was very slight, more child than woman, and he

109

doubted whether she had any breasts to speak of under her coarse hemp dress.

'How old are you?' he asked.

'Same as Moody asked.'

'How old?'

'Fifteen.'

'In truth?' he pressed.

'Will be true soon enough.'

'I brought you this,' said Williams, and offered her the biscuit and cheese.

'A kind thought,' she murmured. 'But I hope that I'm never again hungry enough to eat ship's biscuit.' She began to nibble on the cheese without complaint.

'Where you from?' she asked.

'Caernarfon.'

'Cardiff,' she said. With a shrug she took the cannikin from his hand. She lowered her head to the cup rather than raise it to her mouth. Williams looked away.

'What's your name?' he asked.

'I know yours. Mr Moody told me. Lord Williams.'

He looked at her to see if she teased him, but her small freckled face was filled with large eyes. They were kind, yet cold. She was not a pretty girl, had little more than her youth to recommend her. Besides that, she was a purse of skin and bones.

'Is that what they call you?' she asked. 'Your Lordship?'

'No,' he smiled.

'Me name is Catrin.'

'He was ribbing you,' said Williams. And then, almost seriously, 'Do I look like a Lordship?'

'No. I thought that, when he said that, you might be the captain coming down for me. But I seen you above. You're the fiddler.'

The sounds of Sympson's grunting interrupted the conversation.

'Look,' she said, and pointed at the sack of sugar beneath her. 'When Mr Moody was off searching, I made a hole.' She dipped her finger in it, then raised it to her lips and sucked on its end.

'Sugar already in the punch,' muttered Williams, just to say something to make any noise louder than that of Sympson and his whore.

'Shall we?' she asked.

'I . . .' he said.

'Don't have to be shy,' she said. ''Tis paid for.'

'Stop it,' he spat, and avoided her eyes.

'Am I too skinny for you?' she asked.

'You're a child, girl.'

'And you're a man?' she enquired.

'I suppose you see enough to know.'

'Do you wish to lay with me or no?'

'Slow yourself down, girl, I hardly know you.'

''Tis no matter. Is just a trade.'

'Aye,' said Williams, and nodded twice. 'Perhaps because we're countrymen, but does it not feel a little awkward between us?'

'Certainly,' she said, 'because you prate too

much. Your friend Mr Moody is a simpler fellow.'

'Show me your bubbies,' said Williams.

The girl looked up at him and cocked her head as if she were a dog and thought she heard her name being called.

'Go on,' he said.

She slipped the sides of her dress over her shoulder and it fell to her waist. Her ribs were more prominent than her breasts. Williams reached forward and rubbed the tips of his fingers over one nipple and then the other.

'You'll need be eating more,' he muttered.

Her head was tilted back so that all he could see was the long stalk of her neck caught in the candlelight. It was either pleasure, or the pretence of pleasure.

'Turn over,' he ordered and she complied so that her knees and two hands were pressed against the sackcloth of the sugar. He gathered her dress so that it sat bunched in the small of her back. Spitting in his palm, he put his hand against her, and pushed a finger inside her, up to the knuckle and then out again. Williams dropped his trousers to his ankles and the light of the candle seemed to shudder as he pressed himself inside her. It was, in her experience, a brief transaction, and she was relieved when he withdrew and squeezed himself against the top of her skinny thigh. She breathed hard, and blew out the candle on her first effort.

'What you do that for?' asked Williams. He

could hear her wiping herself with what he presumed was the ends of her dress, then a lack of movement and silence joined the darkness.

'Will you not talk to me?' he asked.

A small sniffle in the dark.

'I'm turning around girl,' he said. 'Take my shoulders and I'll carry you out . . . come on now, or the rats'll be on us soon.'

First one hand and then another closed around him and then she jumped up on to his back and he cradled her thin legs in his arms. It took no more than a long minute for Williams to find his way from the hold. Sympson had left the hatch open, and the dull half-light was obvious to eyes now used to the darkness. He put her down when they reached the gundeck and, speaking to his chest, she asked, 'Will Mr Moody not be looking for me?'

'How far do you lodge from here?' replied Williams.

'A half-mile. No more.'

'I'll walk you to your door.'

'I've not earned my fill.'

'I'll fill your purse,' said Williams.

'And Mr Moody?'

'A friend of mine.'

On the weather deck the music had died and been replaced by a flat singing, a drone loud enough to cover Williams's exit. The young girl ceased worrying on Mr Moody's behalf when they passed his snoring figure lying prone in the coil of an anchor cable. It seemed a long walk in the

113

darkness and no words were exchanged but a soft '*Do bo chi*'. Escorting his charge home served to lessen Williams's guilt and to keep him from the chaos of the *Rover* for a time longer.

Besides, he was glad to know where she lived.

CHAPTER 14

Unsurprisingly, the next day was a quiet one, where noises were railed against – even the lowering of buckets for galley water. The last of the ladies of the night walked off the ship into the curse of the morning sun, where all that went on the night before seemed of dubious distinction and instant regret. The grumbles had already started how one found himself lighter in the pocket than another, or how one man's head was porcelain to another's eggshell.

Williams had thought it best to take his sleep away from the ship. Roberts found him slumped in the crook of a tree just yards from the gates of the dock.

'William,' said the captain, and nudged his dozing countryman with his buckled shoe.

'William, are you awake lad? William?'

Williams opened his eyes and saw his captain standing in front of him, lit by the bright midmorning sun, still dressed in the maroon britches, laced in gold brocade. His dress coat hung over his side, and the cream-coloured shirt had begun to yellow at the collar as if he had slept in it.

'How was the governor?'

'Fat with information. She has been seen.'

'Catrin?' asked Williams, pinching his eyes.

'The *Juliette*,' said Roberts. 'In these waters not two months back. She heads for the Caribbean. A touch, Mr Williams, a faint taste is it not?'

'Well enough for tomorrow,' said Williams and spat a dirty mouthful of spit to the ground, 'but today is for a lady of Cardiff, who spent her time with me last night.'

'Odd's plot and her nails,' cried Roberts. 'A Welsh whore on Devil's Island?'

'No,' said Williams.

'No to what?'

'She's not a whore.'

Roberts laughed at him. 'I forget your age. I think of all that's stopped in your brain pan and forget you've never had a full heart. If you're to fall for a whore tis just as well she's Welsh.'

'She's a girl. A wee thing.'

'And I'm sure that she had the smile of daybreak, and stars for eyes.'

Williams smiled. 'No, Captain, she's a plain one, skinny lass.'

'Come now,' said Roberts, and dredged himself to his feet. 'We've not one but two ships to unlade before you go visiting again.'

Although little of note occurred on the first day in Devil's Island, apart from a general and slow recovery by the crew, the next week was spent with the governor's traders and assessors ploughing their way through the holds of the *Rover* and *Sagrada Familia*. Sympson directed the selective unloading of the ships and stacks of hides sat ten feet thick on the dock, alongside the bales of cotton and silk captured from the *Experiment*. The sugar was carried by cart and oxen to the warehouses that separated the dock from the town. All were occupied by the movement of cargo, save Aged Q who had snapped his ankle on that first night. While kinder sorts suggested that he had been an old goat chasing after young birdies, Kennedy concluded that he was a lame old nag who should be thankful his throat wasn't cut.

The crew were paid promptly by the governor for their wares. If any had the inclination to study the pieces of eight that they received as payment for the sugars and hides, they might have noticed that their own gold, paid out upon the night of their arrival, had already begun to return to them. Of course, it was not long before the circle of coin was complete and the path that separated the *Rover* from the taverns and nanny houses of the town was soon widened by a constant traffic.

It was a sudden turn to be thrown from a year in the company of men to walking the streets of a town where five hundred women lived. Odd to look at a woman, and from the shade of her dress see that she was indeed a lady, perhaps even the governor's wife, and then to tip your hat in her direction, thinking yourself a pretty cove. By the end of their first week on Devil's Island, with only a loose watch to keep, the crew became accustomed to being gentlemen of leisure, and some sat on deck sewing, while others sought out local pricklouses, and they fashioned clothes from unsold material and hoped their appearance might reflect their financial status. It was a rehearsal for the responsibilities of wealth that the *Juliette* would bring. There was, however, a shortage of shoes on the island, and it became the only manner in which the townspeople could sort the *Rover*'s crew. The captain, quartermaster and first mate had all secured shoes – the rest travelled barefoot and their dirty toes mocked their pretensions.

Roberts knew that he would lose command should he try to manoeuvre the crew before their pockets echoed, but to his relief the fortunes amassed so quickly were almost as rapidly spent. There was barely a man who did not see himself as a rum gambler, a drinker and a ladies' man and as each settled upon his 'wife', they competed in the purchase of gifts, in the attempt to create gentlewomen from whores, same as money had made lords from sailor men.

Williams's attentions fell, predictably, upon the Welsh whore, Catrin, whom he treated as if he were the suitor to a grand estate. It had something to do with the burn of gold within his pocket, but it was attention paid in honest romance, and though he had lain with her once he did not rest a hand upon her for the following ten days. Instead, he spent his mornings composing verse or adding to the journal. While his first intent had been to focus his writings on the captain, it was no surprise that a young man courting should turn every thought to the object of his affections:

I turned to Catrin, not one warm hour ago and spoke, 'Thou art fair my love, thou art fair, thou hast dove's eyes within thy locks, thy lips art like a thread of scarlet, thou art all fair my love, there is no spot in thee.' She blushed and told me I was a pretty poet to write such lies about her but I confessed it was not me, but the Bible. She told me I was a hard liar and it took all earnestness to convince her it was the Song of Solomon. I know it wrong for a deckhand to sing holy words to a doxy, but are we not also young and honest in our way? If our alliance is to be brief, so must it be strong. I do not spill my gold in such a torrent as those about me, but I know that Roberts tells true, and when the first of the threadbare begin to mew, we shall take to the sea, and she shall remind us of our equality. I shall spend all my time with Catrin.

The weight of gold had done much to alleviate the surgeon's duties, and men who had complained of aches and invisible symptoms now preened as if they were post captains. Instead the surgeon was kept busy by those demanding, and sometimes paying for, a shave and a haircut. Scudamore would recommend that he complete the service with a six-ounce bleed – seeing as how close to the equator they stood – but none, not even Williams, would succumb to his entreaties.

Unable to grow a thick beard, Williams would request a shave on every second day. There were few as demanding as the fiddler, but the surgeon did not mind putting his books down to tidy his young friend up for an afternoon of courting. Scudamore applied the lather to Williams's cheeks and to the top of his neck, the fiddler's nose twitching to feel the brush pass over his top lip.

'I was thinking,' grinned Williams to Scudamore, 'of taking lodging in the town.'

'She has you crying for home,' said the surgeon, placing his hand back on Williams's forehead and bringing the blade down the side of his face, from ear to jaw. 'How do you feel, son?'

'Never finer. Find my mouth curled up and can never remember the cause of it.'

'I'm talking physic,' said Scudamore. 'You seem a touch febrile to me.'

Williams shook his head. 'I suppose that I been sleeping unusual hard, but that – I would venture – has more to do with the arms that hold me.'

'And the girl, she sleeps as oft as you?'

'At times,' said Williams, 'we spend the day folded in each other's arms. Scudamore, my friend, you have no idea . . .'

'Mr Williams,' said the surgeon sternly, his hands still holding the fiddler's head, 'I am not

120

asking for one of your poems. Lie upon the deck, if you will.'

William submitted, and laid himself flat abeam. The surgeon carefully ran his hand over his stomach, and knocked lightly upon it twice.

'Sit up now, lad,' he said, 'and we'll make you clean for your lady.'

'So doctor,' laughed Williams, 'is it truly a heart aflame?'

'In truth,' said Scudamore, 'I am not fairly certain. I think it capital if you were to gather your sea-chest and take a room in town. I would recommend that you do so this very morning.' He washed the final soap from Williams's chin, and then rubbed at his face with a damp cloth. 'When you've a room, send word to me. I insist that I see you this afternoon, and make the acquaintance of your young lady . . .'

'Catrin,' added Williams proudly.

'Indeed,' said the surgeon, and called up the next of the small line of idlers.

When Scudamore arrived in the apartment, late the same afternoon, Williams, with a swelled chest, escorted the surgeon about his first home, showing his greeting room, an empty study, then hesitating before the bedroom door. 'Catrin,' he said, 'is resting right now, but if you would be my guest for a pot of ale, then I'm sure that she would join us.'

'Thank you, William. My pleasure.'

As the two men perched upon the window sill (the room absent of furniture), sipping upon warm beer, they looked down on the cobbled alley, and watched the people come and go. Rovers walked past, their clothes rarely disguising the peculiar walk of the seaman, as if they never trusted the solidity of the ground beneath them. The two men talked of epigrams, but at the end of the first pot, Scudamore turned to William and said, 'Would you wake your wife now, William? I must see her before I take my leave of you.'

Williams smiled, and said that he would be glad.

No more than five minutes passed before Catrin emerged from her bedroom, looking like a head and dress slung upon a broomstick. She wore a simple shawl of wool pulled tight across her shoulders.

'Miss Catrin Pryce, may I introduce Dr Peter Scudamore.'

'It is my pleasure, madam,' said Scudamore and returned her half-curtsey with a low bow.

'Really, Doctor,' she said softly, 'you do me great honour.'

'Not at all,' said the surgeon. 'Not at all.'

'You are our very first guest,' she added.

'So I hear. How do you feel, my dear?'

Catrin glanced at Williams, and then turned a smile on the surgeon. 'I am in as fine a spirit as I ha' ever been.'

Scudamore took a step forward and placed his

hand on her brow. 'You seem a trifle warm to me.'
She nodded. 'And William tells me you have slept much of late?'

'Ever so heavy,' she said.

'I hope it does not seem impertinent of me, but would you allow me to act as your physician?'

'Certainly sir,' she replied. 'The bawd has us looked over two days of the month by a Spanish doctor, but he is concerned only with the . . . lower . . .'

'I understand, my dear,' said Scudamore calmly. 'Would you be so kind as to retreat to your bedroom, and undress next door.'

'Should I lie on the bed?'

'Exactly so.'

Williams beamed a smile of reassurance and nodded her towards the bedroom.

After she had removed herself, the surgeon turned to Williams and asked, 'Does she always speak like a mouse in cheese?'

'Indeed,' replied Williams. 'Is peculiarly attractive after a time, is it not?'

'I dare say.'

'What is it you wish?' asked Williams and the surgeon pointed to the bedroom door.

Catrin lay there in the last light of day, causing the surgeon to send Williams for a candle, while he began his inspection. He had seen corpses with similar colours and textures. Her skin was a shade of alabaster, only interrupted by a cluster of angry red spots that decorated the concave mould of her stomach. He made her hold her own legs apart while he peered closely. Williams returned and placed the candle by the bed, and then stood back with his arms crossed in front of his chest.

'You may dress, child,' said Scudamore, as he took a seat at the foot of the bed. He swivelled until he met with Williams's gaze.

'I shall tell you both what I know.'

'Go on then,' said Williams. 'Spit it.'

'Is a fever,' said the surgeon. 'It belongs to you both. I have seen it before. It comes first like the bloody flux, but tis a fever and a bad one, and is a form of contagion. You will both remain in your rooms. I shall visit you twice a day.'

'For how long?' asked Williams.

'Must we go nowhere?' asked Catrin.

'It will be a while longer,' answered the surgeon. 'A week or two, perhaps more. Will seem slow for a while, but the time will soon pass quickly.'

'How?' asked Williams.

'Delirium,' explained the surgeon.

CHAPTER 15

By Scudamore's eighth visit, on the fourth day of their internment, Williams had begun to curse and blame the doctor for their current state. Until the diagnosis, the couple had been flourishing under the dose of mutual attention. Even if their bodies were ailing, their minds had not noticed, and the rush of sickness that fell upon the apartment seemed to Williams like a disease ushered in, or at least provoked, by the surgeon. Catrin's fever ran high as early as their first night together in their home and her temperature undulated so that by morning the bed was damp with her perspiration. Her small body was contorted at times, as the pain centred in her stomach burst in spasms through her limbs. Williams remained in good health, but kept a close watch on his own stomach, continually expecting the rash to develop. He sat beside Catrin on the bed and observed her suffering.

The surgeon pressed his medicine upon them both and bled them daily to relieve them of the heat of their fevers. On the fifth day, Williams succumbed to his wife's condition and subsequently had only the cloudiest recollections of the days that passed. The rooms began to take on a fetid, cloying odour, whether the windows were left open or closed. Scudamore, though happy to risk contagion on his friend's behalf, was unwilling to press others into service. He tied their ankles to the bed frame and, though the skin became chafed and sore by their feverous movements, it seemed a safer option than risking a delirious escape into the alleyways of Devil's Island.

Both patients lost weight, but while Williams could afford to shed the remainder of his original belly, Catrin had little to spare. She was reduced from waif to skeleton and Scudamore was thankful that her bed partner was insensate: it was a hard sight to see a good soul wither. He administered his favoured tonic of cinchona to appease the fever and tried to feed the couple a tincture of opium to ensure a steady rest. While Williams held his medicine, Catrin responded as if they were emetics and kept nothing down.

Scudamore feared the worst for her. He had lost many patients from milder symptoms. During twilight on the tenth day, Catrin entered a deep coma. The doctor was unable to feed her, and watched helplessly as her body refused to support her sleeping mind. After two long weeks, he carried her lifeless form from the apartment. Williams, in unconscious mourning, entered a similar coma, and with the greatest of regrets Scudamore considered him lost.

★   ★   ★

It was a strange sound. Two distinct thumps followed by a light pitter-patter and then a swish across the polished floor as a weight was swept forward before the racket was repeated. The sounds grew louder and louder, until they seemed as if they would burst Williams's eardrums. He sat bolt upright in bed and cried out aloud.

'My God,' said Aged Q caught mid-swing on his crutches, 'you're a whore's kitling for having a grown man pacing days for you.'

Williams cast his eyes around the room. 'Where is she?'

'The girl?' said Aged Q shifting uncomfortably from crutch to crutch.

'Catrin, the Welsh girl.'

'Long gone,' murmured Aged Q to the wooden floor. 'Dead past two weeks now. Closer to three, perhaps.'

'You saw her?'

'Saw the surgeon givin' her burial. Wasn't a clergyman who'd come close. So he dug the grave and said blessing all by hisself. People wouldn't let her within town walls, so he buried her a mile from town. Had oxen and carried her out.'

'Two weeks dead,' said Williams to himself, and then looked at Aged Q as if the news were part of an orchestrated conspiracy against which he stood alone. 'Then where is the surgeon?' he asked, growling. 'Why is he not here?'

'Don't raise your voice against him lad. Was Roberts that made him leave, and fairly so. Had spent three weeks mopping at your brow. And hers. Did not leave until you slept.'

'Your ankle?' asked Williams, calming once more, already tiring.

Aged Q gave his crutches a wiggle. 'Been o'er a month, but I'm not a young healer like yourself. Still cannot rest my weight against it. Been keeping you clean, brother, for my sins. Washing after you I have, feeding you what surgeon's left behind.'

Williams's anger subsided. He could not bring himself to resent his friend, a man who had risked infection to keep him alive, even after he had been abandoned.

'Rhode Island sloop came sailing by,' said Aged Q eager to turn the conversation from the dead girl, 'around a week ago, and well . . . Roberts . . . requisitioned her. Believe he encouraged the governor. She was captained by a rum cove, called Cane, struck her as soon as she saw the *Rover*'s flag, and we sailed her in. Cane shared a drink with all, not just Lords, Commons too. Then he shipped out with a ketch bound for the Carolinas, but before he told Roberts he was but a small sister ship to another Rhode Islander, a brigantine that had provisioned the *Juliette*. Roberts relieved him of his sloop, took forty men, and sailed to find the brig.'

'Was the brig rich?' asked Williams.

'Can't rightly say,' said Aged Q. 'Been o'er the week and no signs of her.'

'And the surgeon's with her?'

'Aye, Roberts thought it best he stayed ship-board. Took all the old crew with him. We still have the Experiments down the dockside. Money's pretty thin. Kennedy around too – refused to sail without his coves,' wheezed Aged Q swaying on his sticks. 'Now that made Roberts smile, could not be happier to leave him behind but said that we'd hold *our* share of the prize. Capital lad. Think of it – asleep for a month and collecting sea tax like a king.'

'Capital,' said Williams sourly. 'Why'd he not sail the *Rover*?'

'Reckoned with the American sloop they could sail abeam of her sister without a worry. She'll be easy taking, and a pretty thing.'

Aged Q coughed into his hand, and briefly studied the excretion lying in his palm. 'You must be gut-foundered, lad. I'll bring you some beer and fruit. Something soft for you.' He skipped towards the doorway on his four legs.

'Thank you, friend,' said Williams.

'How does it feel?' asked Aged Q.

'How d'you mean?'

'You've not uttered a word in a score of days.'

Williams managed a nod and the beginnings of a smile, but turned his back on the old man. It was not right for one man to see another cry. He slept for a while, into darkness, and when Aged Q returned, a basket strapped to his back, he found the fiddler had moved himself from the bed where

Catrin died and was rolled in a blanket on the floor of the study.

It was another three days before Williams was strong enough to stand on his own feet for more than a minute or two. Aged Q divided his time between sitting with a taciturn Williams and swinging down to the dock to keep watch for Roberts's return. At night he spent a small sum of gold that Williams had loaned him, drinking alone. The two men had always shared an intense dislike for Kennedy, and Aged Q was careful to keep distance from the Irishman.

Aged Q was not a man who mustered automatic respect. It was the poor combination of too much age and too low a rank that made inferior men consider him a relic. He was, in many ways, an average man, but Williams recognized that it was a singular achievement to have spent forty years sailing deep seas. He thought of their friendship as a trade of experience with vitality.

Not having seen his own image in months, Williams guessed from the pressure of eyes that he felt upon him as he walked the streets that he was much changed. His illness had drained him of colour, and the stains of sun and wind had long since leaked into the sheets of his bed. The whites of his eyes were now pink, and the girth that had been the cause of teasing only months ago was a railing of prominent ribs.

CHAPTER 16

Aged Q forsook his crutches the week after Williams awoke, and the two convalescents found a shelf of rock, sheltered from the sun, that looked out across the ocean, from which to watch for Roberts. Williams did not wish to be alone with his journal. He could not bring himself to write a word; Catrin's name was too sacred for pen and ink and all other matters too trivial. The warm wind blew steadily upon Aged Q and the fiddler as they debated long and hard on the provisions that Sympson would have taken aboard the sloop for a brief chase, and reckoned that they could not last much longer. Unless, of course, they had taken the Rhode Island brigantine and sailed north for the *Juliette*, abandoning the *Rover* and the dregs of treasure from the *Sagrada Familia*. Williams knew it was reasonable to believe that they would abandon Kennedy, retire Aged Q and consider himself long-since dead.

Even the sails of fishing smacks confused the two Rovers as they searched the horizon for the single-masted sloop and the two masts of the brigantine prize. On the twelfth day of their watch, they took their accustomed pews, a jug of ale propped between them, and began to discuss the variables of fate that might have befallen the members of the crew. Williams turned his eyes from the edges of the horizon to the dock beneath them.

'God in heaven,' he said, and rose to his feet, staring in all directions at once.

'What is it lad?' cried Aged Q. 'What do you see? Tell me, goddamn your eyes.'

Williams was already moving off down the path, his weakness compensated by the awful worry that enveloped him.

'Slow yourself,' shouted the old man, limping and hopping after him. 'Avast you bastard,' yelled Aged Q 'take pity on me, you whoreson.'

As they passed through the gates of the dock, Aged Q paused from exhaustion, and looking up, forgot to breathe for a moment, as Williams raced from one end of the dock to another. There was no *Rover*. No *Sagrada Familia*. It took them little enough time to confirm the fact that there was no Kennedy either, nor any from the *Experiment*, and they were now the lone representatives of the *Rover*, welcomed in so royal a manner by the people of Devil's Island.

There followed an extraordinary display from Aged Q including a stomping dance at great risk to his fragile ankle and a lengthy recitation of every curse that he had heard during forty years of seafaring. Williams felt that his own anger had been eclipsed, if only because of the silent satisfaction he derived from the knowledge that Kennedy, whom he had long considered hateful, could now be publicly declared a lick-spitted sharper.

It was then with heavy hearts that a fair-sized sloop was seen bearing to the harbour. The two men stood dockside, as messengers who would confirm what every eye suspected. The majority of the crew were ferried ashore by idle fishermen, and listened with patience as Aged Q related his own tale of the last two weeks. Williams could feel Roberts's eyes upon him, and the gaze of the surgeon, but he could not look up to meet their stares. He had seen their own exhaustion etched upon each face as they had walked up the stone steps of the dockside. Roberts did not speak a word, until he proposed that they all should retire to a tavern and consider their position over supper.

Scudamore took a moment to shake Williams firmly by the hand, as if he was checking for a pulse. His eyes glistened with grateful tears but the Welshman could only manage a hollow smile. So much misery seemed to have been meted out all around that he did not wish attention to fall upon himself. They had survived, yet all had reasons to feel cheated, and more than one could not see the point in their endurance. Bunch's countenance was the most weary of all. If the rest were betrayed by Kennedy, then Bunch had been disowned. While this painful moment was not unfamiliar to Williams, he could not help but break his first smile in weeks in honour of Bunch's unhappiness.

The Rovers had spied the brigantine two days out, and had chased her for the following eight, but the sloop was no match for her sister. Why she had not hove to, none could say, but she ran before them like a bird over water, and when the vote was taken, and the decision made to return to Devil's Island, the wind died laughing at them, and they were left sitting in an Irishman's hurricane. After two days and no sign of relief, they ripped planking from the quarterdeck and fashioned sweeps for the rotting tender. It took three days for the tender to return with water and by then they were at the dregs of a hard ale that had caused a ceaseless vomiting and an increased dehydration. Still, all drank it, for it relieved the mouth of splinters. It was now two days since and the wind had returned, finally pushing them homeward.

It was odd to look about the tavern and see so many faces taut from hunger, so many noses twitching at the aroma of cooking meats. No one addressed their depleted physical state, for they shared the single dominant thought of aggrievement and yet had to bow to the fact that revenge was already beyond their reach.

'Unless there are dissidents present, I enforce my captainship.'

'Aye, Bart,' said Sympson. An uncaring chorus of grudging support followed.

'We're a herd of milch cows,' said Roberts, 'and I hold myself accountable. There is little more to be said of it. This is not the time to turn on one

134

another. The hateful are long gone and your gold is with them. Those that remain are your brethren and do not doubt. We shall learn from this . . . Mr Williams?'

'Aye, sir,' said Williams, staring at his bare feet.

'You shall sit with me and script articles. They shall be read tomorrow and marked by all who wish to sail. We trail the *Juliette*. Any who yet have monies are to give them up to Lord Sympson. They shall be repaid double within a month. Upon my word. We outfit and weigh anchor as quick as Jack Robinson.'

Williams carried a jug of ale to the apartments above the tavern where Roberts had secured a room. It was a spartan space of uninterrupted bare woods, rubbed clean enough, but dirty to a deckhand's eyes. Roberts had set paper and ink before the desk and centred four candles on the table so that the quill and weave of the paper were brought into clear focus while the rest of the room backed into shadows. For once Roberts was sitting close to the light, across the table from the empty chair.

The captain had removed his frock coat and the blackened linen neckcloth. The pretensions of a gentlemanly life had been abandoned, and the streaks of dirt on the cream shirt confirmed the change of fortunes. Roberts had lost a little of the flesh about his face, and his jawline, two days unshaved, was rife with a strong grey stubble. If Williams had not known of the deprivations suffered by the crew, he would have said that Roberts looked well.

'William, you are a welcome sight.'

'And you, sir.'

'The surgeon had me expecting to drop dust over your grave. Interred or unchanged he said.' Williams tried to smile, but it came out as a tic, repeated twice. 'I told him that we Welsh were made of stronger stones.' Williams nodded, and took his seat opposite the captain. 'Am sorry for your wife,' said Roberts softly. 'She ne'er looked a strong girl.'

Williams continued to nod, but his pale skin had begun to redden.

'And did you keep on with your journal?' said Roberts, asking the question that Williams suspected he had been trying to contain.

'Oh yes,' said Williams, his voice tightening. 'Every day when I was talking to saints, I would find a moment to annotate my dreams. I wrote a line or two of you, wrote it in Catrin's sweat and shit, and would have inked it in her blood had I been conscious of her demise.'

'Mr Williams, I have not been courting kings myself,' said Roberts dryly.

'But you left us. Took the surgeon and left us. Went sniffing after your ghosts of gold when we had a full hold and . . .'

'Listen, little prick,' growled Roberts, his voice deepening in opposition to Williams's distressed pitch, 'I'd a hundred men and more and provisions

136

too low to make the Caribbean. It was a simple chance for an afternoon's gain and didn't reckon on a long chase nor adverse current, and you mew and pule like a newborn. You think I show you no concern, is that your trouble?'

'You,' said Williams, standing, 'care for what is of use to you. You use me for a purpose.'

'Aye, fair enough,' said Roberts, 'I make use of you. You should be grateful that you're of account . . .'

'To hell with you, Bartholomew Roberts,' shouted Williams. 'You've shown yourself vain and imprudent – lost half a crew and a pair of vessels and could no sooner win the *Juliette* than a . . .' Roberts pushed the entire table so that it stuttered against the floor and then shot forward into Williams's legs, causing him to fold in the middle and bringing his head within Roberts's reach. The captain grabbed a handful of hair and banged Williams's face down once upon the table, very hard, so that the blood from his nose ran on to the writing paper. Roberts leaned forward, still in his seat. Williams could feel the slenderness and the strength of the arm that gripped his hair, and he tried to fight it off with both his hands.

'This is the sum of all. Do you understand me boy?' He banged Williams's head down again. 'This.' Roberts squeezed the fistful of hair, and the fiddler squealed as he heard strands ripping from his scalp. 'Strength. Strength and a little guile. Tis not hard to understand now, is it?' Williams tried to shake his head in agreement, but the grip was too firm. 'Save diplomacy only for your equals.'

There was a knock on the door. Roberts released Williams's head and pushed him backwards into his chair. Two women, smelling of the grease of kitchens, entered, carrying supper before them. Roberts stared at the dish of brains. Williams, with tears in his eyes, blood still oozing from his nose and a hand rubbing the top of his head, felt great empathy for the sheep.

Smiling at the women as they put the plates in front of the guests, Roberts addressed Williams. 'You cannot afford to stay selfish lad,' he breathed loudly. 'Answer me this. Do you still keep the journal, or is it gone with the *Rover*?'

'I have it,' said Williams, running his cuff over his mouth. 'But it has had no entries for the best of a month.' He spat a mouthful of blood on the floor.

'The world seems agin you.'

Williams did not speak while the dishes were laid out on the table top.

'You've lost a girl you cared for. Had a wicked fever that sucked your health away.' The ladies retreated, waved off by Roberts, and instructed to close the door after them. 'Abandoned by your friend the surgeon, and now beaten by the captain when you've never felt so feeble.' Roberts raised a spoon to him, and gave him a mock salute. 'You're thinking that you would not treat a dog this way.'

'I am thinking,' said Williams, wiping again at

his nose, 'of trading for a dog. I'll kick it to ease my bruises.'

Roberts laughed hard, and wagged the spoon at the fiddler.

'*There* is an answer,' said Roberts, 'and now that we're at supper like civilized men I would tip my hat to you if I wore one, and call you a thick-skinned lad. We may have stood a day or two before death, but you slept next to him. A veritable Lazarus.'

'You're a confusing man,' said Williams softly. 'Sometimes I feel as if I do not know you.'

'Come now,' said Roberts. 'You speak more to me than the rest as one.'

'I know it,' breathed Williams, 'and it means nothing.'

'You wish to know me? You may find me then in the rules that I keep. You and I, soon as this is through,' he said, speaking through a mouthful of mutton, 'shall play at God and set commandments down for the rest to observe. What do you think of that?'

'Is capital,' said Williams flatly.

Roberts concentrated on his food. Finally he slapped the spoon on the table top, rubbed the back of his hand across his mouth, and then ground his palm against the beginning of his whiskers.

'Imprudent . . .' he said, and looked at Williams.

'Come again?'

'You called me imprudent. Before, when you cursed my bones.'

'So I did,' said Williams, and prepared himself to hold the gaze.

'I feel,' said Roberts, 'that it fits me directly. A regular nokes to set faith in Kennedy. I regret it. Drink to an apology, because it is the last that you are ever likely to hear.'

Williams raised his glass. 'You'll never again admit an error?'

'I will never again make one.'

'Then I will stay steady till the *Juliette*.'

Roberts clinked his stone water mug against Williams's jar of ale, and then stood to lower both of their plates to the floor. 'The first commandment,' said Roberts, easing himself into the back of his chair, 'is that each shall remain with only one vote, despite rank. Vittles and drink is equal and open . . . until a scarcity arises. Then the quartermaster shall set rations.'

Williams dipped his pen, and began his scratchings in English.

'To pilfer against crew is to be marooned. Against a particular crew member and nose and ears will be split. The thief shall be set down in some . . .'

'Inhospitable land?' suggested Williams.

'Aye,' said the captain. 'Good. Hardship, but survival.'

'And the third?' asked Williams.

'There is to be no more gambling aboard.' At this Williams looked up and wrinkled his bloodied nose. It seemed to him a ridiculous condition, but

140

the heady throb from between his eyes counselled him to silence.

'Drinking,' continued the captain, 'is to be conducted on deck. If men wish to plot against me, then they will be sober enough to consider their crimes.'

'We're more bound by greed than faith,' said Williams softly, so as not to excite the captain, 'but as the mother hen you've fed them gold and still they strayed. Queer coves, Captain.'

'Fine point, fine point.' Roberts was more volatile than usual. At sea, no man could question the work of a superior ranking. If the chain of command was broken or even strained, then its strength would be reinforced with the lash. The betrayal of Roberts and Kennedy's successful escape had rattled the man, and Williams, despite his crushed nose, was tempted to see a strange sort of decency opposite him. He could also see a man who, as captain, had felt the first shudder of the precariousness of his position. Kennedy's real theft was one of confidence. If the *Juliette* was the enticement through which Roberts led his crew, the loss of the *Rover* was an outright rejection of the captain's ethos.

'How are you lad?' asked Roberts.

Williams touched his hand to his nose, and felt the sharp pinch of dried blood. 'Is nothing,' he said and rubbed his hand over his raw scalp. 'Feel like a pilgarlic.'

'And the fevers? The surgeon told me your stomach was torn.'

141

'Well,' said Williams, 'still cannot trust my arse with a fart, but, as yet, that is my only concern.'

Roberts smiled warmly, a father considering the travails of a son. He pointed at the paper, signalling that he was ready to proceed with the fifth commandment.

'Pistols and cutlasses to be kept in clean condition. No boys or women are allowed among us.' The captain had begun to pack his pipe, carefully balling the tobacco to assure a slow burn. 'Any attempt to smuggle birdies aboard will result in death. Desertion of ship during an engagement or otherwise – death.'

'A strange equation,' commented Williams, and then added, 'perhaps not.'

'Any man who strikes another on board shall resolve the insult ashore. First through pistols, then through sword. Nine shall be that no man may leave the crew of Bartholomew Roberts until he has one thousand pounds to his name. If he loses a limb, four hundred, an eye two hundred, and so forth, according to your fairness. The tenth concerns the allotment of shares. Two for captain and quartermaster. Lords one and a half, et cetera.'

'Ten commandments,' said Williams, dipping his quill in ink and committing the final words to the page, 'and as fast as Moses.'

'The eleventh,' smiled Roberts, 'is a gift to you. No musician shall work on the sabbath.'

'I approve of the new world,' said Williams, looking up from his page.

'Aye,' said Roberts, 'and it almost skipped by me, but we'll have no faithless teagues prancing peacocklike about my deck.' The words were not louder, but more pronounced. 'No Irish. None at all.' Beads of sweat had risen on the captain's top lip, and he reminded Williams of a drinking man. He understood how it could be that Roberts would not touch alcohol. It was already in his blood and he could turn from sympathy to spite in a trice.

'Is a good twelve, then, Mr Williams?'

'Aye, sir.'

'None that you might . . . remedy?'

Williams trailed the nib of the quill down the margins of the articles. 'Looking so close, Captain, I confess that, of all, only the third bothers me. No gambling. You might as well tell a man not to box his Jesuit.'

'Exodus twenty, verse seventeen,' said Roberts. 'I am sure you are familiar with the text. Thou shalt not covet thy neighbour's house, nor his wife, manservant, mistress, nor horse and carriage. Does that not seem strange to you?'

'I'm supposing that I've never thought upon it before.'

'Who knows the workings of man better than his Creator? We are given a commandment that is deliberately set against the nature of man. And so we are forced to sin. For those who believe, they are given reason to repent. Those of little faith will find a thrill in running against the government, and yet they will not strain to mutiny. Of course the men will have at dice, and they are welcome to it.'

'God desires, man distributes,' quoted Williams in Welsh.

CHAPTER 17

When misfortune befalls a crew it is shared among their number. Like gold, it is divided and burns at each sailor to differing degrees, but still is each's first and last thought of the day. On the following morning, they were all driven early from bed by a collective unhappiness and gathered in the tavern to share a meal alongside the fishermen readying themselves for their dawn work. They listened carefully as Williams read aloud the terms of articles, and though glances were exchanged at any mention of gambling, women, or drink, the majority drew immediate comfort from organization. There was a prevailing attitude of anxiety and all were ready to return to the sea and prove themselves at their work. The crew made their marks in a round robin at the foot of the articles.

The same afternoon they were divided into work parties by Sympson, and set about readying the sloop, cleaning her, stocking her with as many provisions as could be bought or traded for. She was renamed the *Sycamore*. Out of the vast fortune that had been captured within the *Sagrada Familia*, less than one thousand pounds had been confessed between them. It was still a fine sum, but money could not buy what did not exist. Devil's Island had been exhausted by the month-long stay of Robert's crew, and Kennedy had provisioned the *Rover* only the week before, and there was little left to trade for.

Such was the breath of relief when the mainsail was finally set that it was almost enough to fill the canvas and blow them from Devil's Island. Those who had left wives behind mourned them throughout the first watch, when clouds and waves had a curious habit of imitating the female form, but the rest reminded them to be thankful for their freedom. Spirits were raised by the end of the first week, when they took not one, but two smaller sloops within a single day. Their provisions were supplemented and then completed when they took a Bristol ship of ten guns on her voyage out. They seized an abundance of clothes, a small portion of money, five barrels of powder, twenty-five barrels of goods, a cable, a hawser, ten casks of oatmeal, six casks of beef and five of her men. Her captain was a pot-bellied Englishman, who displayed his general disdain by refusing to speak with Roberts.

Both captain and crew of the small sloop seemed so grateful for their change in fortune that they did not even punish the English captain for his arrogance, and a vote was taken where it was decided to let the captured ship prosecute her journey to Barbados. Their hold was already beginning to weigh heavy with stolen goods. Three such brief and easy captures restored any doubts that the crew had to Roberts's resilience and luck, and the captain seemed an altogether different man, who drew his prizes mainly from the clothes of the galley, reserving for himself the best and often the gaudiest of suits.

On the day when a second Bristol galley was spied not forty miles windward, Roberts had ordered Williams to his cabin. When the fiddler arrived, the cabin was empty. On the captain's desk lay a pot of ink and the last page of Williams's manuscript. He had not even noticed its absence. Though Roberts could not possibly have understood the words he had, no doubt, noticed the lack of interest Williams had displayed in his work. Only one paragraph had been written since their departure:

Miss Catrin Price (born Cardiff 1706, died Devil's Island, 1720)

I cannot mark a page with tears. Let me say this to you. I regret that I was not awake to hold your hand, but know that I lie beside you. When your eyes were closed, so were mine. As you suffered, so did I. And when I woke, it was without you, and I burned your linen and sent prayers upwards. Godless, I have knelt before your grave. I do not like life without you, but what is left?

He dipped his pen then turned the page.

I am alive again, like a snake that has shed its skin. There is a Bristolman on the horizon and I am forced below to convert myself from lover to scribe. Bunch is the only man who seems to share my sadness, for he has not a friend left aboard the ship, save for Coffin, who holds no influence. And Roberts, dressed in brown lace, makes himself a figurehead, a gentleman who is both at one and apart from the crew. And I? The sun has turned me dark again, my nature is reclaimed by the sea. She has thinned me out, taken my belly and tried to stitch my heart. Let me change my skin again, put down the ink, pick up the fiddle and play a tune for our cannon. Let me forget mine own happiness for now, and let me deserve it when it comes.

It was with great confidence that the black flag was raised. Despite Wilson's admonitions, the gun deck was cleared in a half-hearted and slovenly manner. Hammocks were slung carelessly over the leeward side instead of rolled and pushed against the bulwarks as extra protection against shot. Roberts conned the ship windward of her target. Their laziness in preparing the gun deck did not distract the crew from their general urge to convey their bloodthirstiness. As the galley struck her mainsails, they gathered on deck, with the clatter of hand axes, cutlasses, grenadoes, pistols and muskets. There was a lot of jostling. It was a larger vessel than those taken earlier in the week and, despite the system of sharing, as the first man

148

to spy the ship was granted the finest pistols, the first aboard chose freely from clothes as soon as Roberts had taken his choice.

On the bow, playing sharply at his fiddle, Williams concentrated on emitting a fearful screech heedless of tune. The shriek of the fife, wedded to the continued thunder of the drum and the deep howl of the crew, made them sound twice their number. When they were within a ship's length of their prey, Wilson ordered a warning shot to be sent across her bows. The crew watched patiently, expecting her to strike as they drew ever closer. They kept their eyes trained on the galley's gun ports, well aware that she could outgun their sloop. A Barbados flag rattled up the galley's main mast and a cloud of smoke appeared on their windward side.

A series of deafening roars seemed to begin between Williams's ears, and the *Sycamore* lurched under the broadside. Williams heard a crack and glanced forward to see that one of the bowsprit's shrouds had been severed by a cannonball. There was a hollow pop as a musketball pierced the side of the drum and, with ears ringing, Williams came to the conclusion that the bow was not the safest of places to be. He could determine, as the smoke from the first broadside rose above the ships, that the enemy was setting a stud'n'sail and was keeping a pace with the sloop as she tried to limp past. A quiet blast seemed to emerge from beneath him, and the *Sycamore*'s little four-pounders sounded in pathetic defiance against the heavier guns of the galley.

Williams took four bounding leaps towards the men crowded, or rather divided, on the main deck. A shot from the opening broadside, packed with shrapnel and fired from no more than thirty yards, had bisected the waiting men. As Williams took his fourth leap, the waist of the sloop disappeared under a blinding flash as two of the grenadoes intended for the enemy exploded, sending a thick belch of smoke across the decks. He slipped in a large pool of blood and lost his footing. Pushing his hands against the blood-spattered deck Williams could hear orders barked around him. He sat staring at his bloodied hands through tearing eyes. A piece of viscera, a small wedge of unmistakable gristle, was lodged in between the third and fourth fingers of his right hand. The acrid smell of powder kept him conscious. He was wiping his hands against his ducks when he heard and felt the shudder of the second broadside. Williams thought that they must be so close to one another that their rigging could be intertwined.

It was an accurate guess. Roberts had ordered the helmsman to pass close to the enemy, the sloop's larboard side coming within yards of the Bristol's bows. The second broadside had passed over their deck, save for a great crash that could be heard as a cannonball slammed into the *Sycamore*'s stern, passing through the windows of the captain's cabin, just beneath the quarterdeck. Roberts was staring aloft, trying to assess the damage to mast and sails.

Scudamore had hurriedly set his surgery on the disengaged side of the gun deck and, stirring Williams from his trance, employed him as a surgeon's mate, having him drag the injured towards the medicine chest, where he was frantically preparing dressings. Williams did his best to put aside the piteous pleas for assistance from various quarters of the deck. It did no good to look for friends. Every cry was a familiar tone. Despite the small size of the crew a full quarter of them had received injury from the surprise of the opening broadside.

It seemed that the brig's gunner had handed the firing orders directly to the gun crews. The captain brought his ship around, presenting his starboard guns to the sloop, hoping to sink the *Sycamore* or at least cause so much damage that she would be winged in flight. The ten guns of the starboard side were each presented with a shot at the sloop. Even the rawest crew, such as Williams, bristled with indignation at having to expose themselves so. There were loud cheers from the brig as their shot struck home in the stern of the ship, a mere two feet from the waterline. The second blast was chainshot aimed towards the lines of their mainsail. It whistled as it passed too high, and buried itself in the ocean. Roberts had weared the *Sycamore* so that she now presented a smaller fore and aft target, and only one of the

151

final balls struck, a second ball arriving in the captain's cabin.

Those in full body, including Roberts, scaled the rigging as Williams leaned back, pulling bodies towards the surgeon. It seemed as if all sails were being unfurled. It was an odd moment of the engagement when neither ship was in a position to do more than fire the pop of muskets at one another. Williams tried putting his hands under the arms of one of the injured, but there was no second arm. Only after studying the contorted and bloodied face for a long moment did Williams realize that he was tugging upon the breathless body of Aged Q. Despite the fact that the old man had nursed Williams in his unconsciousness, the fiddler could not bring himself to interrupt the surgeon's ministrations on Aged Q's behalf.

'Here boy,' said the surgeon. 'Hold this.'

Williams took the roll of bandage from Scudamore, as the surgeon unravelled a long strip of dressing and wrapped it tightly around a knee that had been shot through. Even as Williams watched, the blood soaked through the bandage, redness expanding to the edges.

'Rum,' said the seaman, looking anywhere but his legs. 'Give me rum, Williams. Give it me.'

'Ignore him,' ordered Scudamore, and caught Williams's eyes for a moment to confirm the statement. ''Tis a stimulant, rarely recommended.'

They moved in a low crouch to the next wretch, the cabin boy, Coffin. His right side was red with burns that had run up to the crown of his head and melted his ear so that it was no more than a small opening amid angry flesh. The skin along his right flank had already begun to blister, and Scudamore moved on to the next casualty, leaving Coffin behind.

The boy groaned, and took the longest breath that Williams had ever heard. The fiddler wanted to disappear down the main hatchway and pretend that he was under his sisters' oak tree.

'Oil,' said the surgeon, speaking only a yard away, but the words seemed to echo, 'rub the boy down in oils, man. Now.'

Williams looked over and saw the surgeon kneeling over one of the five week-old members of the crew. There was a puzzled look in his eye as he surveyed the wound. What to do with a man whose buttock muscles had been removed right down to the pelvic bone? Scudamore pressed his sticky hands against one another, smearing the blood of many men together. There was blood on his trousers, his shirt, even where he had run his hand through his hair. Williams glanced down at his own chest, noticing that it too was matted in drying blood from where he had first slipped on the main deck.

Roberts had returned to the main deck and was hauling on the clewlines, then running amid men for the braces. The captain stared abaft, watching as the Barbadian brig crowded on sail and swung her yards to follow Roberts's path into the wind.

The *Sycamore* bore as much sail as Roberts dared, and the ship creaked in protest and hurled her bow into the trough of a wave, sending a heavy scud from bowsprit to main mast.

The cabin boy cried out as the spray slapped against his skin, then retreated to a soft and mournful moan as if he had resigned himself to a bitter and permanent pain. Williams slavered his hands in olive oil and rubbed them first upon Coffin's right arm, and then upon the right-hand side of his chest, pausing when Coffin's eyes ran freely and restarting when the patient gained his breath.

Another round crashed into the water, yards from the starboard side. Bow chasers, thought Williams. For the first time, he began to despair that this might be their final fight. It was now obvious, and few had had time to think on it, that their presence in the Caribbean waters had been clearly announced when the empty ship from Bristol had reached her port in Bridgetown, Barbados. Her governor had rapidly prepared a ship that, Williams guessed, held not less than twenty cannon and eighty men. He cursed captain and then crew for their lenience in dealing with their prisoners. Still the *Sycamore* seemed to be accustomed to the demands of such a full set of sails, and the distance between hunter and prey had increased by half a league. Their fire now fell short and the crew busied themselves by sweating the clewlines and reef-tackles, and pouring buckets of salt water over her sails, hoping that the damp canvas might catch more wind.

For two hours it appeared that their simple tactics might prove effective, but by the end of the day it was clear that the distance between the ships was now closing. Though the enemy crew might not be such fine sailors as Roberts's, they were in an undoubtedly finer ship. Come the setting of the sun there was not a man on the main deck, who, looking at the approach of the brig, did not wish himself on board the *Rover*.

CHAPTER 18

Throughout the night the carpenter worked, employing eight men in repairs to the ship, while four more took turns at the pump. There was no likelihood of rest for any man aboard, and sailing before the wind there was little choice in course, with Roberts unwilling to chance an encounter with any of the leeward islands. If they were to be forced to run aground, it was a decision that would be easier to make in the light of day.

Below, the fo'c'sle resembled a field hospital, where an exhausted Scudamore had plugged his ears with cotton so that he could work among the constant cries of pain. There was, he knew, little to do for most, apart from wait and see who had the will to live. He might encourage life by stemming the flow of blood. He could keep busy with the bullet forceps, and the ping of extricated metal was a sound that penetrated his ears, and provided him with succour. Staring at Williams, utterly fatigued, as the fiddler strapped Aged Q to their improvised operating table of planking and lanyards, Scudamore was relieved at the sight of assistance, filled with gratitude to God

156

that Williams had been spared from both the disease and the engagement. He was staggered by the experience accrued in such a young life. Then his eyes turned to Coffin, rolled on his side behind a hefty topsman, and he knew that by these sailors' standards Williams had long since reached manhood.

It was a dismal light in the fo'c'sle; no number of lanterns could provide adequate illumination. Williams squinted as Scudamore made his mark with a scalpel along the shoulder joint of Aged Q's left arm. The surgeon took a pull of rum and then cut into the flesh with his handsaw and began to work his way through the muscle. He tried to use the rhythm of the ship's sway to energize his efforts. Aged Q was already unconscious, but the sound of saw meeting with bone made Williams feel as if his teeth were loose in his mouth, and his stomach turned as it never had on the high seas. He vomited over his own feet and then staggered from the fo'c'sle. Scudamore cried after him, but did not interrupt the rhythm of his sawing, stopping occasionally throughout the long five minutes to brush the wound free of bone splinters.

Williams continued to dry-heave over the larboard side of the bow, coughing wretchedly into the darkness. A hand paused on his shoulder.

'All right lad?'

Williams shook his head.

'Silence, William,' said the captain. 'We must maintain a quiet.' His hand left Williams's shoulder and pointed to the sea. 'She could be a half league from us.'

Williams coughed one final time, and then brought himself upright.

'Come now, lad, the surgeon needs your help.'

'I cannot go back,' said Williams. 'Not now.' But the world returned to Williams: the fresh air, the sound of groaning timber, the continuous squeak of the pump. He gulped one last breath, held a hand up to silence any possible protests that Roberts might have, and returned to the steps of the main hatchway.

Roberts stood beside the helmsman throughout the night, facing abaft, until his eyes grew so tired that the stars on the horizon seemed like an armada of ships' lanterns in pursuit. By his reckonings, they were no more than a hundred miles from St Lucia or Barbados. He was certain that Barbados sheltered no islets in which to lose their pursuers and, while he knew that north and south of St Lucia were a string of smaller uninhabited islands, there was no chance of gaining land by morning. It was a decision that he was loath to make, straining to guess what their pursuers would be anticipating. Either way, they were pushed from the *Juliette*'s course. He set the course to north-north-west and laid down on the quarterdeck, facing the heavens. Shutting his eyes, but not for sleep, Roberts wished that the darkness might last for ever.

All hands were called in expectation of sunrise,

none having slept for more than a handful of minutes. They were doled out cold salted beef and biscuit. No fires were lit, no clue offered to the darkness. Roberts encouraged them to eat well, but there was a distinct lack of hunger, and minimal conversation as each set of eyes was turned to the east, awaiting the judgement of the sun.

Colours spread to the highest point of the skies, a purple that gave way to blood orange. Finally the sun dipped to illuminate the sea, clearly casting the shadow of their pursuer on the water, not three leagues behind them. A few swore, and some looked helplessly towards Roberts, but there seemed to be a resignation, as if they had been handed a writ from Nature. Roberts begged the Lords' attention below, and they descended to the great cabin.

'Exactly what?' asked Hardy again.

'Begin with cannon,' said Roberts, 'then we rid ourselves of powder, oatmeal, spare yard, rum and whisky, then anchors . . .'

'Not the rum,' said Sympson, 'I cannot abide with that. Will fight till death, but some might need rum courage – tis black luck to deprive a dead man of a last wish.'

'While we talk we lose ground,' said Roberts. 'Keep your rum if you will die drunk.'

They hauled the anchors overboard, hearing the loud rattle of the chain burn through the hawse hole, and kept only a small kedge that might offer them a prayer at a future anchoring. Then went

159

the cable, followed by the hawser. To the great concern of the Commons they tipped the cannon over one by one, the small sloop rocking as they were released over the leeward side. The oatmeal, whisky and a great portion of the beef and biscuit were ejected with few protests after Sympson had guaranteed the rum. Only gold and goods were kept, with the hope that they would have the chance to trade again.

The sloop responded positively to the lightened load, sitting higher, not fighting her way through a wave as before, but gently coasting up and down the angles of water. The surgeon grudgingly added to the lightening of the vessel when Peters, the carpenter's mate, and Aged Q were given a brief funeral and cast over the side. Williams barely noticed, his eyes remained fixed on their pursuers, occasionally flitting to the debris of casks that bobbed in their wake.

'A reef in the mainsail,' advised Sympson, approaching the quarterdeck. A worrying creak sounded from the mainyard, to support his case. 'If we lose it, we're lost.'

'If she holds,' said Roberts, 'we live. She cracks, we die.'

'Bart,' said Sympson, protesting.

'Captain,' corrected Roberts, and refused to speak another word.

Only Williams, who had disappeared below with Scudamore to check on the remaining patients, could surmise that there was a difference in distance between hunter and hunted when he re-emerged at eight bells. His cry of excitement caused all heads to turn.

'We're past her,' he cried, and looked a little embarrassed at the gathering stares. 'Can you not see we've gained leagues on her?' This brought about a continued discussion, the conclusion of which was an expletive-filled doubt of Williams's navigating expertise, and several cries of Jonah from the suspicious few who were now certain that they would be dead within the day. Only at about midday did some concede that the fiddler might be right, and Sympson, with an open slant-toothed smile, ordered the starboard watch to put a reef in the mainsail. By sundown, the brig was a speck of litter on the horizon. One of the few remaining casks of rum was broached, widening Sympson's grin.

Though their escape had buoyed the spirits of the crew, it was not a restorative for those still under the surgeon's care. Roberts had sailed north for Dominica, no more than two days of sailing with such a wind behind them. The surgeon reckoned that fresh fruit and land might turn some from their wounds, yet over the course of the first night, when the windsail failed to negotiate the air to the cramped and fetid quarters of the fo'c'sle, five of the remaining eight died, including Brownrigg, who had perplexed the surgeon with his endurance after his buttocks had been shot away. However, he did not leave the earth quietly, hollering curses against the world, his mess mates, bosun and surgeon. No words were exchanged among the crew, though their ears rang with his accusations, heightened by their own well-being, but all wished him dead, and quickly so. When he finally expired his fingers were so tightly wound about the cords of his hammock that he was simply carried on deck, swinging in his bed like a governor in a sedan. Sounding lead was pressed between body and bed and he was committed to the deep.

Only Coffin's recovery surprised the surgeon. He had always been the quieter of the two cabin boys, but also the weaker. It was difficult to discern, in the days he convalesced in silence, whether he was stubbornly hanging on or actually healing. Asides from applying coats of oil to his burned skin, there was little that Scudamore could do from the moment the salt box exploded in his face. It looked as if Coffin's head was covered in candle drippings. His brow had dissolved over his right eye and, where it emerged from behind the skin, the eyeball was covered by a thick white fluid, the like of which Scudamore had never seen before. Coffin sat, tracing his hands over his face, imagining his countenance and dwelling in silent shock.

CHAPTER 19

Dominica lay off the weather side of the sloop, stretched under a bank of rain clouds that covered her length. The island carried a ridge of humps across its spine, too green to be mountains and too large to be hills. As eight pulled on the sweeps of the tender, trailing their empty water barrels on ropes behind them, Williams could see that the forest led down to the very sand of the shore. It was an infinite regiment of palms, mangroves and elephant ferns.

They rowed the tender up a narrow inlet, crossing under a stone bridge that had no path on either side. The forest was so dense around them that one tree's roots crossed over another's, until layers gathered and the floor of the forest looked to be thick in wooden serpents. Small shelled crabs scuttled in their creases. Branches met over the heads of the oarsmen – a vault of palm fronds and ferns that returned the echo of dipping sweeps – and pillars of sun created a path of light along the river. Clouds glided past, darkening their route and wetting them with a thin drizzle of rain.

'Avast,' came a cry from the bank, and a

musketshot erupted from the forest. The sound reverberated all around the boat, and none knew where to look. 'Avast!'

They rested their hands on the oars, and looked to Sympson for instruction. Moody nudged Williams and pointed to the starboard side, but the Welshman could not see a thing.

'What ship are you?'

'From the sea,' replied Sympson to the forest.

'Roberts's men?'

Sympson looked particularly put out. Whether it was because the stranger had such information, or whether it was because he did not like to think of himself as anyone's man, Williams could not figure.

'Are you brethren?' questioned the voice.

'Who do I have the pleasure of addressing?' inquired Sympson in mocking tones of politeness.

'Twenty muskets, you arse,' came the reply. 'You Roberts's men?'

'Aye,' said Sympson. The crew were fidgeting with their pistols, trying unsubtly to rest them under the lip of the boat so that those on shore could not see their preparations, but when they turned their eyes to the forests, there were only a thousand trees to see.

'We wish words with Roberts,' said the voice, 'and have news for him, if he will grant us favour.'

'You're an Englishman, are you not?'

There was a short pause. 'Aye.'

'Then step forward,' encouraged Sympson, 'and show yourself a capital fellow.'

'Tell Roberts that there are a score of men who wish to put themselves in his service. If he'll take us, we have news. All able here. Jack tars through and through.'

'Strange fellow,' muttered Sympson to the crew. 'We came for water,' he cried. 'Can we fill our barrels?'

'Untie them,' said the voice. There was something odd about the tone, something that Williams recognized, as perhaps Sympson had, as not exactly English. The timbre was deep, but the vowels were clipped in a dialect that he did not recognize. 'When you're back with word, they will be filled for you. A kindness showing trust to you.'

'And a damnable guarantee for our return,' shouted Sympson.

The voice broke into cold laughter, and asked Sympson to convey fine greetings to his captain.

'And who shall I say sends these greetings?'

'Bill Magnes and company.'

Roberts returned, taking only Sympson, Hardy and Williams with him, the remaining oars lying flat in the bottom of the boat.

'It was around here,' said Sympson, scouring the riverbank for any discernable difference from the last mile of pulling. Roberts raised his pistol and fired a shot into the air.

'Aye,' said a voice, different from the one that had goaded Sympson earlier. 'You can put that down now.'

'Is that the voice of William Magnes?' Roberts asked the trees.

'It be.'

Roberts laughed. 'And you expect passage aboard my ship, do you?'

'Who the devil is he?' asked Sympson.

'A nocky boy from Minehead,' said Roberts loudly, 'wears a red louse bag, and was a mate on board a fourth rate, same as me, till he hopped the twig. Never heard of again.'

'Really, Bart,' said the voice, 'a kinder introduction for your new shipmate please.' A figure stepped out from behind the thick trunk of a mangrove tree on the east side of the river. As Roberts had promised, his ponytail was secured in a dirty red bag that dangled beneath his neck. He looked to be a heavy man, shaped like a water barrel, with a high forehead and a grin several teeth short of a smile.

'Barty,' he said, 'tis fine chance, is it not?'

In three strong pulls, the tender reached the river bank, and Magnes grabbed the bit of the painter and ran a loop around a limb of mangrove tree. The sailors left the boat, and stood opposite Magnes on the narrow bank. Roberts looked for a long second at the proffered hand before deciding to shake it.

'Good on yer,' grinned Magnes.

'You'll prove yourself a changed man,' said Roberts, 'or I'll not take you far.'

'Runnin' on the navy is hardly a hanging crime compared to likes of you. Was a long way ago, ten or twelve years man, and I been spending time more honestly than your good self.'

Twelve men emerged from the roots and limbs of the mangroves.

'All's good men,' said Magnes, 'fine sailors from the *Revenge*. Portsmouth brig. Taken by Frenchies, who saw fit to be rid of us.'

'A hard decision, I'm sure,' said Sympson. 'That your boy?' He pointed a thin finger at the only black man in the group.

'Not exactly,' said Magnes, and obviously hoped to leave it at that.

'I'll not take thirteen of you,' said Roberts, 'you can draw lots or however, but one will stay. More if you so wish.'

'Leave the nigger behind,' suggested Hardy. The man's eyes shot to Hardy, not in hatred but considered defence. Williams was surprised that he understood English.

'Is he a sailor?' asked Roberts.

'Oh, yes,' said Magnes, and scratched at an itch on his leg.

'As long as there's no Irish in him,' smiled the captain, 'then he's welcome aboard.'

Sympson and Hardy looked a little dubious, but did not openly contradict their captain.

'Well,' said Magnes, and presented his ship-mates with a frighteningly large smile, 'why doesn't our little group retire for a few moments, where we can draw quietly at straws.'

When the thirteen men retreated back into the forest, their sounds were first amplified by the cavern of the river, and then muffled by the leaves of the foliage. Sympson turned to Roberts and asked, 'Is Magnes a good man?'

Roberts was scraping the dirt from his nails with his rigging knife. 'I thought at first, no. And then I remembered to consider ourselves. I thought, twelve month ago, had someone asked my vardy of David Sympson, Is he a rum cove? A capital fellow? I would have spat him down and called Davey Sympson a whore's bastard, and would sooner have sailed with a poxed Spaniard.'

Sympson saw the sense, and nodded, but Hardy began to laugh hard to hear the quartermaster so berated.

'And,' said Sympson, 'had I been asked in my days of honest trade about Richard Hardy, I'd have called him a horse's godmother, and a poor hedge-creeper.'

Hardy ceased his laughter and looked to Roberts and Williams for support. Williams spoke to ease his discomfort.

'A mate on a fourth rate,' murmured Williams. 'Which ship was she?'

'Oh, Mr Williams,' said Roberts, 'always thinking to fill his knowledge box.'

'Against Spain?' guessed Sympson.

'And a mate?' pressed Hardy.

'Aye,' said Roberts, 'third mate.'

'So,' reasoned Williams, 'he must have something to recommend him.'

'He was,' explained Roberts, 'always good at pissing down the officers' backs.'

'Tis a talent in law,' said Sympson, 'but how does he fare asea?'

There was the whisper of voices from far away. Then a loud burst, a voice raised in outrage, suddenly stopped short, the sound of feet pushing against wet ground. Williams counted the men from the *Revenge* return one by one. There were twelve. The black came last. Roberts stood and began to untie the painter from the gnarled arm of the mangrove.

'You made your choice?' he asked Magnes.

'We are twelve, are we not?'

'And the outcome was accepted?' asked Williams.

Magnes turned to him and grinned broadly. The pock marks either side of his mouth curled upwards into bright red crescents. 'The draw was presumed to be weighted. The accuser did not accept the result peaceably. Made the presumption that the outcome was predetermined.'

'Was it?' asked Williams.

'Depends on faith,' pondered Magnes. 'I don't believe he was a Calvinist.'

There were, of course, no formal introductions

when the new members of crew stepped aboard the *Sycamore*, but she being such a small ship it was obvious that the old hands were displeased by the recruitment. This did not unduly worry Roberts, who knew that the sea would sort them or pull them together, and that fine sailors could be forgiven any intrusion. Magnes slept in the fo'c'sle, though his first night was spent on words with Roberts in the captain's cabin. The men, especially the youngest, had no objections to the new recruits but seemed unnerved by the prospect of having a black among them. Old hands had shared space with most every kind of man or animal and could stomach a negro. Space was cleared for him, but it was understood that this was mainly because his associates had a respect for him that none were ready to question.

He was half a hand taller than any man on board, but seemed to be constructed by sinew rather than muscle. It was not an impression of stringiness, but a flexible strength. His eyes were hard to hold because, in their reptilian coldness, they forgot to blink. Only beginning at the crown of his head, his hair grew down to the nape of his neck to give the impression that he was wearing a mask that had slipped backwards.

'The negro,' said Roberts, 'does he speak the King's English?'

'Lord Sympson can testify to that,' smiled Magnes.

'Tis a lie, Bart – I've barely matched eyes with the nigger.'

'Wrong, Davey,' said Magnes, 'who'd you think you were talking to when you first came up our river?'

'No?' muttered Sympson.

'I was walking inland with some laddies, and I told him that if you should come by to welcome you as he did. Saw you anchor and know that's the only river fit for fresh water for twenty miles north or south.'

'Has fine speech?' asked Roberts.

'Tis a pretty tongue,' said Magnes, 'has Dutch, and his own lingo.'

'Damned parrot,' muttered Sympson.

'A wily cove,' said Magnes, taking a drag on his pipe.

'He a Virginia boy?' asked Roberts.

'Straight from the Guinea coast.'

'Caboceer?' asked Roberts.

'Aye, man,' said Magnes, and looked up, impressed by the guess, 'worked with him myself – many a trip. Meaner than a black snake.'

'Ashanti?' asked Roberts.

'Inland tribe,' said Magnes, leaning forward in his chair, 'was a slave himself, for the Fata. Runaway. Came to us, he did. Imagine the balls in that. Offers many Fata, takes us inland and we fill the hold in under two weeks. Lost nary a man to Guinea fever. Good ones, too. Must have got two hundred to Bridgetown. Ne'er thought I'd see him again, but I come back a year and six month later – Fort Charles – and who comes to the ship, but Innocent.'

'Innocent?' asked Roberts.

'Don't rush a tale,' said Magnes, and puffed leisurely at his pipe in revenge for the interruption. 'Had set himself up, reliable like, and quicker than any else.'

'But why's he here?' asked Sympson.

'Not exactly sure,' said Magnes, 'think that he'd fished his pond dry. Not many Fatas left. On me fourth trip . . . we'd always treated him well, he gets it in his head that he'd come with us. There was a preacher in the Fort. Regular martext. Innocent may mimic a voice well, but he can't read. Used to depend on the bluecoat for his learning. He tells the lad about how God above is everywhere. Innocent wouldn't fall for that, got sharp eyes, and couldna see God no matter where he looked. So the martext tells him about the King of Kings, a man, so as he can understand. A cove called Christ. Now, Innocent reckons that the lad's not in Guinea, 'cause he's asked every Christian ten times when last they'd seen Christ. So he comes on with us, talking about how he and Christ must have chat. Captain reckoned he'd make a special sale of him, and invited him on.'

'You're teasing?' asked Sympson.

'Graver than you know,' said Magnes. 'Put him to work too. First-class stuff, sir. Takes aloft like a damned monkey. And fights, man . . . bulldog, hands and teeth, all hands and teeth. Ne'er seen blood like that. Prodigious useful.'

'Innocent,' said Sympson. 'How the stupid arse come on that?'

'He'd be asking about Christ, and whose company he kept. Who's his allies, and enemies. The nigger's true name, what we'd call him afore, was longer than Sunday's sermon. Nobody called him nothing most of the time. But some French lad, when we were taken, he tells him that the Catholics were Christ's best friends. "Who is the King of the Catholics?" he asks. "Why, the Pope," says the French boy. "What do they call Pope?" "Why, Clement or Innocent."'

'He preferred the latter?'

'We preferred the latter,' said Magnes, 'made us laugh. And now he's kept it. Proud of it too, he is.'

'Fuckin' papists,' said Sympson, and spat on the floor.

'He's no papist,' said Magnes. 'Just wants a name of power, so that Christ will share a meal with him.'

'Does he listen to a captain?' asked Roberts.

'Oh yes,' said Magnes, 'see the captain as a god. A small god, but a god nonetheless.'

'A creditable notion,' said Roberts, 'that should be encouraged.'

'Aye,' agreed Magnes, 'but had that been on the *Juliette* then he would have been considered . . .'

A silence dropped so suddenly that it seemed

to Magnes as if even the bilge water had ceased to move.

'You sailed upon the *Juliette*?' asked Roberts.

'Second mate,' answered Magnes, with touch of pride. 'A year since.'

'We look for her.'

Magnes exploded into laughter. 'In the *Sycamore*? First, she would shatter you, but she'll be Africa-bound soon, so how would you propose to catch her? Shall we all stand before the mast and blow smoke in our sails?'

'Your arrival is fortunate,' said Roberts, undisturbed, 'and your words fair. The *Sycamore* is a temporary haven. A little patience, Mr Magnes, and the rewards shall be divine.'

Although Magnes did not answer, it seemed to Williams that he preferred to chew on the doubt rather than swallow it whole.

Magnes was given the task of trading at Roseau, in the north of Dominica, and acquitted himself well, using Williams to aid in translation. They reprovisioned the ship, bartering almost all of their goods. Their twelve crates of India wipes fetched a favourable exchange, and they were able to equip themselves with a pair of decent anchors, and six four-pound cannon. It could hardly be considered fire power, merely the beginnings of a threat. Besides this, they obtained twenty casks of dried fish and a fine supply of rum. Magnes also carried other important but unsurprising news.

They were aware that Barbados had knowledge of their presence in the Caribbean, but Magnes had heard of their arrival through the French, and knew that the governor of Martinique had outfitted two twenty-gunners and offered a reward of five hundred pounds for the head of Bartholomew Roberts. While this served to both flatter and aggravate the captain, he had little choice but to sail his small and lightly armed sloop away from the Martinique squadron. After consultation with both Lords and Commons, it was decided that they would head south to Carriacou, before heading back to Africa in the dead wake of the *Juliette*.

CHAPTER 20

The surgeon, hands covered in paint, squinted against the setting sun and his captain's silhouette before him.

'How goes it?' asked Roberts, indicating the black cloth.

'I am not a great study of portraiture,' stated Scudamore, 'but I believe it the custom, Captain, to include the instruments of a man's trade, even for a flag. Now, were this for my trade, I would be grasping the hands of a skeleton, and between us we would hold the sides of the hourglass. Time being that which separates one from other. Perhaps a saw in my other hand.' He took up the pot of paint, put it down, pulled up the rum and held it to his lips for a long minute.

'Do as you said,' toned Roberts. ''stead of handsaw, an arrow.'

'Why not a quadrant, Captain?'

'An arrow.'

'You are the only man of navigation aboard, are you not?'

'You are the only medicine.'

'A ship may survive without a doctor,' confessed

Scudamore, 'but without a navigator she is but wood upon water. What say, Captain, a quadrant?'

'An arrow, sir,' repeated Roberts.

'At your insistence,' relented the doctor and, before the captain, he began to paint upon the black cloth. At the centre of the piece lay the hourglass. It was grasped on one side by a man wearing a tricorn hat, on the other by a skeleton of similar stature. The skeleton gripped an arrow.

'Tis fine work . . .' mused Roberts. He coughed, then held the surgeon's eyes before asking, 'What do you administer to a cove who finds his sleep slight?'

'Every night?' inquired Scudamore.

'E'ry night.'

The surgeon laughed. 'Had you asked that me when I was at practice off Moorfields I would have settled you with a pot of tea and urged you to seek sea air.'

'And failing that?'

'I would willingly bleed you,' said Scudamore, 'and weaken you to sleep. Or lace your tea with rum.'

'There is little easiness,' said Roberts, 'in being the pinnacle of such a democracy. I wished it, I wished it aloud – my own ship – and I am heavy of it.'

'You are anxious?'

'I am.' For weeks now, Roberts's thoughts had contained nothing but desires, a series of must-haves and must-dos and even when they were not for him they were connected to him. The wishes of a crew, the needs of a surgeon, and always the laws were simple and hinged on the need to inflict loss – the loss of trade, the loss of life.

'You fear you shall not find the *Juliette*?'

'No, no . . . it is the crew. No man is of worth to me . . . and yet, together they act as lice. They scratch the insides of my pate.'

The surgeon raised his pot for another lengthy sip, then placed the vessel softly on the deck and said, 'I see you above them.'

'I pretend the power, Doctor,' said Roberts, his voice lowered in confession. 'What they shall not gift me, I presume. To their agitation, I do not urge patience, but show it in my manner. Tis a mob, Doctor, and longs for barked orders.'

When the captain looked up from the second painting he saw that he had raised a smile upon Scudamore's face. Roberts began to laugh.

'I plead counsel from my surgeon. Expression, sir, is more release than the letting of blood or the saltiest of air.'

'Humours,' insisted the surgeon. 'Tis in the humours.'

Their second flag lacked the subtlety of the first – a bowlegged sailor standing upon two skulls. One marked ABH, the other AMH. A Barbadian head. A Martinician head. Such directness dismissed the advice, both sought and given. Doctor resumed his work as painter, and the captain ran the first flag up the mizzen mast. As the doctor pointed his paintbrush at his handiwork above, Innocent's head appeared from the main top and stared at the flag. Rising from his crouched seat, the doctor approached Roberts once more.

'What do you think of our nigger?' he whispered.

'Our nigger,' said Roberts, 'seems an independent cove. Has found himself a home where none wish to follow.'

'A civilized chap of our own persuasion,' agreed the doctor, nodding.

Innocent had proved to be a solitary man. Most of the crew were fidgeters and had a seaman's habit of keeping at least the fingers working, even when the mind was blank. They sat in groups, whipping or splicing, washing or singing or honing the blade of a knife. Innocent preferred to sit alone and, having none of the seaman's prideful abhorrence of the fighting top, spent his time there, sometimes with his eyes closed, otherwise staring around the ship. It was as if he expected every league of water to speak in different tongues. The crew tried all manner of tricks to goad him to any form of action or reaction. They banged on the drums and begged him for a dance, cursed him to his face, welcomed him into their messes. Pleasantries and spite were greeted with the same unfathomable stare. He had, it was generally considered, spent too much time alone to enjoy the company of his fellow man.

However, as Magnes's tale had displayed, he was absorbed by certain traits of the Europeans, wishing to know the man whom the white nation bowed before. Anyone who might have knowledge of Christ, who might be able to obtain an introduction on his behalf, was worthy of communication. It was unsurprising, then, that few of the ship's company held any interest for him. He was not fond of speaking for the sake of speaking, but he would listen and interpret any conversation that he overheard.

During their fortnight of careening in Carriacou, Innocent observed how all men, save for Williams, seemed wary of the captain, and gathered in groups to speak of him. And though the doctor administered to the captain's body, it was his young compatriot who was his holy man, what the French sailors had called the confessor. Often Innocent had felt the young man's eyes on his own face and, while the crew had grown used to ignoring him, he could feel an interest in Williams's stare. The captain, Roberts, was a small god, not omnipotent like the French god, nor the Englishman who had been Magnes's captain, but Roberts still had a command and a presence that pushed all from him.

Williams swung himself over the edge of the top, avoiding the lubber hole, so proud of his progress as a tar that he did not notice Innocent resting in the shadow of the mainsail. He had come from Roberts's cabin where he had been writing at his journal, while the captain attempted to explain his calculations for plotting their course. Though both knew that it was neither a simple nor an accurate matter, Roberts teased Williams with the speed of the arcane markings that he scratched in chalk upon the table. The captain reckoned them between New Providence and the coast of Florida, only two hundred miles from the colonies of America. While they could hardly disembark, Williams began to feel closer to his own home, knowing that a population not so different from himself lay near.

He edged out to the main yard arm, and helped to put a sea stow on the mainsail, and was skipping back to the deck, when he heard a voice call, 'Welshman?'

Williams popped his head back above the top, and stared at Innocent, who was resting with both eyes closed.

'We shall talk,' said the negro.

'Shall we?' said Williams.

'Now,' ordered Innocent.

'Hardly man,' replied Williams. 'Bosun's whistle's blowin'.'

'You'll come back, after bells ring.' His voice was smooth and practised, the same tones that he had first heard on the stretch of river in Dominica. Williams felt like nodding, despite the rudeness of the words.

'Perhaps I will,' said Williams, and backed quickly down to the deck.

Pure curiosity brought Williams back at the end of his watch. Few had managed to get more than a word or two from the blackamoor. Though Magnes swore on a tattered copy of the Bible that it was indeed Innocent who had teased them upon the river, Williams had begun to doubt the man's fluency in English. He had spent the end of his bow watch fixated upon the playful silver bodies of a group of dolphins that ran before the *Sycamore*, turning and twisting at great speeds.

'Evening,' said Williams, and pulled himself through the lubber hole. He peeked down to ensure that no one had spotted his breach of seamanship.

Innocent held a hand out and pointed west at the sun. The sloop lurched as a wave slapped her bows, and the wind beat against Williams's face. He marvelled at the beauty and the emptiness of the evening. The orange sun was framed with a red ring as it sank over the horizon. When Williams looked back, Innocent directed his gaze overhead to the moon. It was circled by a second, duller shadow.

'Tis strange,' said Williams, noting with amusement that the Africans, as well as the English and Welsh, felt most comfortable beginning a conversation with the subject of the weather.

'A great wave,' said Innocent, and passed his hand over the horizon, back and forth.

'Indeed,' said Williams, and looked out, but could only see the odd white cap.

'They come tonight,' intoned Innocent. 'Perhaps when the sun returns.'

'Ahhhh,' said Williams, nodding twice.

'As on Galilee,' preached Innocent, 'when Christ saved ye of little faith.'

'But Galilee,' Williams pointed out, 'was only a lake. This is an ocean.'

'The waves shall be greater.'

'Hmpphhh,' muttered Williams, looking sideways at his companion.

'I see,' said Innocent, and tried unsuccessfully to trap Williams's eyes with his own, 'that you are Christ's friend.'

'Did I say that?' protested Williams. 'I hardly think I did.'

'You are the man of the captain's head and heart.'

'Even were it true, what would it be having to do with Christ?'

'Before the storm, they are as one.'

'Mr Innocent,' said an exasperated Williams, 'I am the ship's fiddler, not a man of God.'

Innocent's arm shot out and grabbed Williams by the wrist. He twisted it so that William's palm was raised to the dying sun.

'Your fingers are black,' said Innocent, 'like the man of God who taught me.'

Williams looked down at his ink-stained fingers and then quickly wrenched his hand free.

''Tis ink,' said Williams. 'If you must know, I help the captain keep his log.'

'I know ink,' replied Innocent. 'It is used in words.'

'Exactly so.'

'"The word was made flesh and dwelt among us",' quoted Innocent.

'Ahhhh,' said Williams and began to see the vaguest outline of Innocent's logic. 'So by having ink on my hands . . .'

'You are a friend of Christ.'

'That is what the preacher told you?'

'No, he lied to me.'

'So you figured that yourself?' smiled Williams.

'I did,' said Innocent, solemnly offering Williams half a bow.

'Did you never see a man with ink on his hands, who was, perhaps, a purser or a secretary? Someone obviously not friend to Christ?'

'Do not attempt to sway me,' said Innocent. His face held the vaguest hint of something akin to a smile. 'Does the man Billy Fishhooks have ink or pen? Or De Vine? Or Philly Bill?'

Williams thought for a moment, conjuring the faces to match the names of some of the deckhands below. 'I don't suppose they do,' said Williams.

'Then I am certain,' said Innocent, 'that men with blackened hands are better friends of Christ than all others.'

Williams wanted to tell him how it was a matter of learning. How, if you had been taught the art of writing, the chances were that you might also know a little of the good book. It simply meant that you had stayed in school longer than a labourer's son. He tried to find the words but did not know where to start. Innocent had tied together thoughts that most considered separate. To unravel them would be to start a conversation that he did not have the confidence to direct, nor the knowledge to conclude.

'I am not in error,' said Innocent.

'I don't suppose that you are,' replied Williams.

Rising to his feet, Innocent swung from the top of the shrouds, and took a step up, poised halfway between rat-lines.

'Wrong way,' said Williams, smiling, 'the deck and food'd be south.' He jabbed his thumb downward.

'I climb,' said Innocent, 'and watch for the storm.'

'Oh yes,' laughed Williams, finding his feet, 'I forgot the great waves on the small lake.'

Williams jumped on to the shrouds and they moved at an equal pace in opposite directions, the fiddler heading for his journal:

The black is addled. Cooked by the sun until he reached a high degree of irritation and then abandoned in his confusion. I think it is his arrogance that has me riled. I expected a certain humility, a touch of gratitude for my interest in him, and instead I am confronted by the most cock-sure man I have ever met. There is humour in it – the gravity of such a man. He combines the sobriety of my former tutor and the solemn nature of my father; and I confess I smile to see it mixed so. I have noted the distance that such a wily cove as Magnes puts between himself and Innocent and begin to feel there is much to be gained by imitating this action. As for Magnes, his presence and constant chatter of the Juliette *is more effective for the health than all of Scudamore's nostrums. He says that a man must wade through coins to cross the waist of the ship. Of course, I do not believe him, but the tale remains a warming one.*

CHAPTER 21

Deep into the night – how long, Williams had no idea – the fiddler found himself turned from his hammock and landing in a half-inch of water.

'Bunch!' he cried from his sleep. 'Coffin! You damned notches.' The sloop lurched and Williams was turned from his knees and did one involuntary somersault before coming to rest against a thick anchor cable several yards away. The rest of his watch stayed snoring around him, but he realized that he could hear little of their noise as the infernal roar of an angry ocean raged through the inches of wood beside him. For the first time since Williams had been crimped aboard his Guinea-bound brig, he felt an absolute horror in his situation, and felt smaller than the lowest louse on the ship. The sloop rolled back to the starboard quarter, and Williams slid on his arse back to his hammock.

'Damn,' he thought, 'and I'll wager there's no fire to dry my ducks out.'

Seeing little likelihood of a return to sleep in such conditions and sodden clothes, Williams stumbled his way to the weather deck. The main hatchway was battened down, but he could hear the wind scream though unseen cracks and his face was spattered with a steady leak of cold water. He turned around and thought it best that he return to his seachest for more suitable gear.

He rummaged among his fine, unworn silks and searched frantically for tight knits, skins or leathers. In his year at sea, he had had the sublime good fortune to avoid anything other than a brief squall and moderately heavy water and, seeing how their hunting grounds had seemed to be stuck in the permanent grip of high summer, he had had no need of warm clothes, nor given much thought to wet weather gear. Rather than appear on deck in something unsuitable or, worse, laughable, Williams chanced that bare skin would be effective, since the wind remained warm, so he wore only his ducks.

'Eight bells,' shouted Philly Bill on behalf of the outgoing watch. 'Starboard watch on deck, and she's beginning to blow.'

As the sailors stirred and swung their feet into the water that raced about the fo'c'sle, Williams followed Bill aft.

'How hard is she blowin'?' asked Williams, with an attempted air of nonchalance.

'Ahhh,' said Bill, laughing, 'not so bad as for all hands. Hardy'll have you handin' the tops'l first thing I reckon.'

'Really?' said Williams, and headed for the main hatchway, eager to be first and make a show of his enthusiasm to the outgoing watch.

188

The fiddler was greeted by the sight of the white top of a wave surging above the fife rails. He stumbled to the weather side and took a firm grip on the standing rigging. 'Beginning to blow,' he thought to himself, and spotted Moody emerging to join him. He opened his mouth to wish his friend a hearty good morning and was rewarded with a whistling slap of water that crashed against his face, forcing its way down his throat. He coughed and swallowed, and through his tearing eyes he caught Moody's grin.

The sun should have emerged over an hour ago, but she seemed to have forgotten her business, and the wound between the sea and sky had been stitched shut by the thread of the rain. Five minutes into the watch, Hardy mouthed the order for them to head aloft to the top yard. When Williams placed his feet on the lower shroud, he tried to convince himself that his fear was overexcitement, and he used his dread to force himself up past the main yard. He concentrated on his footing and grips as he had originally done when he had feared heights, and tried to ignore the efforts of the wind to rip him from his purchase.

The difference between air and water was lost to Williams, and he found that every breath had to be strained to give his body life. He could barely see the yard in front of him, and drew his only comfort from the fact that the wind would not let him fall. It had him trapped, chest pressed against the yard. For the moment, Williams was glad of it. 'Beginning to blow,' he repeated to himself as he wrestled with the wind, edging towards the yard arm. He had sailed enough to know that, when stowing hundreds of square feet of soaking and wind-lashed canvas, it was an easier job to head for either arm. The sail would bunch in the middle as the men on deck hauled on the bunt and clewlines, and the weight of the canvas would transfer towards the mast, leaving lesser weights for those positioned by the yard arms.

He had his fourth fold of canvas tucked carefully under his stomach when a huge blast of wind made him shuffle his weight on the horse. The sail ripped itself free from under him, and continued to liberate itself along the line of eight topsmen, and they swore one by one, all looking off the starboard quarter and cursing Williams's guts. Once again they hauled in on the canvas, and this time they secured the gaskets and began to edge towards the main mast and the shrouds. In one terrifying moment the sloop yawed in the rough sea, and Williams found his toes searching for a footrope that was no longer there.

All the other hands had already made their way to the shrouds, and the horse danced madly beneath him. The wind pressed his stomach against the yard, and he was pinned. His feet kept kicking as he ran in the air. Finally they caught the footrope and he settled himself for a moment, his eyes burning with terror and yet seized with the crazed happiness of survival. When he finally reached the shrouds, he scuttled down the ratlines as if he were combating nothing worse than a fair breeze.

By the time that Williams's watch ended, there was little he could do save head below with Moody, eat biscuit and cold beef in silence and then collapse into his hammock, with no thought for ridding himself of his wet ducks. Even the pitch and roll of the vessel had been forgotten. The slosh of water against the sea-chests, the constant groan of the ship, even the high-pitched squeals of rats in the bilge – nothing could interrupt the deepest of sleeps. When he was woken once more by Philly Bill, this time with a firm hand shaking him by the foot, he felt as if his four hours had passed in the snap of a finger.

'Blessed bastards,' shouted Bill to the rested men. 'Captain's called for all hands. She's blowin' hard.'

Moody appeared next to Williams in the dim light of the fo'c'sle.

'Come now, you lubber,' he grinned.

'Pox on you,' said Williams, tipping himself from his hammock. He rushed ahead of his friend.

On deck, to Williams's surprise, the conditions had worsened. There was now a light on the ocean that had not been there in the morning. It was as if the sun had battled with the skies to reach them, and finally had been rewarded with a late dawn, even though, according to the bells, she should have turned her thoughts to setting.

Williams stared at the approach of the following sea. It raised their stern, and the vast oncoming wave melted beneath the sloop. Once over the crest, the stern would dip and Williams's stomach would turn as the following wave seemed to grow to twice the size of the one just ridden.

Two men were tied to the sloop's helm, struggling with a kicking wheel, lit by the dull light of the binnacle. They leaned into the steep angle of the ship as the sloop laid her gunwale under the water. It seemed as if they were sailing in a cauldron of boiling milk, and Williams noticed that two jacklines had been hitched fore and aft either side of the deck, so that a man might have something to grab should a wave break over the deck.

'Williams,' called his mate, Hardy, shouting into his ear from no more than an inch away, 'ask the captain if the tops'l should be reefed.' Williams nodded, closing his eyes against the rain, thankful that he had been given an order. He turned for the quarterdeck, having second thoughts about his keenness to convey the message, seeing as how he would be part of the watch sent aloft. The captain nodded. He clapped Williams once on his bare back, and screamed something that Williams could not hear a word of.

Once he had climbed past the main yard, Williams looked down to the deck and could see it appear and disappear amid furious swirls of clouds, driven down to the sea by the wind. He knew from Roberts's plotting that they were days from the coast of Florida, but Roberts had also told him that it was the flattest land that he had ever seen, and Williams knew that there would be no warning from the crash of breakers. They would fall to their knees as the coral tore through the hull, and it would be far too late to clew off. They would die in the shallows.

Innocent moved ahead of him, Moody just behind, then a pair of Magnes's newcomers and Billy Fishhooks and a brace of old-timers. They worked as one, and never had Williams been so certain of a common interest: they all wished to be back on deck. They heaved together, and the reef was tied in seconds. Once again, having shot up ahead of his fellows, Williams was last to begin his descent. Looking off the starboard quarter, he saw a great wall approach, a huge black wave crested by a pure white head of foam. It was gathering its strength, and seemed as if it was intent on the destruction of their sloop, possessing a consciousness unlike its brother waves. The crest began to curl forward. Williams screamed with all his might to the deck, shouting for every man to hold fast, but it was a wave that had travelled across the earth to land against the sloop. As it collapsed into its own trough, it roared with the broadside of a hundred guns, lifting the stern of the sloop and driving her bow under the water.

The fiddler wound his arms and legs between the shrouds and ratlines, and prayed to God. The deck beneath disappeared in a blinding curse of white, and Williams refused to believe that the sloop would ever rise again. Without a sound, the bowsprit came up from the roll, then the head, holding thousands of gallons of hissing water that sped aft, carrying everything and everyone unsecured before them. Even Williams, suspended thirty feet above the deck, had been hammered by the force of the spray. Those who had headed to the topsail yard with him had heard his warning in time and meshed their bodies with the rigging and survived the jolt of the wave. The ship had been turned almost abeam. If the helmsmen had been swept aft, it would be but a short time before the ship was pounded until it broke apart. With the scud and salt still burning at Williams's eyes, it was impossible to see the deck properly. He could tell from the blur of white that it was still awash.

Thirty seconds later, he dropped to the deck and grabbed at the jackline on the weather side, and moved aft, hand over hand, following the topsmen as they made their way past the capstan towards the quarterdeck. He saw Innocent leave the line and lunge as the sloop rode the crest of a wave, reaching for a body that had been lying prone by the larboard pinrail. Williams had not even noticed it through the waters of the storm. Innocent gathered the figure in one arm and fought his way back to the line, where Moody grabbed at the body and together the two men sheltered it as the next wave broke against their bow.

Roberts appeared at the steps to the quarterdeck.

From under a hail of scud, he pointed upwards. Williams's eyes followed the captain's finger until he saw that the topsail that they had just reefed had been shredded and was cracking like a whip in the wind. The fiddler groaned and braced himself to return up the shrouds. A hand landed on his shoulders, and he looked up through the rain to see the giant figure of Hardy, rigging knife in his mouth, shaking his head at Williams, and moving towards the main mast. Innocent followed, and the two men moved up the gear once more, disappearing into the dipping clouds as they prepared to cut away the main topsail.

The captain hauled on Williams's shoulder and pushed him towards the main hatchway. Together they lifted the hatch and jumped down its throat.

'Find all the tarpaulin you can. Bring it me. Now. Now, boy. Now.'

Williams turned and ran forward to the fo'c'sle, turning through the hands' sea-chests, throwing up the lids and frantically searching the compartment for tarpaulin coats. Within a couple of minutes he had found six coats and hurried back under the main hatchway. There were a small knot of sailors waiting there for him, and all donned the jackets, including Williams. No one spoke. Williams wanted to shout, to be heard over the roar of water and storm, but they had settled on silence. It seemed inhuman to Williams not to scream back against the ocean, but the rest merely buttoned their jackets, noting the thickness of tar and wax upon them. Sympson opened the main hatchway and, under the deluge of water that poured through, he climbed into the storm. Magnes followed, then Moody, Pinch, a pair of Magnes's men, and finally Williams, who slammed the hatch closed behind him.

Under bare poles the helmsmen concentrated on keeping the sloop heading straight into the wind but, with the waves still coming from the starboard quarter, she was pitching erratically. There were no sails to manipulate the principles of wind, only the rudder working against the water, but when the waves lifted the stern clear of the sea, the rudder was a useless thing, the wheel spinning impotently as the ship began to turn to face the waves abeam.

Magnes waved them forward and the small group moved along the deck, gripping the jacklines until they had reached the foot of the main shrouds. Waiting until the roll of the vessel aided his movements, Magnes stood on the bulwarks and gained the rigging. Williams, his coat flapping furiously about him, had no idea why they were headed aloft again, but followed his fellows up, only loosening one limb at a time, as he fought his way against the infernal wind. When they reached half mast, Magnes ceased to move. Williams thought that he must be in some difficulty, perhaps too weak to continue.

The six men held to the vessel's web as the sloop pitched sickeningly into the next series of waves.

Then, to Williams's amazement, he noticed that the ship was beginning to wear round. Their small company, banded together, arms and legs laced in the tarred rigging, had replaced the ship's sails, and as the wind tried to tear the tarpaulin from their backs the ship began to turn. It seemed to take an eternity, but no more than three minutes could have passed. Slowly the wind backed the ship, catching the reefed topgallant that Hardy and Innocent had managed to unfurl.

Williams gritted his teeth and began to move back down the rigging. A foot from above landed directly on his fingertips, and Williams howled into the wind. He saw a face peer down, remove the foot in question, and then suddenly both feet were gone. Williams stared upwards at the sight of a body flapping horizontally in the wind. Hanging on with only his hands, the man above was shaken like a piece of ribbon. Williams thought to reach out but the body was seized by so many demons that he dared not, fearing that he would lose his own grip. And then the man was gone, taken by the wind. Williams looked over his shoulder, but there was nothing to see except the black and white of the ocean.

Night lent the storm an added horror. Williams spent the hours alternating between staring into the dark and praying out loud, knowing that the wind swallowed his words. At three in the morning he took his turn at the helm alongside Moody, and the two of them struggled against the wheel to learn the particulars of the sloop's trim and the number of turns required to keep her on course. Roberts stood by, lashed to the stanchion. At dawn the sea still raged, but it seemed softened to Williams, now that the invisible terror of the night had passed. It was not until Roberts rebuked him for shouting so loud that Williams was sure that the wind had abated.

'Stop your praying, man,' ordered the captain.

Williams tried looking down at his own lips and realized that he had been mouthing the words 'Dear God Our Father' for as long as he could remember. He dared a quick glance at Moody. Despite the deckhand's exhaustion, Christopher Moody found the energy to force a mocking wink at Williams to remind him of his rawness.

'Prefer the company of sailors who curse,' shouted Roberts to his countryman. 'Praying men give a captain great worry.'

'To the devil's dugs,' cried Williams. He spat a mouthful of rain water on deck in a pathetic show of bluster. He did not open his mouth the remainder of the watch.

CHAPTER 22

By noon, the waves had decreased in size, no longer riding the pinrails nor sending forth sallies over the bow and across the deck. Roberts kept all hands, allowing rest for no man, and sent the men to the pumps in twenty-minute rotations. Some had now not slept for three days, and Williams, though utterly exhausted, was considered one of the fresher hands. There was close to three feet of water in the hold as the carpenter surveyed it, water slapping against his thighs, with two men accompanying him, not for their knowledge of carpentry, but to guard the carpenter from any casks and barrels that had broken loose during the storm. Despite the conditions, he located three sizeable leaks and blocked them with a temporary concoction of tallow, oakum and canvas. This lent succour to those manning the pumps, who now felt that their spent energy was being used to give the ship life, and not merely prolonging her death.

At four bells, when the swell had died to less than eight feet, Pinch lit the first fire in four days. All hands gathered by the galley, clothes still sodden, but the sun only one night away. Finally, they counted their numbers. Billy Fishhooks was gone, and four of Magnes's men had been lost to the sea. Sympson, Wilson and six others were below, stretched on the gun deck keeping the surgeon busy. They were mostly bruised and broken. Only Sympson, whose right eye was swollen shut and his nose flattened, had sustained a serious injury. He lay below, floating in permanent sleep. Scudamore had waved salts and vinegars beneath his nostrils, before applying a small ball of cotton soaked in bilge water to his top lip, but it brought no change to the quartermaster.

The following dawn revealed clouds of white returned to the ceiling of the sky. Williams walked from bow to stern along the weatherside of the deck, and found Roberts peering through his spyglass at the west. Roberts turned and handed him the spyglass, and pointed at the horizon. There, no more than thirty miles away, lay a flat sandy strip.

'Odd's plot,' breathed Williams. 'Florida?'

'Perhaps,' shrugged Roberts.

Before the larboard watch were sent below to rest, Roberts insisted on having a service for those who had been taken by the sea. The single copy of the Bible could not be found, but then so much that had not been secured had been scattered or destroyed. Williams listened with interest as Innocent volunteered to speak. A bright pink weal trailed from beneath his right eye across his nose, from where he had been lashed by a strip of topsail, two nights before. Since four of the eleven who had come aboard with Innocent had been lost, Roberts thought it right that he should speak. It was a peculiar speech, excerpted in chronological order from the Bible. He started by raising his voice, and invoking the spirit of God moving upon the waters, and ended by quoting John's baptism. Williams saw more than one eye raised in astonishment at Innocent's words. He was no longer considered a dumb savage. None could shake the notion that they were trapped in a country parish.

Then, as was customary, the sea-chests of the dead men were carried to the deck. Lord Hardy sat at the head of the auction, as fellow crew competed at paying nonsensical prices for ordinary articles of clothing. It was a gaudy memorial to a dull funeral and a heartless death, and the merriness rung hollow. Too many had been lost, and there was much to attend to.

Fully half their water had been contaminated by salt, as had much of their dried fish and their only wheel of cheese. With perhaps more solemnity than at the funeral service, the soiled goods were cast overboard and Bunch gave a mock sermon in poor imitation of Innocent. The sloop had been beaten badly and had survived, but several serious repairs were necessary and they could not be done at sea. A faint crack had appeared in the top mast, and the topgallant yard looked as if it had been bent by the winds. Moody said not to mind it, that it had become merely a little too wet and the yards would soon dry into shape, but Williams suspected that the sloop would no longer carry a blow.

They had lost not only a topsail, which considering that it had been tied in furious winds by a single set of gaskets, surprised no one, but had also lost their topgallant when the wind had ripped open a double set of storm gaskets and split the sail seam by seam. The more time Williams spent considering the nature of the storm's damage and the loss of life, the less he could make sense of why the sloop was still afloat. They would have to postpone their pursuit of the *Juliette* until they were both reprovisioned and refitted.

Philly Bill took the job of sail-maker, and when the following day brought a dazzling sun and seas so small that their breaking against the bow sounded like mocking laughter, all able hands gathered on deck and busied themselves pushing their needles through salt-stiffened canvas, creating an extraordinary patchwork of sail. The cooper, Simmons, his chest wrapped in fresh dressings and tied in the surgeon's unique knots, was breaking down barrels by the forepeak, separating nails from bands of iron, and rotting wood from good.

The sun had helped shift the general weariness of the crew and, though there were no cries for fiddle or fife, Hardy sang 'Old Molly Jones' and was asked by Coffin if he'd sing it once more. The lad was such a sorry sight that Hardy complied. Williams had found the storm more shocking than the rest of them. He had been warned of its arrival and had not believed. It seemed unfair. Storms should have places and times, schedules to which they should keep. They belonged off the Cape, in the Orkney Isles, not springing from these warm seas. Twice he had sat in the cabin and tried to describe the full horror of the ocean, but no words could evoke the magnitude of his fear.

The fiddler considered the sea as a moody force. While his fellow sailors saw these moods as the capricious fancies of a cruel mistress, Williams suspected they were the reflections of the face of God. That night he understood that God deemed man a trespasser on the sea. A storm, to the creatures of the sea, was perhaps cause enough to dive a little deeper, but to those who stole across her surface, from port to port, it was a heavy challenge. For a robber, without a port, perhaps the offence to God was greatest. When asked their home port, they would proudly shout, 'from the sea', but when they were caught between giant waves it was as if they had been discovered in a lie, and punishment was duly exacted.

But then how could Williams explain the following two weeks of sailing, a wind neither too strong nor too weak, that did not test the limitations of the sloop, but rather encouraged and nudged her southwards? Both days and nights were clear and filled with sun and stars as they sought the haven of St Barts, an island that would accept their kind, judging men on the weight of their purses.

With Aged Q a fading memory and Michael

Coffin a scarred tomb of silence that conversed with no one, Williams had found that his supply of friends had been severely depleted. Outside of the cabin, Roberts was his captain, inside the subject of his writing, and despite his often generous advice and a feudal sense of a fief's protection, Williams did not exactly see them as friends, the same as he and Christopher Moody. The difference in age and rank presented an insurmountable barrier for the countrymen to become closer than they were.

Innocent had confirmed that Williams was a man of learning by the end of his second week on the sloop. Exactly who had divulged the information was unknown to the Welshman, but Williams cursed him every time Innocent approached. His fiddle-playing for the crew was exhausting enough, and he had been grateful for the penultimate provision in the ship's articles granting him the sabbath in peace, but Innocent had seen that as an opening, the perfect day for the furtherance of his theological education.

The African sat with his legs folded under him and his arms crossed in his lap, and Williams was pleased that his tall shadow protected him from the glare of the sun.

'I know,' said Innocent, 'that to arrive . . . where I aim myself must take patience.'

Williams nodded, unsure of what Innocent was saying. He often spoke in vagaries that eluded Williams's understanding.

'I must wait,' continued Innocent, 'until the end of the summer, in the English year one thousand seven hundred and twenty-nine.'

Williams was surprised at the precise nature of the prediction, and also a little relieved that Innocent did not seek immediate redemption through the fiddler's knowledge, which was close to being exhausted.

'Why then?' asked Williams.

'That is ten years to the day from when I sailed from Corso.'

'In Guinea?'

'Aye,' said Innocent.

'Why ten years?' asked Williams.

Innocent laughed at him. 'You think I do not know the tales of Christ who roamed upon his resurrection.'

'I believe,' said Williams, 'that you know more than I.'

'Ten years of wandering, and it shall be ten years also for me. Ride through great storms, kill the one-eyed man, and when women cry for me, I, like he, will not follow.'

'What?' said Williams. 'Christ *cured* blindness . . .'

'And the house of Aeaea, where all were turned to swine and driven from the cliffs of Gethsemane.' Innocent smiled: it was a Christ that he could understand.

'Innocent,' asked Williams, 'who taught you these stories of the Bible?'

'My first teacher,' said Innocent, 'who wore the

blue coat at Corso, and showed me that Christ was not the weak man that others said.'

'Was this the same Christ,' enquired Williams, 'who journeyed to the land of the lotus eaters, and forced his men from the isle.'

'I have such a plant in Guinea,' said Innocent, nodding. 'I have torn myself from it.'

'And ten years?' asked Williams. 'And you believe that you must suffer what . . . Christ suffered?'

Innocent looked intent. 'No man will suffer in the same way as another. But the sufferings may echo one another, to show direction. I am different from your Christ.'

'For a start,' said Williams, 'he had but one God.'

'One God for you,' smiled Innocent, 'for me, there are still many spirits, and many offerings to make.'

The same evening, Williams sought out Magnes in the same manner that Innocent had pursued him earlier in the day. He spied the dirty red louse bag perched in the arm of the bowsprit, by the foremast stays. Swinging his legs over the edge, and taking three quick steps to the bowsprit shrouds, Williams turned to Magnes and gave him a smile brighter and wider than a fresh bonito.

'We are close on St Barts?' asked Williams.

Magnes sucked at the ivory stem of his pipe, while Williams studied the carving of the bowl. It was shaped like a great wild beast, springing out at whoever the smoker faced.

'Surely not the most profitable of spots?' said Williams absently.

'Perhaps, perhaps not,' said Magnes, 'but for a crew that's outrun the constables there are worse things than a mild trot.'

Williams nodded, and then unconsciously shifted the tone of his own voice, alerting Magnes to a deliberate change in subject.

'Mr Magnes?' said Williams. 'Are you aware of Innocent's beliefs?'

'Aware of them? Certainly. Do I care? I don't give a rat's prick.'

'He does not know the difference between the Bible and the myths of Greece. Was this your doing?'

'Mr Williams,' said Magnes, 'if I congratulate myself when I read a play sign, would I really be citing Greek, or quoting Bibles at blackamoors?'

'I cannot understand it,' said Williams, 'why someone would deliberately deceive a cull like this. To obscure Christ Almighty with Odysseus.'

'Simple enough,' said Magnes. 'I've seen how your eyes roll when he comes looking for you on your rest day. Imagine . . . locked up inside a fort with him for a rainy season. Nobody else will listen to your godly prate . . . then a nigger who speaks your tongue comes along, and he wants learning. At first, you are pleased and teach him all you know. Then he does not leave, wants more. You know not what to tell him. More stories, more miracles, and then perhaps you begin another story, and keep the same names as your first tale. No harm done.'

'But the man cannot tell one from another,' said Williams. 'He thinks Christ a murderer.'

'Well,' said Magnes, 'makes him all the more appealing to the likes of us.' He laughed hard, and tapped at the bowl of his pipe. 'Leave him be on it. There's none to contradict him, save yourself. Will do you no good. He'll believe his first teacher afore he'll trust a swab such as yourself.'

'I suppose,' said Williams, 'that there is no argument to be proffered.'

'There you go, lad,' said Magnes, 'no debate at all. In the eye of my mind, when the storm's above me, I think of Christ the sailor. Innocent thinks of Christ the wanderer, the warrior. Much as himself, you see.'

'I'll let him be,' said Williams, beginning to pack his own pipe from the pouch that Magnes had laid between them. 'How long has it been since you first met Bartholomew Roberts?'

Magnes looked up at Williams, with half-cocked eyes. He was a sharp man – could tell the difference between a liar and a thief at fifty yards – and his eyes fixed on Williams.

'Roberts,' said Magnes, 'I had not seen his hide in fourteen years.'

'What was he like?'

'Much the same as now. Keeping to himself. And an abider of rules.'

'Well,' said Williams, 'that hardly makes sense.'

'Oh,' said Magnes, 'I'd say that he keeps to the rules well, seeing as how he wrote them.'

'Are they not to your liking?'

'Don't play captain's worm with me, boy,' said Magnes. 'They are a quiet set, and easy enough to abide by.'

'I did not mean . . .'

'I understand well enough. Was never inexpert at a game I cared to know.'

'I'm no sharper, Mr Magnes,' protested Williams, 'surely you can understand the need to know where a man sprang from?'

'A need,' said Magnes, 'is an insufficiency. I's a bastard and know not where I'm from. There are men, who lie open for all to sniff, like summer flowers, and then there are men like the captain who are shy with talk and kindness.'

'My point exactly,' said Williams, 'so if you would tell me what the man was like before.'

'Did he turn willingly to this way?' asked Magnes.

'No sir,' said Williams. 'Doctor said he remained in faith to his captain. Davis had talk with him and carried him off.'

'That'll tell you something of the man,' said Magnes. 'He's as fine with chart and compass as any I ever seen. If I was to meet with such a man at sea, I would like to convince him aboard myself.' Magnes kept his bowl burning with a slow inhalation. 'Roberts was like any other, back then, against Spain. Except in knowing what he knew. About sun and stars and seas – more than midshipmen, officers, masters and captains. Don't think that he could ever figure – don't think that he ever spent enough time inland – to remember to forget that it's not talent that advances one man ahead of another.'

'But birth?' guessed Williams.

Magnes nodded. 'Aye. Or luck and money. And now he has both, and rigs himself like gentlefolk.' Magnes laughed, shaking his head. 'All right by me, enjoy myself watching him go at it.'

'And shall we find the *Juliette*?'

'It shall not be so hard to *find*.'

'She a pretty sail?'

'Take the fairest maiden that you have ever wished to wap. Then give her the constitution of a highlander and the speed of a burned cat and you have her essence.'

CHAPTER 23

Three days from St Barts, Sympson woke from his deep sleep, but his eyes could not stand the presence of the sun and her shadows for long. The quartermaster no longer appeared during the day, but kept his watch at night, complaining that the sun shook his head roughly. His appearance grew dreadful, his eyes becoming redder, his hair darker and his nose edged westwards across his face as if it was offsetting the sway of his teeth. Sympson's recovery was seen as a doubly blessed affair when Innocent discovered the *Samuel* against the horizon. To Roberts's relief she struck but those boarding found no officers in her waist, only deckhands who lowered ladders in silence and gathered in a herd on the bow.

She was the most daunting ship that the Sycamores had spied in a year, with black-raked masts and an elongated rapier bowsprit in imitation of a swift sloop. Though her three-masted square rigger may not have been as manoeuvrable as their sloop, she weighed close on three hundred tons and had a main deck of one hundred and fifteen feet. Most importantly, to the optimists among the *Sycamore*'s crew, she had a large cargo capacity and the sort of bulky seaworthiness that might carry them safely to the Guinea Coast.

The captain of the *Samuel* and his mate were standing outside the great cabin, holding a white stretch of canvas and two pairs of pistols a person. Those who had boarded first, coming from the sloop, were perplexed at how to deal with the contradictory situation and strolled past the steadfast men with the odd curse and the promise to see to them later. Since the *Sycamore* had not been fired upon, the red flag of no quarter remained furled. The curses were empty, their safety was ensured by custom.

'Captain Cary of London, sir,' said the oldest man, attempting to bow but really only creasing the tailored globe of his stomach. His silver wig inched forward over his brow. 'My first mate, Mr Neale.' The man in question gave a smaller bow.

'My name is Captain Roberts.'

Cary wrinkled his nose at the assumption.

'Are you a man of honour, sir?' asked Cary.

'Depending on the man I have dealings with.'

'A gentleman, sir,' said Cary, bowing again. 'I have in this cabin eight ladies. I number my wife among them. They are quite besides themselves, sir. Finding the ocean dreadful enough, you have put a fright upon them. They had not thought to fear their fellow man.'

'They'll come to no harm,' said Roberts.

'Good, sir. Very good, sir. I take it that your rabble know orders.'

'As I hope,' said Roberts, 'does your wife.'

Cary bowed once more, reversed his pistols and handed them hilt first to Roberts. Roberts held them before him and his fingers traced over their barrels.

'They are not primed,' added Cary.

Roberts looked up, surprised.

'I have no intention of letting blood flow in the presence of women, and disarmed them despite myself.'

Roberts smiled and nodded, thinking Cary white-livered.

'Come, Captain,' said Roberts. 'Let us have this door opened and introductions made. What say you to that, Lord Hardy? Mr Magnes?'

'I'm not so sure,' said Magnes, 'that I have ever shared a room with a genuine lady. I venture that stripped of jewel and powders I'll recognize the girls beneath.'

'I would have to insist,' said Cary, breathing through his nose, 'upon my honour, that my wife is left garmented.'

If Magnes was overeager to enter the cabin, he was no less enthusiastic in his attempts to rapidly remove himself. The ladies in question, upon a mild interrogation conducted by the well-mannered Williams, proved to be the wives of elderly Bostonian men of position. They were

English to a fault, and though their words were modest their accents could not abandon a native arrogance. Much more importantly to Magnes, they were a queer-looking bunch of old hens, especially Captain Cary's wife, whose coarse grey hair crept from under an ill-fitting wig.

'Damn,' said Magnes, spitting the floor next to Hardy's bare feet, ''tis a coven full of mothers' mothers.'

'Ne'er make an old cock crow,' said Hardy, sharing his shipmate's disappointment.

Roberts stepped around the small cabin, noting the thickness of the powder and the obvious lack of jewellery.

'Ladies,' asked Roberts, 'did you not bring servant girls to soften the journey?'

'A distinct lack of room,' explained Cary.

'Lord Hardy, Mr Magnes,' said Roberts, 'if you would stay and keep the ladies company until the surgeon's arrival.'

'Surgeon?' whispered Mrs Cary.

Williams, Roberts and Cary gathered in the great cabin, where the *Samuel*'s captain presented his captors with a multitude of purser's papers that the fiddler waded diligently through until he discovered the list of crew. Cary wound tight circles in his cabin, talking incessantly about how gentlemen were made and not born.

'Captain,' said Williams, 'thirty-two it says here, including mates, but I counted but thirty-one myself on entering.'

'Perhaps,' suggested Cary, 'you miscounted.'

'He's a sharp one,' said Roberts. 'Would you care for him to count again?'

'Oh, then,' answered Cary, 'perhaps you'd be missing our late friend, Glasby, struck down by stomach pains but one week out.'

'Harry Glasby?' asked Roberts.

'Aye,' said Cary.

'Have heard the name before and used with much respect. He'd have been your sailing master?'

'A terrible loss,' nodded Cary. Roberts continued to stare at him. 'Quite dead I assure you. Dead, dead, dead.'

'Williams, go alert the crew to keeping an eye open for the coveted Harry Glasby.'

The famed navigator was found by Moody and Philly Bill, secreted in a cask, curled in half an inch of dried fish. He was beaten to the maindeck by the flats of their swords, his thin frame shivering with fear. Glasby was not many years older than Roberts, but looked as if he had suffered from the sea, not from hardships, but from an awful anxiety that had led to his weak disposition and halting stutter.

Ha-Ha-Ha-Harry Glasby, who might begin a sentence slowly, but could finish one at a sprint, was known as Laugher within the hour. Every time the crew forced him to speak his Christian name they would howl with amusement at the Ha-ha-ha, and by the time the second syllable was pronounced it was inaudible for the shrieking around him. Glasby was uncommonly thin for an officer, and had a terrible one-eyed squint from spending so many years measuring the height of the sun. High winds had also removed most of the hair from his head, sparing two tufts north of either ear, which were marked with strands of white and grey. His wizened frame resembled a scrawny chick, and his entire pate, pronounced by his sharp beak, turned fiery and sweaty at the endless mocking.

Scudamore walked past the gang tormenting poor Harry Glasby, trailed by Bunch, Williams and Pinch, who carried between them seven bowls of food for the ladies' dinner. Pinch had long been used to a series of insults directed at his cooking since he had first made dinner in a ship's galley, but that evening he had attempted to exercise his culinary expertise. The salted beef would not only taste fine, but would be presented in an original manner. He had wedged the ship's biscuit into the hunk of meat so that every bowl had the thin grey fin of crust rising from the grizzle of dark beef. So it was with great offence that Pinch looked upon the ladies as they turned their noses from his grand effort and pushed their bowls away in repulsion. He promised that none would see the rum-drenched plum duff that he had hoped to confound them with at pudding.

'Come now, eat,' roared Pinch, and Bunch smirked at him. The surgeon merely took a seat and waited patiently.

'Does one have to eat the biscuit?' asked one lady.

'Does one have to eat the biscuit?' mocked Pinch in a high whine.

'I fear my teeth are weakening,' added the lady.

'Ah,' sneered Pinch. 'Scurvy.'

Bunch and Williams nodded, and then backed from the room at the sign of a quick wink from Scudamore.

'No, ma'am,' said the surgeon. 'You may leave the biscuit, but we must insist on the consumption of the beef.'

The women seemed encouraged by the politeness of the surgeon's address, and the fairness of his compromise. To Pinch's delight, they began to eat their meal without further complaint.

'You will note,' said the surgeon to the chomping mouths, 'a vague aromatic flavour to your meal. A touch of orange peel or some such scent. It is the tamarandi spice.'

'How pleasant,' said one woman politely and nodded at Pinch.

'If you should feel a small rumble grow,' continued the surgeon, 'do not worry yourself unduly. Perfectly harmless, I assure you. Tamarandi has been used by our Indian cousins for thousands of years as an expeditious emetic.'

Bunch pushed open the door to the great cabin with his shoulder and struggled into the room carrying one large bucket filled with sea water. Williams followed, toting an empty bucket and

217

three chamber pots. All the receptacles were placed on the table.

'Really,' said Mrs Cary, 'I should like to see my husband.'

'In a little while,' said Scudamore.

The lady with the weak teeth belched loudly. Confounded, she raised a hand to her mouth.

'Mr Bunch, you may leave us now,' said the doctor.

'Think that I'd prefer to stay, sir,' said Bunch.

'I know that you'd prefer to stay,' said Scudamore.

'My Lord,' said a rosy-cheeked lady, and suddenly stood, raising her hands to cover her mouth.

'Go on,' said Scudamore. 'Get you to Hardy, and make yourself busy.' The cabin boy left very slowly, eyeing Williams with disdain, but the fiddler was looking at a pair of eyes peeking from under a bale of fabrics beyond the women. They blinked at him. He took an unaffected piece of salted beef and held it between his fingers. The dog moved cautiously across the cabin, all skin and suspicion. It took the beef, folded its tail between its legs and sat on Williams's feet.

Mrs Cary leaned towards a bucket, looked into its depths for comfort, and then, in a manner noted by the surgeon for its attempt at gentility, vomited loudly into the empty container. The ladies were entirely used to vomiting, having encountered heavy weather rounding the English coast, but never had they suffered such a pure chain reaction.

Scudamore had sensibly placed one of the pots on the floor, allowing a greater access for the sudden rush of desperate women. It was an unpleasant cacophony, and even Pinch, who had sailed seas as rough as any of the crew, felt a certain nausea creep over him as his dinner was returned before his eyes. To counter the effect of the noise and stench he stood, whooping and crying, 'Come now, old bitches, shit through your teeth.'

The fiddler had turned his back to the fray, kneeling now to scratch the grizzled dog's stomach, but Scudamore sat silently, having wrapped a scented handkerchief around the lower half of his face. He looked on calmly as they tried desperately to help one another out of their dresses in time, abandoning all sense of propriety and squatting naked over pots and buckets. When finally the spasms halted, and the room echoed only with the embarrassed sniffles of the women, Scudamore looked across the room at the grey and ageing flesh, the splatters of shit and vomit, and saw Pinch standing by the small window, gasping for air.

'By my own dog's balls,' said Pinch.

'Avast,' said the surgeon, rising to his feet, 'tis now the unholy part.' He knelt down to his small leather case of medicine and withdrew a small wire sieve, and a fine silk seine. Scudamore took three steps towards the first chamber pot.

'Lord, Lord,' moaned Pinch, 'smells worse than twelve long dead.'

The surgeon trawled the pot and raised the seine

to the poor orange light of the lanterns. He banged it upon the table, and poured sea water across its contents. A score of small gems sat dulled by their sordid layer. 'Thank you, thank you,' said Scudamore to the ladies. 'A large reward for such a small effort.'

The women scraped together enough clothing to cover their fronts but still lay sprawled in varying positions on the cabin floor, none deeming herself worthy of a chair. Scudamore, so used to dealing with cases of the bloody flux, sieved through the warm mixture of solids and liquids, collecting a fair pile of diamonds and the occasional ring.

'Doctor . . . ?' said Mrs Cary.

'Yes, my dear?' said Scudamore, with professional sympathy.

'A cloth,' pleaded Mrs Cary.

'Why yes,' said the doctor, 'water and a cloth. And a fair night's rest. You shall have all of these, ladies, but not tonight I fear.'

CHAPTER 24

September 1720 – The Sargasso Sea

The *Samuel* was exchanged with the creaky *Sycamore* and renamed the *Fortune*, Williams's dog was christened Ketch and Captain Cary and his brood were released. Only Glasby was retained. He cried out to his shipmates to remember his impressment and then was promptly sick upon the deck, so distressed was he at his situation. They reached St Barts in three days, where the sight of their twenty-six-gun brig was enough to stir a steady stream of recruitment. Roberts's name had travelled before him. He was thought to be both pistol-proof and rich as the Grand Mogul. With the added hands to help in their careen they stayed ashore not two weeks.

On their final day Williams wrapped portions of salted beef carefully in parcels made from palm fronds and walked with his dog to the western side of the island. There was little change in tide and he followed the beach around in its slow golden arch. He was forced inland by a series of small cliffs. As he climbed the loose, straited slate the fiddler looked out upon the ocean to see the light line of a barely submerged reef circling the island, just a cable offshore. It seemed a pretty sight, a vein that skimmed across the skin of the sea. He sat under the sun, his dog in the shade of a palm, and devoted his attention to his journal:

I have taught Ketch to sit upon my lap. He ran in dizzy circles when I was aloft and has a strange habit of finding himself under the bosun's feet where he has endured many bruises. The rest of the men are as fond of him as they are of their new ship. While I am now thin as planking, Ketch grows daily from Pinch's administrations and has become an affectionate emblem of our success. Throughout our stay at St Bart's, he joined the surgeon and me on our walks, and proved adept at sniffing out turtles in the sand. We have collected some sixty of them and rest them on their backs in the hold, pouring water over them to ensure that they shall live until their meat is needed.

I introduced the surgeon to the strange philosophies of Innocent and at last we have confounded the blackamoor. He was convinced that he should not see his home for ten years, but since we now sail for Africa, tis more likely to be ten weeks, but he was not perturbed by the news – indeed, he smiled smugly, as is his habit, as if he knew better than the rest of mankind put together. He further irks me by referring to my dog as Argus and ignoring my proposal that Christ was a man of peace and atonement. 'Innocent,' I said, 'you travel with those who

222

lust only after women and gold.' He merely nodded in his irritating fashion and said, 'Was not Christ different from his disciples?' Magnes is correct. It is impossible to teach the blind to see.

The longer that we stay at St Barts, the more we bear of actions to be taken against us. It seems as if the British, also, have become resentful of our stay in their waters. The threat of one ship, and trade is interrupted – so we shall sail after our Juliette. Only Glasby seems upset by our imminent departure, though he has begun to wilt under the weight of the captain's flattery. They talk well together of the art of navigation that so eludes me. I believe the captain is much relieved to have another schooled so well in sea and stars. With our heavy numbers, Roberts tells me, we shall have a second ship and shall be stronger than His Majesty's Navy. The captain shall con one, Glasby the other. The topic of navigation seems endless and the two converse daily on the matter. I am not jealous of the captain's time, only I feel that in his efforts to win Glasby through kindness he quickly forgets the mariner's initial conviction and hatred of our trade. But Glasby is a small, ugly man and can do no harm in such close quarters – if one eye is kept upon him.

Even after they had sailed from St Bart's, Williams found himself with much time to increase the volume of his pages, describing the new arrivals in unparalled detail and so making the acquaintance of all. His continued presence in Roberts's

223

cabin, wryly stirred by Bunch, brought much whispering about the fo'c'sle, yet the majority of the newcomers were impressed by Williams's access to the captain and saw it as proof of his wickedness. Even Bunch and Coffin – still cabin boys and yet now among the older hands – lorded it over the younger newcomers.

While Roberts was forgiven for not enjoying his ale because he was already removed and accepted as different from the men, the abstemious Harry Glasby was greeted by all but Roberts with deep suspicion. A man who would not share a drink could never be trusted with a secret, and yet Roberts paid close attention to the sailing master, constantly engaging him in debates over the various theories of longitude. At the end of their first week of sailing together out of St Bartholomew's, Glasby had begun to warm slightly to Roberts. He was, by nature, a fairly jovial man, despite his nerves, and had relented to Roberts's pursuit of conversation. Within days they plotted the position of the *Fortune* together.

Glasby took up much of their time expounding his belief that the riddle of longitude lay in the skies above, and that an accurate calculation could be made by studying the motions of planetary moons and their eclipses. If the eclipse of a certain moon could be predicted by the speed of its orbit around a planet, then the appearance and disappearance of this moon would act as the hands of a divine, lunar clock. Roberts asked him how the planets' moons would be visible by day, to which Glasby winked and told him that the answer was worth twenty thousand pounds of His Majesty's monies.

There was, he said, a brass helmet, built by an Italian over a hundred years ago, called a celatone, that let a man read the moons with ease. And while the Paduan had discovered the measurement of time in the heavens, he had not figured out the manner in which the planets could be measured at sea. In other words, said Glasby, how could a man prevent the very movement of the sea? And then he nodded once, as if to let the captain know that this was the secret that he held.

Their seventh day's sail eastwards was remarkable for two reasons. The first, noted by all, even a restless Ketch, was the absence of wind. The ocean stretched in all directions like a taut sheet of satin. Second, and only noticed by a handful of the Lords and Williams, was the disappearance of Roberts from the quarterdeck. Williams descended to the cabin, and entered silently. Roberts looked up for a brief moment, and then returned his concentration to the charts.

'Have you come to write, William?' he asked.

'I have,' said Williams, opening the drawer of the captain's burry, and removing the oilskin pouch that contained his growing wad of papers. He pulled a chair back to take a seat. It brushed against the floor.

'Quiet man,' growled Roberts.

'Is something amiss?' asked the fiddler.

'Nothing,' said Roberts, 'but your prate. I need quiet. Kindly remove yourself.'

'I shall only scratch here in silence,' whispered Williams.

'You shall leave lest I box your ears,' said Roberts, not looking up from his charts.

Williams joined Innocent in the tops where he sat alone, whistling for the wind. Ketch paced the deck beneath, occasionally craning his neck to keep a watchful eye over his master's dangling feet.

'How is the captain?' asked Innocent.

'How would I know?' said Williams, already beginning to regret his visit to the tops.

'Most are on deck,' answered Innocent, 'but the captain is not. You leave quietly, return with your nose wrinkled. This you always do when you think you smell unfairness. It is childlike.'

'Well,' said Williams, 'then why don't you tell me how the captain is yourself?'

'He did not wish to see you. He pores over water charts.'

Williams stared at him, not entirely in shock, but impressed by the accuracy of his assumptions. 'What does he do?' asked the fiddler.

'He cannot understand where the wind is. He will trace his course, back one day, then another, and finally he will conclude that he is in error.'

'He has never been wrong,' said Williams.

'He has never conferred with another man,' added Innocent.

'Glasby?'

Innocent nodded.

'Are we out of the Trades?' asked Williams.

'If we press for Africa and his *Juliette*, our skin shall be paper, our teeth chalk.'

'We have been at rest but one day,' said Williams.

'The captain knows. Glasby knows. He tries to kill us all. He martyrs himself by the hope of salvation. Our bodies are his steps to heaven.'

Williams, despite remembering Innocent's accurate prediction of the storm, could never accustom himself to the man's tone. Everything was so certain for the blackamoor. It wasn't that the man struggled to be right, he simply was. He neither savoured nor relished his exactness, and that bothered Williams even more. He could recite Bible and book and yet he could not write, a negro who slaved, a man who could spot the contradictions and absurdities of others, but did not question his own tenets.

'So we're dead, are we?' asked Williams. 'The whole damned lot of us?'

Innocent shrugged.

Williams laid back, stretching his arms out, his legs moving back and forth in a gentle swing. 'This dying business,' he said, closing his eyes, 'is capital for a man's health.'

The sun slowly drew the oils from his bare chest and baked his skin. There was little, if anything, to do, and Williams was not called upon by the bosun. Instead he spiralled into a deep sleep under the high sun. When he finally awoke, after dark, he had a sharp headache and a pair of suns burned behind his eyes. Innocent had abandoned him. Williams hurried down the shrouds, continuously blinking, and immediately sought out the surgeon to see if he had any solutions to relieve his aches.

While William's headache was swept away by the darkness and several long pulls at a hogshead of water, no wind arrived to push them for the coast of Guinea. Instead, the sea seemed intent on impersonating land. A great swath of seaweed was gently swept by the current towards the *Fortune* until she was firmly enmeshed in the green strands of the sea's own hair.

On the fourth day of the calm, the surgeon enlisted the help of William Williams and Christopher Moody and had them row him from the ship in the tender. The effect of the sun upon the seaweed-infested ocean had produced a purple glow. The morass of vegetation harnessed the light, stripped it of its joy, and then released it in a muted effulgence.

While Moody and Williams struggled to dip their sweeps in and out from among the seaweed, the surgeon pulled and poked from the stern of the tender with a boat hook, fishing aboard small clumps of seaweed and any life that was attached.

'It is a city,' murmured the surgeon, holding a soldier crab in the palm of his hand. 'A floating city.'

Moody smirked at Williams. 'Tis the Sargasso Sea,' he said. 'No place to tarry.'

'I do not know if I share your opinion,' said the surgeon. 'There seems to be much to learn.'

By Scudamore's reckoning, the seaweed averaged a depth of no more than a foot and supported an entire network of life both in its tresses and beneath the strands that trailed in the water. Moody hooked an eel from the waters and held it wriggling to the sun.

'Extraordinary,' said Scudamore. 'A large fish could not venture among such thick vegetation for fear of entanglement, but the eel is ideal. The ideal eel. How perfect. There must be smaller fish to support them.'

Williams pulled a small clump of seaweed aboard and draped it over his head as if it were a wig. The water soaked his hair and cooled him.

'Sargasso?' he said to Moody. 'And does the wind ever visit?'

'Surely,' answered Moody. 'Upon its own whim.'

The next day Williams and Moody returned to the tender. The surgeon remained on deck, examining his specimens from an iron pot, donated grudgingly by Pinch. Williams and Moody now shared a sweep and were part of a team of twelve men tugging the *Fortune* through the vegetation. Four men hung from the martingale and the bowsprit shrouds, using boat hooks to try and sweep an easier path through the weeds. The coast of Guinea was already a dead dream and the *Juliette* a vision postponed. Now they headed for the nearest coast, that of Surinam, but seven hundred miles separated them from fresh water. By the calculations of quartermaster Sympson, more familiar with the division of gold, it would take a steady breeze to bring them there without the ravages of scurvy or a torturous death from dehydration.

Innocent, remaining in his familiar perch, looked in all directions and saw no relief from the vast cloud of weed that had settled upon them. They rowed in shifts through the nights, quitting for the few hours when the sun seemed to burn from directly above. He knew that the time was not right for Guinea, and acknowledged the wisdom of retreat.

The continued calm encouraged much gambling on board, that Roberts, despite his articles, turned a blind eye to. Any captain preferred the most dreadful of storms to such a cloying calm. While a storm was forthright in its intentions, a calm was insidious and ate at the mind before reducing the body. After their second week without more than a teasing sigh of wind, still gently draped in their expanse of seaweed, Sympson consulted with Roberts and orders were given that all liquids on board, including rum and beer, were to be strictly rationed.

There was talk of omens, of the bad luck of renaming ships, and potential Jonahs were turned over in the crew's mind. However, such had been their good luck before the calm that all were reluctant in their accusations, knowing that a sudden wind could catch them in their foolishness. But lips began to dry under the reduced rations, until slowly they cracked, blistered and bled. No matter the number of times that a man passing by the mainmast drove his knife into the wood, the wind would not come.

The salt beef, the dried fish, the biscuit, all seemed like recipes invented by the Devil, and it became hard to swallow a mouthful when there was so little saliva to wet the way. The turtles, bathed twice daily in sea water, were eaten one by one, and Scudamore and Williams were toasted when lips were finally wetted, because the turtle, normally such a dry meat, now seemed more succulent than venison. It became apparent that the lack of liquids affected every man's appetite, and they would have given a cask of beef for a mere barrel of water to share between them.

Within the next three days, the first signs of scurvy were spotted. It was easily enough noticed in others: the sudden lethargy that grew to perpetual exhaustion, a nervousness that made even dull daily chores seem like life-threatening tasks. Philly Bill collapsed first. He was one of the strongest men of the *Fortune*, much admired for his ability to sweat the stiffest of ropes, yet he fell in front of all, trying to stand after an hour's splicing under the noon sun. His messmate William Main told the crew that Philly had had an unusual aversion to turtle and could not stand the thought of ingesting the meat, indeed, had declared that he'd sooner eat the bosun. This brought relief to many minds; the fresh meat, as long as it lasted, would prevent the spread of scurvy.

Both the turtles and the remaining water barrels were placed under guard after the last keg of beer was mysteriously drained in a single night. There were many suspicions, some saying that it had been drained by the sober Harry Glasby, but a number of hangovers proved otherwise. Thirst was a stranger thing than hunger. Hunger started with a growl, but came and went and could be parried by the knowledge that the ocean was filled with food. But thirst shrivelled the body. Lips stuck to one another, cheeks joined behind them. Even the creases in a man's brow seemed to deepen. Skin was no different from soil, and the erosion began deep down before surfacing.

Every man found a nail, pulling them from the ship's planking if necessary, and sucked continuously on it through day and night to keep the mouth moist. Philly's exhaustion leaked throughout the crew. Two days after the last turtle was consumed the first of the men, including Pinch, came out in large blotches across the skin, giant welts of blues and purples.

At the end of the third week, they had their hopes raised and dashed. A dark cloud gathered above them, and a firm wind took hold. Those who had thought that the last of their strength had long gone were momentarily energized by hope, and rushed aloft to release the canvas. The wind was followed by a heavy rain, and every stitch of canvas, every yard of cloth was hung out to gather rain water. Within an hour both the wind and the rain vanished. Their only consolation was that they had been stirred long enough to emerge from the seaweed.

When they squeezed out the water from the canvas and clothing, they groaned to taste it and spat out the poisonous concoction of salt and tar. Only the water that had fallen directly into the barrels, no more than three days' worth at their present rations, was potable. The rest was poured in silence over the side. It echoed as if the dirty stream were a toxic cataract.

A depression came fast upon the crew. As their minds went, so their bodies followed. Old wounds began to reopen. A childhood scar on Williams's shoulder grew, then blistered and yawned, and he looked upon it with the curious attention of one who sees something long thought gone. Pinch's stump split open that night and, if it caused him pain, he was too tired to relate it to Scudamore. Philly's legs had swelled so that he could no longer walk, and his flesh lost its elasticity so that it hung from him like a dotard. His gums were inflamed and his breath became so offensive that few could bring themselves near.

Within four days they were down to their final

barrel of water. Roberts gathered the Lords to tell them that they were now so far south that winds would surely come within the next few days. He was dressed as if orating before the king's court and, while the marks of scurvy were apparent on the other men, Roberts kept the extent of his own disease a private matter, hiding beneath a white silk shirt and a long blue frock coat, and lightening his face with skin-toned powders.

That night, a small wind blew up just hours after they buried Philly, and the stronger hands crowded on a fair amount of sail, reluctant to push their luck, knowing that none had the will to deal with an emergency caused by their own hands. Still, there was no land in sight.

When the wind died for the third time, with Roberts reckoning them only eighty miles from the coast of Surinam, any man could tell that the heart had gone from the crew and they had resigned themselves to a slow death delivered by a vengeful Lord. Sympson had a dozen men carry their spare mainsail from the fo'c'sle and lower it over the side of the *Fortune*, creating a shallow canvas pool, that those who could not swim might cool themselves within. All trappings of civilized men were now forgotten. Those who were too distressed by the itching of the insect population that bred in their clothes and too tired to beat the vermin out simply wandered naked about the *Fortune*, clasping sailcloth to them if they sat under the burning sun.

Williams had been approached on three occasions since the consumption of the last turtle and had been offered up to two hundred pounds for the sale of his dog. Ketch had sensed the thirst in the men as they talked to his master. Of course, it was not only his meat that they were after, but his blood. He had told them both the first and second times that his dog would not be the first to die upon the *Fortune*. And though it had sounded very swashy at the time, Williams regretted his ultimatum, and with Philly drifting to the ocean's bed he had no choice but to give Ketch up.

When Main and Mackintosh and Hardy first tried to lay hands on the dog, Ketch gathered his strength and leaped at them, drawing blood and causing wounds that would not heal. They backed off and beseeched Williams to kill the dog himself. He sat by the surgeon's trepan and, holding the dog between his legs, drew the scalpel quickly across Ketch's throat. With a firmness of grip that surprised him, he resisted the spasms of death and spilled not a drop of his blood. They shared it among themselves while it was still warm.

Ketch's death was not regretted until the following day, when the communal thirst reached such a pitch that there was great competition in the hunting of rats. The dog, master of this vocation, had missed his calling, and the hold was filled with seamen climbing over bales of silk and casks of salted beef, all in search of the freshness of raw meat.

CHAPTER 25

During the first days of the calm, Harry Glasby, sailing master, had managed to persuade the cooper and the carpenter to raise two large barrels from the deck, and had the deckhands fill them with sea water. Before he, too, fell prone to the exhaustions of scurvy, he tried to show Roberts how the sway of the ocean might be counteracted by taking the measurements of the sky from a suspended position within a container of sea water. Roberts stood by him as the sailing master immersed himself, watched by every member of the crew desperate for entertainment.

He floated, naked on his back, balancing an hourglass on his head to show how successful the application was. Williams observed him – the sailing master was the only man who seemed to have forgotten that they were in a calm – but remained detached amid the laughter of the crew. When Glasby dragged himself from the barrel he was thrown a small piece of canvas to dry himself with, and slapped hard on the back by many hands, and called a precious fellow for holding his humour when they were so hard-pressed.

Now Glasby's tank was used for an altogether different application. Hardy, who remained among the more active of the crew, captured a rat, and took the original measure of greasing the side of the barrel with lard and plopping the rat into the sea water. He began by collecting wagers as to how long the rat could swim before it would perish from exhaustion. Pinch ran low, reckoning it could not swim for more than three turns of the glass, while Innocent, refusing to put money upon it, guessed that it could last an entire watch. It was an easy sport for men suffering from scurvy to watch, for it involved little movement and the sight of something suffering more than them.

The rat, its fur slick with the combination of lard and water, struggled furiously at first to climb the sides of the barrel, but Hardy's preparations had been thorough and the rat began to travel in circles around the circumference of the barrel, followed by its bright pink tail. As its life expired it brought back a certain energy to the men, some calling for it to swim for another hour, some wishing it dead minutes ago. When it drowned after three hours of curious paddling, Bunch had come within the closest minute, and collected almost one hundred pounds in gold. Its blood was then drained by the cabin boy, who chose not to share his drink.

Hardy, who had lost only a few guineas, was asked if he could provide similar entertainment again. Williams found the rat, a large male, who had somehow evaded the attentions of the crew, and brought it on deck the following day, dangling it by its tail. The expert wagerers noted its size, the length of its tail and the sedate manner in which it accepted its fate. Generally, it was reckoned a plump and unfit beast, certain to sink at a quicker rate than the previous contestant.

This time, after all the wagers had been placed, the outside of which now stood at five hours, Hardy bet them it would last double the longest, at ten hours, and asked for direct wagers. Over three hundred pounds lay against the mate. The rat tried to climb from the barrel in the same frantic manner as his predecessor, and once again submitted to his fate of swimming in tight circles. After the turn of the third hour, when its paddle was slowing, and the pink tail seemed to be swaying mainly from the ripples in the tank, Hardy leaned in, plucked the rat by the tail, and smacked him twice against the side of the barrel on the crown of his head.

The crew laughed. Pinch cried, 'Don't kill the bastard, he's got another turn in him.'

'Let him be,' shouted Main, still short of his projected time.

Hardy dropped him back into the centre of the tank, and he resumed his circles.

'Come on boy,' spluttered Pinch. 'Look alive, look alive.' It was hard to determine the cook's words. His gums had swollen, and his teeth were so loose that they seemed to drop every time he tried to break a smile. Even Roberts had come on deck to watch the struggle, and Sympson had stretched stiffened canvas over a tricorn hat, leaving him plenty of shade to protect his eyes.

During the seventh hour, the rat paused to squeal and shriek.

'Sink, you whoreson,' shouted Main.

'Sink, you bastard,' screamed Bunch, who had wagered the entire of his previous winnings against Hardy.

Instead, the rat reversed his course. When midnight came, most of the men dispersed across the deck, the rat still swimming after fourteen straight hours. When they awoke, and they slept long after sunrise with no chores to encourage them, the rat still swam. Only at noon, twenty-eight hours after he had begun to swim, did the rat finally stop, floating dead on the surface.

If Williams had not placed a substantial bet of his own he would have been under immediate suspicion for having forced the rat to ingest some agitative concoction before bringing him to deck. There was a lot of grumbling when Hardy urged his debtors to settle their accounts at once, but so few believed that they would ever spend another ounce of gold that Hardy was not forced to grip either of the pistols that he had slung over his shoulders.

Magnes was the most argumentative, continuously pointing to the fact that Hardy had raised the rat from the water and beaten him across the head when he had seemed ready to sink.

'Even if twas true,' said Hardy, 'and you docked

me the three hours afore, I'd still have taken your money by a day.'

'You've cheated every friend you own,' said Magnes, with some note of admiration. He pulled his debt, in coin, from his pocket. 'Is a rum trick, and one I look forward to . . .' Magnes coughed, and brought his hand to his mouth. 'Damn.' He spat the loose tooth into his palm, and slipped it into the empty pouch that had held his gold.

'The vitality of the rat,' said Hardy, 'is reminding the vermin that he desires life.'

Williams spent his time leaning over the taffrail of the quarterdeck, laying out the sounding line, forcing himself into dull occupation just to prevent his mind from stagnating. He could not find the invention within himself to take a seat in the captain's cabin to keep his journal. Besides, he thought, the adventures of William Williams and Bartholomew Roberts were set in storms, not calms. Hunger and thirst shamed a man. The mere sight of his captain revived the mocking memory of the *Juliette*. He had no energy to expend on such high hopes.

Instead, once every hour or two, Williams would let out the sounding line to its full depth, and reel it back in, always carefully studying the application of tallow to see if there was even the vaguest report. Two more had died that morning, including Pinch. The old man had perished surprisingly quickly, seeming to think that death was, at this stage, the speedier relief. Once more, Innocent spoke words over the bodies, and Williams, in a small affectionate gesture, sewed both beef and tobacco into the cook's clothing.

Pinch was lowered into the ocean with the second body. Unfortunately, no one had remembered to weigh them with stones from the ballast, and the two men, stitched in their hammocks, floated all day just yards from the boat. It was an inspired moment in the life of Phineas Bunch, who took a small fizzgig and speared one of the bodies from a dozen yards. He attached a line to the taffrail, and kept both eyes on the six feet of bait in the water. Bunch sat patiently on the quarterdeck, alongside Williams, holding a brace of muskets, waiting for the first shark to arrive.

The captain climbed the shrouds at a slothful pace. When he reached the fighting top of the foremast he found Innocent lying flat upon his back. The African was still, save for his jaw, which chomped in constant circles. On hearing a step upon the boards, Innocent opened his eyes for a moment. He did not see fit to adjust his position as his captain slumped against the mast.

'Beer,' said Innocent softly.

'Sorry?' returned Roberts, sliding the nail from one side of his mouth to the other.

'Rum,' said the African.

Roberts leaned forward.

'Water,' murmured Innocent with hushed laughter. Roberts began to smile and found himself shaking with good humour. He wished to cease but could not stop. When, finally, the laughter died, they sat in silence together. Their shadows became long and merged.

When the *Fortune* was finally visited by a shark, it was dark and two-finned, and swam in circles around Pinch's floating body. Bunch levelled his musket, and the blast roused the ship but left the shark undisturbed. Those members of crew who could still move of their own volition gathered on the starboard side to watch Bunch's second shot. It missed.

'Have you ne'er shot at fish?' said Magnes. ''Tis a feat, unless he's a big bugger and passing right beneath.'

'Aim ahead of him,' recommended Wilson, but Bunch's third shot lodged in Pinch's body and turned the sea around the hammock a milky shade of red, which had the effect of tightening the shark's circles. Finally, he could resist no longer and, to a cry from the men, the shark grabbed the body and shook it vigorously as if he could pull it apart.

'Good luck to you,' said Magnes to Bunch, who was busily reloading his musket with a large charge of powder.

'I could clear a six-pounder,' mused Wilson.

A second, larger shark, the colour of sand, stretching twelve feet from head to tail, joined the first as they tore Pinch's body to pieces. The second body drifted not fifty yards away, but unnoticed by the sharks.

'If you pull 'em in, William, then I can get

me a close shot at them,' pleaded the cabin boy.

Williams ignored the froth of feeding, and let his sounding line out once more.

'You'll have the liver,' offered Bunch, but Williams did not turn.

He fired at the foaming mass and struck flesh, but the larger shark had torn the body from the fizzgig and swum under the ship.

Later that night, another fin was spotted, and the *Fortune* seemed to have gathered her own family of sharks. By noon, four fins appeared and submerged at the stern of the ship. Bunch, obsessed beyond reason, kept up a steady artillery fire remarkable for its constant inaccuracy. The sharks had learned to swim either out of range of Bunch's fire or, when swimming close, to sink to a depth at which the shells of lead were already cool as they floated beyond the predators.

The final barrel of water was now half empty and, though the morning had brought four less heads to provide for, it would not last them another two days. At sunrise Roberts had risen to find Coffin dead under the chart table. His mouth was blackened, his entire chest covered in a dark, thin bile, and his eyes clenched shut. When Roberts lifted the boy from beneath the table, there was the sound of glass rolling across the floor. The captain looked to his feet to see an ink pot come to a rest. Whether or not drinking the ink had been the cause of his death or the final act of the dying,

Roberts grew angry. He carried the child up the main hatch-way and up on to deck, where the bodies of three of the deckhands already lay side to side.

He placed the cabin boy beside them, and then returned to his quarters, asking Williams to send the sailing master to him at once.

'Have you noted this morning's tally?' asked Roberts.

'Five,' said Glasby. His speech was cracked, jealous of every word spent, as if silence was the secret of survival. The final tufts of his hair had been removed by the scurvy. His scalp was now irritable and red, covered in a prominent layer of dead blisters.

'Including Coffin.'

'Hmmm,' crackled Glasby.

'These are your own deaths,' said Roberts.

Harry Glasby almost began a smile. He had been waiting so long to be confronted over redirecting the *Fortune*'s course, and yet now he was so tired that he could barely bring himself to converse, let alone defend himself.

'There is hell for you, Glasby.'

The sailing master tried to answer, but his speech had dried up the remaining moisture in his mouth. His head hurt terribly, but he did not care. Did not care whether he expired or was run through, whether he incurred anger or joy, but he regretted the pride that had brought about the becalming. He may have wished them all dead, but a rope was sweet mercy compared to this prolonged wake they were forced to endure every day on deck. To his surprise, Roberts said no more, but rose and left him to thought.

Wilson carried his own muskets, a fine Spanish pair taken from his counterpart on the *Sagrada Familia*, and hobbled up the steps to the quarter-deck. He had strapped a Dutch short-barrelled flintlock across his back and, laying all three guns before him, began to prime them with great care. Bunch watched the gunner with curiosity.

'Too little charge,' said Bunch, waving his musket in the gunner's direction. 'You'll barely break water.'

'If,' said Wilson, 'you've a head thicker than the beast you hunt, you'll remain gut-foundered and dry-tongued. Now, Mr Williams, will you give a man a hand?'

Williams tied a bowline to his sounding, tethering it to the taffrail and, with a gap-toothed smile, walked past Bunch to the gunner's side.

'Lick Arse,' muttered Bunch.

Williams paused. 'There is a chain of command. You are the last link.'

Though the sea rarely left men pretty for long, scurvy could take the finest of visages and ravage them beyond recognition in a short fortnight. It left some, such as Sympson and Scudamore, untouched for no apparent reason, but both Bunch and the fiddler had been mocked by the first stages. Williams had lost three of his frontmost teeth, his eyebrows, and sporadic clumps of his sandy hair. It left him good for scaring crows and children, or for the sea. The malicious smirks exchanged between Bunch and Williams were particularly gruesome and, though both were quick to note the disintegration of the other's face, it had not occurred to either that their own looks had been equally savaged.

Wilson and Williams dropped large chunks of salted beef into the sea by the starboard side of the *Fortune*, and discharged their muskets at the first shark to pass. It was a process that they repeated again to Bunch's silent amusement. Slowly, the largest of the sharks, a dark-skinned fellow with thin pale stripes that rippled down his flanks, adjusted the depth of his passing until a man could have reached and grabbed at his fin. Finally Wilson put a heavy charge in his short-barrelled flintlock and, filling it with scattershot, handed it to Williams. Then he primed both his muskets and loaded them, propping one against the taffrail.

Williams fired first, waiting upon the gunner's orders and then unleashing his salvo at the sleek body as it rippled the surface. Wilson followed the fiddler's shot with a blast to the shark's head, and then, throwing one musket to the deck, grabbed the second gun and unloaded his second shot into the frothing water. Together the two men threw a weighted rope tied with a reef knot into the water behind the shark. They passed the loop over the shark's tail and secured the rope to a timberhead.

The power of the shark surprised all on deck. It seemed to pull the entire *Fortune* south, rocking her arrhythmically, causing several cries of men begging for peace, to have the shark cut free.

It took every fit man – and their numbers were no more than eighteen – to heave the shark up into the waist of the ship. Wilson slit open the shark's belly with a well-honed cutlass. The stench of digestive juices discouraged Scudamore from moving closer for a moment, but soon he was propelled by professional curiosity and, wearing his dark surgical gloves, he began to rummage in the shark's belly. He removed the head of a tuna, the unbroken shell of a tortoise, the stump of Pinch's right arm, and a simple leather boot that Bunch claimed to have belonged to Philly Bill. It gave Williams a peculiar sense of dread to see the boot, stained by stomach acids, as if the *Fortune* was merely a floating larder, stocking the beasts of the deep.

Without Pinch to prepare the meat, the fittest of the crew shared the duties between them. Wilson, in what Williams presumed a magnanimous gesture, offered the entire liver to Bunch. The cabin boy, too thirsty to want to commit the meat to flame, began to eat it raw. The rest sliced their meat thin, and seared it only for a moment, hoping to keep the majority of the juices intact. Roberts appeared on deck carrying a bottle of rum. He remained dressed for an appointment with an ambassador, today choosing a suit of gold brocade and a black felt hat embroidered with a Spanish coat of arms. The suit sloped from his shoulders, an ill-fitting garment that mocked the vanity of wealth. Despite the disguise, it was easy to determine that scurvy had touched upon their captain the same as it had spread among his men. His gums were so engorged that he resembled a Gibraltar ape. Williams prayed that he would not mention the name of the *Juliette*.

'Before we feast,' he said, 'I offer my crew the last rum of the ship. You know I am not a drinking man, but I have touched my lips to liquor to loosen them. You are prime coves, and if this is God's choice, then to the Devil we go. So take a last tot, and drink each other's health.'

CHAPTER 26

The combination of fresh meat and the taste of rum temporarily lifted low spirits but several reacted poorly to the shark flesh, most notably Bunch, who turned puce then yellow before his skin blistered and began to peel from his body. The physical symptoms were accompanied by a vehement urge to itch, so that Scudamore was forced to strap him to the mess table and hold vigil throughout the night. But no man was capable of keeping watch awake and the surgeon slept fitfully, waking every now and then to Bunch's moans. The first rays of sun that slipped through the gunport revealed the cabin boy to be a skinless wretch, a weeping rawness of red flesh. All remaining hair had fallen from his body. Scudamore had never seen such an extreme reaction to poison while life still held, and could only bathe the boy in scentless oils to prevent his wet and exposed skin from adhering to the woods.

Williams could feel his strength ebbing, no longer even bothering to raise the sounding line to examine the tallow. Instead, he devoted his energy to his last words, words he hoped to commit to paper. When he finally hobbled down the main hatchway towards the captain's cabin, he could feel the thick alienation of his swollen legs, filled with undrinkable liquids.

Roberts was snoring from his bunk and Williams quietly opened the burry to remove his manuscript. He noted with disappointment how he had not set ink to paper in over three weeks. It came to him suddenly, as he searched for the small green vial where he had kept his precious ink, that to die and to leave his journal encoded would be no better than to never have written it at all. It froze him for a moment, but he could not face the question without the ink. It was not in the recesses of the burry, nor in the chart drawer, nor on the captain's table. Nor could Williams find the larger pot.

'Captain,' he whispered. The word came out as a small cough. 'Captain,' he repeated, and shook Roberts gently by the shoulder.

Roberts opened one of his eyes, as if Williams did not deserve his full attention.

'The ink, captain, I cannot find it.'

'Tis gone,' said Roberts, 'drunk by Coffin.'

Williams was struck by a second wave of panic. They were about to be turned from the world and the careful preparations that they had taken to preserve the history of their year were to count for nought.

'I shall be cursed for it,' breathed Roberts. 'The pistols,' he pointed weakly to his pair of silver-handled flintlocks. 'On the ribbon is the vial you seek.'

Williams took the two steps from the bunk and untied the vial from the ribbon. He flipped the brass cap from the neck of the vial and dabbed his finger against the opening. Raising his finger to the exhausted light of the lantern, the ink seemed watery and sticky.

'I bled the boy,' said Roberts. 'Tis enough for a fast goodbye and your cross.'

'But,' said Williams, 'what of our code?'

'Two choices,' said Roberts. 'Consign the code to the start of your journal.'

'I have not the strength,' said the fiddler, slowly shaking his head.

'Then live.'

Williams nodded and left the cabin without inscribing his final thoughts. He headed to the hold and for twenty minutes sat in darkness without moving. Finally he heard the small scratching sounds that he had been waiting for. He knew that the rats were at least as desperate as the men, and he waited until he could feel the chill of sharp claws move up his leg. Williams reached out and, forgetful of the knife he carried, squeezed the life from the rat. Opening its throat with his teeth, he sucked the warm liquid from the malodorous fur. When he was sated, Williams returned to the deck and, nesting in the shadow thrown by the setting sun, fell asleep.

Under an ashen moon, Roberts walked barefoot

about his quarterdeck. Slats of light pushed across the water, illuminating the bow watch, Harry Glasby. Roberts sucked the nail in his mouth and took another soft turn about the mizzen, then looked once more at the sailing master. Soon, sleep began to drape her arms about the captain, lending his eyes a heavy-lidded warmth. Chewing down upon the nail, he fought her, curling his toes upwards, stretching them out. Roberts defied the urge to lower his body to the deck. He stood throughout the night. Just before sunrise, the sailing master was lulled by the unchanging horizon. Glasby's head nodded into sleep.

As Hardy emerged into daylight to ring the bell, Roberts signalled for his attention.

'Mr Glasby,' said Roberts, 'has drifted at his watch.'

Hardy nodded. 'As do they all.'

'Glasby is to be lashed to the mizzen. Able hands on deck.'

Delirious from the remnants of sleep and the assault of scurvy, Glasby could not perceive his crime nor even the nature of his punishment until the first knot broke across his back. Roberts began by administering the lashes himself, surrounded by the few Fortunes who could still stand. The captain handed the whip to Williams. The fiddler looked down upon the raw flesh, stripped of its skin. He did not see that he could cause the man more pain and passed the whip to Magnes.

Magnes twisted the whip's hilt in one hand, the bloody knots in the other, and brought it down into the flesh. After his fifth swing, Scudamore relieved Magnes of the whip and, with Williams's help, carried the unconscious sailing master below. Roberts retreated to his cabin. His crew hushed as he passed.

When Williams emerged that afternoon he looked around the ship to find, once again, only an unruffled blanket of bluest ocean. The *Fortune* was littered with bodies lying prone under various makeshift canopies so that it was no longer possible to tell the living from the dead. He untied the sounding line from the taffrail, ran a slip knot over his own wrist and settled backward into sleep. Three hours later, he felt a small tug on the line, then another, and turning his head violently, he knocked his nose against the taffrail. Moody let go of the line, and huffed a breathless laugh at the Welshman.

'Uncommonly amusing,' breathed Williams.

Moody waved at the stink of Williams's breath, and then, as repayment for his humourless prank, he began to wind the sounding line up on deck, forming the tight clockwise coil. When the tallow weight finally appeared over the bow of the ship, Moody tried to say something, but there was no moisture left at all in his mouth. Williams almost felt guilty for not having shared his prize. He looked up to see that Moody's eyes were wide. Christopher Moody thrust the tallow into Williams's hands.

Stuck to the bottom were a few grains of sand, and Williams could not have been more elated had they raised the *Juliette*.

Roberts, drained from his watch, accepted the news with an exhausted smile, and deferred to Sympson. The quartermaster, along with Scudamore, was the only man who still showed no signs of the scurvy, though thirst had reduced him the same as others. Sympson could not speak loudly enough to address the *Fortune*, but instead spoke to Williams and Moody and had them spread the news and subsequent orders throughout the ship. Though they were in reach of land, still they were not in sight. To drift another week to the shore would be the death of the entire crew of the *Fortune*. The strongest must row for shore and return with filled water barrels and it must happen as soon as possible if they were to have any chance.

With the guilt from his private feast rapidly increasing, Williams was the first to volunteer, along with Sympson, Scudamore, Moody and four of the most recent arrivals. It took a full turn of the hourglass to lower the pinnace, instead of the usual five quick minutes, and another half hour to secure the small chain of three barrels with a long painter to their stern. Harry Glasby awoke, and his sobbing carried over the still waters to the crew of the pinnace.

Their pulls seemed slow, as if the ocean were a thick glue that fought to hold the sweeps. There was no energy expended on singing, nor even counting time, and they pulled in silence throughout the remainder of the day, all well aware of the brace of fins that had abandoned the *Fortune* for their company. They slept bent over their oars come the darkest of the night and, without even wind to stir the music of water, it was easy for Williams to imagine that they were the last men left on earth.

Dawn brought with it the enticement of heavy cloud and the cries of a pair of man-o'-war birds who splashed into the water ahead of the boat until a circling fin sent them soaring once more. By dusk the clouds grudgingly admitted that they clothed land and then quickly relented, welcoming the desperate men with a windless downpour. Though none could see because they all had their necks craned skyward, Williams wept for the mercy.

Sympson pushed his hands through his soaking hair and began to laugh. It was as if they had been murdered and resurrected by the same hand. Though not all shared their quartermaster's laughter, it did not seem incongruous, just a deeper echo of the rain. The downpour continued for eight joyous hours before passing over them in a north-easterly direction that all reckoned would soon embrace the *Fortune*. Roberts had determined them just north of the Marowijne River. To hear the words coming from the captain's mouth was one thing, but to see the river emerge from the contours of the land, to see thousands of gallons of fresh, drinkable water, to be able to wade in the very substance that had seemed so precious for so long – it seemed unfathomable.

At noon the following day the keel of their small craft ground against the shores of Surinam. Williams moved along the shoreline, gathering shellfish. He returned to the pinnace with arms laden and the crew used a stone to crack the shells open, sucking the moisture from inside. While they were so engaged, Sympson noticed a native dugout paddling not a hundred yards from shore. He waved weakly at its four occupants who, after a brief conference, decided to head ashore. It was not until the Fortunes saw the reflection of horror and pure pity in the Caribs' eyes that they had some notion of the devastating effects of the last month. Even disregarding the damage of scurvy, the sun and dehydration had turned their skins to stretched parchment. They resembled the dead returned, and thinly papered.

Sympson tried addressing them in English, which brought about many shakes of the head. With Williams's aid, they settled upon French, a language that one of the Caribs proved to have the slightest of familiarity with. The fiddler explained, using his hands – though his bloody smile, his blackened armpits and red freckled skin spoke louder than any language – how they had been adrift for close on forty days, how many of their shipmates were already dead, and how the remainder depended on this small party for their very lives.

One of their number, the oldest, whose brown face was smooth and creased as crumpled silk, withdrew to their canoe and brought back a calabash of fresh water, some dried fish and small pieces of cassava. Though none would so much as look at the fish, the water and cassava were greeted with happy nods from all the men. Despite the surgeon's urging for moderation, the calabash was quickly drained by the Fortunes, which the Caribs not only allowed but found positively amusing, pointing and laughing at the grateful men. Sympson retreated to the pinnace and, with a great show, dropped to one knee as if he were before the King of England, and presented the man with his own salt-stained tricorn hat and silver-hilted rigging knife. This prompted more talk by the Indians, the upshot of which was that both companies would be divided. The weakest of the Fortunes would accompany the old man and one other to their village, the other two would take Scudamore and Sympson and head up river, fill the water barrels, and make the journey back to the *Fortune*.

CHAPTER 27

Williams could not imagine a place that he would rather be. He swung in one of the village's only three hammocks and, after a mere two days of drinking a fine broth made of pigeon and the leaves of a lemon tree, he felt a dozen times stronger. Unfortunately, his body still lagged behind the recovery of his mind, and he struggled to stand, failing completely in his efforts to walk. An old woman visited Williams thrice daily, and though she did not see fit to return even one of Williams's alarming smiles, she bathed his body in a decoction of tobacco and a wad of plants that Williams failed to recognize. He was roused from an afternoon's doze by the touch of her crabby hands on his left arm. Opening one eye, Williams was horrified to see her squeeze firmly either side of his reopened wound. A small squirming ball of worms erupted, writhing on the surface of his skin. His nurse gathered them in her calloused hands and clapped once.

The following morning he was lifted in his hammock and carried half a mile from the village and suspended between a pair of lemon trees, where the old woman continued to visit him, covering his body in plantain leaves. In the evening he was returned to the village where he was anointed with a golden oil extracted from the tails of the bright red soldier crabs. It was in this state of regal relaxation that Williams was discovered by the survivors of the *Fortune*, six days since he had seen them last. Sympson and Scudamore had returned to the ship, not only with the water barrels, but with several bushels of plantains. They had further covered the bottom of their boat with shellfish, so that those Fortunes who had persevered had already regained a portion of their health. Out of the one hundred and twenty-four men, forty-one lay dead.

'You look well used,' said Roberts, using a switch of banana tree to steady his walk.

'Tis a terrible life,' replied Williams, smiling with his remaining teeth from his hammock.

Roberts peered at Williams's face. 'You are,' he said, 'a touch plainer than before.'

Williams could not stop grinning, so great still was the thrill of survival, to know that you had been measured against your fellow men and, where they had shied, you had stood tall. He looked at his captain. Roberts's dark skin showed no signs of the yellow hue that discoloured the rest of the crew. He seemed a little pinched, but his gums had ceased to bleed and his cane was more affectation than necessity.

'You are hardly fit to dispatch the birdies *either*,' said Williams.

Roberts allowed himself a close-lipped smile. 'The *Fortune* has bred an ugly crew indeed,' said Roberts, groaning slightly as he propped himself against the trunk of the tree. 'She has weaned from her the runts of our litter.'

Williams leaned forward in his hammock so that he could still focus on Roberts's face. 'Do you reckon us stronger than afore?'

'Soon,' said Roberts, 'ne'er get such care from a naval physician.'

'And how keeps Scudamore?' asked the fiddler.

'He attends to the men in the village. Shows nary a sign of scurvy, and now takes note of the herbs they pound and boil.'

'An invaluable soul,' said Williams.

'That old Carib has told him of a tree that enlarges a man's eel, and Scudamore erred in telling the tale to Magnes. Now I've got eighty men, barely strong enough for standing, begging the surgeon for bark. Some sleep with it over their pricks, others boil the bark in water and drink its tea as it were rum.'

Williams snorted with laughter that shook his teeth. He put his hand up to make sure that none had fallen.

'And belly-aching it would be,' continued Roberts, 'were it not the tamarandi tree. The shit flows so thick in that village that you'd a thought you were sipping on the bilge.' Roberts sniffed at the scents of the land, and pulled at the soft grass beneath him, smearing it between his palms. It was the action of a man who had never expected to set foot ashore again.

'Extraordinary,' mumbled Williams from under his blanket of plantain leaves, 'such people of a natural kindness.'

'It shall be returned,' said Roberts defensively. 'They have a taste for the broadest of our hats. They trade frequent and are not to be bought with black beads and rum.'

'Not that we have any,' said Williams.

'Still, their kindness shall be returned twofold.'

Within three weeks the company was quite recovered, men moving slowly from hammocks to crutches to the steadiness of their own feet. More than one deckhand was seen to wink from beneath the shade of a lemon tree, shifting in the gentle breezes of the afternoon, unworried by their lack of prey, their lack of women, their lack of rum. Despite the general convalescence, and repugnant visages of the crew, Williams reckoned that he had never seen them so happy. No one spoke of those that had died. Death, in this case, had been a weakness. The determined had been rewarded by a life of temporary peace.

Even Bunch, tortured and skinned by the shark's liver, began to grow strong once more, under the care of the same old woman who had quickly nursed Williams to his feet. Bunch received a similar treatment, but, to Williams's amusement, when he finally emerged from under his dressing of plantain leaves his skin remained as scarlet and luminous as it had been the first evening of his illness. Though clumps of his hair had grown back, it was as if he was vulnerable to the very air that he breathed.

Glasby recovered quickly from the double blow of disease and punishment. He spoke little and sat with his back to the ocean so that he could watch men approach. After Scudamore changed his dressing, Glasby would don a shirt so that none might see his scars. Sleep did not come easily, but was grabbed in broken minutes. He always woke suddenly, casting his gaze about the shore. After seven days, his nerves seemed to settle. Williams believed that he had accepted his punishment as just and resigned himself to the regime of Bartholomew Roberts.

Scudamore and Williams resumed their walks together while the rest of the crew savoured their coddled state. Despite the heat, they sported frock coats and britches over long leather boots, and smothered the bare skin of their hands, neck and face with an oleo of crushed termites, employed by the villagers as a mosquito repellent. The forests were much thicker than they had been on St Bartholomew's and filled with the unidentifiable chatter of tree life. They thought it sensible not to stray too far. On their first two outings, they requisitioned a guide, who seemed comfortable in his surroundings for about a mile or so before prompting them to turn back. The villagers were essentially fishermen. Their women proved expert at the pounding of cassava into meal and the gathering of shellfish, but hunting inland was an art that had never been practised.

The tribe was, Scudamore had ascertained, neither nomadic nor agrarian but followed the seasons along the coast in a deliberate pattern, taking their canoes across the southern edge of the Caribbean to Tobago before winter. The doctor had begun to understand the use of many of the plants that the villagers used to aid the Fortunes' recovery, but he could not hide his excitement when their guide stopped them in a clearing early one morning, and pointed to a thickly branched tree that stood at perhaps ten or twelve feet.

'This,' said Scudamore to Williams, 'they call the genipa tree.'

'Genipa,' said the guide, and pointed upwards. The tree was laden with a heavy fruit, ashen in colour, and the size of two fists.

Scudamore removed his frock coat, the arms bearing many signs of the surgeon's strange stitches, and proceeded to climb to the first level of branches.

'Pppssssssssss,' said their guide.

'What's that?' asked Scudamore, looking down.

'Pppssssssss,' repeated the guide, and swished his arm back and forth like a horse's tail.

'Snakes,' said Williams. 'I think he is warning you of snakes.'

'Of course,' said Scudamore. 'I shall take every precaution. Catch, sir.'

Williams was hit square in the chest by a large piece of genipa fruit. The fiddler picked it off the ground, rubbed it against his legs, as if it were an apple from an English orchard, and then sunk his teeth into its flesh. He received a sharp smack on the side of his face from the young guide.

'Bastard,' spluttered Williams, spitting out the mouthful.

'What's that?' said Scudamore again from above.

'The whoreson just knocked the fruit from my trap.'

'A good thing,' replied Scudamore, heaving himself up another branch and now quite lost in the thickness of the boughs. 'Thoroughly poisonous, man.'

Williams looked weakly at the guide. His thankful nod was ignored.

Soon the floor of the forest was littered by the fruit of the genipa tree, and Williams and their guide busied themselves with making a small pile of it beneath the tree. When Scudamore finally descended, he was grinning ear to ear.

'An experiment, sir,' he said. Gathering an armful of fruit, he began to walk in the exact opposite direction to the village.

After their guide had called for the surgeon's attention and the three men had returned to the village,

Scudamore and the old man proceeded to pound and squeeze the genipa fruit in a wooden bowl. Williams sat by, fascinated by the dark poisonous flesh that he had happily bit into only two hours ago. The mixture was strained through a weave of manioc, producing a thick black juice, which Williams presumed was used to cover arrowheads, only he had seen neither bow nor arrow.

The surgeon took the feather of a man-o'-war bird from within his pocket and dipped it in the genipa juices. Pulling his edition of Wafer's *New Voyage & Description of the Isthmus of America* from the inside of his frock coat and opening it to the title page, he briefly inscribed in a florid hand, *To William Williams, maker of music that lingers. Your honest friend, Peter Scudamore.*

'Ink,' cried Williams after he was handed the book. ''Tis as good as India ink.'

'Surely not,' smiled the surgeon. 'You might begin your charts again, but I suggest you pause a week before relying on the genipa fruit.'

'Why is that?' asked Williams.

'Patience,' cooed Scudamore.

On the seventh day after Scudamore's kind gift of the book, Williams was halfway through his third reading, embroiled in a description of exotic fauna. He picked up the volume after a lunch of a spinachy-looking vegetable and boiled fish. Turning to the title page, he was astonished to see that the surgeon's kind inscription had vanished.

He flipped forwards, then backwards but could not find the words anywhere.

'Mr Scudamore, sir, Mr Scudamore,' Williams woke the surgeon from his post-lunch rest.

'William?'

'The ink,' said Williams excitedly. 'Vanished.'

'As if,' continued the surgeon, 'pen were never pushed to paper.'

'How did you come by the knowledge?' asked the fiddler.

'I enquired,' replied the surgeon.

In the following days, Williams collected several baskets of the genipa fruit and, with the surgeon's aid, filled two of the empty rum bottles with their disappearing ink. Roberts proved true to his words, and conducted the village elders on a tour of the *Fortune*, allowing the men to have their choice of goods from their holds. Sympson had long since secreted the more precious objects, from golden cups to chandler's stores, that the Fortunes reckoned that they could not do without. The elders chose carefully, having some sense of what their own kindness had been worth, and emerged from their visit with a dozen lanterns, twenty cutlasses, a ragged mainsail that the bosun was happy to part with and a large box of ladies' hats.

Without alcohol to stir their libidinous natures, even the lowest reprobates of the crew had behaved as if they were in a reverend's house and did not see fit to touch the Indian women. Most were still occupied by the question of how the tamarandi tree should be employed and, once the captain had announced his intentions of departure, every tree in the surrounding dozen acres had been stripped of its bark.

It was not as if the Fortunes had been seized by an old hunger to acquire or to destroy, nor had their time adrift off the Surinam coast transformed them into a godly ship of missionaries. The quiet sojourn had been a time of convalescence, and perhaps a final prayer for their delivery. With the rebirth of their dreams and desires, the utopia in which they found themselves was almost transformed to a constricting land of disenchantment.

CHAPTER 28

December 1720 – The Caribbean

The *Fortune* sailed north for Carriacou, where Sympson encouraged them to remember that they were once men enured to hard labour. The ship was careened in three weeks. The crew found their voices returned, if only so that they could loudly protest at their lack of rum to the long empty strands of sandy beaches. More remarkable to their captain was the fickleness of the wind that carried them to Carriacou in less than ten days. It was too soon for him to push for Africa and the *Juliette*. Instead, he decided that they would hunt amid the Caribbean trades, waiting for the disposition of the crew to be buoyed by success before attempting the Atlantic again.

On leaving the island, the heat of the season fell upon them. Both the tender and the pinnace trailed in the *Fortune*'s wake. Planks had begun to buckle upon their respective decks and, on Sympson's orders, they were lowered into the ocean, following in the billowing shadows of the canvas like ducklings. Sometime during the hours of Williams's rest, Innocent had slung food and water over his back, and shimmied along the line connecting the pinnace to the stern of the *Fortune*. It was a foolhardy manoeuvre, but the wind beat strongly, keeping the line taut despite Innocent's great size. Come morning, a shocked boat watch reported Innocent's new position to the captain upon his arrival on the quarter-deck. Roberts stared aft and broke a smile at the thought of the man's struggle to bring himself into the pinnace. One slip and he would have been lost to the seas.

'Perhaps,' said Roberts, 'he is diseased in the mind. Will the surgeon be making a call at his house today?'

'No, he will not,' said Scudamore. 'I think,' he added with a grin, 'that it might be cured through cutting him loose.'

'A strange cove,' mused Roberts.

'Finally,' said Williams, 'he is captain of th' ship.'

Though they smiled at the suggestion, it was not far from the truth that had urged the man along the line. Men acquire different habits to pass their time asea, and Innocent had decided to practise his speech. To do so among his shipmates would have brought derision. With the *Fortune*'s mainsail filled from a wind angled slightly abeam, Innocent deemed it safe to speak aloud, presuming his voice would be buried in the swell rather than carried to the ship.

He waited until the end of the sun's journey, then looked out across the seas, and squinted, until they seemed wine-dark to his eyes. 'I have,' he quoted to himself from his contorted scriptures, 'a heart that is steeled against suffering . . . for in my day I have had many bitter and painful experiences in war and on the stormy seas. So let this new disaster come. It only makes one more.' He wrapped a blanket around him and, pretending it a tunic, prepared himself for a sleep soft enough to leave Poseidon undisturbed.

The *Fortune* held course for Barbados but within the space of two days they came upon a pair of ships so richly provisioned that they were at liberty to have no course at all but wander in the shipping lanes. The *Greyhound*, bound for Philadelphia and a mere two days out of her home port of St Christopher's, was treated kindly by the Fortunes who forgave them their homeland once it was discovered that they were carrying a cargo of rum. The following day they took a Rhode Island brigantine, the *Sea King*. She was an eighteen-gun vessel sailing windward under a fine set of fore and aft sails, deeply laden with both sugar and lemons, a giddy coincidence that brought great excitement to Roberts's crew. To find the two most essential ingredients for rum punch upon the high seas was so happy a twinning of fate that it was voted that the *Sea King* was a serendipitous ship and should be retained as the *Fortune*'s sister in service. Valentine Ashplant, who approached his captain in both age and temperance, was set aboard to command the prize, and those crew who did not join Roberts were packed in her tender and wished farewell. Ashplant was ordered to take Harry Glasby with him, whose skills as a navigator were gifted to the *Sea King* in case a sudden storm should arise and the two vessels become separated.

Williams could see the confusion of his captain the first day when he walked about his deck amid so many strangers. He was quick to note it in ink, stolen from the cabin of the *Sea King*:

We are now a heavy population. Our core is quite outnumbered by the surrounding flesh. It seems as if this lies against Roberts's captaincy. Despite the commandments of the Fortune *that all have signed, the true rules of Roberts's command have remained simple. Every man, especially myself, is an instrument and every instrument had a use. But now he must consider the men as a mass and it is not so easy to find the strength of an individual among the numbers. Another five ships have been taken and dismissed, none of great wealth, but we sit in the lanes, and few have even dared to run against our armidilla. Roberts tells me that soon we shall be bunted. We must be, for the trade is truly diminishing before mine eyes. In honour of our successes, Innocent retreated to the pinnace and slit the throat of a hog captured from the* Mary and Martha. *He started a fire in the boat, but was forgiven when he returned to share the meat. Our days of deprivation are now dried puddles of memory that have no bearing on our future intent.*

271

It seems as if it is only Roberts who is worried by the threat of His Majesty's Navy. Perhaps he is merely anxious at the distance we remain from the Juliette.

They were followed for a long day by the trunks of separate squalls that seemed to be set at the four corners of the surrounding horizon. The blue sky above tried to separate the thickening legs of rain. Williams's writing was interrupted by a worried Innocent, who believed that they were trapped beneath the belly of a beast of great magnitude. However the following morning brought a blank horizon. The supposedly inescapable set of converging squalls had sent the *Fortune* and the *Sea King* rushing for the leeshore of verdant St Lucia, and it was there, rounding her coast under the Grand Petons, that prey was sighted by an overexcited Bunch, happy for the chance of new pistols.

The Grand Petons were a strange pair of mountains for the Caribbean, rising sharply like termite hills from the southern edge of the island and casting a vast shadow that covered land, beach, and a stretch of water beyond the reef. There, in the gleaming waters, whose sparkle was accented by the shadows close by, sat a Dutch interloper, the *Elisabeth Puerto del Principe*, with her yards and topmasts down, only recently righted from an extensive career. The *Fortune* and the *Sea King* approached her under reefed topsails in full confidence that, by taking her seaway from her and through their luck in surprising her in such a naked state, she would submit.

The eager men, pressed against the larboard rails of the *Fortune* could not have been more surprised to see her buffeted by bulky fenders of chaffing gear and running out both her jib and studdingsail booms, all in preparation to defend the *Elisabeth Puerto del Principe* from an attempt to board. The Fortunes observed the frantic activity of the interloper with a touch of horror. Empathy quickly dissipated when the interloper delivered a full broadside that severed the *Sea King*'s bowsprit and sent a ball ripping through her mainsail. The cannonade seemed to reverberate against the walls of the Grand Petons. For a moment it seemed that the Dutchman had fired not one but a series of broadsides.

Roberts ordered the red jack of sansquartier to be run up alongside the black flag and then handed control of the *Fortune*'s gundeck to Wilson. Still a quarter of a mile from the *Elisabeth Puerto del Principe*, the air above the *Fortune* was heated by a rush of roundshot and chain. The *Fortune*'s topsail yard sagged like a broken limb as the chainshot wrapped itself around the wood, severing it with heat and power.

Wilson, a handspike stuck with sweat to either palm, was hurrying from gun crew to gun crew, altering the angles of the cannon to concentrate their fire not only on the interloper's gundeck but also on their bow. Roberts stood on his quarterdeck, glass raised, and watched as the first broadside of the *Fortune* ruptured the interloper's bulwark amidship, sending splinters tearing through her waist. Another shot struck at the foot of the bowsprit. The twisted metal of her bowchaser was torn from the deck and propelled overboard.

The sounds of drum and fiddle replaced the blast of the cannonade, over which Roberts could hear the bosun call the order to lower the pinnace and the gig from the *Fortune*'s sides. Both boats were lowered off the weather side of the ship, protecting their men from the last cannon still turned towards the *Fortune* and the *Sea King*. Despite Wilson's angry admonitions, the twelfth gun crew abandoned their cannon and rushed into the crush of men that competed for a space in the pinnace. She was lowered, until water lapped gently over her sides, and pulled away to a great cheer. The pinnace was rowed in a wide circle, trailed by the gig, approaching the *Elisabeth Puerto del Principe* by her bows, allowing not one of her guns to bear on the closely packed men.

Wilson aimed another broadside ahead of the Fortunes, whose pinnace was now half submerged and visibly sinking in the water. Her crew were so concentrated on the fight ahead that they had not considered the prospect of drowning. None thought to bale. The *Sea King* raked the *Elisabeth Puerto del Principe*'s fighting tops with grapeshot, chasing out any musketeers who had hoped to climb to gain a purchase for repelling the potential borders.

Williams sat in the middle of the pinnace, the water lapping at his lower thighs, wondering if any missed his playing on the bows of the *Fortune* and even more intrigued as to why he had thought to join Moody and Innocent as they made their way ahead of so many new hands, determined to board. They began their fire when they had closed within a hundred yards, sending balls from their flintlocks over the bows of the interloper, trying to discourage her men from making sport of them when they sat so vulnerable and low in the water.

The *Elisabeth Puerto del Principe* was riding two anchors from her bow, providing ample opportunity for the first of the Fortunes to leave the pinnace and take to the Dutch ship. The first man was no more than three links up the chain when the hawse hole screamed with the shot from a blunderbuss, tearing at both his hands and his head as he fell backward. Moody swung his graplin high above the bowsprit, finding purchase on the martingale, and Innocent, a pair of pistols strung over each shoulder with red-laced ribbon, shimmied quickly upwards.

Meanwhile, the gig had come about on her leeside, giving Wilson an opportunity to deliver one last gravel-laced broadside across the stern of the Dutchman. By the time that Williams had gained the bowsprit, Innocent had proceeded to the aft timberheads, and the Dutch were in full

275

retreat to their quarterdeck, where they had turned their stern chasers upon their own deck. The Dutch gun crews were emerging through the aft hatchway, joining their officers on the quarterdeck, some, perhaps, for the first time.

The stern chaser exploded across the waist of the ship, and the Fortunes were caught by a blast of grapeshot that screeched above the deck. Williams raised one of his four pistols and without taking careful aim at any Dutchman in particular fired in the general direction of the quarterdeck. The gig had finally been brought about to the interloper amidships, and poured her men over the side. Innocent grabbed at Williams's arm and shouted, 'Now.' They leaped over the carcasses of a pair of sheep and ran fast along the larboard side of the ship, forcing the officers commanding the stern chaser to make the desperate choice of which oncoming party to fire at.

The roar of the stern chaser coincided exactly with Williams losing his footing and crashing to the red deck amid the deafening echoes of musket fire. The fiddler rolled once and screamed, convinced that he had been shot through. Once again Innocent reached down and hauled him to his feet, almost picking him up to throw him inside the upturned longboat. He fell amid the squeals of four terrified piglets who galloped back and forth amid the fetters and oars that lined its bottom.

Williams turned on his back and breathed hard beneath the sun, preparing to leave his temporary

1aven. He could see the silhouettes of some of the Fortunes climbing the foremast shrouds and stepping into the damaged fighting tops. Moody took an eternity to lower and aim his musket at the quarterdeck, before glancing down at the longboat and waving his friends forward. Innocent and Williams clambered out just as another group of Fortunes rushed past them, carrying not a pistol between them but roaring louder than any report and gripping reefknives in one hand and cutlasses or boarding axes in the other.

Body met body on the quarterdeck. Williams saw a figure rise above him, a rapier thrust at his chest. Without hesitation he raised his pistol and fired, from four feet, into the man's face. The shot seemed louder to Williams than any twelve-pound broadside, perhaps because the gun smoked in his own hand, perhaps because he was now surrounded by the clash of metal against metal and the precarious screams of men. The ball shattered the man's nose, he raised his arms, and his body fell backwards before Williams. The fiddler followed the body down, to end his life, to save it, to see the wound, to confirm the hit. Teeth and mouth and nose were a confusion, slammed aside by a hole that tore through the centre of the head. Williams recoiled, rejected the taste of bile, forced himself upwards. He tried to wiggle his toes. They were sealed by blood. The fiddler did not know if the fight had been won or lost. He stood with loaded pistols and was not engaged. Thoroughly confused, he retreated from the quarterdeck. As he descended the steps he was relieved to see many of his fellow Fortunes climbing over the sides of the *Elisabeth Puerto del Principe*. They looked at his bloodied visage in shock, and then passed to the quarterdeck to see if there were any last rites to help administer.

There were over eighty bodies pressed against the deck of the *Elisabeth Puerto del Principe*. Many of the corpses lay over one another. Without the division of uniform it was difficult to account for the dead. The remainder of the interloper's crew – all but five or so were wounded – lay kneeling in an orderly row on the quarterdeck. Sympson, who had appeared with both Roberts and Scudamore after the worst of the fighting was over, sought to save on shot and powder and carried a large blade. The quartermaster had devised a thin veil of fine black silk that he had sewn across the inside of his tricorn hat. Though he could see through it, it remained thick enough to shield his eyes from the acute pangs of the sun. He walked down the line of men, all tied like hogs across hands and feet, and hacked at those who struggled in their bonds, quickly dispatching those who offered a clean sight of their necks. By the death of the last man on the quarterdeck, Sympson was slathered in blood, and removed himself to the scuttles so that he could clean his veil.

Scudamore, accustomed as he was to bloodletting, did not know whether to turn fore or aft.

There was a remarkable silence about the ship, as if even the wounded Fortunes were dumbfounded to find themselves amid so much carnage. Finally the sound of chains moving against chains drifted to the deck. Moody ascended from the main hatchway, preceded by six Africans, fettered and manacled. They stared at the bloodied deck and the dozens of their dead captors, but seemed only disturbed by the sight of Innocent, as if they could not place him within the equation before them.

'Three score more,' said Moody to his captain, pointing with the tip of his cutlass to the waist of the ship. 'Five dead from splinters, another two relieved of their wounds. A foot of water in the hold.'

A group of Fortunes attended to the pumps while Bunch, having already seized pistols from the dead captain of the *Elisabeth Puerto del Principe*, oversaw the slaves, instructing them to remove the clothes from a body, and having them separate the Fortunes from the Dutchmen. He kept the clothes of those officers who had not died the bloodiest of deaths, and carefully relieved them of gold chains and rings using a mixture of salt water and blood as lubricant.

CHAPTER 29

Buckets of sea water were raised by rope and, using the hard-bristled brushes, the Fortunes began to clean the deck of the interloper. Roberts took hold of Williams and together they descended to the captain's cabin. It contained four broad-based copper vases, filled with bright orange flowers, the sight of which made the fiddler pause. He could not help in the translation of Dutch, but found the bill of passage from Accra, from where the *Elisabeth Puerto del Principe* had sailed with over three hundred slaves. Seventy remained, but it was impossible to know whether the rest had been sold at neighbouring islands or perished upon the open seas.

'Is that not the name of the *Juliette*?' asked Roberts, tapping the page with his finger.

'I do not know,' said Williams, 'I have no understanding of the tongue.'

'I think it is. They passed one another a month back. She sails for the Gold Coast.'

Do we follow?' enquired Williams.

'Will return only when the season passes and the rains have gone. We have much time.'

'Do we sell slaves, Captain?' asked Williams. 'They would be worth much, would they not?'

'Thirty pound a head in St Lucia for the best of them.'

'We sail north along the coast?'

'We sail for Martinique to parade our wares.' Roberts pulled a series of signal jacks from the burry. 'We sail in the Dutchman.'

'Over two thousand pound,' calculated Williams.

'Will take five times that,' said Roberts.

Williams looked up, and saw that Roberts had no intention of gifting him with an explanation. He would be forced to let time unwind the design. Under Roberts's silence, Williams took a loose leaf of paper from the table and, raising the Dutch quill, made a brief encoded entry. He noted the number of dead, the heads of cargo and guessed at the ship's draft. A translator of his text would have been forgiven for presuming that the taking of the interloper was an action of little consequence to the author. Only the jagged tremors in the script and the dispassionate tone gave any clue to Williams's harried mind. And yet, after the fiddler had blotted the paper with sand, folded the sheet and tucked it within his shirt, he turned and talked calmly with his captain, as if the truth lay not on the deck above but in the paper against his chest.

All men gathered on the deck of the *Fortune*, including those from the *Sea King* and the slaves of the *Elisabeth Puerto del Principe*, still manacled but free to walk. Their ankles were blistered and most were unsteady on their weakened limbs, having lost the desire and ability to stand after months crumpled on shelves in the hold.

The service for the twenty-seven dead Fortunes was held at sunset of the following day. Already, under the tropical heat, the bodies had begun to rot, attracting circling crows from off the shores of St Lucia. Bunch shot them from the sky. The Dutch dead had been thrown overboard, and could be seen swept by the currents around the southern coastline.

It took three days for the carpenter to render the *Elisabeth Puerto del Principe* serviceable and, though he could not altogether disguise the battered look of the ship, once the bosun had set her yards and sails, she seemed a fair vessel. Roberts gathered over one hundred of his men, leaving the remaining twenty-four as crew for both the *Sea King* and *Fortune*, who sat peaceably at anchor in the bay. He sailed north for Martinique, only half a day's sail with a fair wind.

Keeping most of his men below deck, and forcing all his slaves above, Roberts followed the westerly coastline of Martinique, running both his Dutch flag and the green jack used by the lowland interlopers to show that they carried a full hold of slaves. The French planters, always eager to circumvent the taxes demanded by the Royal Africa Company and her delegates throughout the Windward and Leeward Isles, would be quick to inhale the ruse. The *Elisabeth Puerto del Principe* proceeded to tack south, returning to their small squadron but standing off some miles north of her.

Roberts sat against the taffrail of the quarter-deck, looking down the ship across the backs of the shackled slaves, speaking to Williams of his days as trader. Innocent came up the quarter-deck's steps. Since they had taken the interloper he no longer roamed the ship barechested, but covered his trunk with coarse Manchester cotton, differentiating himself from those taken.

'Captain,' said Innocent.

'Aye,' replied Roberts, 'are you heading for the gig, or would you care to take seat and smoke?'

Innocent sank to his haunches, but refused a pipe of the captain's tobacco.

'I converse with these men. They are Yoruba. Good people, they wish to return.'

'Indeed,' said Roberts, packing the bowl of his pipe. 'How do you speak their tongue?'

'At Corso,' said Innocent, 'when I learned from the bluecoat the tale of Christ Father and the search for His kingdom, I also moved along the coast. We take many men, and we head upriver for sennights and more. They called me talking nigger, and I learned many tongues of many men to trade. These are Yoruba. This man,' he pointed to one of the Yoruba, who was resting his head upon his knees, his arms locked together around his legs for support, 'he is the bluecoat of his people. Among these here, they are mostly Yoruba, they are to listen when he speaks.'

283

'What of it?' said Roberts, staring at the man in question. His face was scarred with swirling blue circles, intricate patterns that had been drawn by needles both into his cheeks and across his forehead.

'He is a man who sees ahead. He is friend to chance.'

'Obviously not,' said Williams. Roberts glanced aloft, at where Bunch hung in the mizzen, anxious for the sign of the first sloop.

'Innocent,' said the captain, 'I fear that we shall shortly be busy. If you wish to speak plainly, then so engage me.'

'I want to be captain over the Yoruba. I want you to give me all Yoruba and ship. This ship.'

Roberts looked into Innocent's eyes. The African obviously believed that if he stared at the captain long and hard enough then he would get his wish. 'You will have no ship, Innocent. You have signed articles the same as all others, and you are held by them, as every nail has its purpose on this ship.'

Innocent continued to stare at the captain.

'What of the Yoruba?' he asked. 'Are they to be sold?'

'I have not decided,' said the captain.

'We vote,' declared Innocent.

'If we vote,' said Roberts, 'then they will be sold.'

'Give me *Sea King*.'

'When you have a thousand pound, you are free to leave, and then you shall have truck for your own vessel. Achieve this, and I shall not stand in your way.'

'Sail ho!' cried Bunch from the top of the foremast as the *Fortune* rocked gently in the soft coastal swell of St Lucia.

'Innocent,' said Roberts, 'perhaps you might encourage your Yoruban friends to stand a while and show their health for the benefit of our Martinquan armies.'

'I do not think so,' breathed Innocent.

'You may choose from the able hands among them in two days' time. We shall carry no women nor children, as is laid out in the articles, but you may choose from the Yoruba.'

'They are mine?'

'You shall buy them from your divides. They in turn shall purchase their freedom from you.'

'It is done.'

'Shakes?' said Roberts, offering his hand.

'We have words,' said Innocent, turning and walking to the closest party of the Yoruba.

With the slaves circling on the deck like sheep driven by the threat of dogs, the first sloop stood off and lowered her boat, heading innocently for the *Fortune*. By nightfall eight other sloops and ketches were anchored off the square rigger and the *Fortune*'s great cabin was the forum for a group of agitated French planters.

Morning brought seven more vessels who had sailed in the darkness across from the neighbouring island of Martinique. Seeing such a busy trade and so many rivals gathered around the *Elisabeth Puerto del Principe* they brought the oars of their gigs down sharply across the water, knowing that the quality of slave was high to have attracted such attentive bargainers. No man carried less than five hundred pounds' worth of gold dust, and some close on a thousand. The planters, appearing over the bows of the interloper, were disconcerted to see such a rum collection of slaves on deck. None were oiled, as was customary. Those who had come with measuring sticks of silver, brass or wood, to compare statistics of head and body, slapped the rulers against their palms or twisted them in anxious circles. They were not greeted with the usual keen salutations nor handed a glass of wine. Instead, they were invited below, where they joined the knowing smiles of neighbours who took a small pleasure in unravelling the deception to their fellow dupes.

Roberts, clad in beige silk britches that ballooned about the thigh and gripped the calves, and wearing a shirt of the lightest and whitest cotton, carried neither pistol nor cutlass. He was escorted to the great cabin by both Hardy and Sympson. If Sympson was a sight for some concern, with his toppling lemon teeth and his silk visor pushed back across his head like a lady's bonnet, then Hardy, clad in the acrid fetor of dried blood that clung to the seams of his ducks, was a worrisome apparition. Williams followed behind them, his pistols slung crossways with black ribbon, so that a dark X covered his sun-kissed chest.

'We welcome you,' said Williams in French, 'and thank you for your promptness. If you have the suspicion that you are to be cheated of your gold, then put such worries aside. However, it seems a shame to have called so many men from their homes with no promise of business. We wish to serve you as our Dutch friends would have desired before their departure.'

'Where have they gone?' asked a man, whose wide-brimmed hat was decorated with peacock feathers. He was hushed by his compatriots.

'Captain Roberts does not wish to make any man pay less than five hundred pounds for his purchases.'

'You have more *negres*?' asked the same man.

'No sir, we have no more than you observed upon your entrance. Besides, they are not all to be delivered to the island of Martinique. In breeding gentlemen, you would not ask brothers to lie with sisters. These are not animals, sirs.'

'You have how many for us?' asked the peacock hat.

'How many can we spare, Captain?'

'Forty,' said Roberts.

'Forty,' repeated Williams in French, but the mumbling had already begun.

'Sirs,' interrupted Williams. 'If you believe it a scandal to pay eight times the customary rate, I would encourage you to place a value upon yourselves, and add said sum to the equation. I think you should agree that we find ourselves all content with the bargain struck.'

Each small sack thudded against the table of the great cabin. Soon only the petals of the dying orange flowers could be seen above the small hill of gold dust. While Roberts and Sympson remained to weigh the gold upon the Dutchman's scales, Hardy and Williams marshalled the planters to the interloper's deck, where Scudamore was busy separating the slaves according to his captain's orders.

The women and children were herded to midships and urged down the Dutchman's ladder to the planters' gigs. Since the blue-cheeked Yoruban stood beside Scudamore as he conducted his examination, none of the men resisted the doctor's probings: white fingers pushing aside lips, rolling back the foreskin of the penises, having them bend to check their anuses for flecks of blood. Scudamore selected thirty men for the planters, in the end dividing them not through age nor through sickness (for almost all showed signs of the bloody flux). He selected them through their eyes, choosing those who held the gaze of their scarred elder and rejecting those who looked away or boldly met his own eyes.

Williams led both planters and their acquisitions to the waist of the ship where each planter pulled a coloured handkerchief from his pocket and hailed his gig to carry him to his respective ketch or sloop. The fiddler had each sign his name upon a receipt that he boldly gifted them, a present of his own invention. The lopsided transaction was recorded in unabashed detail in the temporary ink of the genipa fruit. Williams took great pleasure in imagining the parcel of enraged planters gathered in their governor's house, presenting him with fifteen pieces of dissolving evidence – enough to hang the entire crew of the *Fortune*.

CHAPTER 30

With seven thousand five hundred pounds' worth of gold dust sitting light in their pocket, they fired the interloper late in the same evening, covering her in a thin coat of pitch to help her burn. Under the light of this spectacle, where the flames lit the bulky masses of the Grand Petons, creating shadows lighter than the night-time sky, the Fortunes drank freely on her gun deck. The interloper crackled and hissed until she was shattered by a grand explosion from some undiscovered keg of powder.

They sailed north with the trades behind. Roberts kept the slaves on board the *Fortune* and filled the *Sea King* with those men who caused him some suspicion, whether it be from their voice, their manner or their actions. He had only his instincts to guide him and, though he sometimes reasoned there were no good men present on either ship – and he included himself in this assessment – he kept the oldest of the crew close around him, leaving only Lord Ashplant to con the *Sea King*. He relied on Williams to inform him of those he had knowledge of and encouraged the fiddler into much writing. While Williams would read aloud his passages concerning the men he felt should be pushed aboard the *Sea King*, he elided several paragraphs from his narration:

I avoid it. He would have pressed his blade through my body, maimed me, killed me. Prevented me from writing these words. Instead, he fell before me. Yet, I am plagued by the question of justice. As a man, I was justified in my decision, this I know. Yet as a hand among the crew, I was not. It was a decision that I made months ago, even if I have not seen the depth of my judgement until now. I shall witness, I shall not partake. No blood shall flow from my hands.

It was unnecessary carnage, brought on only by the temperament of the interloper's captain. And what did he seek to protect? Slaves. I asked Roberts, is the slave a man? Should he be treated as such? He replied that it was best to think that a man was a man, until he was a slave and could only recover his humanity once his bonds were broken. I do not know if this is wisdom or merely reasoning to let a man continue in the trade. Roberts considers Innocent a man. Indeed, I believe he holds him in more respect than I do myself, telling him that they shall shortly return to Africa.

We have passed St Christophers, where, once more, Innocent showed his worth by leading a party ashore to round up a flock of sheep for vittles. There was much joking between the surgeon and myself

291

about how Innocent had met a Cyclops. We have decided between us that this is not a portion of his lunacy, but a matter of great wonder. While I have set about creating the heroics of our ventures, Innocent lives in a world of myth all the days of the week. And while he is an arrogant man he bows before the captain and now muses over our possible return to his native shores as a likelihood. We shall careen at speed in Hispaniola, and soon the swells of the Atlantic will bring sweet relief to Roberts. Now he can hardly sleep, vexed by the size of his crew and the surely that we are hunted. These are oceans, and should we choose to bow our heads, none should find us. However, I suspect that the Juliette *will hold to waters thick with traffic. These are the worries of a captain though, for a mere fiddler shall walk free of His Majesty's wrath to peddle his wares in London, but a fiddler should keep his hands from blood.*

Roberts led them to Bennet's Key, where hogsheads filled with sugar were placed one upon the other and ordered in the shape of a horseshoe, forming three walls to a saccharine house. Taking the *Sea King*'s mainsail, the bosun and his mate lashed it over the hogsheads, creating a canvas roof that would shield them from the sun and the rain. The entrance to their encampment looked directly out upon the Gulf of Samana and, while Roberts had had no quarrels with the Spanish, he appointed three lookouts and had Wilson line their cannon in two rows, facing the water.

Hispaniola held the largest concentration of Spanish in the Caribbean. For this reason Roberts had sought to avoid conflict with her ships, knowing that the supposed creed of warring against all men was an impractical decision in such divided waters. While the west third of Hispaniola had been ceded to the French, the Spanish governor-general held his seat in the east, from where he issued decrees and determined appeals from the entire of the Spanish West Indies. Though it was an island marked with the scent of European monarchical power, it remained wild, traversed by a mountainous range that ran across the Spanish borders to French territory, filling the two tines of the forked peninsula that dipped to the sea in the west.

The waters in the Gulf of Samana were ideal for the heavy work of careening both the *Fortune* and the *Sea King*. The beach head was protected by a vast peninsula that absorbed the Atlantic swells, but behind the stretch of sand lay thick entwined fingers of forest. Reckoning themselves distant from both plantations and cities, it was with considerable surprise that Bunch, rushing from his lookout post atop a small platform made of thirty hogsheads and a mess table, declared that not one but two sloops were sailing directly for their anchorage.

They were in roughly the same position in which they had caught the interlopers. The crew was filled with fear that they had been tracked by a Barbadian or Martinician squadron and were now caught between the densest forest that any man had ever seen and a thin coil of rope. Roberts did nothing more than climb the platform with his spyglass tucked in his belt, and sit patiently until he could clearly discern their flags.

'You may douse the linstocks, Lord Wilson,' cried Roberts, 'save fire a shot in welcome. They are a pair of black flags.'

Hardy busied the men by having them plant their topmast in the sands and running their own black flag skyward. The fear had passed through minor permutations of relief and now the crew awaited the anchoring of the sloops with the same conspirational excitement that two poachers might find coming across each on the edge of a vast estate.

Captains Porter and Tuckerman, unknown to any of the Lords and certainly to Roberts, had sailed south from Virginia with their crew of thirty-eight, and had been unknowingly sharing a hunting ground with the superior force of the *Sea King* and the *Fortune* for close on a month. Porter was a stout fellow, whose body was covered in the thick hair of an ape. He was prone to the habit of twisting his arms to pluck infested tufts from his back. His head was as bald as his body was hirsute and, if it were not for the uniformity of his tan, he would have seemed torn from some ancient mythology, a lowly cousin of the centaur.

His ally and confederate Captain Tuckerman was of a similar barrel build, but his chest and back were covered not with hair but in a remarkable mixture of scar and tattoo, where the white welts from old whippings had been enclosed in the blue lines of India ink. Each scar was defined and then topped with a triangle of ink, so that it looked as if his back were laced with arrows caught in flight.

They carried with them a span of tobacco that they laid at Roberts's feet as if they were plenipos returning with favours for their king. The captain welcomed them and bid that they share a drink. Like most of their kind, they accepted heartily, and the three sat down together, joined in their circle by the majority of the Lords. The crews of the two sloops also came ashore at Bennet's Key, bringing with them a barrel of their darkest rum, and other gatherings formed as men met to contest the latest news of their native lands, the potential knowledge of mutual acquaintances, and the stories of their chosen profession. Innocent did not stay with the Yoruba, who sat among themselves, granted water but not liquor, but chose to join the circle of Lords, captains and the fiddler, who had edged to the periphery of the enclave from where a man could listen unseen.

'Captain,' said Porter, addressing Roberts. 'Tis an odd thing in our trade to meet with stronger ships and take pleasure in the chance.'

'Gentlemen,' replied Roberts, 'though our numbers, both men and cannon, may outweigh yours, had you been delegates of the Crown, I think perhaps that we would now be standing trial.'

'Bartholomew Roberts,' said Tuckerman, as if to himself, 'we have followed in your feet like tykes. Your name has carried across this sea. You are held in contempt in Barbados, in Martinique and more islands than man can put word to. They say that trade slows . . . stops . . . when they breathe word of you.'

'I have heard them say, sir,' said Porter, itching at his back in discomfort, 'that you had taken a fleet of treasure off the Spanish Main, and had built a fort in an unnamed isle.'

'Aye,' said Roberts.

''Tis true?' asked Tuckerman.

'E'ry last word,' said Roberts.

'Thousands of moidores?' asked Porter.

'Thousands upon thousands,' said Roberts. Captain Porter began to sweat from conjuring the close relationship between the man before them and the wealth of which he dreamed.

'And where is this fort?' asked Tuckerman.

'Upon,' said Roberts, 'an unnamed isle.'

The circle erupted into laughter.

'Do you make sport of us?' asked Porter, looking at his pair of pistols that he had placed on the sand in front of him.

'Ne'er,' said Roberts, 'would I make game of a man who suffers as we suffer. Indeed, let me play patron. What can I present as my gift to you?

Innocent, tell us, is that not the way for a host to treat welcome guests?'

Porter and Tuckerman turned their heads to the left to see who could possibly travel under the name of Innocent. When they saw the man, his cheek scarred from the storm, his eyes unyielding, they awaited to hear his words with amusement, as if the captain had asked an opinion of seal or turtle.

'"In the palace of Alcinous,"' said Innocent, quoting his scriptures, '"Christ was gifted with a golden chalice, so that the guest might remember his host when drinking to the gods."'

'Golden chalice,' murmured Porter, overcome by Innocent's words and suddenly forgetful of his elocution.

'It was also said,' continued Innocent, 'that there should be moderation in all things, and it is equally offensive to speed a guest who would like to stay as to detain one who is anxious to leave. Treat a man well while he's with you, but let him go when he wishes.'

'Fine words,' said Sympson.

'Christ preached,' persisted Innocent, 'that nobody should be sent away with empty hands, and that each host must present at least one gift.'

The pirate captains paused for reflection.

'Well, sirs,' said Roberts, 'as holy men, we will not depart from the words of the Bible. Isn't that right, Williams?'

'Holy words,' chimed Williams, from the last ring of the circle. 'Inviolable.'

'Shot,' said Tuckerman. 'We are low on shot.'

'And powder,' added Porter.

'And mutton,' said Tuckerman. 'We have had nothing but the meat of fish or turtle for eight week and more.'

'How you have suffered,' sympathized Roberts.

'Uncommonly so,' said Porter, shaking his head.

'This black duster,' said Tuckerman, 'is he the only one of his kind?'

'We have thirty more blackamoors,' said Roberts.

'Your other niggers,' said Porter, 'can we make truck, a fair exchange between deckhand and nigger?'

'It is,' mused Roberts, 'a heady equation.'

'One civilized for three savages,' said the hairy Porter.

'I would not hear of it,' said Roberts. 'Let us say – one of my civilized for a mere *two* of your savages. I insist.' The circle broke into laughter, especially Innocent, who enjoyed the response, as if his captain were the finest of the court's wits. But his smile lost its curl when Roberts added, 'I will trade you two blackamoors for one of your sailors.'

The other two pirate captains exchanged glances.

'We are friends,' expounded Roberts. 'I offer each of you nine, for four of you. A kinder offer I cannot make.'

Tuckerman nodded at Porter, who considered him for a moment, before clapping his palms together in agreement.

'Our quartermaster, Little David Sympson, shall see to your needs,' concluded Roberts.

The Lords looked at their captain to see if he was in jest, but Roberts rose to his feet and removed himself from their house of sugar, lit his pipe from the embers of their feast and moved off down the beach.

'Captain,' said Innocent, running to catch Roberts, 'do you mean to sell Yoruba? Do you not forget one promise by making another?'

'I made one promise. It does not compromise another.' Roberts did not look into Innocent's eyes, but stared dead ahead as he spoke. 'A ship is sailed by seamen, not labourers. I did not number your black crew, but I keep my word, Innocent, and gift twelve to you. I have thought hard on the numbers, sir, and I figured that, as Christ's ally, you would not need more than the same twelve disciples.'

Innocent made to object, but closed his mouth without utterance, and nodded twice at the captain's wisdom. He turned back towards the Yoruba, leaving Roberts stepping across the caked beach, breaking the crust of the sand with each of his steps.

CHAPTER 31

Sympson saw to his captain's wishes with a slothful regret. To give away powder, shot and fresh meat, three of the more essential ingredients of a successful venture, was an enigmatic gesture that held the scent of pomp and pride. Though the quartermaster would not doubt his captain aloud, it was obvious from his behaviour that Roberts performed as if his position was secure, treating the Lords like knights gathered to serve their king. And yet their luck had held through storm and calm, and Roberts was, despite Sympson's reservations, a more amusing and light-hearted cove than when he had first served under Davis.

The quartermaster ordered two barrels of powder to be unearthed from the depths of their temporary storeroom of a dozen sweeps supporting a curtain of canvas. He then pointed to a pair of crates of rusted shot, and lightened it considerably. Finally, Sympson selected a brace of their mangiest sheep, loading the gifts into the *Fortune*'s pinnace.

There was much excitement the following morning. Tuckerman and Porter, heeding Innocent's words of welcome and unwelcome guests, saw fit to cut short their stay and departed. Most of the encampment were in a state of quietude, having competed with the crew of the sloops in the intake of rum, when they were disturbed by a loud grunting noise by the rear of their makeshift structure. At first, the sounds were presumed to be coming from Hardy, known for the frequency with which he boxed his Jesuit, but then the barrels began to quake, as if the chief mate was now beating his head against the casks. It was not Hardy, but a pair of large, black bristled wild pigs, which had trotted harmlessly through men sleeping on the beach. However, they had become unhinged by the scent of sugar and their passions awakened even the darkest of hangovers. Though Innocent had tried to stand between man and beast, crying about Circe and the need to count their numbers, the pigs were attacked by an angry horde of deckhands. In the fray Innocent attempted to save them but was gashed in the leg by a tusk and could not prevent the swine from being rapidly reduced to breakfast.

Scudamore had only just come from bandaging Innocent's calf before the scrutinizing eyes of the blue-cheeked Yoruban when Williams burst in to interrupt the doctor and the captain as they sat before fruit-laden plates.

'Captain,' said Williams, breathing heavily, 'you may wish to rise to support Innocent. Some crew gathered about the Yorubans and inquired of

Innocent why these men had not been traded for whites. One asked which isle they would deliver the rest of the blackamoors to, and Innocent said that they would remain with the *Fortune*.'

'And what did he reply?'

'He called Innocent a vagabond soothead, and told him that he would rather bunk with Satan's children than unwashed blackamoors. Then Innocent knocked him to the sand. When he stood, he knocked him down again.'

'I suppose that I'd better make my way,' said Roberts, smiling, and took the doctor's proffered hand, and stood.

'Twould be prudent,' said Williams.

'Prudent, William, do you see how prudent I have become?'

The vanquished, a man called Blake taken from the *Greybound*, was still sitting in the sand with his hand cupping his bloodied nose. Innocent, despite his recently bandaged leg, was standing five yards away, staring down a group of twenty or so of the crew. Roberts looked at the cloud of blood seeping through the white bandage, stressing the darkness of Innocent's skin.

'Captain,' said Innocent, 'tell them.'

'Would you be so kind,' said Roberts, 'to leave? Find an unoccupied spot, and rest your leg.' Innocent turned to the Yoruba doctor, speaking softly. All the Yorubans got to their feet and followed Innocent away from the house of sugar, down the coastline. Innocent suppressed a limp.

The captain sat down in the sand, not two yards from Blake. When Innocent was out of earshot, Roberts encouraged all around to take a seat and, while four of the thirty backed away, now that a fight was unlikely, the rest dropped to the sand.

'Mr Blake . . . men of *Fortune* and *King* . . . is that you arear, William Magnes?'

'It is,' said Magnes, pinching sand between thumb and forefinger.

'We don't want niggers,' said Blake through his hands.

''Tis a decision of small time,' said Roberts soothingly, 'that shall profit all.'

'I'll not crew with niggers,' emphasized Blake.

'How come the profit?' asked Magnes, above the others.

'Mr Magnes, you have always spoken highly of Innocent. Why do you haver now?'

'Innocent is different from those, that much I know. He's never been slave to whites, and has a harder heart than any man among us.'

'And you are familiar with the Yoruban tongue, and know how each of these twelve are?'

''Tis in the man's eyes,' said Magnes. It sounded weak under such a strong sun morning.

'These men are to be the first barricade after the bulwark is breached. Sacrificed to cannon if you will.'

'But him as goes first aboard takes finest clothes,' said Bunch.

'No blackamoor'll have portion of the *Juliette*,' declared Blake.

'Yes he will,' said Roberts. 'They will have quarter share, same as cabin boys, and if they live to see gold, then they are full of daring or luck, the like of which you'd wish to see.'

'If,' said Magnes, 'you only wish to grant them quarter share, then you cannot say that any one among them is a man.'

'No, Mr Magnes, I believe that you are wrong sir, and will admit so,' said Roberts, increasing the volume of his tone. The lilt of Welsh was replaced by the clipped vowels of a rising anger. 'I believe I would ne'er grant a full share to a man who could not sail. These soots are lubbers, and remain so until they learns ropes – unworthy to share. Seeing as the blackamoors shall not remain among us till they're able, they shall not rise above half shares.'

Magnes nodded, and did not press his captain. Instead Blake resorted to a more basic effort to undermine Roberts. 'They smell worse'n swamp heads.'

'If odour were disqualification for crew, Blake, we think you'd ne'er been taken from the *Greyhound*. Besides,' added Roberts, 'upon reaching Africa, they will buy their freedom of the crew at a heady rate, and return to whence they came.'

'When do we sail?' asked Magnes, thoughts turning to the becalming.

'We shall dry trade up in these lanes,' said Roberts. 'You heard the noise of captains last night. We are noted among all islands, and they shall rid themselves of us. They will appeal to the Jamaicans, and bandy together. We shall leave them for a while, and let them drink themselves safe. We head east to meet the *Juliette*.'

'Africa,' said Blake, quietly. 'Nigger women,' he breathed, and then looked along the ranks of deckhands, to see what they thought of the proposition.

One hundred and thirty-four votes were cast. The ballot was not decided by the placing of shells or pebbles by a man's feet as was their custom, but by an open division. Hardy sat in the sand, and those that wished to sail to Africa stood on his right, and those content in the Caribbean went to his left. Every Lord and seasoned deckhand sided with Roberts and his decision to head for Africa. A group of four, including Glasby, abstained. Thirty elected to remain, but when they saw the manner in which the vote swung, they also moved to Hardy's right, so that the only evidence of opposition was the impression of feet in the sand.

The men continued to careen their two ships, scraping away the weeds and worms that had impregnated the hulls, and soothing their timbers with holystones. All wished that the *Fortune* and *Sea King* might sail firm and weatherly, in the weeks across the Atlantic and run before both storms and calms.

CHAPTER 32

Seeking Harry Glasby for a palaver on astral movement, Valentine Ashplant was distraught to discover that the sailing master had vanished from their encampment. First, he cursed the sailing master's name, and then devoted ten minutes to extolling his virtues, blessing the man for all that he had taught him aboard the *Sea King*.

'A precious fellow,' crowed Ashplant. 'Godly cove as could not play party to wickedness.'

'That,' said Magnes, pointing to the trees that grew as close as nettles behind the first ring of palms, 'could tear man in two. He'll not go far.' It was impossible to tell where the branches of one tree ended and another's began.

'I am,' snorted Roberts, 'of the same opinion as Mr Magnes. There seems little point in pursuit. Daresay there are few stars in the scrub to navigate by. It seems uncommon close.'

'But he's run with two recruits,' countered Sympson. 'The man has eaten at minds like toredo, gnawed at the sense of the thing. If the woods be so dark that no man may see, then my

306

peepers'll ne'er had such comfort.'

'And do you trust to find yourself, should you wander many miles?' asked Roberts.

'If I cannot find them, I will head for the coast, Captain, and follow her round. Why a child might find his way back.'

'Might I accompany Lord Sympson?' asked Scudamore, with a naive nonchalance as if he had requested a cup of tea.

'And I?' asked Williams eagerly.

'No,' said Roberts.

'I would find an extra hand plenty help,' said Sympson.

'The doctor is needed close by crew. I'll not risk him that,' answered the captain.

'And William?' asked Sympson, smiling. 'You've another Welshman in Skyrme now. So let me tread with William.'

Roberts considered the proposition for a moment. 'Very well. You shall set an example for the doubters. In three days, if you find no trace of them, you return.'

''Pon my word, Captain.'

'And little good that has ever been,' said Scudamore, peeved that his examinations of flora and fauna had been so easily rejected.

A hundred yards from the beach the forest closed about them. The sounds of men working and singing were extinguished by the damp leaves and boughs knitted over their heads. It was dismally sweaty, and the ground beneath them varied between damp and swampish, so that Sympson's and Williams's knee boots would sink to their very tops in a sucking mess of water and mud. The quartermaster led their way, hacking at thin ropes of foliage with his well-honed blade. After a half-day of walking they paused in the hollow trunk of a dead tree and shared water and dried strips of mutton. They ate in silence, then pressed inland, hoping to find a stretch dry enough to have held a footprint, but the dampness prevailed. The two slept draped across the arms of a tree. When he woke in the morning, Williams found that an army of ants had used his torso as a span to carry their leaves up and down the trunk. He jumped to the ground, where he howled and danced until an irritated Sympson descended and, stripping him of his shirt, swept the ants from his body.

'Glad as I am of your company,' said Sympson, 'I can't figure what gain your presence brings.'

'I only came to join the doctor,' moaned Williams. 'He knows a capital amount of all the vegetation. Learned it from Innocent. We would have noted all that we found.'

'You three,' spoke Sympson, 'regular Dick Snary triplets, each with a fuller brainpan than the one behind.'

'Well . . . said Williams, humbly.

'And yet brought to your marrow bones by creatures not half the length of a thumb nail.'

He walked ahead. The fiddler followed, wishing,

many times over, that he had stayed among the comparatively erudite to work feverishly in his journal. Instead he kept the surly company of Sympson and the possibility of conflict with a man whom he had nothing against.

The gradient began to steepen and the ground became harder. They could not look above to judge their whereabouts from the stars, for it was rare to get a glimpse more than a patch of the night sky. On their second day, when they had traversed a series of small inclines, Sympson asked Williams if he had a notion of where they were.

'I expect we've climbed a share.'

'And,' asked Sympson, 'which way do you suppose the *Fortune* to be?'

'That I do not know,' said Williams with a smile. 'I am but the nimble fiddler, in service to His Lordship.'

Sympson nodded and flashed his awful grin of tombstones at Williams.

'I suspect then,' said the quartermaster, 'that we'll be vittle for the beetles.'

'We are not lost,' said Williams. 'You told the captain that a shaver could navigate his way.'

'That was before the ups and downs befuddled me,' said the quartermaster.

'Oh,' said Williams softly, and suddenly became very serious.

'We shall walk tonight, and trust upon our luck.'

It was not hard to tell exactly when twilight died,

because a suffocating darkness fell about them, suffused with watery air. The thunder began in the distance, but brought no illuminating blasts of lightning. Soon the rain began to fall. They could hear the wind blow hard above, but it could not penetrate the canopy of leaves and branches that protected them like a house of stone. Though they could not feel the bite of heavy rain, it seemed to be funnelled from leaf to branch to trunk, so that great gushes of water came pouring down some trees, even after the storm had long departed. Sympson stopped under one of the thicker canopies and pulled his pack from his back before lowering his head to the trunk of the tree and letting the water pour directly into his mouth. Williams followed suit.

Sympson removed his tinder box from his pack, brought the lantern about, and began to strike flint against steel, waiting patiently for the spark. He was an old hand at the sport and could normally find a light in under ten minutes, but half an hour later he thrust the instrument in Williams's face, disgusted with himself. Williams had similar luck. They sadly packed the tinder box back into the pack, and attached the lantern by a lanyard.

'How do we find our way if we walk in darkness?' asked Williams.

'We are just as blind by day,' answered Sympson. Rising to his feet, he began to move along the soggy ground, heading downhill whenever the gradient allowed.

It seemed to Williams as if the sun had not shone for a sennight, though it was still an hour before dawn, when Sympson, cutting his way through a dense patch of fern and nettle, emerged into a strange clearing, where five palms stood in a circle, creating a thick, leafy shelter. The rain echoed from the bellies of the enormous fronds. From the edge of the glade, the five trees seemed like a royal pavilion to the exhausted travelers.

'What is that?' whispered Sympson, and dropped to his knee. He had already worked his knife into his hand.

'Where?' asked Williams, wiping water from his brow, and straining his eyes.

'Between the trees. A light.'

Williams looked hard ahead. There, in between the palms, was the strange flickering light of a fire. It seemed implausible in such weather. And yet it could not have been fire, for they were downwind of what small breeze there was beneath the leaves, and there was no smell of burning, nor did the light have the playful dance of wood aflame.

'Tis not right,' said Sympson.

'I will look upon it,' whispered Williams.

Sympson held his arm, but then released it, pressing his own knife into the fiddler's hand. Williams crept forward through the muddy ground, ignorant of the small snakes that writhed amid the wetness, until, with his heart blasting above the thunder, the fiddler was presented with the most beautiful sight that he had ever laid eyes upon.

There, dancing between the five palms, were a thousand fireflies – ten thousand – a dense cloud of light protected from the rain. They flew in strange amorous formations, attracting and repelling one another, joining in haloes then scattering like the stars above. Their glow revealed Sympson's shadow close by Williams.

'God's good grace,' murmured Sympson, and stood entranced by the fiddler's side. They watched the insects at play for ten long minutes without moving or even swaying in their stance.

'Tis like fairies,' said Williams, and Sympson nodded.

'Gather them, man,' said the quartermaster.

Williams pressed his hands together into a hollow cup, and swept them into the air before him. He peered inside his hands, and saw three blinking lights turn his skin to a dull orange.

'Not in your hands, man,' laughed the quartermaster, 'in the lantern.'

The two men stripped their shirts from their backs and, walking with their eyes closed under the pagoda of palms, held the damp cloth before them, so that the fireflies would be gathered against the cotton. They returned to where their lantern lay and, opening its gate, they swept the fireflies into the glass container with gentle motions of their hands. Hundreds escaped and burned and buzzed about them, so that they made one more round, until the lantern was choked with the intermittent flashing of the flies.

Their light burned brighter than twenty candles. Sympson and Williams reluctantly departed from the five palms, looking over their shoulders at the undiminished splendour of the sparkling circus.

Even with their own light the path was still not clear. The ground was plagued by fallen and rotting trees, and seemed to force them first upwards and then downwards so that it was impossible to tell if they made progress or were moving further from their friends.

Daylight made a poor attempt to break through the dull, dripping green of the morning, and they depended on their lantern of flickering fireflies to guide them through the murky shadows. The land was wetter than before, sucking at their boots and making every footstep a matter of effort. They came to a small river, no more than a stream ennobled by the rains of the previous evening, and stopped on her banks.

The fiddler plunged into the river with both feet at once and seemed to sink forever, until his boots made contact with a rocky bed, leaving him covered up to his nipples in the fast-flowing water.

'Well done, lad,' said Sympson, and followed him into the water.

'How about caiman?' asked Williams.

'What?' asked Sympson, holding his pair of pistols and powder horn above his head.

'Caiman,' said Williams, over the sound of the rushing water. 'The doctor described them.

Lizards, large as a man, swim like fish with hide tougher and teeth sharper than steel.'

Sympson moved past Williams on his right, intent on speed rather than caution.

'And snakes,' continued Williams, frightening himself into a similar pace, 'snakes as long as anchor cables that swallow men whole.'

But the quartermaster had already scurried on to the banks of the far side of the river, and now peered into the light cast by the fireflies above Williams's head, aiming his pistols back and forth should any of the monsters appear. The fiddler pulled himself from the river, and collapsed in exhaustion into the deep mud of the banks.

'The sea,' said Sympson, 'is a simpler place.'

Williams looked up, and laughed. They were coated from head to toe in the mud of the river banks. Under the strange light cast by the insects, they looked like two red pieces of sun-baked pottery discarded beside the kiln.

They continued to walk, finding no reason to pause, even eating as they pulled themselves through mud. Neither had any notion of time that had past. They might have been wandering for hours, or minutes, and were each lost within the lists of their private regrets, when a human sound rose far above the constant chatter of the insects.

'We have returned,' said Sympson, grinning at the fiddler. 'I told you as much.'

Williams nodded wearily from relief, and called ahead, 'Who goes there?'

'T-T-Tis I,' came the voice, 'Harry Glasby, with Crossworth and Proudlove.'

Sympson pulled his pistols from his pack.

'We'll kill them here,' he said.

Williams shook his head. 'M'Lord,' he whispered, 'five heads might find *Fortune* sooner than our two lost souls. 'Sides, a master mariner might have better chance with this navigation than us fools.'

Sympson and Williams approached under the light of their strange lantern.

'We've but a musket between us,' cried Crossworth as the fiddler and quartermaster neared. Sympson lowered his pistols.

The two men stopped a yard from the trio, the forest so dense that even at such a close range they were still separated by the thin rake of ferns. It was hard to say which party was the dirtier. Each man was so stained with mud that he seemed like a melted figurine, but even the mud could not disguise the mutual misery of their condition.

'You've qu-qu-quite a nose about you, sirs. We've had a hard time of it, couldn't figure ear from arse, till I had to shimmy a palm like a monkey.' Glasby showed his torn hands to his old shipmates. 'I stared at the stars for mo-mo-moments between cloud and thunderclap, and yet the two of you have sniffed us out like hounds for badgers.'

'Was Sympson,' said Williams, noticing tears well in the sailing master's eyes. 'He has an uncommon sense of direction, land or sea.'

'W-W-We saw your light,' said Glasby, 'and praised God that we were not to perish in this hell.'

Crossworth leaned towards the lantern. 'We were,' he said, 'tracked by many of the Lord's creatures.'

'Can you gift us food?' asked Proudlove. 'We thought that God would feed us, but tis hard to know what should be eaten, and what should be put aside.' He cast his hands above him in an arc, 'It seems a place of devils.'

Williams looked at Sympson, who nodded. The fiddler delved into their pack, pulling two strips of mutton, and offered them to the men.

'I . . . I . . . assure you,' said Glasby, through a mouthful of sheep, 'that we were aimed for harbour, and rue with great regret our decision.'

'You remember the consequence?' asked Sympson, puzzled.

'Aye,' said Glasby, 'but we hope that you take our return and utmost re-re-regrets into consideration.'

Their fate was not further discussed. Their mutual predicament was the only shared concern. All wished to see the ocean once more. No matter what sentence was passed upon the escapees, it might be deemed kind compared to the gnawing fear of the forest.

'Wh-wh-where do you figure us?' asked Glasby.

'Oh,' began Sympson, 'not far now, I believe.'

'A mile or so, north,' said Glasby. 'I think but a few hours of hardship before the sea.'

'We think as one,' lied Sympson and, gathering the small company to their feet, insisted that Glasby should lead the way.

They were even closer than they imagined and, emerging from the band of palm trees that separated forest from beach, felt slightly foolish to have been wandering in circles so close inland. It was a short walk along the amber-strewn sand until the stranded shapes of the *Fortune* and the *Sea King* appeared on the horizon, more welcome than any smoking chimney or familiar cry. Now the trio's fear of being eaten by forest denizens was replaced by the anxiety of their return. The company paused to wash the caked mud from their bodies in the warm salt water of the Gulf, and Glasby, Proudlove and Crossworth petitioned the fiddler and quartermaster for their kindness, as if their testimony would prove invaluable to their continued existence.

CHAPTER 33

When, finally, they entered the encampment, four days after they had set out, both Williams and Sympson were greeted as heroes, returning laden with booty. The carpenter made a small hut from the barrels of salt beef, and the three escapees were thrown roughly into the pen.

Scudamore harassed Williams until he had revealed the size and shape of every plant and animal encountered. The doctor took great delight in the flickering of the fireflies that continued to produce their awesome glow for a second night. Williams retrieved his manuscript from his seachest and, finding a quiet corner of the beach, away from the surgeon's relentless pestering, he began to make an entry in his journal. He wrote of the forest late into the night, interrupted every now and then by watchkeepers, who stopped by looking for a flame for their pipes and stayed to marvel at the contents of the lantern.

There is much relief to see the ocean again. I never reckoned that she would have such a hold on me and, were I not ordained for London society and authorship, I think I should spend my life this way. There was perhaps a more constant fear among the darkness of the forest than I have ever felt at sea. The search for Glasby mattered not, though we could not part with only one sailing master. But the fear also held wonder, though I do not know the room for awe had I travelled alone. Moreover; I am surprised at the patience of Roberts for the Juliette. *The crew begins to talk in earnest of her riches once more. Indeed, she is the basic conversation that binds us, replacing even the weather and women in the volume of our talk.*

With his knees cocked in front of him, and his back pressed against the trunk of a great palm, Williams fell into sleep while holding his journal propped before him like an easel.

Come the morning, Williams was woken by his captain, who had sought him out to extend his congratulations of their unlikely search. Williams nodded with pleasure at the lauding, but the position in which he had slept had left him sore, and he could not concentrate on Roberts's kind words. He excused himself, begging nature, and waded waist deep into the sea. His body wracked with aches and shivered despite the warmth of the water.

The fireflies began to die the following day. As their tails ceased to flicker, Williams opened the gate of the lantern and let those who still lived fly free of the bodies of their compatriots. Glasby and his two confederates remained in their cage of salt beef. Williams brought them water three times during the first day. From a crack in the wooden walls he could see that, despite the heat that had baked the prisoners for close on two days, they seemed fit enough. They had breached the side of one of the casks and feasted on a heavy ration of salt beef.

'What news, William?' whispered Crossworth from within. 'I cannot stand this another day.'

'Will dig our way out,' moaned Proudlove.

'The Lords have elected to serve you fair trial,' said Williams. 'You shall stay within for no more than a day more.'

'God bless, William,' said Glasby. 'And sp-sp-speak kindly on our account.'

'I shall,' swore Williams, 'if I am called upon.'

The fiddler did not receive the opportunity. By nightfall his limbs were so swollen that he felt comfortable neither standing nor sitting and lay stretched upon the sand, as if he had been struck down mid-stride by God above. The doctor was called and Williams was carried within the walls of the sugar casks, where he was propped upright upon a bed of cotton, three sheets deep, upon Scudamore's insistence.

'And how do you feel?' asked the doctor kindly.

'Does it not seem,' whispered Williams, 'that sickness seems to be selective in her intentions?'

'Swamps, sir,' said Scudamore, 'are never the

kindest of places. I thought perchance if I filled your mind with caiman that fevers might let you be.'

'So tis a fever,' said Roberts from behind the doctor.

'Not a fever, sir, but a weak ague of some nature or another,' said the doctor. 'Rest a while Williams. You are not threatened.'

Though Roberts did not spend the night at Williams's side, he discovered the fiddler's sea-chest and ensured that his manuscript was safe inside. At first light the following morning, he returned to check on Williams's progress, and found him much disfigured over the course of the night, his limbs swollen as if he had been pumped with water. His ankles were as fat as cannonballs, and he wheezed as if he had to strain the air for goodness. The surgeon was administering an application of sulphur and, looking up, wished a good morning to his captain.

'A word, sir,' said Roberts.

'Within the moment,' replied Scudamore.

They walked together down the beach, at a distance from any man, so that none might hear their conversation.

'I have heard the word dropsy before, doctor, but what of it?'

'It is,' said Scudamore, 'an oedema, the swelling in the joint of serous fluids.'

'And what harm may it do a man?'

'Great harm, Captain. Great harm. Take the

beating from a man's heart, the very breath from his mouth.'

'Can it be cured?'

'Well, sir, I am feeding him a tincture of sulphur of my own device, and also an aromatic bark of the sassafras root. I hold him from water, no matter how he cries for it. Dry the man out sir, before the waters rise high enough to drown him.'

'Have you bled him?' asked Roberts.

'No sir,' cried Scudamore, positively alarmed, 'the last thing I would do.'

'Is there nothing else?'

Scudamore paused in the sand. 'Innocent came by, during the deepest of the night, with the blue-scarred Yoruban, the one they call Owaba. He looked long at Williams, and told me, through Innocent, that he sees much of this in his home country.'

'What cures from Africa?' asked Roberts, and with this admission of interest they resumed their walk.

'He recommends that he should be buried unto the neck in sand, and left there for one exact turn of the glass.'

Roberts laughed, but saw that the doctor did not share his smile. 'He's a Welshman, not a turtle's egg. The Yoruban jokes us.'

'No sir, far from it. Perhaps a sensible measure,' reprimanded the doctor. 'I suppose it is the Yoruban equivalent of keeping a man under blanket and fire and feeding him boiling tea for days. Sweat it out, Captain. And all in a half-hour. Remarkable,' said Scudamore, 'if it works.'

'Then we shall bury him.'

'And, if he does not survive,' said the doctor, 'then we need not dig again.'

Roberts nodded once.

'A jest sir. Medical humour.'

The captain smiled at the doctor, and they walked together back to where Williams lay.

Bartholomew Roberts sat on the centre barrel amid the constellation of Lords, flanked by the majority of the Commons, save for those posted as lookouts, who slept quietly further down the beach. Several of the Lords, most notably Hardy, had begun their drinking early in the morning, and were seated with dried seaweed covering their heads, both as protection from the sun and to mock the justice that they were about to dispense.

'Who will speak on your defence?' asked the captain, addressing the three deserters who sat cross-legged in the sand, each with a pot of beer before him to calm their throats after the dryness of their prison.

'Wh-wh-why, I will, Captain Roberts,' spoke Glasby.

'I do not think so, sir,' said Roberts, 'or we shall be at this all day. I hereby appoint Crossworth to speak in your defence. Glasby, you may interject. Mr Magnes, who is no member of the House of Lords, and yet esteemed within the Commons, shall prosecute the case. Be careful with your words, gentlemen, e'ry man has but one vote, and Magnes has a gifted tongue of gold. We promise you a fairer trial than any court in England. There shall be no strutting cursitors, no twisting of the laws, no canting terms of complexity, no bribing of witnesses nor straw booters. Mr Magnes, let us try those who endangered the common pursuit of the *Juliette*.'

William Magnes, wobbly on his feet from three glasses of undiluted rum, was not at his most fluent, but still encouraged empathy from the vast jury, most of whom shared his state of early intoxication. He teetered for a moment, then began, 'The seventh article according to the captain's commandment, and may I quote? "Desertion, during an engagement, or otherwise, is death." May I repeat? Death, gentlemen. A simple article, one we may all understand. This case shall be brief.'

'Mr Crossworth,' asked Roberts, sucking on the stem of his pipe, 'do you have anything to say on behalf of your three?'

Neither Innocent nor any of the Yoruba were in attendance for the trial of the three deserters. Under the eyes of Scudamore they had dug a skinny trench, close to six feet in depth, at the high point of the dune. The sand was dry at first but, as they dug, it became damper, holding its intended shape, a coffin for a standing man.

Williams, whose hair matched in colour the wet sand exposed by the shovels, was lowered slowly into the hole by Innocent, Owaba, and several other of the Yoruba.

The blue-cheeked elder laid down flat beside the erect body of the fiddler and began to pack the sand against his body, pressing downwards at first, making sure that the sand hugged his body, from his legs to his chest. Soon he was clumping the sand against Williams's throat, applying pressure and creating a small cushion of sand on which the patient might rest his chin. Scudamore looked down upon the head, poking from the sand as if it had been severed from the body by a great stroke, and then scratched at his own chin. His shadow lay across the fiddler's head. Owaba placed his hand in the surgeon's and gently pulled him to the side, talking fast in his own tongue, and then laughing hard with his fellow men.

'He says what?' the doctor asked Innocent.

'He says that the fiddler is like an egg to be boiled. We must make sure his insides harden.'

'Very amusing,' said Scudamore.

Williams muttered something.

'Sorry William?' said Scudamore, lowering himself to his haunches.

'I have an itch,' breathed Williams, and managed a slow wink.

'M'Lords,' said Crossworth, with an ingratiating smile, as if the mock trial could never result in anything other than a mock verdict, 'we went in search of meat, and returned, having failed in our quest.'

'You did not return,' said Magnes, 'you were apprehended, were you not?'

'Ma-ma-may I?' asked Glasby.

Roberts shrugged, and Hardy waved him on.

'Fir-fir-first and foremost,' began Glasby, haltingly, 'I ne'er signed my name to any articles. I was hard pressed.'

''Tis true,' said Roberts.

'What may play as rules for those who committed in ink cannot stand as rules for those who chose not to sign.'

'Mr Glasby,' asked Magnes, 'does this mean that by attempting to desert you did not consider yourself in violation?'

'Zactly,' said Glasby, and pointed at Magnes with his forefinger, grinning with having nailed the word first time with his tripping tongue.

'It is indeed a method by which you might preserve your own skin, but you merely condemn your fellow men. Does he not?' Magnes petitioned the jurors. 'You may ne'er have inked your name, but these two were in agreement surely as the rest of us.'

A low mumble of agreement returned.

'Mr Crossworth,' said Magnes, 'what say you to that?'

'Was his idea,' said Crossworth, pointing at the sailing master. 'Would deckhands, noddies as ourselves, have trusted our skins to forest if we did not trust in a master's direction? It was him that put us up. String the leader of the mob, not the innocents within.'

'And yet,' said Roberts, 'tis generals who are ransomed and soldiers abandoned.'

'I propose to the jury,' said Magnes, 'that each is as guilty as the other, and should be hung by the neck, till they is dead, dead, dead.'

The sea of jurors concurred, and the men began to shift as if the trial had reached its conclusion.

'I have known Glasby closer than any Lord,' cried Ashplant, rising to his feet and laying both his pistols on the barrelled seat he had just risen from, 'and he is near God and clean in spirit. Would think it a curse to our cause should he be hung to gibbet on some godforsaken stretch of sand. You wish to hang him, then you must hang me.'

'So many gentlemen at court today,' said Roberts, 'and all of such noble intention. We will consider each man's case against the other, and vote for life or death on three separate occasion.'

The sun beat down upon the sand. Though Owaba walked slowly between patient and ocean, and ladled salt water over Williams's forehead to give him an illusion of cold comfort, the sand began to get hot under foot. The Africans did not seem to notice, but the surgeon removed his frock coat and sat on it to put some distance between himself and the boiling grains. He could only imagine the temperature of Williams's body, and pressed his hand against the Welshman's brow every few minutes, out of professional interest of the body's endurance.

Owaba made several clicks with his tongue. Innocent and the Yorubans sprang to their feet, and began to dig frantically at the sand around Williams's head. Slowly the fiddler was disinterred. It was impossible to tell if his swollen limbs had subsided. His whole body was moistened with sweat through every pore, a film of sand coating it from toe to chin. He resembled a large crustacean.

Scudamore hurriedly escorted him, with the help of Innocent and Owaba, to the shade of a giant palm, where they covered Williams in woollen blankets. It was the most prominent point of their harbour, from where the surgeon could observe the remainder of the trial. Williams had ceased to wheeze – seemed to breathe easier already – but the surgeon did not know if it was a cure or a temporary reprieve.

'What does he say?' the surgeon asked Innocent as Owaba chatted away.

'We are to leave him, let him sleep for afternoon and night. Keep him warm and unwatered. Tomorrow he shall be fit again. Weakened, but in health.'

''Tis time you taught him the King's tongue, Innocent, so that we may all speak as one. We have much to tell one another.'

Innocent repeated Scudamore's words to the Yorubans. Owaba spat out a brief sentence, and the black skins erupted into laughter. The doctor opened his arms, in plea for a translation.

'He says that if your tongue was stolen from a king then he would rather use his own.'

'Marvellous,' said Scudamore, 'a fine effort at jest, and yet profoundly unamusing.'

Trusting Williams to the group of Yorubans, the doctor retreated back towards the encampment and his old shipmates.

'How now?' asked Roberts at the surgeon's approach.

'And with you?' replied Scudamore, taking a seat on a vacated barrel by the captain's side. Lords and Commons had dispersed to vote, and only the captain and the three defendants remained seated.

'How did our man fare?' asked Roberts.

'He is afire,' said Scudamore, 'covered in ten thousand grains of sand and wrapped in blankets, surrounded by cackling fools and yet, sir, I suspect them of intelligence.'

'Let us hope so.'

'We must feed him well. If we were on a Kent farm, I would say hogs' feet, cows' heel and a jelly broth. And eggs, sir, plenty of eggs enrich the blood.'

'And if we were on the coast of Hispaniola?'

'I daresay salt beef and turtles' eggs will do.'

Scudamore smoothed his thin grey hair over a burned patch of his scalp. 'And these three? What of them?'

'They are voted on, each as to his own. I suspect the crew will have themselves a hanging.'

''Tis a plain case,' said the surgeon, shaking his head, 'and a sorry one. Only an execution seems so . . . parliamentary. Is it not what we spurn?'

'Spurn, sir?' asked Roberts, genuinely surprised. 'A fair trial is a rare thing.'

'With no priest to administer rites?'

''Tis a regret,' admitted the captain. 'A good ship has need of a priest.'

'Christopher Proudlove,' said Magnes, 'of Hednesford is found guilty of desertion. Horace Crossworth, of Newitton, guilty of desertion. You shall be taken from this place, and hanged by the neck, until you are dead, dead, dead.'

Proudlove, who had been kneeling, now lowered his head till his brow rested against the sand. He began to weep, hiding his tears so that none might see. Crossworth looked ahead, out past the ships, to the calm waters of the gulf.

'Harry Glasby,' continued Magnes, 'is pardoned of his crime. Why, I cannot say. I would have had you dead, sir.' Glasby did not raise his eyes, for there were no gentle looks of forgiveness cast in his direction, only weighted gazes that would have further burdened his heart.

'My, my,' said Scudamore aloud, but in the

330

silence his voice carried and, though he had not cast his ballot, many men who had voted were just as surprised to see Glasby pardoned of his crime.

The prisoners, their wrists bound tightly together behind their backs, were heaved on to sugar barrels under the sloped trunk of a palm and their legs held fast by their executioners. Their necks, seeming strangely thin and fragile to the onlookers, were passed through nooses.

'Do you have any last words?' asked Roberts, standing with his back to the ocean, facing both the men and the forest behind them.

'Look closely upon us,' said Crossworth, 'and observe the manner in which we pass, for you shall all follow us. Our souls have long been damned and marked for hell, and I shall keep beds warm for all.'

'Mr Proudlove?'

Proudlove shook his head and closed his eyes.

'Gentlemen,' said Roberts. Hardy pushed at Proudlove's barrel. It hesitated as the seaman sought to keep his balance for one last breath of life, but then keeled over on to its side, rolling a couple of yards in the sand. As Proudlove fell, so Crossworth's weight was momentarily lifted from his platform, and Magnes heaved it forward from under him. Their loads were counterbalanced, and the two deserters spun violently before each other, not a yard apart, legs clashing and eyes locked in communion.

The lone figure of Glasby sat between the

hanging palm and the encampment, and seemed to represent an isolation that had invaded every mind, as if they had set themselves on a course of disaster, that because of the rules they had chosen to abide by, could no longer be diverted. The captain approached Glasby, blocking the light of the sun. The sailing master looked up.

'Why?' he asked. 'Am I not dead?'

'I think . . .' said Roberts, '. . . you would be as happy to die in our company as you are pained to live in it. A man with such prominent morals must find the onus of two more deaths uncommonly weighty.'

Glasby returned his gaze to the sand.

'You are my error,' continued Roberts. 'I wish upon you a long life as my companion.'

'God,' murmured Glasby, 'has swifter plans.'

CHAPTER 34

The deserters were rocked gently by the breeze, twisting together and away, like partners caught in a country dance. By sundown, their flesh, or perhaps the flies that covered it, attracted a group of small blue birds with sharp yellow beaks. They paraded in pairs about either head, finding purchase on the ears, then clambering on to noses for the soft meat of the eyeballs. Though most of the crew had returned to the encampment, there were still those who sat contemplating the justice that they had doled out. Hardy returned before the last light died and, severing the cord above Proudlove's head, saw both bodies collapse to the sand in front of him. He cut free the nooses, and carefully coiled the rope. Neither of the deserters were buried, but were dragged by the feet behind the row of palms and committed to the forest.

Williams sat upright on his pile of blankets, unabashed in his nakedness, still high from the scent of his own survival. The blue-cheeked Yoruban was propped against the fiddler's sea-chest. Grinding his boots in the sand, the doctor stood before them.

'Have they fed you?' Scudamore asked his patient.

'They beat turtles' eggs for me, and a cup of its blood, but I am awful parched.'

Scudamore took off his shabby black frock coat, and spread it in the sand to Williams's right. After lowering himself to its folds, he proceeded to examine the fiddler's limbs. He paused as he held his patient's right hand, and squeezed at the muscle under Williams's thumb.

'I have no sense in it,' said Williams.

'Rest it between us,' said the surgeon.

Williams laid his hand with the palm exposed to Scudamore's view. There was the sound of feet scuffing sand, and Owaba neared them with a pair of glims. Under the candlelight, William's fingers seemed like the legs of an upturned beetle.

'Move the smallest finger,' ordered the surgeon.

William's brow creased in concentration, but no movement came to his hand.

'Hmmm,' growled Scudamore. He took a long needle from his case of instruments. Leaning in towards the light of the candle, he watched as the needlepoint penetrated the flesh of the palm. Still Williams did not move his hand.

'It is obvious that the hand has no life, but as to whether your condition is permanent or temporary, I cannot say. Most disappointing,' said Scudamore, shaking his head. He broke into a practised smile. 'But hardly troublesome. Asides from this inconvenience, you have made a remarkable recovery, and owe some thanks to the Yorubans.'

Williams's visage held no thanks.

He gained enough strength to return to his feet, and wandered around the encampment in a daze, seeming to lack the mental ability to deal with his handicap. While his shipmates caulked the hulls of the *Sea King* and *Fortune*, and smoked and swept their holds, Williams sat, fixated on his hand. Even after they had stripped the canvas roof and begun to pull down the wall of sugar, the fiddler could not bring himself to aid his fellows. His sea-chest seemed to mock him, filled with his fiddle, his layers of manuscript and pen and quills long accustomed to the angles of his right hand.

Innocent walked past him and, without a greeting, took hold of the fiddler's heavy sea-chest, groaned and raised it to his shoulders.

'Leave it be,' said Williams sharply.

Innocent returned to his haunches and deposited the chest back in the sand.

'Stand,' ordered Innocent, 'we can raise it together.'

Williams had returned his gaze to his hand.

'What does your doctor say?' asked Innocent.

The fiddler breathed out in one great breath, as if he were snuffing candles. 'He said that it is rare to see the dropsy rise so high in a man. It prefers the lower half of a body, ankles and his legs, and rarely creeps so high, but it rose to my heart.'

Innocent laughed. 'We both know.'

'Sorry?' said Williams.

'The heart is the sister of the mind,' said

Innocent, and knocked his temple with his finger. 'She is vital as the brain. We can live without hand, eye, leg, but pierce the brain, pierce the heart and man is undone. They are the sisters of life. If one ails, then the body must make sacrifice.'

'Ahh,' said Williams, 'I begin to see.'

'Christ made many sacrifices before He gained His kingdom back. He burned bulls, and sheep, and ate and raised the rest in smoke. You did not heed the gods, so the sacrifice was taken. You have been saved and scarred, and you have had your music torn from you for your pride.'

'What pride?' asked Williams. 'I am not a proud man.'

'"What a lamentable thing it is,"' quoted Innocent solemnly from his private scriptures, '"that men should blame the gods and regard us as the source of their troubles, when it is their own transgressions which bring them the suffering that was not their destiny." You take pride in your music, and the captain is unwise to take pride in his dress. You will fail.'

'I'll wager you a hundred pound,' said Williams, angered by the words against Roberts, 'that the captain shall guide you to your Guinea Coast again.'

'And I will wager you two hundred,' replied Innocent, 'that he will not return you to this sea again.'

'Tis done,' said Williams, and offered Innocent his left hand.

Innocent smiled, for he truly believed it was an account that Williams would be unable to settle. Together they raised the sea-chest and made their way towards the *Fortune*'s gig, walking in between the shadows of the *Sea King*'s masts, raised once again to the skies.

Glasby was taken aboard the *Fortune*, and Ashplant made a successful petition to be relieved of the command of the *Sea King*, and followed his charge aboard the flagship. The brig was now populated almost exclusively by tyros, and it was Roberts's obvious concern that he surround himself with his old hands. He did not heed what tempers brewed aboard their sister ship. The *Sea King* voted her own captain, one Thomas Antsis, a man who tried to dampen his arrogance in Roberts's presence but could not quench his eyes of sly ambition. In an unspoken wager between Roberts's sense and his presumption he laid money on how long the *Sea King* would sail alongside the *Fortune*. He reckoned she would take her leave during a long night, or the first sign of heavy weather.

Occupied only by a sense of general uselessness, Williams could find little to do aboard a ship that did not require the use of both hands. It was as if the land had stripped him of his ability to either serve or defend himself against the sea. It was not easy to tell whether Williams distanced himself from his shipmates, or whether they now judged him different from them, and did not seek out his company. Even the jocular Christopher Moody seemed to revel among new friends and spared little time for his old mate.

Like most injured seamen, Williams gravitated towards the galley where he helped Nanny Joe prepare the fires and food. Nanny, Pinch's replacement, had no sympathy for the fiddler's handicap, and took a swing at Williams with his wooden foot for being so slow upon two good legs.

'I looked truck and tail, but I couldn't find the sorghum,' confessed Williams to the cook.

Nanny looked up from a cask of molasses that he was prising open with a marlinespike, and said, 'I said sorgo. Sor-go. Tis a syrup, you noddy.'

Williams turned, without further word, or faint protest, and made to head below.

'On your way to hold,' said Nanny, 'your captain wishes words.'

Roberts sat before his table, a web of sea charts open before him. His unlit pipe protruded from the side of his mouth. He played it back and forth against his teeth with the tip of his tongue, and the sharp clatter of enamel upon the ivory stem rose above the creaking timbers of the *Fortune*.

'William,' he said, 'three days you avoid me once more.'

'You must have heard, has the surgeon not told . . .' Williams stayed close to the door as he addressed the captain. 'I cannot sweat a rope, I cannot take a trick upon the helm.'

'You were ne'er the best of sailors.'

'And how does a man play at the fiddle?' asked Williams, and raised his dead hand before him.

'Well,' said Roberts, and seemed lost for words.

Williams nodded, and stared at his own feet, and said in a peculiarly small voice, 'And sir, I cannot write. Twas why I did not come.'

'I know,' said Roberts, 'and have given it much thought. You shall take Bunch as your scribe, and teach him all he must learn.'

The young Welshman snorted. 'Impossible,' said Williams. 'T'would take a lifetime to teach that dullard a code and five tongues.'

'Then teach him one tongue, and do not tell a code,' shrugged Roberts, and Williams smiled as if the thought had occurred simultaneously to him.

'And you can have practice,' said Roberts.

'Practice?' asked Williams, an edge of worry to his voice.

'You shall begin by teaching the negroes the English tongue.'

'I will not.'

Roberts warmed to hear such command return to the fiddler's voice. Self-pity had been buffeted by his stubbornness.

The fiddler was at the centre of many good-humoured jests from the crew. He made great shows of his exasperation, often repeating in a theatrical bellow whatever crime the guilty Yorubans had committed against the King's English. It was an understandably hopeless attempt at communication that Williams refused to continue after the third day. Instead he sat with Innocent and devised a manner of teaching where each of the lines was named after an animal familiar to the Yorubans. The starboard fore topgallant inner buntline was reduced to the 'red ant', and her larboard companion was renamed the 'black ant'. In this way, Williams learned many words of Yoruban, and, alongside Innocent, was seen to stand in the liminal space that separated the worlds of the black and the white sailors.

After two days of call, response and continuous echo, the Yorubans could recite the names of the lines in two languages. Any man takes pride in the acquirement of knowledge, and Williams grudgingly confessed to himself that he also took some pleasure in its transferral. He saw faces that had been dredged under the chains of slavery now blossom to know that they were learning the mechanics of the ocean, the methods that might ensure their return.

At night, upon Roberts's insistence, Williams retired with Bunch to the captain's cabin, and began his education. It was apparent, before he had even presented the cabin boy with a book, that Bunch knew neither reading nor writing. It puzzled Williams how to approach his pupil. It was not a simple matter of pointing and repetition as it was with the Africans during the day, for they could see, touch, haul on the objects of explanation. Great realms of language separated Bunch from Williams and, if it had not been for the captain's orders, neither would have been willing to cross them.

The one-handed fiddler had not thought for a moment that Bunch would be harder to teach than a mob of Africans, but he was resistant to knowledge, positive that Williams could add nothing of importance to his life. He would sit, his skin as scarlet as a soldier crab's, and glare at Williams with his dark eyes, remembering every occasion at which their paths had crossed. Bunch had always thought of Williams as a mewling babe, protected by the shadow of the captain's name, and it was only after an entire week sitting at leisure in Roberts's cabin that it occurred to Bunch that he could now be viewed under a similar light.

Williams made the decision to teach Bunch Latin, determining that if he were to wallow through several languages the process might take years. Instead of informing Bunch that he was learning Latin, he told his pupil that it was his native tongue of English. Williams taught him straight from his own simple code, so that, in future, when Williams dictated, Bunch would respond automatically in a script that only the two of them might understand.

Though, at first, Bunch was angered at having to submit to Williams's superior knowledge, as soon as he gathered a basic vocabulary he began to take enjoyment in his lessons, almost pitying Williams. Within ten days, Bunch could form letters at five times the speed of Williams's hand, and even had a delicate flourish that both master and pupil took pride in.

There was only a single moment when Williams's ruse threatened to collapse about him. He had entered the captain's cabin to find Bunch sitting at the desk, a copy of *Dampier's Voyages* before him. From where the fiddler stood, it seemed as if Bunch's eyes scanned the page in patient comprehension. Williams was rooted, certain that Bunch had connived to learn English despite his efforts to impart only coded Latin.

'What is this?' asked Bunch, looking up from the page. 'What language?'

''Tis Spanish,' lied Williams.

'Cannot be Spain,' insisted Bunch. 'Why would Roberts be surrounded by the books of Spain?'

'Give it here,' said Williams, and Bunch rose and passed him the volume.

'You are learning quickly,' said Williams, his face unwavering in deceit, ''tis indeed not Spanish – tis Welsh, the captain's native tongue.'

''Tis a damn hard thing,' said Bunch, 'pot hooks and hangers to me.'

'We will learn it too, if you so wish,' returned Williams.

'I do not wish,' replied Bunch. 'A man does not need more than the one tongue in either head nor hand.'

'Well said,' praised Williams, and returned the volume to the burry, bringing the cabin boy back to their pages of coded Latin.

CHAPTER 35

They set course for Africa under moody April skies. From a vessel intercepted and released off the Turks, the Fortunes confirmed that their fame had spread back up to the Colonies along the Eastern Seaboard. It was even reported that Governor Spotswood of Virginia had ordered over fifty cannon placed at points along his coast to defend the colony from the man they called Black Bart Roberts. Proud of their captain's moniker, the crew relaxed as if they reclined in the house of heroes and were luminaries by association. At eight bells that day, Scudamore gave Roberts a small speech of amused congratulation from one of Shakespeare's sonnets, closing with a low bow, 'For I have sworn thee fair, and thought thee bright, Who art as black as hell, as dark as night.' Their notoriety was welcomed with a quick blush at fame, and a solemn nod to signal that such repute was deserved.

The humour of the day was lost before morning. A night of thick cloud brought fever to their captain and an opportunity for the *Sea King* to kiss the *Fortune* a soft goodnight. To Scudamore,

343

standing over his ailing captain, the illness seemed a premonition of betrayal. The loss of the *Sea King* meant little to the doctor, filled with men he did not know, carrying little of importance, but the news ate at Roberts. If Kennedy's actions were sudden and treasonous, then the departure of the *Sea King* was an insidious rupture that Roberts had expected.

Owaba and Scudamore combined their potions, and together brought the captain back to his feet within six days. Wrapped in blankets against the damp April chills of the Atlantic, he woke to find the surgeon poised above him, surrounded by the mist of his own breath.

'G'morning to you, Captain,' the doctor said. 'A capital recovery. For a while, I was convinced you were in need of a trepan.'

Roberts sat up.

'Eyes are filled with blood,' continued Scudamore, 'but they shall recede, sir. Like the tide. Being a nautical surgeon, like the tide. Ebb, neap, spring and lunar.'

Roberts grunted.

'Pardon?'

The grunt was louder.

'Peace?' asked Scudamore. 'Yes, peace. Uncommonly sensible of you, sir. Silence is best for now. Humour shall wait.'

'Bring me Sympson,' said the captain.

The quartermaster closed the door behind him

with great care, as if deliberateness might block the sound of voices from both escaping and penetrating.

'Are we set for Guinea?' muttered Roberts weakly.

'Aye.'

'Who takes the conning?'

'Glasby,' said Sympson, to which his captain groaned.

'Tis fair enough,' said Sympson, 'I told him of the great fort at Cape Corso, and at Annabon, Wimba and Apan and, without painting it in the very words, I made him see that we were closer to the Crown in Guinea than we were in the Carribee. He thinks he steers the executioner's cart, and is uncommon deliberate in his sums. Every hour, Captain. Every single hour.'

'Our course?' asked Roberts.

'We hold straight,' said Sympson, and to Roberts's questioning eyes, added, 'I beleive Glasby. He be spaniel tame for now, and will not bark till he sees the bores of British guns.'

'Thank you,' murmured Roberts and held his hand out to his friend.

'I believe we shall need another ship to face the *Juliette*,' said Sympson and Roberts nodded in agreement.

The poor state of the captain's health was a timely excuse for both Bunch and Williams to make a more or less permanent home in the great cabin. The doors were closely watched by all the

Lords, and many of the interested Commons. Sympson had informants walk frequently back and forth throughout day and night to see who might presume to enter Roberts's domain. Both cabin boy and fiddler were excluded from the equations of power. Seen as attendants of the status quo, they came and went as they pleased.

'*And then, with a great stroke,*' dictated Williams, '*the captain raised his sword.*'

'Was not solely the captain,' said Bunch. 'Was Hardy too. And was not a sword, but an axe.'

'Mr Bunch, how much literature has passed before your eyes in your lifetime?'

'Nary a word,' confessed the cabin boy.

'I have played audience to much of it,' said Williams, 'so I know how a man should sing.'

Bunch obediently, and unwittingly, translated the fiddler's words into his arcane coding of Latin. He sipped at his cannikin of rum, and looked down upon his scarlet hands. The tips of the fingers from his right hand were stained with Indian ink.

'What if the captain dies?' asked Bunch.

'From an ague? A mere ague?'

'Almost did you in,' sniped Bunch.

'I doubt he is so much as febrile,' replied an irritated Williams, 'more likely plotting the demise of the *Juliette*.'

With Bunch performing the duties of scribe, the manuscript was reduced to a description of actions and the swerve of Williams's words were corralled in his head. This was when the pain in his dead hand was greatest, when his vision was silenced. Black thoughts converted death to murder, his share to theft and he stacked them at the sides of his mind. The relief that his creation brought him was denied by the necessary presence of Bunch, and he felt himself adrift.

By the end of the week, Roberts emerged through the aft hatchway and walked to the steps of the quarterdeck, where he sat in silence under a pair of oiled hides, staring at the wind, described by rain against swirls of scud.

'Mm-mm-my,' said Glasby, alone at the helm. 'You're still as plain as a rotten grape.'

Roberts ran a hand over his swollen features. 'You must be wrenched to see I breathe.'

Glasby gave an honest nod.

'You'd have conned us straight to Corso, would you not?' asked the captain.

The sailing master nodded again. 'I will give my eyes to see you hang.'

'You flatter me,' spoke Roberts softly, 'but it will not be so. The sea will have me. Let us take reckoning.'

Many of the men had sailed these seas before and, as they southed along the coast of Africa, driven by the dying hamattan winds that left their sails stained red with Saharan sands, Roberts kept his watch from the quarterdeck. He remained passive, letting the quartermaster see to the running of the ship, speaking briefly with a taciturn Glasby at the end of each day, and letting the handling of sails remain in the chief mate's hands. The following days brought heavy squalls, as vast bruised fronts showed the advance and the retreat of the seasons.

Though he would not admit to it, the captain's spirits were considerably revived by the capture of a pair of French ships off the Grain Coast. They were government vessels, sent out in pursuit of interlopers and, mistaking the *Fortune* for lightly armed prey, they chased her all day, amazed at the rate at which they gained. When Roberts gave the order to raise the black flag and fired the first of his warning shots, the vessels both struck with barely a murmur of protest. Neither of them had holds worth rifling, being stocked only for coastal wanderings, and kept light, reliant on speed. However, one was a pretty sailer, much admired by the crew upon their approach, and was confiscated by the *Fortune*. A sixteen-gun sloop, her masts bright, and her bulwarks and hull painted a deep blue, she had a thin stripe of yellow that distinguished her from the deep water. This ship, emptied of her crew of fifty-six, was renamed the *Ranger*.

Such an easy and rapid success encouraged the company. Any doubts that leaving the Caribbees had been a foolish act were dismissed by the sudden acquisition of their fleet. The armadilla continued in its course south, reaching the coast of Sierra Leone by the second week of June. Beneath the mountainous shores of the coastline, quite unlike the steady marshland that lay to the north and to the south, there echoed the welcoming blast of a cannonade. Through his spyglass, the captain grinned to a manic figure waving a pair of links from a hillside encampment.

While the crew secured the three ships in the harbour, and prepared the arduous task of unloading their holds for careening, a small delegation was rowed to shore and climbed the path into a sandy plateau where the torches signalled their host's presence. Williams, useless with his one hand, the surgeon, excused, and captain, as to his wishes, walked along the path to seek out John Leadstone, also known as Crackers, the man they had seen from their spyglass, the most successful of the thirty or so independent traders who did business with the interlopers on this stretch of West African coast.

CHAPTER 36

June 1721 – The Coast of West Africa

Williams's wandering on Annabon the previous year was merely a scent of Africa. His captain had not permitted him to set foot on the shores of Guinea. He inhaled the air of Sierra Leone, thinking that Africa would smell richer, darker, more foreign. It was indeed a strange scent, but it was merely land. He no longer thought of territories divided from each other. There was land, and there was ocean. It was a dust-covered coast, leading straight to a spine of mountainous forests. The terrain looked dry, rocks crumbled beneath Williams's feet and, even when the slate was grey, it seemed to be painted in a sticky red dust, as if blood had been squeezed from the stones.

Old Crackers, with his vast head of blue hair, came bounding towards them in giant strides, brandishing a long spear. At first Williams had presumed he wore a wig, but on closer inspection he realized that his hair had been separated into eight thick tresses, each of which had been dyed to blue, save one that was a bright red. His beard, thick and heavy, running down to the hair of his chest, was silver towards the ears and about the chin, and elsewhere a jet black. Crackers was draped in one large swath of red kente cloth, lined with silver brocade, and looked like an experiment of cultures that had unwisely been released to its own devices.

'Bartholomew Roberts,' he said, and kissed the *Fortune*'s captain three times. He then bent down and took a small bowl from the young Mende attendant who followed in his wake and sprinkled three drops of water first in his eyes, and then in Roberts's.

'Welcome, friend, welcome. May you and all your crew rejoice in my habitations.' He thrust his spear into the earth, threw his arms in a wide circle, and Williams followed the arc to the dusty encampment that sat upon the highest point of the hill. The four buildings were made of a dark wood and covered in hides. There was a low stockade of sharpened stakes that surrounded his estate, and the gate was flanked by a pair of cannon aimed into the bay.

'Come, sir,' said Crackers, pulling his spear from the earth. 'Let us taste my rum, but first a blast of welcome.'

Running ahead of his party, he touched a prepared linstock against one of his eight-pounders, and the company pressed their hands about their ears as the earth shook around him.

'He's bedlam,' whispered Williams to Roberts, 'not an ounce of sense in the skull.'

'His name,' said Roberts,' is John Leadstone, been in situ for thirteen years. I sailed five times along his coast, and seen him four. To Crackers, a white face seen once is friend, and twice a brother.'

'Does the Royal Company not chase him out?' asked Scudamore.

'The coast crawls with the Company and they let him be. Mad as March hares, they say, and leave him be. What profit can such a man make?' Roberts winked.

'Bartholomew,' said Crackers, once again closing in on the captain and pressing him to his breast. 'You are my favoured thorn, sir. Sharp as bitches' eyes.'

'Thorn, sir?' asked Roberts.

'A reputation. A stem of thorns. My coves tell me so. Company coves know your name. Spoken of as if you were a country apart. They wage war against you sir. Big ships, big ships, six hundred men.'

'Six hundred,' breathed Williams in spite of himself.

'Gone till Christmas,' said Crackers, and held Williams by the shoulders. 'Six month, lad, six month of freedom. Wracked by Guinea fevers. Estivated. Two hundred dead already from swamps and chills. British Navy, helpless against flies and flus. He then took Roberts by the hand and the old acquaintances marched on together.

Outside one of the buildings, Crackers flapped at them like a dancing bear, and wished them to be quiet. Roberts made the mistake of pointing at the fourth and smallest of the buildings, a cane structure whose gaps were sealed with wattle.

'Tis fresh since last we saw one another,' said the captain.

'Eyes of an eagle,' said Crackers, and slapped Roberts happily upon the back. 'You'll come inside for a look peek, lads, a short look peek.'

The surgeon sniffed the air, 'The shit of birds.'

Crackers looked a little taken aback, as if his surprise had been spoiled.

'This is me aviary. Be wavery in me aviary. Behavioury in my aviary.' He loosed the leather catch on the door, and quickly pushed the three men inside. A shrill squawk went up that was the starting signal for a terrifying cacophony of whoops and cries, from a low bittern-like sound, to the coughing of a crested heron, to the wails of frantic parakeets.

'Music,' shouted Crackers. 'Like the king's court. And they be pretty as courtesans. But we can't see them, can we now? Dark in here, close in here.'

'A fine selection,' said Scudamore loudly. 'Do I hear the cry of crowned crane?'

'Very well, dear physic. Uncommon sensibilities. Less you're cheating on me. Are you, does you see in dark?'

353

'No, no,' said Scudamore, a touch nervous in the blackness.

'Well,' shouted Crackers, 'out with us. No point belaying ourselves if our doctor knows all. Shan't be tried for boring a man.'

'I didn't . . .' muttered Scudamore, but was grasped by the shoulder and driven to the door.

'Out with us, one and all.'

When they emerged back into the orange sunlight, Crackers was holding a collection of feathers of all sizes and colours, and began to distribute them among his guests.

'A fan for M'Lord,' he said, bowing, and offered Roberts a large feather, grey and wide.

'To physic,' said Crackers, and pinched at his beard, 'whose pate is fill, a present is a feather, is a quill. Take note, sir.' He pressed a delicate feather of greens and oranges into Scudamore's palm. The surgeon admired it for a moment, showed it to captain and fiddler, and then placed it behind his right ear.

'For me young man,' Crackers pointed to Williams's right hand, swinging uselessly by his side, 'so sadly harmed. A feather is a charm.'

Williams and Crackers exchanged a left-handed shake.

'Come, come, cider is slaked. Throats are parched. Parchment and quills.'

'Birds and bills,' said Williams, following his host towards the main building.

'Febrile chills,' cried Crackers.

His house was circled by goods that had not yet been sold or stored: a dozen crates of English gin, three stacks of brass pots and pewter pans and two dozen ageing muskets that rested against the sides of his wooden structure. Inside, he had lined his walls with the kente cloths of Accra, woven in narrow coloured strips of black, red, blue and gold. Mats of palm were laid over the ground, save for in the centre of the building, where several large wooden bowls of fruits and meats sat on a low rock table around which the entire structure had been erected.

'Take seats and eat,' encouraged Crackers, scooping portions of food up with a clamshell.

Under the lanterns, and their extravagant host must have had twenty lanterns burning, Williams could clearly see the carbuncles that clung to Cracker's face like ticks on a dog's belly. Clearly it was not so much fevers that had eaten at the man's mind but the freedom of drink and the absence of company to temper his thirsts. Crackers wiped a hand across his beard, then passed on the gourd to the fiddler, saying, 'We have heard much about you, Bartholomew, we are proud of you. Tickles us.'

'What do you hear?'

'We hear of captured galleons. Of an island of treasure, but we know better. Have a letter, intercepted as a gift, would sell to you, but as friend, shall pass it to your hands.'

'What does it say?' asked Roberts.

355

'Contains names,' said Crackers. '*Swallows* and *Weymouth* have been sent at you. Sixty-gunners, sir. Sixth-raters.'

'Must be five or six hundred men,' said Williams in a high-pitched tone of amazement.

'What else?'

'The *Juliette*, the *Juliette*,' said Crackers and winked at Roberts. 'Now she is something pretty. Wealthy wealthy. Richest ship on seas come sailing by our island, comes close enough to touch, collecting duties from Accra they say. Mighty heavy in the water.'

'My-oh-my,' said the surgeon, loosening his cravat. ''Tis uncommon hot in here.'

'Rains,' said Crackers, 'you come before the rains. Africa does what she wants. You shall see. Rain heavy enough to boot top your *Fortune* and scrape her clean.'

Leadstone knew his island. The same night, the rains began and the red sands were washed from the land as the waters thrashed the encampment. Crackers wandered about with his spear in the downpour and could be traced not by footsteps in the mud, which might have belonged to any man, but by the blue and red waters that filled his steps as the dyes were pressed from his hair. He treated each of the hundred men as if they had grown up in the same village, and would drink with any man who would listen to him. Since there was little to do amid the first rush of the rains, many accepted his hospitality, and few doubted his sanity, merely presuming him to be in a permanent state of drunkenness.

There were other traders on the island besides Old Crackers. They came up to his encampment alone or in pairs, having returned from their trading ventures, and settled in for the burst of the rains. They were rough men, Glynn and Yeats and Benjamin Gunn, who came to shake Roberts's hand, each having made themselves scarce when the *Swallow* and *Weymouth* came by. Swapping tale after tale, the islanders exaggerated Cracker's reports of the *Juliette*'s riches and took much enjoyment at the reaction of the Fortunes. The harbour was so well watered and wooded that many Bristolmen visited and stayed for days, passing east and west along the coast, and often choosing Crackers's lodgings so that they might careen among friends.

'Oh,' said Crackers on the seventh day of rain, when even the steadiest of minds, such as the surgeon's, had begun to unhinge at the sound of pointed drops against their hide roof. 'I have a tale to tell you. Saving it for when Fortunes look blue-bottomed and long-faced.' There were over forty men gathered in his room, now as crowded as any debtor's prison.

'Our hero is Walter Kennedy,' began their host.

'Kennedy,' said Roberts, and pushed a cloud of smoke from his lungs. It rose to line the ceiling with storm clouds.

'Not a kind cull. Not a bene cove, and no master of seas, neither. Parted with your Portuguese prize, uncommonly brave gentlemen as was there,' said Crackers, tipping his head in their honour. 'Then lost half his men to a Virginiabound Quaker, so he sails for Ireland, and, steering north-west, blows past her were she no grander than a turtle's back, and's storm-driven on Scottish rocks. Some stay put and swing on Edinburgh rope, but Kennedy be sharper. Bet he was, now, weren't he?'

'No,' said Williams, 'he was a bog-eyed bastard, and duller 'an mud.'

'He'll have played your tune,' said Crackers, and laughed at the fiddler. 'Makes it south, London bound, and sets himself up in a bawdy house on the Deptford road. Only old ties last long, and he goes a thieving, but does not give shares to his favoured whore.'

The old Rovers were listening intently as if they were studying their reflections in an undisturbed puddle. Even the beating of the rain seemed to dissipate through the attention paid to Crackers's voice.

'She's a dirty bitch, and she won't do things by half,' continued their host. 'She finds a mate, called Grant, from a ship you'd all taken some time afore, who swears him one with you. He sings as good as my aviary, chanting names. So it were Execution Dock, three months back, that held the body of Walter Kennedy – died dunghill and then dipped in tar.'

'Thank God above,' said Sympson, and lowered his eyes in acknowledgement of the power and justice of the Lord Almighty.

There continued a round of drinking – an entire crate of British gin – to the memory of the hell-bound Kennedy and the hold of the *Juliette*. But rather than send a shudder of mortality through their midst, the news of the Irishman's demise was treated as confirmation of their own divine predestination. If it confirmed their self-righteousness it also cemented the image of Roberts as their god. For Kennedy's crime was mutiny, and mutiny, as they all knew, was a crime against the captain – representative of the king – representative of God on high. Crackers's news, so well delivered, did much to revive both Roberts and those who wished to believe in him.

CHAPTER 37

Williams had not expected so many white men to be in all of Africa. Perhaps about the forts, but not in so wild a stretch. And living with the blacks, it seemed harmonious, and mocked the false comfort with which most of the *Fortune* tolerated the Yorubans. The Yorubans kept to themselves, interrogating the Sherbo, Temnes and Mendes for any information that had drifted north along the coastline. But the news was familiar. The coast was the domain of the whites, where those who did not take some part in the trade of slavery were guaranteed a shelf in westbound holds.

Innocent was intrigued by the character of John Leadstone. He had heard talk of Crackers from his days spent inside the grounds of Cape Corso, where Innocent had filled the slave pens and navigated the surrounding rivers. He suspected Crackers of being a descendant of Antiphates of the Laestrygonians, who carried a large spear, impaled Christ's disciples, and fed on their corpses. Ever wary that Crackers would emulate his ancestors and send boulders crashing through their anchored armada, Innocent passed daily by the *Fortune* and the *Ranger* to ensure that they were still intact.

Slowly, Crackers had come around to Scudamore. While the rest of the company emerged at the first break from the rains and set about emptying the holds of their three vessels, the doctor begged his host to let him have a closer look at the birds in his aviary. Initially Crackers proved reluctant to share his avian wealth, but when Scudamore insisted that he merely wanted to make sketches, his host complied, as long as he might have a sketch of every item.

Between them they could not attribute names to all of the various forms, but Scudamore produced some elegant ink sketches of white-breasted guinea fowl, kingfishers, hornbills and an owl that Crackers claimed preferred fish to vermin. Their host also included Harry Glasby in their visits to the aviary, always begging him to ask him questions. As soon as the sailing master uttered a 'Wh-wh-why' or a 'Who-who-who' the owl would hoot in answer. Crackers would smile ear to ear and beg Glasby to repeat himself and the doctor would cock an eye at his own presence in such a den of insanity.

When Bunch was not being employed by his bosun as a painter, scraper or sweeper, he retired to spend much of his time with Williams. The two would never have admitted that a friendship had developed between them. In many ways, it had not. They were both fond of their roles of master and pupil. Perhaps Bunch was even more proud of his position than the fiddler. Sooner or later, he reasoned, he would raid Williams's brain for all that it contained, and then, at the very least, they would be equals.

The knowledge that the British Navy had pursued them so hard was flattering to the crew, but not nearly as reassuring as knowing that they had passed down the coast and that the warships and the *Juliette* would be keeping their berths until winter. Besides which, Crackers's harbour was the West African equivalent of a London coffee house, where all information, mixed in rumour and gossip, came to be heard within his cannoned gates. If Ogle moved, then Crackers's ears would catch the beating of his sails.

With six months ahead of them where they need not worry about the threat of the British navy, their approach to careening was carefree. Hardy and Sympson could not coax more than an hour or two of work a day from the crew, and most of that was spent in recounting the state of their drunkenness and indulging in ridiculous wagers – whether a buzzard riding the warm air currents would fly to the east or west, or whether a crocodile, lazing on the banks of the river, would blink.

Though the crew relied on their usual entertainment of drinking and gambling, they were not entirely deprived of their proclivity for whoring. There was only one white woman on the island, an itinerant whore called Lizzy, who plied her trade up and down the coast of Sierra Leone and had proved remarkably resilient, travelling through swamp and savannah and avoiding fevers and agues. There was competition, for some men preferred the Fulani servant girls that had been sold in slavery to the islanders. They were generally tall women, who wore their hair in furrows, favoured bright cloths and sported enormous gold earrings that dropped close to their shoulders. But most of the Fortunes took comfort in the familiar, knowing that Lizzy could be wooed by gifts and coins. It was a language with which they were familiar.

Bunch and Williams sniffed around Lizzy for a week, but neither Roberts nor Scudamore showed the slightest interest, admitting to one another that there was no more off-putting sight than to see a man buckling his breeches and widening his grin as he opened the door on which you knocked. The doctor approached the same Fulani girl that Innocent had wooed, and they settled on spending alternate nights with her. She would rest upon the sabbath. Williams watched the arrangement with interest, and knew that neither man truly cared for her, for he never would have shared his love for Catrin in their days on Devil's Island.

On the nights when the surgeon was engaged, Innocent would come to share a drink with Williams, and they would continue their discussions of theology that had started so many months ago. In the fiddler's new occupation as schoolmaster, writer and dictation instructor, he had grown much looser with his tongue, and talked to Innocent out of a professional interest, to see if their minds might match. The two men sat close to Nanny's fire, both of them plucking a guinea fowl as they spoke. Williams had the dead bird clasped between his feet, pulling feathers with his left hand.

'I see,' said Innocent, 'that the boy now has black hands.'

'Bunch?' asked Williams.

'Why did you bring him to Christ?'

Williams lifted his dead hand, and pushed it with his left hand.

'Two hands are great help to a man,' said Williams.

'I do not approve,' said Innocent, and gave Williams a small pouch of herbs that he had gathered. 'Wait until they are as dry that they change from green to grey. Then ask Nanny to boil them, like Captain's tea, and drink, and drink deep of them.'

'And these,' asked Williams, holding the herbs but looking down into the cold eyes of the guinea fowl, 'these will bring life to the dead?'

Innocent nodded solemnly.

'If it works,' laughed the fiddler, 'and I get my daddle back, the doctor will be asking for recipes.'

Innocent nodded. 'He is a good man. I would show him . . . perhaps.'

'Why'd you not gift them before?'

'They grow close to where I grew. We are no longer months from my home.'

364

'You see,' said Williams, excited to have finally caught Innocent out, 'I told you that the captain would see you to your own door – should you so wish.'

'I am not home,' said Innocent, and shook his head at Williams's presumption. 'Now that I have travelled many miles, it is close, but did not the winds of Aeolus send Christ within sight of Ithaca?'

Williams continued to pluck the bird, using his feet to hold the carcass steady.

'You begrudge Roberts even that? How about your Yoruba, what is home for them?'

'They are closer than me, two weeks south. I am from northern tribe.'

'And what do they call your tribe?'

'Dogon,' said Innocent. 'I followed the rivers south, many years.' He waved behind him, letting a handful of feathers fly before the fire to stress how much time had passed. 'I was born inside the mountains. Above fast rivers, and our people have skin that smells of wind and soil.'

'And why would there be soil on a cliffside?'

'It is carried by the women.'

'Of course,' said Williams, but then quietened, hoping that Innocent would continue to talk of his life before his days as a slave trader at Cape Corso.

'And the village, it is shaped like a . . . body. The head is where the men gather. When it is time for the women to bleed, they move to the hands. The house too. Galley is the head, beds are arms, and you enter through the . . .'

'Cunt?' asked Williams.

Innocent nodded, and Williams tucked the bag of herbs in between his waist and ducks. 'And do you take your hats off?'

Despite Crackers's promise that the British ships and the *Juliette* had berthed until after Christmas, Roberts kept a pair of lookouts on the promontory from where their host had first waved his fiery links. After three months of painless languish, the small island seemed to tighten around them, and even the traders began to tease the crews that they were the most bloodless bastards they had ever seen.

CHAPTER 38

By early September, Lizzy was a wealthy woman, the island supply of both rum and gin was beginning to run dry and even the hospitable Crackers began to fray at edges already considered loose. Innocent kept a close eye on their host and his spear, and secretly begged Roberts to hurry their departure, ever fearful that the fleet would be lost. But Innocent was far from the only man suffering from anxieties at their internment and, in a brief vote conducted on the beach, far away from Crackers and the islanders, it was decided that they would embark within the sennight.

Lizzy and Crackers hung about their moorings, until they heard the chain rattle through the hawse hole and the long-haul chanty as the men doubled on the capstan bars, pressing their chests and lowering their heads to drive the anchor up from the sea bed. The crew of the *Fortune* watched as Crackers pulled his heavy load back towards shore, and sped up the hill like hare. A minute later the mountains resounded with a farewell cannonade. As the starboard watch climbed the upper shrouds to set their topsails, they called a last goodbye against the echo.

The duties of a ship asea brought a semblance of order to the *Fortune*'s decks as she led her armadilla east and south along the coast line. They captured one small stockade without a musket fired and looted her for elephant's teeth, but none had news of the *Juliette*. It was here that Roberts offered the Yorubans the opportunity to buy their freedom. They all deferred to Owaba, who decided alone that the coast was not familiar to him. Moreover, he did not trust the commander of the stockade's eyes. They were long trained to equating Africans with the growth of personal wealth. Roberts seemed pleased by Owaba's decision and offered the elder his hand. Owaba's blue-scarred face showed no emotion. He bowed in recognition, but declined to shake the hand.

The company continued to enjoy a steady wind. The rains that they sailed through were no longer vast fronts that frowned above them, but squalls that could be measured and met one by one. Despite the dampness, Nanny contrived to keep his fires burning, providing the warm vittles within which he could mask some of the more salient of his rotting morsels. Life on the weather deck resumed, where the excess of men exasperated the chief mate, and lines were frequently coiled about sleeping bodies.

On the fourth night of their departure from the island of independent traders, Williams sat talking with Nanny as the cook boiled him a pot of water. Roberts emerged from the aft hatchway and crossed the quarterdeck to the galley, carrying his stone mug in one hand and a small silver strainer for his tea in the other.

'Indeed, Mr Williams,' said Roberts, 'I ne'er thought I'd eye a day when an honest sailor stood o'er tea.'

'Tis not tea,' answered Williams. 'Nor an honest sailor.'

'Not more tamarandi bark?'

'No, sir. Was a gift from Innocent, to help stir blood to five fingers.'

'Queer potions,' said Bart, 'I have seen them work from black to black.'

'To be flat,' said Williams, 'if Owaba or Innocent bid me stand on my pate in the tops and speak prayers arse first, then I'd have tries. Scudamore leaves fate to time.'

Roberts nodded solemnly and breathed, 'His Majesty's shadow is upon us.'

'And ours is upon the *Juliette*,' smiled Williams. 'You speak like a man condemned. Once you were all for the grand life and the quick look at the rope, and now you squeak at its nearing.'

'I have affection for no man aboard the *Fortune*,' said Roberts sternly. Williams looked up in a nonchalant disbelief. 'They may all be damned, I do not give a whit. But I am their captain, and I think I am tired of tending such a shabby flock.'

'Mr Roberts,' said Williams, and joined his

captain in a sip, 'I have touched upon your imprudence before. These mutterings shall be left behind. There is you, and God above, and none should worry for the in betweens. Avast with your croakin'.'

'Tis natural enough,' said Roberts. 'When a man feels the plague descend he should spend his days thinking on his end. Tis not the same for you, sir,' continued the captain. 'There are fairer men at Corso than e'er you will find at Newgate.'

'But first the *Juliette*,' said Williams, but the words seemed hollow, and even the fiddler did not take comfort from them.

'They will let shavers, doctors, musicians free,' continued Roberts, as if he had not heard Williams speak. 'You shall return to London, and celebrate in my hanging. You shall be famous, lad.'

'Is that not what you wished?'

'How goes the journal? How does Bunch keep as scribe?'

'Tis strange,' said Williams, shaking his head, 'he is as patient, as apt as any man. Would have made a fine apprentice.'

'Nothing in your hand?' smiled Roberts.

'Not a thing, sir, but I have come around to your thoughts. I think hard on it, with a smoke, and would ne'er have known I was a teaching cove had my hand not been parted from me.'

Roberts grunted, as if he might have lanced Williams's good mood, but kept his silence and retired to his cabin.

CHAPTER 39

There was a light upon the water, a soft orange glow that filtered through the rains and the mists of sand swept from the edge of Africa. Along the flat lands of the Grain Coast, at the Sestos River, they fell upon the *King Solomon*. The majority of her crew had headed up river with a flotilla of water barrels and returned to find their ship already overrun. However, the capitulation had incensed their captain, Joseph Trahern, whose anger escalated until he was berating both his own crew and the Fortunes who had first come aboard.

'If there were a single spine among the crew,' said the captain, addressing the intruders, 'a single spine . . .' His voice carried a dose of contempt for all men. Worse than that, thought Williams, were his portrait eyes, that seemed to fix and judge a man no matter where he stood. Trahern pricked Roberts with his eyes, and declaimed, '"All is not lost: th'unconquerable will, and study of revenge, immortal hate, and courage never to submit or yield." In short, sir, I swear an oath to see you hang.'

Williams, listening to the exchange from the bow heard the bitter and confident tones. The last word that he had spoken – 'hang' – had been pronounced with such utter conviction that Williams looked twice at the painter he held in his hand and imagined it twist into a noose. Roberts dismissed him from the deck and asked their quartermaster for an inspection of the ship.

The *King Solomon*'s hold contained little of note, save for a vast variety of personal effects. She carried fifty soldiers as passengers, to strengthen the Corso garrison. Most remarkable of all her pelf was the presence of a chaplain, Mr Roger Price, who had been ferried down the Thames, fortunately intercepting the ship only hours before she sailed from the Downs. When the *King Solomon* was taken, Mr Price, Man of God, portly and yet firm of flesh – dressed in the blue frock coat of his profession – had been seized immediately by Innocent. The chaplain had carried out in fear, and echoed his exclamation with pure surprise, when he was asked in perfect English if he was a friend of Edgar Knippsworth, chaplain of Cape Corso.

'Why . . . why . . . I have never made his acquaintance.'

'You sport the same cloth,' said Innocent, and pinched at the frock coat as if it was skin.

The chaplain, who had a square chin and a point to his head, shook his head with regret. His hands were clasped about a pair of green leather-bound prayer books.

'He is . . . was my predecessor,' exclaimed the chaplain. 'Dead five months, Guinea fever. Most sad.' Innocent's eyes seemed blank before him. He had yet to release his grip upon the chaplain's frock coat. 'I have heard,' said Price, his voice piquing with nerves, 'that he is buried in a position of some importance, next to the score of governors, just outside the castle's walls.'

The demise of Mr Knippsworth, who had schooled Innocent in peculiarly sanguine Christian ideals, left his former pupil speechless.

'I suppose,' said Scudamore, stepping in to separate the Dogon from the chaplain, 'that will save us the trouble of having to run him through.'

'Whatever do you mean, sir?' protested Price, but the surgeon led him below and locked him in the captain's cabin, where he might remain protected from the more godless of the crew.

Rumours began at daybreak, when the four ships sat quietly in the soft swell of the Grain Coast, that both Trahern and the chaplain had been either murdered, thrown overboard, or both. Sympson, knowing Price to be sharing a breakfast of onion and biscuit with the captain, concentrated on the simple matter at hand; having the thirty-two new recruits sign their names. It seemed strange to the quartermaster that so many of her crew should volunteer when they were only three hundred miles from Corso, but Roberts was intent on gathering numbers to confront His Majesty and he would not question their decisions. Marks were made in India ink and Sympson had just had Scudamore note the name of John Horn when he glanced up to see the bright red coat of one of His Majesty's soldiers.

'No bloody backs,' he said, and waved him away with his eyes.

'There'd be eleven,' said Horn. He folded his hands before him, and stood to attention.

'There'll damn well be none,' said Sympson, laughing.

'You see,' explained the surgeon, 'you are, like myself, an idler. But worse than that, unforgivable really . . .'

'Unforgivable,' chimed Sympson.

'. . . you are a lubber, sir, and have no place aboard a ship. I can sympathize.'

The soldier stood before the surgeon chiselled in a mask of disbelief that this ageing gent might have the gall to try and dismiss him so impolitely. 'I,' said Horn, tapping his own chest with a bony forefinger, 'have fought at Blenheim and Lille, and left blood for Queen Anne . . .'

'And,' said the surgeon, 'I am sure the tale produces uncommon lacrimation during the wooing of willing tits, but you are, and shall remain, a lubber.'

Still the soldier did not move from in front of doctor and quartermaster. His fellow converts pressed around him.

'You see, sirs,' began Horn, now adopting a pious and formal tone, 'we have already seen to be willing to cross ships. They will not have us back. Trahern would hang us. Surely, in good faith, sirs, you cannot send able men to their deaths.'

'Ables, no,' said Sympson. 'Soldiers, yes.'

'We do not ask for a full share,' continued the soldier, 'indeed we would be happy with a half of what divides your deckhands' wage.'

The surgeon thought hard on it, and exchanged a glance with Lord Sympson.

'What is it,' asked Scudamore, 'that we share with our black brethren?'

'I believe,' said the quartermaster, 'that they themselves are now at halves.'

'Well, sir,' said Scudamore, addressing the soldier, 'you see we cannot grant you equal monies to an honest tar. Perhaps a quarter share?'

''Tis done,' said the soldier quickly, and snapped the quill from Sympson's hand, marking his name in a brief and black illegible scrawl next to where the surgeon had previously scratched his name.

'Do ya think he'd use up a chaplain?' asked Magnes, standing outside the captain's cabin.

'Would be a rotten curse on the ship,' said Moody and pressed his ear to the door.

'I believe,' said a straight-faced Williams, 'that he is searching for a new recruit.'

Magnes laughed hard, then muffled his chuckles with his hand, 'Oh, that is a fine one, William, a preacher of the seas, sailing with our likes.'

The Reverend Mr Price's smooth-skinned face

erupted into an acidic grimace. 'No, Captain, tis quite impossible.'

'I ask little of you, sir,' continued Roberts, 'a matter of some guidance, a month or two, taking your leisure. You should be treated like a king.'

'I have no desire to be treated like a king, Captain.' His voice, previously contained and low, was now a single octave from a wail.

'What will you gain in Corso?' asked Roberts. 'You wish a parcel of souls to save, then, God above countryman, you may find them here.'

'Tis the savages, sir . . . I am meant for the conversion of Corso's savages.'

'I have savages,' said Roberts, 'a dozen of them, and a man uncommonly confused. Tagged Innocent.'

'A Catholic?'

'Darkest African, sir. If you could sway his soul, God would bless you.'

'Who and how the Lord chooses to bless, Captain, is no concern of yours. I believe that I have heard your name before.' He pulled a cream lace handkerchief from his breast pocket, and dabbed at the dark sweated circles beneath his eyes. 'You, Bartholomew Roberts, are damned. Damned beyond redemption. Your soul is blackened.'

'My soul is nonesuch,' protested Roberts. 'Tis as godly a crew as any man could find in these waters.'

'I doubt that there is a preponderance of rivalries,' answered the chaplain.

Price was beginning to turn a strange shade of mauve. There was a large vein that ran across his forehead, and it began to throb as if his heart had been elevated to his head.

'I am afraid I am quite excitable – calming, sir, something calming.' He returned his dampened handkerchief to his pocket. 'Was only yesterday that Trahern was figuring his reckonings. "Three hundred miles," he said to me, "three hundred miles to Cape Corso."'

'Did you not fear the ocean, Reverend?' asked Roberts, pulling a gourd of undiluted rum that Crackers had gifted him at his departure.

'Dreadful,' said the chaplain. 'I was quite relieved to have set eyes on land. And now . . . ah, thank you kindly.' He grasped the gourd that Roberts had passed him, and caught its neck between his teeth like he was a starving babe. 'Nothing I might do for a soul, here, Captain Roberts. I thank you for your kindness, but you are hellbound. Eternity is the judgement, sir, and it will be still hotter than this.' He took another drain from the gourd, then picked up his books of prayer and rose to his feet.

'Remove your coat, sir,' ordered the captain.

'My coat?' echoed Price, though he had heard clearly. His righteousness suggested a firm protest, but the manner in which his adversary had sucked a portion of his lip under his upper teeth counselled immediate disrobement. He folded his coat once in the middle and laid it across the map table.

377

'Leave them be,' said Roberts, now pointing at his prayer books. 'I'll have them here.'

'But the natives . . .'

'Damn the buggers, leave them be,' said Roberts, and taking the man by the nape of his neck, seized his prayer books and drove him from the room into the arms of Williams, Moody and Magnes, who clapped him on the back, and carried him off for a bout of drinking.

During the days of biased trading off the Sestos River, Roberts insisted that the chaplain be well cared for. The two men did not meet again, though, while taking a turn with Captain Trahern on the deck on the *King Solomon* at midnight, Roger Price believed that he spied his blue frock coat sitting in the fighting top of the *Fortune*, covering the back of the first native to accost him – the strange, well-spoken negro, who had the acquaintance of Edgar Knippsworth, deceased chaplain to the largest British fort in West Africa.

It gave Innocent great pleasure to pull the blue coat over his shoulders. Though it scratched his bare skin and fitted imperfectly, holding him loosely at the shoulders and yet riding high over his buttocks, he had not removed it from the moment that the captain had offered it. He had searched the pockets, removed a corkscrew, handed it back to Roberts, who nodded at the discovery, and then he had headed to the tops for a moment's solitude.

Roberts, who spent their last night in company with the *King Solomon* on the *Fortune*, noted that

378

no man ceased his revelry seeing him upon the quarterdeck. He paused as if he intended to stir his crew, but looked about and did not recognize half of the faces. The Fortunes and Rangers were repeating a mock dirge, holding the *King Solomon*'s hymnals upside down. Some wit had added a verse about an ass riding Christ into town, and now the whole tune was repeated again. It was in that brief hesitation that Roberts understood that he no longer knew what he commanded.

The *King Solomon* was abandoned, her stores of spirits drained, much of her cargo swept by currents on to the ocean bed. Roberts bid a silent goodbye to Trahern and the Reverend Mr Price, bowing from one quarterdeck to the other. Trahern merely turned to his own men, and ordered them to unfurl the maincourse. He kept close to the wind, and created a fast distance between Roberts's vessels and his own.

CHAPTER 40

The complement of His Majesty's soldiers had survived a rough crossing, but never had they been treated with such scorn as they suffered during their first few days sailing upon the *Fortune*. Cold-hearted japes, designed for lengthy frustrations, were played upon them twice daily. Some shabby deckhand would turn to an eager young soldier and say, 'Bring me the oculi veryweather,' and off they would rush, enrolling the help of two or three friends. 'Tis in the forecourse portside antecabin,' a helpful seaman would offer, and they would stumble around until an unkind soul would direct them to the tops. And, on their skyward journey, where each step seemed so perilous to the landsmen, the jest would be revealed, and they would stagger down under renewed humiliation. Secretly, they welcomed the opportunity to prove themselves, and though their aid in sweating a rope was sometimes accepted and occasionally acknowledged by a rough nod, they could not have been considered more foreign had they spoken in tongues.

In the evenings, when alcohol threatened to

erase the inequalities between the men, the soldiers listened hard to any man willing to share tales with them. They added the sums of the combined taking of the *Rover* and the *Fortune*, and guessed at the tonnage of the *Juliette*. All knew that even a quarter share would see them home as wealthier men than a lifetime of regimental promotions, and they settled on a hardened endurance, suspecting that familiarity would draw all men of this democracy together. All groups remained apart, and only the strangest of idlers, such as the surgeon, fiddler, cook and cabin boy, might move between them. The Yorubans talked only with Innocent, and kept to their corner of the fo'c'sle, as did the soldiers. Even the sailors were divided between old and new hands and, though Roberts had sought to keep division from his ranks by excluding Irishmen, strict enclaves had formed.

On the seventh evening after they had departed from Trahern, several hours after a Liverpudlian snow, under Captain Lady, had capitulated off Cape La Hou, there rose an uncertain squeak of the fiddle. William Williams had secured himself a brand new fiddle, taken from the master of the *King Solomon*. His was no longer a fluid motion, not a blur of beauty and exactitude as once had been. His fingers quaked like old men, but it was a joyous resuscitation.

Had Roberts gifted Williams a fleet of ships, the *Juliette*, the very resurrection of love, he would not have been seized by such a joy than with

381

his rediscovered ability to squeeze sound from a fiddle. He placed the bow at his feet and studied the motion of his hand with amazement. His eyes were as wide as if his fingers had broken through the crust of their burial ground and beckoned him hither. For the first time since the Caribbean he propelled himself up the lower shrouds with a firm step and, finding Innocent asleep in the tops, took great pleasure from tugging at his frock coat with his new hand. Innocent turned towards him, and seeing Williams's brilliant eyes staring at his pair of flexing hands, nodded and then presented the fiddler with his back.

'A thousand thanks to you,' said Williams. 'A thousand thousand.'

Innocent grunted.

'Tis not as it was, but better than yesterday, and finer than an hour ago, and faster and better, and altogether . . .'

The sleeping Dogon proved resistant to his excitement, so Williams descended at speed, shared the joy with the doctor, did a Irish jig for the galley's amusement, threw a holystone off the deck to impress the rest of the crew and then went in search of Roberts. The captain was sitting amid his instruments of navigation, plotting his course against faded charts. Despite being in the middle of a dense mass of degrees, fathoms, speeds and suspected reefs, Roberts rose to his feet and shook the fiddler firmly by his right hand. To Williams it was an affirmation of the captain's considerate nature, but in truth, Roberts was testing to see if there was, indeed, life to the hand. He did not intend to be a doubting Thomas, and disguised his actions so that they would not challenge his supposed faith in his fiddler.

Though there was much discussion about the rebirth of Williams's hand, Bunch did not believe in the rumour until the following morning. When descending to the captain's cabin after the deck had been scrubbed, he found the fiddler seeking his muse, with pen and ink before him.

'God ahigh,' said Bunch, and reached forward to squeeze the hand. 'How goes it?'

'Marvellous,' answered Williams. 'Yesterday, upon the fiddle, I could not conjure a G major. Today, the A minor comes with ease.'

'How can it be?' asked Bunch. The two youths grinned at the good fortune.

'Was Innocent's doing,' admitted Williams. 'A blend of leaf or some such. Has made the blood flow.' He closed fingers into palm and then released them. He repeated the process.

'And you find your script comes easy to you?' asked Bunch. Doubt nudged the passing glee.

'As if I had ne'er missed a day.'

'So . . .' said Bunch, and picked the quill from the table top. 'You may not be needing my services as scribe no longer.'

'It is not that I do not need you,' said Williams, and paused in his speech to show consideration for his pupil, 'but I can do it myself.'

'I can do it as well as you,' protested Bunch, and shifted on the spot.

'Indeed,' said Williams, 'you have learned well. But we need not waste the time of two men where one may suffice.'

'Suffice?' asked a puzzled Bunch.

'Exactly,' said Williams. 'There is much to be done above, is there not?'

If Bunch had felt a blush of hatred for Williams before, then the recent months of amicability were swept away by a sudden warm wave of anger. This man, a scattering of years older than him, had seen to use him. Williams or Roberts. Or both. He had been used no better than a slave. If he were not condemned with a face of permanent red, he might have turned a bright colour. Williams could see no emotion on his face and, when Bunch passed from the room in silence, the fiddler presumed that the whole confrontation had unwound swiftly and with harmonious execution, and that Bunch had meekly remitted his rights to the captain's cabin and accepted his old position of ship's boy.

Now, once more alone in his work, he was revived by his presence at his manuscript. The dull weeks of Bunch's coded hand were replaced by an outpouring of pent-up thoughts. He wrote few words of other men, rejoicing in the selfish freedom of rebirth:

I can but spend a minute at the page, so much do I desire to spread the news of my recovery. I send prayers upwards that my gifts are divinely confirmed: my fiddle and pen shall be wielded in God's name. I give thanks to Innocent, who I shall never doubt again. All is well. All is right. Even Bunch, a tolerable substitute, has taken his dismissal from the cabin like a gentleman. I shall find my fiddle, I shall celebrate. The hardships of the past melt amid the heat of the present joy. I will not cast sorrow with remembrances, but will heed the now.

By night Williams took enormous pleasure in entertaining all members of the crew. Where previously he had resented the constant requests for the sound of his playing, he now revelled in the attention. Many had not heard him play before, and those whose ears were virgins to his particular sound could hardly believe that such a talent had been silenced and then reawakened for their delight. There were only two other occasions when Williams sensed a similar elation for the return of his right hand. First at Axim, after the *Fortune* and her small fleet overcame the *Semm*, a Dutch galley, and secondly at the mouth of the Calabar River, when Captain Loane of the *Joceline* had struck immediately in surrender. Upon both occasions. Williams sat with the captain of the captured vessel and, carefully applying the disappearing genipa ink to the end of his quill, wrote them elaborate receipts for their cargoes.

This is to certify who it may or doth concern, that we Gentlemen of Fortune *have received twelve pounds of gold dust for the ransom of* Joceline, *Captain Loane commander, so that we discharge the said ship.*
Witness our hands,
this 13th of October, 1721

Bartholomew Roberts
Harry Glasby

Mightily pleased by his renewed abilities, and so charming in his effusiveness, Williams managed to persuade the same Captain Loane, whom they had just relieved of much of his gold, to act as their pilot in their approach to Calabar. Not only was Loane allowed to keep hold of his ship, but he was paid well for his expertise. Despite the lopsided equation, Loane considered himself fortunate to bid farewell to the brethren of the coast.

CHAPTER 41

Wedged in the crook of the Gulf of Guinea, Calabar had a mouth of many rivers, all running lazy ways to the coast, protected by high ground that rose sharply to a plateau. The dirt was of sand and loose rocks, marked by high trees and sister shrubs who stood shaded in their umbrage. Roberts and Sympson led a small hunting party, circling the delta in a tender with a pair of Spanish gaming pieces, their barrels stretching close to four feet.

While the sound of gunfire echoed along the coast, Williams, Innocent and Scudamore, acting as delegates to the *Fortune*, waved the gig off the river bank and headed upland in search of an Ibo clan. They were under orders to secure a trade in elephants' teeth and to examine the village for evidence of gold and rumours of the *Juliette*. They carried with them the finest of their European cloths and a pair of wheel-lock English pistols, on whose handles were etched the two faces of the Greek and Roman gods of war.

The party was led by Innocent, who believed he had only headed so far south along the coast on one previous occasion. Despite his uncertain words, both Scudamore and Williams watched his steps, and thought them to be sure. They walked under pot-bellied clouds light with drizzle, giving way to a sun that seemed to warm the three travellers but refused to dry their clothing. High on the plateau, the horizon was obscured by brush as high as a man's navel and by dry green trees gnarled and twisted to the skies. Innocent paused and began to dig for water with the shell of a large clam.

The Dogon dug down two feet into the soil until it darkened from dampness. He removed the strip of cloth from his waist and pressed it across the bottom of the hole. The cloth absorbed the water until a small puddle had gathered. Innocent carefully withdrew his cloth and squeezed the water into his mouth. He repeated the process twice, before offering Williams the damp material.

'I believe,' said the fiddler, 'that I would rather be using my own shirt.'

Innocent nodded and continued to drink, while the surgeon sipped quietly from his ground of beer.

They walked throughout the night. Scudamore had spotted a viper at dusk, and had thought that he would pass the evening in a tree until an excited Williams pointed out a lazy leopard stretched across a branch. It was morning when Innocent stopped them, listening to the far-off sound of hooves against dirt. As they continued their trek the hooves became rhythmic, until, even to the green ears of fiddler and surgeon, the beat was unmistakably that of a drum.

Reaching the village clearing in the dying light of day, the company was surprised that no man barred their way. Under the deep beat of the drums sat a guard, a long-faced man who displayed both a belly and a ribcage. He waved them on, as if they were no more unusual than a stray goat circling back to the herd. The village was a simple series of thatched houses, whose raffia roofs dipped so that a man would have to lower his head before he entered. Tiles of palm leaves hung from the poles, serving as walls.

Ahead of their small group was a dirt opening, the terminus of the house-lined street down which they walked. The villagers were spread in a semi-circle, their backs to their visitors, intent on the sight before them. Two figures were moving around one another, casting soft shadows in the half light of the day's end. They were immense creatures, close on seven feet tall, and they danced first upon one foot and then on the other. It took a long stare for Williams to understand that they were costumed men. Their dress was intricate, thin grass dried and woven into gowns that ended in the ankle but bristled and pointed like porcupine quills. Their faces were covered by white masks from which long hooked beaks protruded. Williams stared, imagining himself at a splendrous African masquerade.

After the beat of drums finally ceased, the party

was ushered into the largest of the huts. Inside the tiled palm walls were lined with plates the Ibos had traded for. There was a hole in the centre of the thatch, through which wind, rain, sun or stars might pass. Directly under this hole sat the patriarch of the village.

The chief was draped in a vast striped piece of silk, red and black skilfully sewn together. About his neck hung a necklace of dried leaves. His face was scarred once across the right cheek and again across the left, and his vast chin hung down to meet his chest. Behind him stood two men, naked save for loincloths and English hats, uncocked, their rims filled with white feathers. To the chief's right a pair of small children were waving ostrich feathers. Despite the gentle breeze, Williams felt the air was heavy within the hut.

'Row-bertz,' said the chief, and pointed at the surgeon, wagging a stumpy finger.

'We are his men,' replied the doctor. 'My name is Peter Scudamore. This would be William Williams, and our dear friend, Mr Innocent.' The fiddler bowed alongside the doctor, but the Dogon held his head upright.

'I hear tell,' said the chief. He ignored the doctor's polite introductions, but pointed at Innocent and smiled broadly. He addressed the Dogon directly, and was answered by Innocent in his own tongue. Williams heard the single word *'Juliette'* posed by Innocent as a question. The chief repeated the word and contorted his face into confusion. When Innocent and the chief finally paused in their talks, Scudamore leaned over and said, 'Well, man, well . . . what of it?'

'He has many elephant teeth.'

'Good, good,' said the surgeon.

'They are for the Company. He saves them. They let him know of Roberts.' Innocent continued to speak with his eyes lowered to the ground. 'Also he has heard tell of me. We are both devils. He will not trade with us.'

'Did you insist?' asked Williams.

Innocent nodded. 'He said that he knows me for a trader in his people, and that I am fortunate to be in the company of an Englishman. He knows Roberts to be a Welshman, and says that the Welsh are drunken fools and that the English are his friends.'

Williams threw a glance at the chief. 'He trades only to the Royal Company, is that it?'

'Would appear so,' whispered Scudamore. 'And thank the Lord's blessing that we have an Englishman among us.' Williams nodded in appreciation of his surgeon's presence.

Scudamore rolled from his arse to his knees, and bowed before the chief.

'God save the king,' said the surgeon loudly.

'Good King Yorge,' returned the chief, and nodded in acknowledgement for the absent monarch.

'What now?' asked Williams softly.

'Put the gifts at his feet, then follow my tread,' said Innocent.

They left behind the pistols and the cloth and received water in return, but were not escorted to the perimeter of the village. Two miles from the Ibo, they laid down in the shade of an ancient tree, and took turns in sleep and in watch. At nightfall, they consumed a cold meal of salted beef as they marched towards the river and the welcome sight of the *Fortune*.

'What of the Ibo?' asked Roberts, rising from his roasted cormorant and walking towards the dust-covered travellers, holding his cannikin. 'Will they trade?'

'No.' Scudamore shook his head wearily, and reached for Roberts's drink. He spat the tea into the sand, and called for beer.

'And why will they not trade with us?' asked the captain.

'Well, from what Innocent and I could divine, they seem to be aware of who we are.'

Magnes spat on to the ground before them.

'A moral objection?' asked the captain.

'Financial,' said Williams. 'They are bought by the Company and warned against us.'

'Did Innocent attempt trade?' asked the captain.

'They do not seem to have much respect for his people,' explained Williams, puzzled as to why Roberts had not asked of the *Juliette*. Perhaps he did not expect such cooperation.

'And the Yorubans?'

'I mentioned them, but it brought about a very dark look indeed,' expounded the surgeon. 'They trust neither black nor white. I think they believe we would carry them to the coast and pack them in our ships.'

Roberts looked up, and raised a hand to silence Williams's anticipated objection. 'His Majesty turns all against us. We must protest.'

Most of the Fortunes had never fought a landed engagement in such number, but it was of great encouragement to them all that they were facing an unarmed enemy who had no knowledge of their intentions. The company was not dressed for the sake of camouflage, but in bright colours, outrageous clashings of reds, yellows and oranges, scarlet ribbons tied about tricorns, bows looped through hair. They would rush at the village, close upon dawn, but from the east, so that the Ibo would think they were being flushed by a thousand screaming suns. Each man took great care in preparing his pieces, priming then emptying and repriming until the motion was almost automatic. The march began in darkness, the column moving under the light of links, following Innocent as he snaked up to the crest of the plateau, and on to the escarp of shrub and lean trees. Once again Innocent marched through the day then through the night, until at first light on the second day he waved them to a silent standstill.

'Doctor,' said Roberts, seeking Scudamore out from among the first eager line of men, 'I do not think it wise for you to be so far afront. If you wish a closer look at blood perhaps you might hold back. You may staunch it as you walk.'

Scudamore looked down at his pair of pistols and lightly pressed his fingers to the trigger.

'Any fool can make another bleed,' added Roberts in low tones, 'but few can cease the flow.'

'Yes, yes,' said Scudamore nervously, 'you know, Captain, I do not feel secure in our convictions. Perhaps we might attempt one more bargain for trade.'

'Thrice applied, and thrice denied,' said Roberts. 'No man should treat another so.'

CHAPTER 42

The soldiers were set at the front of their column, marching in step, a thin line of red that heralded the unruly rabble, no man carrying less than two pairs of pistols, powder and ball, and a knife or sword. They did not hesitate in their march. Their numbers were too many, their noise now too great for any sudden surprise. They merely marched onwards, the line trembling with the glint of metal in first light, and then spread from a line of pointed verticality to a gloved hand, wide enough to envelop the village.

The initial fusillade issued by the *King Solomon*'s musketeers was the first and last display of order during the engagement. The villagers all seemed to pause for a divine moment of communal disbelief. They scattered under the advent of noise, naked children, women still rising from their tasks, men half drenched in sleep. The motion was odd, the movement of buzzing flies who chose not to settle. Some ran in circles, others from building to building, and, though cries arose, and a few men emerged from their huts grasping bows, no order was left among the victims.

There was little gunfire. The villagers who had armed themselves with bows and arrows or reached for spears were shot down immediately. The remainder were overwhelmed by the first muddy tide of Roberts's men, who howled their way from one end of the village to the other, then swept in upon themselves, like a wave returning from a cliff face.

After the initial maniacal burst, the morning turned to one of celebratory sport. The Fortunes separated into small hunting parties, clearing out the women and children who had run into the trees and the chest-high undergrowth and dragging them back into the centre of the village before executing them. Hardy gathered the smallest of the corpses, those of children of five years and less and, piercing the flesh underneath their chins, threaded vine out of their mouths, and hung them like lanterns from the largest of the trees.

The Fortunes removed one hundred and twenty bushels of grain from the Ibo warehouses and, leaving a pyre of flesh at the centre of the village, set about firing the buildings. The flames took hold as if the brittle structures were anxious to be engulfed, and the village erupted into a brilliant heated roar of branches embracing fire. The morning sun was obscured by a black and putrid smoke. Williams turned from the stench of burning meat and walked from the blood-drenched dirt, away from the village. He held his arms tight to his side, as if to prove to any who looked down upon him that he was blameless in the bloodshed.

Under the trails of smoke, Williams saw Innocent bending over the knee-high grasses. The surgeon joined by Williams's side, and together they approached the Dogon. He did not look up, intent on his business.

'Dear Lord,' said the surgeon, 'What savagery is this?'

'"There with a pitiless knife,"' quoted Innocent, standing over the brutalized body of the Ibo chief, '"they sliced his nose and ears off: they ripped away his genitals as raw meat for the dogs, and in their fury . . ."' Innocent paused, took careful aim, and brought his boarding axe downward, '". . . they lopped off his hands and feet."'

'You nigger bastard,' breathed Magnes, nearing the small congregation. His voice conveyed that he was thoroughly impressed by the body's devastation.

'Ask Williams,' said Innocent. 'I do this as Christ before.'

'Odd's plot,' breathed Williams slowly, staring down at where Innocent had bored a fleshy hole in between the chief's thighs. He wiped a hand across his eyes, pretending to wave away smoke.

'When Christ found Melanthius,' said Williams, 'in His kingdom . . .'

'The business,' said Innocent, 'is finished. Come, Christ also says, '"It is an impious thing to exult over the slain."'

Innocent took one step from the body, and then leaned over and wiped his bloody hands on the long grasses.

Though many bodies were burned, while some swayed from trees and still more lay still in the undergrowth surrounding the village, Roberts instructed his men to retreat as quickly as possible. If there were survivors, and the captain was forced to make the presumption, then their tragedy had transformed the living into messengers. The Fortunes had little knowledge of the terrain and no information of the surrounding countryside and they did not wish to fall foul of an Ibo war party. The curved teeth of elephants and the weaved baskets of grain were raised on to shoulders and they marched again.

Innocent, leading the returning column alongside his captain, began to recount the stories of his childhood. Only the permanent smirk on Roberts's face revealed that he had encouraged the Dogon's unusual garrulousness. Speaking with precise enunciation, Innocent told of the spiders who come after the rains and lay crystal webs to snare birds, of the hyenas whose cries are the harbingers of misery and death, and of the great lion, friend to the Ibo, who are said to trail and gut their enemies. During the last hours of daylight, the stories wound their way slowly back down the column and were the cause of amusement, more than a few imitative howls and roars. Marching through the darkness, the stories returned up the ranks, and a sudden feral coughing that arose from the bushes served to speed the column into daylight.

Their pace weakened at dawn, but fear had passed, and by sunset they reached the mouth of the Calabar, where the *Fortune* and *Ranger* rose to meet them. Innocent dismissed the Yorubans, then tilted his head at the captain and, in a clear Welsh accent, wished him good evening. Roberts tipped his tricorn in response, and they walked together towards the gig. There were no birds to be spied above them, no fish to be seen in the dark waters beneath, and the coast was deserted in either direction. Roberts looked at the emptiness that surrounded his command, and felt as if pressure were being exerted upon him in dread silent motions. Crew were content enough, water was fresh, prey expected. He dipped his tricorn in the water and brought the hat back upon his head. It was not a force exerted from outside, but from within.

The small number who had remained behind had filled the water barrels and, with alacrity and not a single tot of gin, the ships set sail. Once they had left the insect-laden coastal waters, several brace of the freshly killed fowl were tied off upon the lower shrouds and left to hang for three days. Finally, when Nanny deemed them ripe and seasoned for feasting, he lit a fire, and roasted them, three at a time. The fire was not dampened until the fifth day, when all fresh meat had been ingested and the wind had stirred the tails of the waves into lines of streaming white. The fire hissed and smoked and expired beneath a bucketful of salt water, as the *Fortune* pitched and rolled through the troughs with great ease. Morning brought a fresh set of gales and heavy rain. Yards and topmasts were lowered. The following evening the *Fortune*'s maintopsail split and its replacement, stolen from the *Joceline*, was hastily bent. No sooner was the sail bent than the wind died, the sun burned through a watery haze and the ocean died to swells gentle enough to rock a child to sleep.

Innocent sat below the fiddler, his legs draped over the sides of the top. They were steering for Cape Appolonia, a port that only Roberts and Innocent boasted any knowledge of. Initially Williams had clambered up the lower shrouds to jaw with the Dogon, talk to him of the lands to come, of what shipping frequented the coast so far south. Innocent did not acknowledge his presence, and even if he had been in a garrulous mood, the intermittent clap of the wind in the sails would have prevented anything other than a loud conversation that might have had the bosun whistling them to the deck. After his third attempt to hail Innocent, Williams retreated to his own world, automatically scanning the horizon for a sail, before sinking into thought and constructing his next entry:

I feel a confusion. I try to remove myself from the worst deeds of this ship, yet it is impossible, I am tied to its fate, closest to her captain and must obey his rule. The slaughter of the Ibo seemed senseless, yet I work beside the doctor, aiding in the staunching of blood. Above all, we are witnesses and if blood still turns me somewhat, then let it be so, let me record it, let me avoid it.

It seems that, despite all that has passed, an equilibrium has returned to Roberts that has been absent for some months. Since Crackers revealed the presence of His Majesty's warships, he has calmed instead of panicking. It is as if he has been flattered on a regal scale, receiving a bow of acknowledgment from King George himself. Perhaps he dwells more upon this than the Juliette, for he concentrates on filling our ranks with numbers enough to counter the king. Yet, if we do not find our Juliette, then surely such numbers will be divisive. It would take an admiral, not a captain, to maintain a command without our objective.

Discipline about the ships did indeed unravel with the additional numbers. Sympson began to add his own interpretations to the signed articles. It was not in outright contempt of their signed rules of conduct, and Roberts deemed it an obvious flexing of muscles. Talk had begun even before their success at Calabar, and those who talked most, such as Magnes and Sympson, murmured of their wishes to command. Williams presumed it was empty prate encouraged by full stomachs and pockets still heavy with gold.

The *Fortune* and the *Ranger* sailed towards Whydah, the most likely haven for the *Juliette*, through a thick haze broken by sudden squalls. They would spend the mornings under mainsails, then furl the courses and, by the time the sun dipped, would often be found scudding under bare poles. They dared not beat too close to land, lest one of the sudden storms decided to drive them on to the shores of the Gold Coast. On a night of thunder, where bulbous low clouds threatened rain, Roberts woke from a brief sleep. The swell had turned him back and forth and, while it had not disturbed his sleep, it had unsettled his mind, and all about him he felt the presence of the living God. He turned from his rest, and dressed only in breeches, the scars on his back white and shiny from sweat, he rose through the aft hatchway, to find Moody and Williams sharing a trick at the helm.

'Innocent?' shouted Roberts against the thunder.

Williams pointed to the fore tops.

The captain scaled the shrouds. He could see the bosun and his mate working above him on the fore t'gallant yard. They swung under bare poles, travelling sixty feet through the air with every roll of the *Fortune*. The captain pulled himself through the lubber hole. Innocent had his back propped against the foremast, and opened one eye to greet Roberts.

'Innocent,' said Roberts, 'I have been thinking on the *Juliette*. She comes to me in my sleep.'

The Dogon shook his head sadly, and glanced at the darkening haze that floated about them. A slight rain descended and hung about the skin like sweat.

'We have much in common,' said Roberts. Innocent let the words settle. He did not nod his head, nor dash into agreement. 'I have many men. I am no captain according to the powers of the navy. You have Yorubans. My chief mate is Hardy, yours Owaba.'

'Roberts,' said Innocent, 'you tell me there are two captains on one ship. It is not so. Why do you tell me so?'

'I wish to ask of you a favour.'

Roberts made to talk, but Innocent added, 'Then I also will ask favour.'

The captain nodded. He wished to spill the very dreams that had brought him so abruptly to the Dogon. 'I have seen my death before me. It comes fast. I am not due for hanging.' Innocent showed no emotion. 'If I am not drowned, I wish to be cast into the sea. Not buried, no psalms passed across my body. I charge you with this: raise me and cast me into the sea.'

Innocent nodded.

'Ensure I am dressed in my finest clothes.' The captain thrust his hand towards his neck, and pulled at the gold chains that formed a loose noose about him. 'I will be buried with gold.

Line my pockets if you will. I will pay my tolls at the ocean's bed. You will do this?'

'I swear upon Christ's blood,' said Innocent solemnly.

For the first time since Roberts had pulled himself through the lubber hole he allowed himself to rock back from his haunches. He unwound his legs before him, and emptied his lungs against the growing winds.

'I wish more men,' said Innocent.

'You wish an army?' asked Roberts. 'Or do you broaden the flock?'

'You tell me how we are alike. I say yes, I wish my own men. Soon my own ship.'

'You shall have them.'

'When?' asked Innocent. He had learned from bargaining with Roberts upon Hispaniola that, though the captain was true to his word, his word was subject to a personal interpretation. By sticking the particulars, Innocent hoped to force Roberts's hand.

'Whydah,' said Roberts.

'How many?' insisted Innocent.

'What number do you wish?' countered Roberts.

'One hundred,' said Innocent coolly.

'You shall have fifty in Whydah.'

Innocent nodded and smiled at his captain. Roberts rose and lowered himself around the outside of the foretop. Innocent appeared and, holding on to the shroud, offered a hand to Roberts.

'Tip daddles,' said Innocent and, with the first full smile that Roberts had ever seen from the Dogon, they shook hands over their respective promises.

The port of Whydah appeared after seven days of rains and intermittent winds. Smoke had gathered over it, black mist of ashes that rose to thicken the low ceiling of cloud. Flying an English ensign, the *Ranger* tacked close on the port but, finding few ships moored, came about and returned to within hailing distance of the *Fortune*. Together, they passed down the coast, an anxiety beginning to boil among the crew. Whydah was the richest, the most active port, but it had lain empty, even of the *Juliette*. Either their timing had been inexpert, the tale of their arrival had preceded them, or there had been news of fresh supplies of slaves close by.

Thirteen ships were anchored not six leagues east of Whydah. It was a peculiar place to land, large breakers exhausting themselves on beaches in all directions. In conditions as poor as these it was customary for the slavers to be escorted into and out of the beach by those more familiar with the crash of the waves. When slaves were bought, it was a poor effort to lose them within minutes to European ineptitude.

Both the *Fortune* and the *Ranger* anchored in the road alongside the mainly English and Dutch slavers. There were no interlopers, Whydah being too well patrolled for letterless ships to expect commercial consideration. Roberts sent Williams as the chief delegate in a tour of the thirteen vessels, none of which, to a ship, were manned by more than twelve hands. Most men were ashore with their captains, trading for and selecting slaves and competing against countrymen. While the presence of Magnes and Hardy ensured that William Williams was not taken lightly, the resident mates maintained that they had little of value, few ships having reprovisioned for the journey west, and all begging that their gold had been taken ashore for trading.

A meeting of the Lords was called for, the Commons now too vast, unruly and drunk to be any help whatsoever. It was settled that each of the slavers might be returned to her captain for seven pounds of gold dust. There were few volunteers to accompany Williams ashore until, amid the silent stares of the reluctant, Owaba offered to land among the breakers. Innocent joined their small party, and they were lowered into a slim pettiauger, taken from the Liverpudlian *Porcupine*, a grubby vessel, already low in the water and considerably overslaved.

Their craft waited patiently behind the breakers. No man had trusted Williams with a sweep, and he sat clenching the sides of the narrow vessel. Innocent was in the bow, Owaba at the stern and, at the Yoruban's cry, they beat a quick rhythm towards the sloping waves, and suddenly were among them. Caught in between the cresting formations, Williams could see neither land nor a single mast of the fifteen anchored ships. It was an angry, liminal world, where rock was humbled to sand and horizons were mocked and obscured by the enormous shadows of raking waves. When Williams tried to turn to watch a wave loom behind them, he was slapped across the face by Owaba. The Yoruban gestured that he should look only ahead.

Riding on deafening tails of white, they were thrown towards the beach. All save Williams jumped from the pettiauger, seized her sides and ran fast through the receding water before the next wave might break upon them. Their progress was watched by a large contingent, numbering close on forty. Few had even brought their arms to shore.

As they moved towards the slavers Williams could see their professional eyes creep about the Yorubans and the Dogon. A lean man, with shoulders so rounded that his arms appeared to grow from his neck, stepped out from the gathering to address Williams upon his approach. He wore an old French drummer's coat, pleated and hanging to his knees, dusty and ragged, but still having most of its twenty gold buttons. His eyes travelled between the black flags and the young man who stood before him. Innocent stopped on Williams's right, Owaba on his left. The remainder of the Yorubans stood behind their doctor.

'You have our ships, we have you. Tis an equal trade,' stated the man.

'Sir,' said Williams, 'do not presume that you

407

deal with fools. Look about you. I am but a fiddler, sent among blackamoors. To keep me from my business would be to ensure that e'ry ship is fired.'

'If we trade not with you, then with what?'

'Gold, sir.'

'He wishes gold for our own ships?' The brown drummer's coat turned to consult with his fellows. The question was repeated quickly among them, in both English and French.

'Twenty pounds of dust would do.'

'Sir,' said an English captain, 'there is bare twenty pounds 'tween us. My ship is full slaved.'

'You came to stroll upon the beach?'

The man smiled in silence.

'I will pay five pound for my ship. Tis sense gentleman. Think on your cargo,' said another, his voice smoothed by French accent.

'I will not leave without a receipt,' said a Dutchman.

'Of course, sir,' said Williams, 'it shall be forthcoming.'

'I know you,' said another, pointing at Innocent.

'Who are you, sir?' asked Williams.

'Fletcher, captain of the *Porcupine*. This man's a Corso negro. Trader.'

Innocent did not glance at the man, nor acknowledge his presence. Fletcher turned to the fiddler. 'I shall do no business with you. Not an ounce. My ship is not worth the sum demanded.'

'The *Porcupine* is a poor tub, tis true,' said Williams, 'but do not separate her worth from her cargo, lest you make the gravest error.'

'I will have no business with your kind,' confirmed Captain Fletcher.

'I shall explain your wishes to my captain, and return forthwith.' Williams gave a low bow, removing his uncocked hat from his head to reveal the missing patches of sandy hair, and then retreated to where the Yorubans had settled upon the beach.

The conversation on the *Fortune* was muted by the constant pounding of the breakers. Occasionally there would be a brief respite, no more than a second of silence, and the next wave, even larger and louder against the quietude, would shatter with a clamorous reminder of the ocean's power.

'It seems,' said Williams, 'that though most are close to slav'd, a party came down river with thirty blacks.'

'Yoruban?' asked Roberts.

'I did not stand to consider,' returned Williams. 'They were not kindly disposed to me, seeing my mission as competitive to their own. I shall return for the gold. They request a receipt of me.'

'Indeed?' asked Roberts, smiling.

'The Dutch especially. They presume it a better thing to account to their owner with the proof before them. I deemed it a fair trade and returned for ink and paper ... a moment, if you will.'

While Williams retreated to the captain's cabin to prepare a sealskin wallet of receipts, including both the finest of his quills and the bottle of the disappearing genipa ink, Innocent searched out Roberts.

'I wish the men upon the shore,' said Innocent, sidling so close to Roberts that he might have touched his tongue between his lips and licked the captain's ear.

'Tis a tricky business,' whispered Roberts. 'See five into the longboat with you. Visit the ships already stocked. Gather the men of your choice.'

'Fifty men,' said Innocent, reminding the captain of his promise.

'No more,' said Roberts.

Williams was moving at such an eager pace when he emerged from the hatchway that he caught his left foot upon a strut by the capstan and fell to his knees. Recovering his balance, and a portion of his dignity, he stood. The doctor appeared behind him.

'Innocent shall not return with you,' said Roberts.

'I shall take Scudamore in his place,' answered Williams.

The captain nodded.

'Fine day,' said Scudamore.

'No wandering, nor mapmaking, nor sketching of natives,' said Roberts. 'We shall not hang close to Whydah.'

They nodded obediently.

'There was . . .' added Williams, 'one commander. His ship the . . . *Porcupine*, an Englishman. He protested and dared us to do what we would.'

'Echo once more, his ship will be fired.' He turned from Williams and Scudamore, and summoned Innocent. 'Empty the *Porcupine* of her cargo. If she holds plenty, you may choose your men from her.'

Williams turned to the surgeon, 'We are close to the *Juliette*. Can you not taste her, Mr Scudamore?'

CHAPTER 43

Williams, having successfully returned to the beach, set up table on a palm stump. He used small stones to weigh his papers against the wind, then asked the captains to step forward, alone, so that he might make out their receipts. Dipping his quill in the ink of the genipa fruit, he inscribed:

This is to certify whom it may or doth concern, that we Gentlemen of Fortune *have received eight pounds of gold dust, for the ransom of the* Hardey, *Captain Dittwitt commander, so that we discharge the said ship.*
   Witness our hands,
   this 13th of January 1721–1722
                                       William Williams
                                       Bartholomew Roberts

The doctor was looking over the case of an unfortunate seaman who had had his ankle snapped navigating the breakers. Occasionally the fiddler could hear the man's pained cries rise over the crash of the waves.

'Does this cause pain?' asked the doctor, and pushed down just above the man's ankle. The mate of the *Carlton*, out of London, stood over his charge.

'Argghh,' he screamed.

'And this?' said the doctor, probing another spot.

'Arghhh,' repeated the man.

'Once more?' asked Scudamore.

'Argghh,' he insisted.

The mate leaned over Scudamore's administrations.

'Do you seek your freedom, doctor?' asked the mate.

'Sorry sir?' asked Scudamore.

'Do you wish to be freed of the robbers?'

''Tis an amusing question, coming from a slaver, no?' asked Scudamore, peering up from the ankle. 'No, sir, thank you kindly, I need no rescuing. I am of prodigious use aboard the *Fortune*, sir, uncommonly appreciated and unbothered.'

'They will have you hanged,' warned the mate simply.

'There are few professions,' continued Scudamore, 'save your own, where in times of peace a man may witness death as I have. I could name you a thousand deaths worse than hanging, and many sir, might be caught in land such as this.' Scudamore sniffed at the air suspiciously, and smiled as the mate unconsciously imitated his actions. The doctor returned to the more difficult task of making a splint for the deckhand.

Within the hour, the ink of twelve receipts already dry, one hundred and six pounds of gold dust lay at William Williams's feet. He opened the first of the bags and ran the fine grains through his hands. Carrying it from under the shade of the palm, he waited until the sun squinted against the riches to confirm it as gold. He separated the bags between them, no man caring for more than two. The doctor, having comforted the injured sailor to the best of his abilities, tied lanyards about his own cuffs and attached the bags. For the last time, the fiddler approached Captain Fletcher of the *Porcupine* and made the same offer as he had made to the other captains. Again Fletcher declined the proposition.

'What shall you do,' asked Williams, 'when you see her afire?'

'I only hope that Mr Roberts sees how un-Christian an act he meditates.'

'You have,' said Williams, 'a touch more hope than you should presume. Just a touch.'

Fletcher nodded, then turned on his heels and marched to where the captains of the ships sat in a circle, contemplating the righteousness of their actions. They watched doctor, scribe and the Yorubans gather the gold, then right their pettiauger and turn to the ocean.

The responsibility of the gold weighed heavy upon Williams. He wiggled in the pettiauger,

414

concentrated on finding his perfect centre of balance, but was distracted by the swells that gathered, thrusting themselves at the shore as if they wished to suck life back into the sea. They pushed off through the surf, prepared to ride the crest of the first wave, and plummeted down her back. Williams, leaning to the side, wobbled. He felt the whole craft turning under the oncoming wave, was sure that they would perish, and then realized, as he leaned too far to the right that the pettiauger had corrected itself. The oncoming surge caught the fiddler's hand and tore him from the boat.

He was turned three times underneath the water until he no longer knew where the air could be reached. Swallowing a gritted mixture of salt and sand, he found himself knocked by a second wave, with his lungs so pained that he thought his insides would combust in a bloody explosion. The gold, tied to his belt, seemed helpless to anchor him against the currents that moved silently beneath the breakers. The power of the water turned his legs over his head, landing him squarely on his knees in six inches of sandy water. As soon as he wheezed air into his sodden lungs, he let loose a thin stream of vomit. He checked his body for the two bags of gold dust, located them, and them plumped back on to his arse and walked side and backwards like a crab, out of the edge of the surf. The group of captains watched him from beneath the shade of the palms. None moved to help him.

It took a quarter of an hour for the Yorubans to make it out past the breakers and then be persuaded by the doctor that, though they were correct and the fiddler was a fool for falling from the pettiauger, they should return to the beach to see if the gold at least had washed ashore. Grudgingly, they complied. Williams was retrieved and made to lie in the bottom of the vessel. It was a position he was grateful for. His fear of the breakers had not diminished with his survival, but his respect for the ocean herself had multiplied once more.

'A beneficial dip?' asked the doctor cheerfully.

Williams shook his head, then managed a weak smile, and revealed to his friend the two bags of gold that still hung about his waist.

'An extraordinary assumption of priorities,' concluded Scudamore.

Innocent was already aboard the *Porcupine*. He had ordered all the slaves brought on deck. Many sat shivering, despite the sun. They were not Yorubans, mostly Ibo, and Innocent did not wish to pick his men from among them. Still he paused to examine the misery of over two hundred men, women and children. He knew, from days of trading in Corso, how some had already spent weeks in their fetters. A few must already have perished. He called for a woman to approach him and bent her across his knee. The flux had begun. One Ibo played a flute in the corner. He could only coax three notes from it, and their dull repetition was smeared with a doleful acceptance. Calling orders for the two longboats that rode under the *Porcupine*'s aft to pull for her waist, Innocent stepped into the bow and moved to the neighbouring ship, the *Carlton*.

The Fortunes gathered about the Yorubans as they placed their gold around the mizzen mast. It was a painless wealth, created through threat, without even the waste of a single cannonball. Roberts's eyes darted from bag to bag.

'*Porcupine*?' he asked.

'Presumes on your mercy,' said Williams, adding his two bags to the pile.

'Remove her cargo,' said Roberts, 'then fire her. Be quick about it. We sail at once.'

Bunch, Williams, Moody and Nanny, accompanied by ten of the Yorubans, pulled their crowded gig across to a Frenchman, the *Count de Thoulouze*, where they immediately requisitioned her longboat. They transferred their buckets of pine tar that would aid in the speed and intensity of the conflagration of the *Porcupine*. Williams dipped his finger in the thick substance, then wiped it repeatedly on his britches. His finger remained blackened.

They found the *Porcupine* in a similar state to how Innocent had left it. Slaves, men fettered in pairs, women alone. The deck could hardly be seen beneath the intertwined bodies of the

417

cargo. Bunch was first aboard, and after a brief consultation with the five remaining members of her crew, disappeared beneath deck with them in search of casks and canvas that might add to the birth of the bonfire.

The *Carlton* shared the same vehement odours of shit and rotten detritus as the *Porcupine*, but her cargo was fresh in comparison. More importantly to Innocent, he had located a ship stocked almost entirely with Yorubans. It was not that he had a profound respect for the tribe, but he trusted Owaba and had faith in the man's power over his people. He believed that his choices would soon evolve into a well-run crew. African sailors, who might sail under his command for the seven long years ahead.

Seated in the bow of the boat, Williams picked at his teeth with the long nail of his forefinger. 'How many?' he asked, and jabbed his finger upward at the *Porcupine*.

'One hundred men. Sixty-eight women. Fourteen children,' said her first mate.

Moody leaned over the waist of the ship and, hanging to the lower shrouds, called to Williams.

'Hundreds of 'em up here,' he said. 'How many'll we take?'

'Forty now,' said Williams, turning his head to examine the capacity of the longboat.

Bunch had herded the Ibos to the bow of the

boat. He slopped the pine tar across the quarter-deck, then trailed it down the steps towards the mainmast. Nanny emerged from the aft hatchway, a bundle of canvas rags under his arm. He dropped them to the quarterdeck. Eight of the Yorubans lowered themselves into the longboat. Moody followed.

'And who exactly,' asked Williams, 'is going to be lowering the negroes down?'

Moody shrugged.

'Who has the key to their fetters?' inquired the fiddler.

'Dunno,' mumbled Moody.

'Captain stressed speed.'

'Come on now, you bastards,' cried Moody, standing in the boat, rocking it back and forth.

No reply came from above. Still the same simple three notes from the flute.

Wisps of clouds passed overhead. The remaining two Yorubans descended. The clouds grew thicker.

''Tis smoke,' whispered Williams. 'Bunch, Nanny,' he cried. 'What happens on deck?'

Bunch appeared at the waist, and began to lower himself. Nanny followed close behind.

'Cast off,' shouted Nanny. A cry of panic came from above. It was joined by a second scream and the sound of the flute ceased.

Nanny landed in the bow of the longboat.

'Cast off,' he cried. 'She is afire.'

Williams turned to Bunch. 'The negroes?'

'Do you wish to burn with them?' asked Bunch, and propelled them from the ship with a pull of his oar.

There came the sound of a muffled explosion from the hold, a barrel of powder sparked. The first lick of fire spat from a gun port on the starboard side, and the chaotic sound of panic raged across the deck and travelled very clearly across the water to where the nineteen men sat watching from the gig and the longboat. The emptiness of their own craft was apparent to them all.

'Did you release their darbies?' shouted Williams to Nanny and Bunch.

Nanny stared at the *Porcupine*. Bunch shook his head.

Innocent, prodding the last of the Yorubans aboard the *Fortune*, ignored the stares of his shipmates and walked straight to the quarterdeck, where Roberts stood, looking across the water to the *Porcupine*.

'Fifty,' said Innocent. 'From *Carlton*.'

Roberts did not respond.

'Fifty,' repeated Innocent, and when still the captain did not answer, he followed the man's gaze across to the smoke breathing from the *Porcupine*'s gun ports.

The boards of the ship were dry. Her quarterdeck, smothered in pitch, erupted into flames and the crackle of fire sounded like a sharp gust of wind cracking sail. The timber began to heat before it caught fire. Some of the slaves, pushed in panic against the bow, began to climb along the bowsprit, edging out along the martingale towards the jibboom. Two small children, the only Ibo in sight who were not chained, had begun to climb the foremast.

Bunch and Nanny pulled on their sweeps and edged the longboat further from the *Porcupine*.

'Pull her about,' ordered Williams. 'We'll pass under the bowsprit.'

'No such thing,' said Nanny. 'They'll sink us.'

'I'll not sit here,' said Williams, and rose, peeling his shirt from his body as if he made to enter the water. Moody grabbed him by the britches and pulled him down to his seat.

'Tis wasting ground,' said Moody. 'Thick with shark.'

The flames approached the first of the Ibo. Already, the topmast capstay and the topgallant backstay had been seared apart. Fire engulfed the main stay. In moments the mast fell forward, separating as it fell, throwing one of the children climbing the foremast shrouds back to the deck. The other continued to climb. Those standing closest to the approaching flames held their hands up against the heat, but a gust of wind burned them like dragon's breath. Two leaped overboard, sinking quick as stones under the heavy iron manacles.

The screams stopped within ten minutes. Most had met the fire. The child hanging to the fore topgallant yard could not commit himself to the air. Williams had convinced those in the longboat to row close, and called out against the flames for the child to leap. If they might pluck him quickly, he might still be saved. But the flames rose until they closed around him, and he did not drop, but hung, wound about the yard, a tiny charred body, adding to the choking stench of smouldering flesh.

Williams counted almost twenty fins that moved about the water of the *Porcupine*. He looked about and none would meet his gaze. The Yorubans pulled upon their sweeps. All looked down.

Even Bunch seemed immersed in his own shame. The shell of the *Porcupine* remained afloat, a blackened testimonial, still held by her anchor and cable.

'We are bound for hell,' said Williams. 'E'ry one of us.'

They pulled in silence back towards the *Fortune* and, coming aboard, did not pause to consider the gold heaped about the mizzen. The deck was thick with men, Fortunes, the crew of the *Porcupine* and the Yoruban slaves that Innocent had selected from the *Carlton*.

'Mr Williams,' ordered Roberts, approaching the fiddler, 'You will tell me what happened.'

They passed down the aft hatchway, and did not speak until the captain closed the door of his cabin behind him.

'I wish I could, sir,' said Williams, 'I was in the boats with the Porcupines. Moody came down first. Then the last of the Yorubans. Nanny next. Bunch last.'

'Who set fire?'

Williams shrugged.

'It does not matter,' breathed Roberts. 'Not a whit, not the wings of a bird. Tis all the same. They will say I've done this. Sit down, man, sit down. Tell them the truth of the matter.'

Williams drew himself up to the table, and an anxious Roberts stood behind him for close on an hour. Though he could not read a single word of Williams's coded French, he pored intently over the writing, as if his very presence brought the guarantee of truth:

He stands above me and wishes a report of the matter. I cannot write of it. Burned flesh is still heavy in my clothes. I know what he told me afore. That a man in chains is not a man, but it is not true. Or even were it true, that is not a fate I would condemn a pack of dogs to. I am thick with shame. I write only that he may think I translate the truth. I will have none of it. None of it. If a man observes, but does not act – I presumed that innocence was inaction, but what if I am wrong? What if innocence requires reaction? I wish the Juliette *and then a departure from these shores.*

After ten minutes, Williams paused and, swivelling in his seat, asked Roberts if he could make a list of the men recruited from the slavers. He could not look his captain in the eye, but had to change the mood of his mind.

'And the new blackamoors?' asked Williams. 'What manner of men are they?'

'Yoruban.'

'We are uncommon crowded,' whispered Williams.

'Owaba is almost returned to his home. He asks Innocent if he is free to take his leave. I insist he remains until the day we find the *Juliette*.' Roberts clapped his hands together softly. 'Tis easier if he should take on the students. Unless you would rather repeat the process.'

'I welcome their presence,' said Williams, after a considered pause.

'You see,' said Roberts, 'still we have damned more souls than we have saved.'

CHAPTER 44

Bartholomew Roberts's crew were, once again, men of substance. They were well provisioned, having removed the remainder of the livestock from the slavers in the Whydah road. Besides, there was gold in every man's pocket, and not a limb lost between them. To Roberts's despair, under orders from the quartermaster, a vast space in the *Fortune*'s hold had been devoted to gin, rum, beer and wines taken from each of the captured ships.

There was no murmur, not even a trace of dissent, as Roberts informed the crew that they would careen at Cape Lopez. Williams was watching the captain closely. He could not figure whether the edge of desperation in Roberts's voice was a device used to silence complaints, or a genuine disturbance. Perhaps his position as commodore of a squadron of three ships and over two hundred men had unnerved him. The fiddler did not believe this. He knew it had to be the burning of the *Porcupine*, knew that Roberts often dwelled upon judgements and, while he excused himself from the laws of man, he feared God more than any hand aboard.

Cape Lopez was a calculated choice of destination. Surrounded by an intricate set of sandbanks, it was an impenetrable fortress for shallow-drafted ships such as the *Fortune, Ranger* and the *Count de Thoulouze*. Though most of the Royal Navy's vessels were mere sloops, frigates or snows, Roberts only feared the ships of the line. The banks of Cape Lopez would provide adequate protection from the fifty guns of the *Swallow* and the *Weymouth* and a fine plateau to spy for the *Juliette*.

The *Fortune* had been pulled on to her larboard side by the crew. The *Ranger* and the *Count de Thoulouze* sat in the shallows offshore watching their wounded brethren. Roberts had counted the full complement of his men the day before. Two hundred and twenty-one. Encamped on the shore, collapsed in the shade of canvas lean-tos or gathered in groups around dice and cards, they constituted an entire village. It included the untested, the liberated, the old hands and the lubbers, the godless and the fearful. He was apart from them. Strange faces tipped their hats as he walked among their company. Whether or not the acknowledgements came from a genuine reverence, even the most cynical among them appreciated his longevity and success. A man, melted by fierce fire so that his neck and visage were joined and the chin destroyed, stopped Roberts as he walked past. He handed his captain a pouch of tobacco, and nodded again and again as Roberts filled his pipe. He blew on the end of

426

a stick, and pressed the ember into the bowl of his captain's pipe.

'What ship are you?'

'Tom Robbins of the *Carlton*.'

Roberts nodded, examining the man's face.

'Spain,' he said in explanation, and ran his hand down the thick scars of his neck. Then, ''Tis long now for the *Juliette*, Captain?'

'No,' said Roberts. '*Swallow* and *Weymouth* soon upon us. Tis time to leave these seas.'

'They'd be up at Corso, no?'

'I would not trust news from eyes and ears other than my own. We'll be safe from Her Majesty when we've sailed and he knows not where.'

'There is a cove called Armstrong.' Tom Robbins coughed hard, and spat into the sand. 'Came with us fore Whydah. Ran from the *Swallow*. Could not take bosun who could not take him.'

'I would like to meet Armstrong,' said the captain.

'He would be as pleased himself,' added Robbins.

The process of careening did not go as smoothly as the commodore wished. Though Roberts would have liked to bury the blame for their ineffectiveness under the discarded casks of gin, it was a cruel climate. All morning the equatorial sun would burn so fiercely that even the darker of the Europeans, such as Roberts, could feel their skin sear. Those who drank hard were plagued by variations of gout, and the surgeon was busier than the crew of all

427

three of the ships together. Most suffered only from swollen ankles, where the alcohol seemed to have pooled in the heat, and Scudamore lanced and squeezed the liquids on to baked sands.

Each afternoon, black clouds rolled over the rain forests, miles inland from the marshes and sandbanks of the coast. They brought with them a thunder and lightning that silenced the drunkest of men, and then spat sharp rains that ran up and down the beach, leaving pellet marks upon the sand. The crew sat beneath their leaking canvas tents, and pulled their hats around their ears. Between the heat of the day and the daily release of the heavens, there was little time to organize work parties. Sympson would attempt to stir the men between six and nine before the sun rose high, but the efforts were always tempered by the spirits consumed. On two occasions Roberts attempted to locate the deserter Armstrong of the *Swallow*. Both times he found him in heavy sleep, where even the end of a boot in the small of his back did not disturb the man from his slumber.

Roberts was disturbed under the thatch of his own lean-to during the death of an afternoon thunderstorm. 'Ah,' he said from his private darkness, 'the Yoruban delegation.'

Innocent and Owaba arranged themselves with crossed legs opposite the captain. The Dogon pointed at the Yoruban. 'We have talked for many days. Owaba has come to understand Christ and we petition you in his name.'

'"The plunder,"' quoted Owaba from Innocent's teachings, '"is taken and divided so that no man lacks his rightful share."'

'Tis in the articles,' shrugged Roberts.

'Tis also written,' added Innocent, 'that host should let his guest leave according to his own wishes.'

'You wish to leave?' asked Roberts.

Owaba nodded.

'And you?' Roberts asked Innocent.

The Dogon shook his head. 'I remain.'

Roberts wagged a finger at Owaba. 'I am not your host, nor you my guest. We have a written agreement. Do you have faith in it?'

'No,' said Owaba. His tattooed brow creased as he spat the word.

Roberts laughed. 'Will you take my word as oath and promise?'

'Yes.'

'I shall not remove you from your coast.'

'Many months?' asked Innocent.

'I tire of Africa,' said Roberts, shaking each man by the hand. 'One month – no more.'

There were no promontories within calling distance of their fleet, so watch was kept from the main topsail of the *Ranger*. The outgoing watch would merely row the gig to the beach, rouse his successors and watch their own progress to the *Ranger*, before catching drink, smoke, sleep. The remainder of the time was spent upon gambling. Cards were marked, fulhams discovered, and fights frequent. Roberts could not comprehend the attitude of his crew. There were no women to squander their pelf upon, no taverns, no news of hometowns and friends in the trade. He had presumed that they would attend to the careening with an eagerness so that they might reach a port where they could woo women with full pockets.

Despite the fact that no man worked more than two hours of the day, by February the *Fortune* was almost smooth-bottomed and smoked. Perhaps an unconscious understanding of their own boredom had finally been attained. On the very day that Williams led a party aboard the *Fortune* to scrub her down with vinegar, sand and sea water, a cry came from the *Ranger*'s fore top.

Roberts himself climbed the shrouds of the *Ranger* and pulled the glass away from the unfamiliar who held it. He sat patiently, the ratline caught in the crook of his elbow. After three hours, he descended relieved. It was merely one sail, and not the power of the *Swallow* and the *Weymouth*. Despite his serenity, Roberts called for reports on the half-hour. By nightfall, it had been decided that the sail was heading directly towards their squadron. Though Roberts remained strangely composed, it took little time for the sail to be supposed the *Juliette*.

There were no lack of volunteers to fill the *Ranger*. The Lords, however, remained faithful to the *Fortune*, and the captaincy of her sister ship was handed to another Welshman, James

Skyrme, who replaced his uncocked hat with a sateen tricorn, and asked the surgeon to retie his pair of red ponytails so that he might look the part. Come morning, the sail was still headed for them but, under clear light, two hours after the rise of the sun, she spotted the black flag flying from the *Ranger*, and wore, heading fast for the open sea. The *Ranger*'s maincourse was unfurled and, with one hundred and thirteen men aboard, they soon came under full sail, hoping to catch her quickly. His Lords held their fury at their captain and it was only when Magnes seconded Roberts's opinion that it was not the *Juliette* that a calm returned.

In the *Ranger*'s absence, the watch was doubled. Roberts had caught something of the ship through the glass. She was undoubtedly a large vessel, three-masted and lying low in the water. Perhaps a Portuguese, laden with sugar. If it was so, then she would not outsail the *Ranger* for long. No man expected to see her sails soon, an excuse for even greater lethargy. Only Nanny, busy at his pot, and Scudamore, forever wiping his instruments against his britches, could be considered active in any way that was of use to their expedition.

Williams kept his journal faithfully. He was called upon frequently for play at his fiddle, but his position, though not equal to the Lords, was of such consideration that he was bothered less and less. Always he noticed Bunch's absence. For a short while their mutual dislike had been replaced by a professional association and an enjoyment of their respective roles. Now, with Williams witness to Bunch's late departure from the *Porcupine*, the cabin boy avoided the fiddler. It was a matter that he did not wish to discuss, even though, in truth, Williams had no wish to discuss it either.

I have considered my own misfortunes – crimping, a case of gleet, Catrin's death, dropsy, fever, scurvy, the burning of the Porcupine. *I am either a lucky man or blind to omens of demise. It has been so long since I have even turned my thoughts to home. Perhaps this is foolish. I now have a journal that, published, would be thicker than my thigh. And if these signs are begging for my return, then perhaps the time is nigh. There is gold in my pocket, over two hundred piece and that which shall be taken from the* Juliette. *How can I say my farewell? To Scudamore, Moody, Innocent? To Roberts? I shall betray no man. I shall have talk with the captain. It is after all, his own intention that I return. Besides, we are now a fleet of three ships. Many men. Too many men, we are a colony. To walk about the shore is to greet good friends in sandy streets, to make the introductions of strangers, to share gin and tales. An absence of one shall not be missed, especially if I aim my departure for the time of celebration.*

Dawn was interrupted by a cry louder than any farmyard rooster. A ship, creeping through the night, was close upon the cape, sailing before

432

the wind. Even the direst of inebriates staggered to their feet to watch the masts pass over the headland. It was not the *Ranger*, nor the ship she had pursued, for both carried three masts. This intruder was a snow, carrying a fore and aft trysail from a slender pole aft of her mainmast. Despite clear sight of the two larger ships, she continued towards them.

The *Neptune* had sought out Roberts's squadron, and came bearing the good wishes of Crackers. Though the *Neptune*'s intention was to engage in trading, the fact that she had found them caused Roberts to feel great unease. He watched their gig pull up to their beach head, and stepped forward to greet her commander. Captain Hill, dressed in white britches of unnatural cleanliness and a blue dress coat marked with buttons carved from the spines of shark, was a sly man. To look at him was to gaze upon a face that could not be trusted, and yet, when he talked, his words were so sweet, so disarming in their weighted innocence that they called for an immediate re-examination of his features. After all, his beak was not so pronounced. Perhaps it was the sun that caused his eyes to hide beneath their lids, and the scar that he wore like a chin strap was most likely the unfortunate result of a noble action.

The visiting captain caught Robert's hand firmly in both of his.

'Captain,' said Hill, 'it has been long since I first heard tell of your name.'

Roberts nodded and withdrew his hand.

'You are not well liked among traders, nor soldiers.'

'And what manner of man are you?' asked Roberts.

'A friend,' said Hill, and clapped Roberts upon the back. 'Do not worry yourself, Captain, I am not the worm but the magpie and come to trade for the glitter of your gold. They talk of your wealth from Wimbe to the Isle of Saints.'

'Then you may stay among us,' said Roberts and returned Hill's amicable gestures with an overly heavy slap on his back. Hill coughed. 'You will find many soft pigeons to prey on,' continued Roberts. 'Give them drink and then strip them of their gold.'

Hill nodded twice, unbalanced by his host.

The Neptunes were welcomed in the encampment as the bearers of news and wares. Carrying with him limitless yards of cottons and silks, the finest clothes of the European courts, Captain Hill gifted the crew a case of fine wine and immediately found himself in their favour. While the Fortunes sorted through the clothes, fingering the materials until their edges began to blacken with dirt, Hill was being rowed shoreward again, having recovered a heavy box, mysteriously draped by a golden cloth. He had his men remove it carefully from the gig, and carry it towards Nanny's fire, where it was deposited, adjacent to the largest of the iron pots.

'What would that be?' asked Moody in passing,

and attempted to lift the skirt of the material to peek inside. Hill slapped at his hand.

'Tis for the entertainment of those who aspire to gentility.'

'Then I'd wager you are lost,' said Moody, and resumed his walk.

Hill sat by the covered box until night fell and the drinking was well underway. After all had eaten of a stew of porcupine and shellfish, he twisted his shark bone buttons, removed a miniature pistol from his belt, and fired it into the air.

'Come gentlemen,' he said, 'let us gather round.'

To a man, their interest was aroused. They formed a circle around Captain Hill, the Lords and Roberts closest to the golden drape. Hill cleared his throat, called for attention once more and then began. 'Two hundred years before the birth of Christ, Hero of Alexandria, a man of vast erudition and inquiry, did stumble upon an invention.' Hill patted the cloth twice. There was the faint sound of liquids bubbling. 'Lost for five hundred years, it fell into my possession in the eastern seas. What did I trade for it? You may ask yourself, "What *did* he trade for it?"'

'Go on,' shouted Magnes.

'My own sister, sir. So great was such a thing that the ties of blood, the morality of such an action was overshadowed by the advent of . . .' Once again he tapped upon the golden sheet.

'On with it,' cried Bunch.

'And why not, sir?' asked Hill. 'For the gentle-men of *Fortune*, I show you a sight ne'er held by kings' eyes for five centuries.' With a half-bow and a great flourish of his left hand, Captain Hill stripped the cloth from the cage.

Sitting on the branch of a ceramic tree were four birds, coloured silver and gold. On the trunk of the tree sat a bright red owl, his back turned to his prey. A rumble moved through the Fortunes. They did not know what they were looking at, and gathered closer as if proximity might lead to understanding.

'They are statues,' said Sympson from the first row.

'Invented a statue? Tis like inventing a stone,' called Bunch. The grand joke evoked withering laughter, directed both at the motionless birds and Captain Hill, who stood silently by their side. When the laughter continued, Hill made one slow circle of his discovery. Finally, there was silence.

'They are not birds. This is no owl,' said Hill. 'They are automata. Made from the finest metals in the known world. Neither,' he continued, 'are they statues. A statue is what?'

'Stone,' called Magnes.

'And stone cannot move of its own accord, nor can it speak nor sing. One moment of silence is all I beg of you.'

His request was granted, and in the sudden serenity the sound of chirping birds could be heard coming from the metallic throats of the thrushes. The Fortunes did not take a breath between them. The birds cocked their heads first to the left and then to the right as they continued their tune. Even Williams, skilled in the pitch and placement of music, thought that their song was as sweet as any he had heard in field or hedgerow. After a full minute of their perfect singing, the red owl suddenly swivelled his head, and the four birds each flapped their wings once in fright and ceased their melody. It was supposed to be a comic finale, but the Fortunes were so entranced by the contraption that they did not think to laugh.

'Again,' said Roberts, and Hill, bowing deep to the silence, made one more circle of his design and the thrushes once again lifted their voices, and the owl once again turned his back upon his prey. Hill reset his machine six times before the first man moved from the galley fires. When Hill saw that interest had waned only a touch, he threw the golden drape back over the machine, and bowed before them.

'Tis a mechanism of extreme delicacy,' said Hill, 'and while it would be a delight for the performance to be repeated on the morrow, tonight we must put our birds to sleep.'

The tune that the mechanical birds had sung sifted through Roberts's head throughout the night, and woke him from his sleep twice. Men still drank around him, and talked not of the *Ranger*, but of the extraordinary property of Captain Hill. While Roberts admired the intricacy and the achievement of movement without life, it seemed a diversion. Come the morning, he vowed, he would not sit and pass the time listening to the avian chorus, but would take himself alone, and hunt along the marshland of Cape Lopez.

It was the third time that Roberts had rowed himself alone in a gig since their arrival in Cape Lopez. He found the doctor and the fiddler engaged in discussion about their morning walk. They watched as the captain dropped his gaming pieces into the bottom of the gig. He pushed off without greeting his men.

'Tis a poor mood,' said the doctor, watching the captain bend against the oars.

'You have pleasure in your books,' said the fiddler beside him, 'I in my music, the crew with Captain Hill, but our captain prefers solitude of a more sanguine nature.'

Roberts rowed a full league east from the *Fortune*, towards a vast flock of guinea fowl sitting off the coast, until the bottom of his boat glided over the shallow marshlands of the inlets. He paused to bring a hatful of water over his head, but the ocean was as warm as blood and seemed to hold at his skin. The *Fortune* herself was so very busy. A man could not lie upon her deck without pressing his own flesh against another man's. Roberts had gathered men, brought them so thick around himself that he could not be seen and all were motivated and maintained by the promise of the *Juliette*. To face the *Weymouth* and the *Swallow*,

438

a pair of fifty-gunners, would take many of their lives. And yet, to oppose His Majesty so directly and to defeat him, would show a man to be as strong as a nation.

The gig ground its way into a narrow bank, and sounded the metallic shiver of sand turning against itself. Roberts removed his boots, and then stepped out on to the shelf. The glutinous water came to the back of his knees, heavy and darkened by the sediments of land. He organized the three gaming pieces side by side in the bottom of the gig, waited patiently to judge the wind, and then fired a pistol into the air. The soft wind was replaced by the gust of five thousand birds taking wing, a wave of sound and force that made Roberts squint. He had a full thirty seconds to discharge the muskets as the flock passed above him in their heavy feathered cloud. Standing alone, so many in flight, the majestic choice of life-taking. He did not fire the third weapon, but replaced it on the bottom of the gig.

The brace of fowl had fallen a hundred yards apart, no more than a stone's throw from the bank of sand on which the captain stood. Roberts peeled his damp breeches from his skin, then removed his shirt, and waded naked down the side of the bank. The water rose past his hips, then covered his chest. He arched his neck back and held his arms above him as if he carried great gifts. The water licked his Adam's apple. A granular concoction of mud and sand sucked at his feet. Roberts reached out and pulled the first bird towards him, then waded

439

silently to the second and, as it flapped in his hands, he held it under the water until it ceased its struggle.

He sat alone, naked in the gig, while the sun stained his white thighs pink. Bartholomew Roberts thought on the guns of King George while he plucked the fowl, feathers drifting in the water around him. By the second hour, hunger stirred him and, dressing, he rowed quickly towards the *Fortune*. He could hear the tune of the mechanical chorus a mile from the encampment.

The captain had only just given the plucked brace to Nanny, who had commented on the thoroughness of his job, when, once again, a cry came from the *Fortune*'s fighting top. It was another sail, this time the *Ranger* for sure, and it was generally recommended that she should be given a shot of welcome. Roberts stood upon the deck of the *Fortune* and peered through his eyeglass at the approaching sail. She was definitely three-masted, and moved with great speed for a ship not careened in almost four months. A deckhand came scurrying down the shrouds. He balanced for a moment on the port timberhead, then leaped straight to the quarterdeck.

'Richard Armstrong,' said the man.

'I know,' replied Roberts.

'I think tis the *Swallow*, sir,' said Armstrong, pointing towards the sail.

'Tis the *Juliette*,' said Williams, shaking his head.

440

'She flies the French flag of the *Ranger*,' replied Roberts, still looking through the glass.

'Tis the *Swallow*,' echoed Armstrong.

Roberts took the glass from his eye and handed it to the deckhand.

'On the honour of God's right hand,' said Armstrong, one eye closed against the sun, 'and upon my own life, I would know her trim at double the distance – tis the *Swallow*.'

'It matters not which ship she is. Sympson,' called Roberts to the shore. 'We set sail at once.'

The ship was still two hours from them, but the *Fortune*, having been run into soft mud for the career, would take half that time to be removed from the banks. Roberts descended to his cabin. The shore was a chaotic scene. Sympson attempted to organize his men, but so many were hampered by their days of drinking that they knew not where to go nor what to do. Eventually, two long boats were tied with thick cables to the *Fortune*'s bowsprit and she began to ease herself from the mud. The *Count de Thoulouze* was left unmanned, and Captain Hill and his crew watched the adventurers undergo their transformation to a fighting crew from a comfortable position on the beach, just to the right of the mechanical tree.

Bartholomew Roberts opened his sea-chest, and pulled out a suit of red damask. Dressing with care, he placed a scarlet feather in his tricorn, added two more chains to the thick band of gold already circling his neck, and then wrapped his pistols about a sash of black silk and hung them over either shoulder. He twisted his gold buttons close, lifted his sword, weighed it in his hand as if he judged it anew and finally headed for the quarterdeck of the *Fortune*.

Magnes was at the helm. Armstrong, Williams and Sympson stood behind him. The hundred and twenty men of the *Fortune* had been gathered, the cable slipped and they were under way.

'This is a bite, we shall get clear or die,' Roberts said aloud. 'Mr Armstrong?'

'Yes, sir.'

'If it were the *Swallow*, how does she sail?'

'Best upon a wind.'

'You hear, Mr Magnes, we shall go before the wind.'

As Roberts put the glass down, the fiddler, unheeded, took it up. The ship was no longer a three-masted blur. Her colours could be seen, her cannon counted. Alone, against the dark clouds and the faint blue promise of the evening behind her, she was magnificent, sailing with the ocean as if she were the shadow of a great wave. Williams had never seen a ship so large. Her two decks were freshly painted, her chainwales and catheads dwarfed those of the *Fortune*. Her beam must be close on forty feet, he thought, and her masts split the horizon. Through the pulses of lightning raking the skies, Williams could discern gangs of musketeers gathered in her tops. She yawed in the water, moving to reveal the brightly painted name of the *Swallow*. Williams remained frozen in horrified disappointment.

Roberts knew that there were few decisions to be made. He might pass close to the *Swallow*, under full sail, and receive her broadside before they returned a shot. If they followed this course, they might well be disabled. Should the maincourse, or any such sail be shot through, or should a mast fall, then they might make a run at the point of the Cape. From there it would be every fellow for himself, and they would fare among the natives. Otherwise, they might board the *Swallow*, but they would suffer terribly in the approach. To damage the man-o'-war they would have to ignite their stores of powder and destroy the pair of ships. He looked about him, saw the expectant faces, men unaccustomed to defeat, few having suffered even a fair fight. They had been drunk so long that, despite the sobering sight of His Majesty's fifth-rater, they were filled with a quivering bravado that emphasized their unfitness.

The ballad of the *Black Prince* rose from Sympson's throat, but few joined him. The Yorubans were handed muskets and sent to the tops under Innocent's command. The remainder of the men attended to their stations as the sky began to darken and the familiar afternoon rains approached. Had they arrived sooner, the *Swallow* might have held off, but now they would have to face her with waves stirred and wind gusting.

It darkened and the wind proved fickle. Thunder

peeled overhead so loudly that it seemed that it was sound and not the wind that drove the two ships towards one another. It was a moment of the day that Roberts usually cherished. Off Cape Lopez, each rumble of thunder lasted longer than a minute, a sixty-second echo that shuddered the beams of the *Fortune* and silenced David Sympson's singing. Roberts sniffed at the afternoon storm. Sound, smell, sight, touch, taste – it was the path of the storm. Thunder was always the first and often the last sign of Cape Lopez's storms, both the premonition and the ghost.

This evening the lightning cut low across the sky, so low that every man on deck cringed or turned his back. The storm was immediately overhead, and it seemed as if the bolt had pierced the ship like a brilliant javelin. And the thunder boomed over the *Fortune*, and the ocean itself retreated from the sound. Roberts's only grace was that, as the ships neared, the *Fortune* preparing to pass the *Swallow* off her larboard side, the wind steadied. The *Swallow*'s English ensign was raised. Roberts replied by hoisting the black flag. His scarlet apparel grew dim under the half light. The winds now rose and died, carried rain, then ran dry.

'Brace the yards. Lord Sympson. Bunch, pump the fresh water. Now, boy, now. Pump it all.'

The *Fortune* turned before the wind. Despite the fury of the heavens, the churning dark waters around, not a man aboard feared God, only the extended hand of King George. The *Swallow*'s

444

first broadside seemed louder than all the world's thunder. The fore topsail parted, chainshot hissing and ripping as it cut through the yard itself.

Three bodies tumbled towards the deck. But the *Fortune* had survived the broadside, and the gap was open, the opportunity to run granted. For a moment, the wind died. Simply ended. Then, to Williams's relief, it blew again. The quarterdeck emptied in a second, and Williams found himself alone with Magnes by the wheel. Under his beard was a look of unholy anger. And only then did Williams realize that the wind had reversed itself, and that the *Fortune* had been taken aback. They were open to the *Swallow*'s fire, and could not even manoeuvre themselves to answer with a single broadside. The *Swallow* bided her time, approached close enough to accept the sting of the *Fortune*'s bow-chasers, and then delivered a line of musket fire from her fore tops that had members of Roberts's gun crew fleeing their stations. Bringing herself slowly about, the *Swallow* raked the deck of the *Fortune* with a blast of grapeshot.

Williams had pressed himself so deep into the quarterdeck that he believed he had become a part of the ship itself. He gathered himself to his knees, then leaped from the quarterdeck to the fiferails of the mainmast. Men were running in every direction. He could hear the cries of Sympson and Hardy. Innocent and his men were descending from the shrouds. There, absurdly calm, not eight feet in front of him, sat Roberts upon a coil of cable.

He crawled the last feet to his captain, and shouted, 'What should be done, Captain? What should be done?'

Roberts's hands were cupped about his stomach. Despite the shrieking chain, Williams stared for a long moment before he understood that the captain was holding his intestines, glistening and weeping with blood. Roberts did not follow Williams's gaze, but saw the horror in the fiddler's eyes. He pursed his lips to an O, and breathed calmly in and out under the thunder. Reaching forwards, Williams tried to push his captain's guts back within his chest. Roberts turned his head to ignore the ministrations. There was no skin to stretch across to hide the breach. Williams pulled the red frock coat about him. When he looked up, Roberts's eyes were frozen in surprise.

Innocent appeared beside the fiddler. He lifted Roberts's lifeless head by the gold chains, then let it slump. Another broadside racked the *Fortune*. With a sharp crack, her main topmast plummeted to the deck, snared above the crouching figures of Innocent and the fiddler by a web of lines.

Sympson saw the strange terror in Williams's visage from across the deck. Deaf to the blasts of the *Swallow*, deaf to the pleas of his own wounded, he crossed in private silence to where Roberts sat. Others watched him, their eyes following the quartermaster to their captain. The fiddler brought his hands to his head and spoke unheard words to the cannonade. He never noticed Sympson stand beside him, nor the deckhands that gathered under the thunder like a bloodied chorus. No man exchanged words, or even glances, for it was apparent to all that the *Fortune* was dead.

The Dogon pushed his arms under his captain. Straightening his back, he arose. He carried the lifeless form of Bartholomew Roberts to the unengaged side of the ship and, with an astonished Williams walking in his shadow, musket balls wailing around him, cast his captain overboard. It seemed for a moment that the body would float, as it rose high upon the first swell. Slowly, the weight of gold dragged Roberts under, and the sea ran over his face with a thin white foam, urging him to her depths.

No men were left at their stations, except for Peter Scudamore. Ears plugged against thunder and cannon, the doctor attended to his business in perfect calmness. Williams descended through the main hatchway, and joined the doctor on the lower deck. He was tending to a Yoruban, whose jaw had been shattered by a musket ball. The man made no noise. The fiddler looked at him and thought him dead. Another broadside crashed against the *Fortune*. She did not return fire.

Scudamore looked up, and saw his blood-soaked friend.

'Are you struck, William?' he asked.

'He said nothing to me.'

'Who, William?'

'Tis not my blood,' said the fiddler, 'but Roberts's.'

Scudamore met his eyes for a moment, and saw their wounded truth, then returned his hands to the work of bandaging the new recruit.

'If the flag is not lowered,' said the doctor, 'then bring it down yourself.'

Williams shrugged and drifted in an impotent stupor to the deck. His skin itched. Peering over the chainwales into the shallows he searched for some sign of Roberts's body. One hand squeezed the other, and suddenly the fiddler felt vulnerable, even to wind and driving rain.

The *Swallow* remained aloof, fearing that the most desperate of the men would sink the *Fortune* by blasting her stores of powder. Her boats came and went by the hour, slowly transferring prisoners and depositing a prize crew upon her deck. Williams was among the last to leave, found wandering about the lower deck of the *Fortune*, insensible to all around him, his ears still singing with the roar of cannon. He did not think of gold, nor freedom, nor even his precious manuscript, still dazed by the change that half a day had brought. He was discovered in the powder room, drinking idly by himself. Glasby preceded the soldiers. He ran in and begged the fiddler not to blow the *Fortune* up and to send them all to hell. It was not Williams's intention. He walked to the waist of the ship and descended peacefully into the *Swallow*'s longboat.

CHAPTER 45

March 1722 – Cape Corso, The Gold Coast

Cape Corso Castle jutted from a rocky peninsula, incongruous with its sharp lines of majesty set against the dry yellows of sand mountains behind. Beside the castle was a series of thin streets, houses divided in grandeur between the English traders, the negroes they traded with and the pens of the negroes they traded. There were two slave pens, one within the walls of the castle, and the second at the edge of the town. The more genteel of the small township, most notably the wife of the governor of the Gold Coast and the established bawdy madams, would dip their handkerchiefs in scent and hold them to dainty noses, lest they catch the fetors of the slaves as they promenaded past the pens. If half the senses could be removed, if eye could see but hands had no desire to touch, if ears could absorb the sound, but the kerchief repel the odours, then such suffering could be tolerated.

A short distance from her walls, the previous agent-generals of the castle had planted a garden. It too was walled. The twenty private acres abounded with pineapples, lemons, coconuts, guava, pomegranates, grapes and limes, and the cassava tree. They were meticulously planted, creating shaded avenues that would guard the stroller from the intensity of the African sun. Behind the garden, Corso's walls stood fourteen feet thick, with four great bastions and seventy guns. She lorded it over her coast, queen of land and water. For fifty years a vast British flag had hung from her main tower like a giant fan sent to cool His Majesty's subjects. Standing on the battlements a man could see the coast's business stretch east and west, the waters cut by pettiaugers and sloops which bustled across the harbour outfitting ships and trading cargoes. Frigate birds perched on crenellations and cocked their heads. From a distance the castle looked rigid, polished and organized by British fervour. It was only her sun-baked walls that suggested she was poised on the edge of the dark continent.

Africa visited constantly. She crept inside the castle walls and passed from caboceer to slave to master, and spread dizzying sicknesses, forcing yellow bile over discoloured tongues. Of the two hundred and eighty men who had sailed out in the *Weymouth*, sister ship of the *Swallow*, over two hundred had perished on African shores, and only a single man to anything other than disease. They were buried outside the castle walls, and the graveyard snaked like a curious tail leading from the castle's gates.

For three weeks the men of the *Fortune* and

Ranger sat within her dungeons. The castle's slaves had been removed to the outer pens on the edge of the town, and every man captured off Cape Lopez was now imprisoned in her depths. The entirety of the crews wore fetters about their feet and hands, which were linked to a single iron chain. It trailed about the length of the dungeon. A man could stand, but none might take more than a hobbled step in any direction.

An initial solidarity had been transformed to an independent fear. Even those who were practically assured an acquittal, such as those French and English taken at Whydah, who had not stepped upon any prize, began to feel a tightness about their necks as they slept. Glasby's absence and a report that the *King Solomon* had been sighted in the harbour heightened their anxieties. All knew that the sailing master would sing, but none could predict the melody nor the length of the tune. It was certain that, if he wished, he might hang them all. Even Valentine Ashplant, who had saved Glasby's life upon Hispaniola, did not consider himself immune.

The Fortunes were ashamed of their actions, or rather lack of them, though many knew it to have been a vain cause, once the main mast had been shot away. The *Ranger* had fared little better, tempted to the open ocean by the *Swallow*'s captain, Chaloner Ogle, out of sight and sound of Cape Lopez. They had pursued in full arrogance, expecting an easy prize. Finally, the

Swallow had allowed her to come within range. Skyrme confessed to any who would listen that he was excited by the chase, and was within musket shot before he rightly realized his mistake. The *Swallow* had turned to starboard, hoisted her colours, and fired.

In the darkness of the dungeons there was no truth to the event. Every man was anxious to add his version to the mixture, either to extricate himself from fault or bow humbly before the blame. Skyrme had ordered the black flag run down. Then he had ordered it back up again. They had set sails. They had furled them. Finally they fought, Skyrme slowly trying to bring the *Ranger* about so that they might board the superior force. The *Swallow* stood off, and let her cannon devastate her opponent. Her third broadside removed Skyrme's leg to the thigh. At his own request, it was cauterized against the fiery rim of one of their own cannon.

They had lost only ten men when the main topmast came down about their heads, but another twenty had been wounded, and the *Ranger* sat lamely in the water, receiving fire, neither capable of fight nor flight. The last order Skyrme remembered giving was to lower their colours. The black flag was wrapped about a cannonball and committed to the sea.

Blake, who spoke through a face of melted flesh, told how he and six others had retreated to the magazine and fired a pistol into a barrel of gunpowder in an attempt to sink both the ships together. The flash blinded every one of them, and killed John Morris. It had propelled William Main out of the cabin gallery and into the ocean, sending a sliver of wood through his hat. But it was the final resistance. Main was plucked from the sea, and quarter was granted. The Swallows had spent two days patching the *Ranger*, accounting for the absence that had worried their shipmates. When the *Swallow* bore off to engage the *Fortune*, the *Ranger* was sailed through Prince's Island for Corso.

Under the castle, the crews had lost twelve more to their wounds. The doctor was inconsolable. At first Williams had presumed that it was due to the loss of Bartholomew Roberts and the *Fortune*. But Scudamore refused to talk with him. As musician and doctor they were guaranteed an acquittal. He gained the truth on the seventh day of their internment.

'Did he not tell you?' asked Magnes.

'What?'

'He was carried back separate from the rest. Same ship as the Yorubans. Just him and them and those that watched him. Good doctor tells the niggers he knows navigation. They could win the ship between them he says. He was seen talking in tongues to the blackies, then one sees fit to peach to the captain, and now the doctor, deemed forced – natural enough – will be hanged with the worst of us.'

'He's ne'er raised his hand,' said Williams.

'Mutiny,' said Magnes, 'is no show of faith in Crown . . . Remember him, William, for you shall get not a word more from his lips. He talks only to God. Asked for prayer books and reads them thrice over.'

Williams strained against his chains and nodded to the only slit of light that braved their cell.

'If I could see,' he said wistfully, 'I would wager all my gold that the *Juliette* sits in the harbour.'

'Come now, William,' whispered Magnes.

'I'll wager she does.'

'Then I would take all your pelf.'

'Have you seen her at Corso?' asked Williams.

'She has never been, William,' spoke Magnes softly.

'Never been where?' asked the fiddler.

'Never been built,' said Magnes. 'Except in the mind of Roberts and those of us who supported her . . . construction. Was a dream, boy . . . and was always meant to be. Held a crew of two hundred together and pushed them prettily, did it not?'

Williams wished to doubt, wished to ask another question, but now it was he and not Roberts who could not speak.

Days would pass without a word spoken between the two hundred men, but when silence broke all wished to share their thoughts. Privacy was equated with conspiracy. No man wished to be looked upon as a peacher, especially when he still lived among his fellows, no matter how lowly their dwelling.

'Do you think we'll all be hanged?' asked Bunch.

'Some of us three times over,' said Sympson.

'And tarred?' insisted the cabin boy.

'You shall not feel a thing,' answered Sympson.

'Will they grant us green bags?' asked Bunch.

'You shall speak for yourself if asked,' said Magnes. 'Trial'll be held under a captain. Means I shall be heard before I am taken by my scruff.'

'Can we not give gloves?' asked Blake.

'Aye,' chimed Bunch. 'Those that are forgiven can grease fists.'

'And what will you grease with? Goodwill?'

'What will be done with our gold?' asked Bunch.

'It shall never be found,' said Magnes, 'and Captain Ogle shall buy hisself a county and end his days Lord of Admiralty.'

'We were rich men a month back,' murmured Skyrme with a mournful nostalgia.

'We were free men,' said Magnes, 'and now we are ghosts.'

When finally they were called, a silence fell upon them. Glasby had sung. First called were the most recent recruits. Then musics and boys. Finally, all the negroes. The rest remained. Bunch winked at Williams as the single chain that linked their shackles rattled through the rings. Their black gaoler motioned for them to head for the lighter shadows of the doorway.

'Tis home for feast days for us,' said Bunch, and waved the fiddler ahead of him. Despite an absurd flavour of fear and relief, Williams could not raise a smile. Their calling had only deepened the gloom of the dungeon and the surgeon had not looked up from his feet.

The African captives were marched slowly up the stairs ahead of their European counterparts. While the Yorubans tended to keep their heads bowed, as if they were seeking anonymity, Innocent held his head high and did not look at his captors. They held no interest for him. As he passed, he nodded at Williams in the same manner as he used aboard when he wished to engage the fiddler in a discussion. Williams watched him disappear up the stone steps, and did not doubt that he would see him again.

The remainder of the crew were brought before the *Swallow*'s surgeon, and were asked for their name, age and birthplace. Finally they were requested to yell loudly to check the dampness of their lungs. Then they were dismissed, marched to the gates of the castle, and abandoned. They headed to the nearest tavern, the Coastal Queen, to watch the Yorubans and the single Dogon as they were marched towards the slave pens. Bunch and Williams drank calmly together as if they were the best of friends. On their third pot they were assailed by the milk-eyed tavernkeeper, who carried a bottle of English gin and asked them for their stories. Small flakes of skin fell from his ears as he took a seat between the Fortunes on his bench. He coughed twice, and caught the rising phlegm in his hand, wiping it on the underside of the table. Williams would not speak, so Bunch talked for two, and included the fiddler through frequent gesticulations as he gave a lengthy, embellished account of their lawless wanderings along the Gold Coast.

The tavernkeeper begged off in the smallest of hours, pleading that he would be rising early to listen to the proceedings against the first and most wicked who had been selected from the *Fortune*'s crews by their sailing master.

'The most wicked?' asked Williams.

'Them that they're most itching to hang,' explained the keeper as he excused himself.

'Will they all hang?' asked Williams.

'On account of their ages,' said Bunch, grinning. He wiped his fingers along the inside rim of his cannikin and sucked them clean. 'The Lords will hang straightways. Sure as sure.'

'None of us no less guilty than others,' breathed Williams.

'Think on the captain,' said Bunch. 'A capital cove as died like man should. Lords'll hang like weasels when they's stripped on gibbets.' He seemed comfortable with the thought.

'What shall we do?' asked Williams tiredly.

'I cannot speak for you,' said Bunch. 'I will claim our chests tomorrow, if I may, and then find a way from this hell quick as Jack Robinson. I'll find an English-bound as'll have me, and spring quick ere they change their minds. Would not trust Glasby. Whiddler through and through.'

'I shall speak tomorrow,' said Williams, yawning. 'Speak in their defence.'

'You'll only hang yourself,' said Bunch, standing up from the table, and downed the dregs of his pot.

'Phineas Bunch,' said Williams lazily, 'do you mean to see your shipmates hang?'

'I care not,' said Bunch, 'whether I see them hang or no. I shall be gone from this place and a curse on every devil's mother.'

Williams sat alone. He listened to those who slept about the tavern, and considered how much had been lost, how much of substance. So why, he wondered, had he dwelled upon the loss of the *Juliette*, a mere idea, since Magnes's revelation? At first he had felt stripped of his memories, as if he had never known the man he had deemed so close. Yet now he remembered that what Roberts sought first, before the myth of the *Juliette*, was his services as biographer. And if the *Juliette* were the lie, then it was *his* role that was central. The preservation of Roberts's name was all the captain wished. The *Juliette* was simply the means of manipulation through which Roberts could ensure that a crew would hold long enough to guarantee his notoriety. And so it was in peace that Williams headed from the fire, in the understanding that his words had always been Roberts's principal instruments. Tomorrow, providing that the Admiralty had not employed a decoder, the pages would return to his hands. Once edited of his more sinister actions, they would provide him with a glorious future and Roberts with an afterlife. Finally, before he passed into sleep, he thought of the men beneath the castle, and of Innocent chained within the pens, of Roberts's weighted body anchored to the seabed.

CHAPTER 46

The seven inquisitors acted as the commission. They were to be both judge and jury, and sat along the heavy oaken table with their hands folded before them, as if there was merely one way for a gentleman to sit, and it had been declared. Williams loitered at the back of the room, an acquitted freedman, merely observing. Sympson, Magnes, Hardy, Moody, Ashplant – all had their backs to the fiddler. As the secretary charged in, he dropped a mess of paper. Williams helped him gather his bundle, then begged a sheet from him, and folded it carefully so that he might later make notes upon the trial. He sidled against the walls, positioning himself next to the tavernkeeper who broke off from scratching at his right ear, and nodded in acknowledgement of Williams's presence.

'Who are they?' asked Williams.

'That grand noddy,' said the tavernkeeper, pointing at the largest man, who sat in the middle of the seven, 'called Heardman. He's been here an' his ship f'ever. Lost most of the Weymouths. Came almost three hundred strong. Got fifty hands left, an' they been crimpin' for months. Is why they only sent *Swallow* after yous. Couldn't find men to sail the *Weymouth*.' He cast his eyes back to Heardman. 'There's many that likes him round – I got a penny whore who says her captain's equine among the undergarments.'

'Who has the gold brocade?' asked Williams.

'Phipps,' the tavernkeeper spat on the ground before him. 'Honourable Phipps. General of the Coast. Like being captain of a frog's pond. On his right, Edmund Hyde. Rich as any nigger king here abouts. Rest are queer coves. Have to have seven to hang a man. Got us two merchants, Boyce and Dodson – Boyce has gout – and two shavers, from *Weymouth*, added for numbers. They'll hear them out.'

'Good, good,' said Williams.

'And then they'll hang the lot of them.'

Mungo Heardman, the captain of the *Weymouth* stood before the courtroom. He faced the prisoners. Behind them sat several rows of merchants, the odd lady, and a smattering of sailors and traders who had come to remind themselves of the long reach of His Majesty. Williams, sitting in the last of the pews, could see Heardman's jowls quiver as he stood. The captain had a large nose, creased like an arse, and his eyes seemed to be always wide, as if they were constantly offended by the presence of the nose. If there were more faults to be seen, then they were cleverly disguised by a large grizzled porcupine wig that trailed down either side of his

461

red frock coat. He rapped the large table in front of him with the heel of his hand and addressed the prisoners.

His voice produced its own echo as if two men spoke together. Under the stoned cavern of the great hall it sounded as if the Lord Himself had descended to pass judgement upon the Fortunes.

Heardman did not look a grim man, but the very table, the hall, the links lit despite the early morning, spoke of a funereal solemnity that no jest could shudder.

'According to the laws of this court, you shall be granted a fair trial. Any man among this commission of seven may intercede in the lines of questioning if he deems he may aid in the deliverance of the truth. Lieutenant Fanshaw shall conduct the examination of the witnesses.'

The man in question, no more than mid-twenties and with the tart smile of a midshipman who wielded his father's name, stood and bowed before resuming his seat. He was so thin that, had he turned sideways, the court may have missed his introduction altogether. Heardman nodded at Fanshaw and then continued. 'After the witnesses have spoken, and only after, shall the prisoners be allowed to speak on their own behalves. I am the captain of the *Weymouth*. Those of you who have sailed with His Majesty before know that you shall be granted a fair trial.'

'And a fast one,' called Magnes.

'Prisoner,' said Heardman, 'should you wish

to speak again, you shall be returned in chains to England and shall be tried there, fairly, or elsewise.'

Magnes bowed in deference to the wisdom of future silence.

'Lieutenant Fanshaw, if you would call forth your witnesses.'

It seemed vaguely comical to Williams. The opening and closing of doors, the uneven trudge of sailors across the carved floors of the great hall. Only the commission seemed comfortable in their surroundings. The rest looked about them as if they were in the belly of a whale.

Lieutenant Charles Fanshaw, whose journey through the ranks of the *Weymouth* had been accelerated by the untimely deaths of so many of his predecessors and rivals, almost shouted his first words, as if experience could be replaced by volume. 'Lieutenant Isaac Sun of His Majesty's *Swallow*. Ralph Baldrick, bosun of same said ship. Daniel Maclaughlin, mate of same said ship.' The three men in question were polished for the occasion. Their hair was contained by ponytail, drink had been avoided for some hours and they had encouraged one another into their Sundays. It was a grand opportunity to speak in front of the Admiralty. Their backs were rigid with a disciplined deportment.

One by one they gave evidence that the five prisoners before them had all been present on either the *Ranger* or the *Fortune* when the ships were given quarter by the *Swallow*. Showing much disappointment that they were not needed to expound on the prisoners' guilt, they were led from the hall by a wigged attendant, who escorted Captain Trahern to the end of the table, where he took his seat. It was the same bitter voice that Williams had heard from the ship's bow, and the same portrait eyes that now judged the five Fortunes as one.

'I, Joseph Trahern, do solemnly promise and swear on the Holy Evangelists to bear true and faithful witness between the king and prisoner or prisoners, in relation to the fact or facts of piracy and robbery he or they do stand accused of. So help me God.'

'These are the men, sir. Most active every one. Brisk as any. Know more faces than these. Him on the end, they called him Sympson.'

'Lord Sympson,' corrected the quartermaster.

'Silence,' said Heardman.

'He not only boarded the *King Solomon* in a state of improbable drunkenness, but he took an axe to much of my cargo, sir. Pointless sir, quite illogical, and that which he did not wish for himself, he did not think to share among his fellows, nor to return to myself, but did cast the lot overboard. Bales of fine cotton, sir. A man's livelihood, ruined for drunken spite.'

'Mr Sympson,' asked Fanshaw, 'do you have anything to say in your defence?'

'Speak, can I?' asked Sympson.

'Indeed.'

'Should ha' murthered 'im.'

Fanshaw paused to let the words echo about the Great Hall, and then said, 'You feel no sorrow for your actions?'

'Nary a spoonful of feathers,' said Sympson, 'e'ry man in this room is as guilty as each other. We're robbers one and all. Only difference is rich and poor. And none so poor as us rogues.'

'Indeed,' smiled Fanshaw, and ceased to question the prisoner, feeling that he had made his points adequately. 'Mr Magnes, or perhaps, Lord Magnes.'

'Ne'er a Lord,' said Magnes, 'you can paint me brisk as you want, but ne'er called forth to join the House.'

'Mr Magnes,' said Fanshaw, 'do you have anything to say in your defence? Captain Trahern has testified that you were most active in the taking of the *King Solomon*.'

'He's telling it plain but not all.'

'We beg your pardon.'

'We done taken the *Solomon*, fair enough. We recruited, tis true. Men joined us freely. But you ain't asked why they would leave their ship with . . . such precipitation, now have you?'

'Would you care to enlighten us?' asked Fanshaw, his voice cloaked in disbelief.

'He was a bugger, wasn't he?'

Sympson snorted with laughter, and Moody hollered.

'Preposterous,' cried Trahern, and gripped the sides of his chair.

'Young lads and all,' said Magnes. 'We was not committing an act of robbery upon the high seas, was a rescue. Was why so many came aboard. Give their arses a rest.'

Captain Trahern stood to attention. 'Gentlemen of the court,' he said, 'I do not have to subject myself . . .'

'Chain him fore he nabs us,' shouted Magnes.

'He ain't takin' none of mine,' cried Moody, and made fists at the witness.

Mungo Heardman rose to his feet and levelled a finger at the prisoners, which seated Moody and silenced Magnes. 'Mr Magnes, though it is in all of our interests to see that you obtain a fair trial, unsubstantiated accusations have no place in this court of law.'

'Sodomy is a hanging offence, is it not?' asked Magnes. 'For His Majesty's Navy tis a hanging offence, and therefore, sir, I believe it a serious matter.' Heardman had not interrupted him. 'Besides,' continued Magnes. 'I have us a witness.'

'And where would that witness be?' asked Fanshaw, raising his bony hand to his ear and cupping it.

'In this very room.'

Fanshaw looked across at the captain of the *Weymouth*, and received a nod.

'His name?' asked Fanshaw.

'William Williams,' said Magnes, and Moody

made a poor attempt at controlling his laughter until the quartermaster silenced him with an elbow to the ribcage.

'William Williams,' asked Lieutenant Fanshaw. 'Under an oath of God. Did this man, Captain Joseph Trahern, attempt to *know* you at any particular time that the *King Solomon* lay alongside the *Fortune*?'

'He did, sir,' said Williams.

'And what did he do, sir?' asked Fanshaw.

Williams looked at his feet, and wrung his hands together. He shook his head.

'And what did he do?' repeated Fanshaw.

'Buggered me,' blurted out Williams, and Moody snorted once more.

'You were buggered by Captain Trahern?'

'He tried to mount me like bull on cow, sir. Only we were both bulls.'

Trahern had turned a very deep shade of purple, and had begun by staring intently at Williams. But once the fiddler had spat out the word – 'buggery' – the captain of the *King Solomon* no longer knew where to place his eyes at all. The accusation was so dreadful, its punishment so severe, his position so very awkward that he felt even the slightest of false movements might turn this lie into truth in the eyes of the commission.

The court paused as if they did not know how to deal with the matter. Heardman shook his jowls, and squirrelled a finger in and out of his ear.

'Mr Fanshaw,' said Boyce, 'I understand the importance of the matter in His Majesty's Navy, but we must remember that Captain Trahern is commander of a merchant man and, though he is accused of a heinous crime, it matters not whether he is a bugger. His ship was taken, his goods stolen and destroyed.'

'You cannot,' cried Magnes, 'push aside the testimony of a writing man.' He wagged a finger at Williams. 'He is erudition. A scholar would not lie before God Himself.'

Heardman looked up directly at Williams and raised his hand.

'You are an écriteur?'

'Yes sir,' said Williams. Heardman seemed to consider his course of actions for a long moment. The evidence of slow machinations disturbed the serenity of his features. The eyes of permanent surprise closed for a full second, only reopening as he declared, 'I do not believe you. Come hither. Take up this quill. Scratch me a word or two.'

Williams rose from his chair, and walked awkwardly to the long table of the commission of seven. He took up Heardman's own pen, and then paused, scratching a bare patch on his skull.

'What should I write, sir?'

'*God have mercy on your soul,*' said Heardman. Williams wrote out the line as instructed and then began to walk back to the chair of the witness.

'You are excused, Mr Williams,' said Mr

Fanshaw. 'The trial shall continue. Thank you kindly.' The lieutenant turned his gaze towards the row of prisoners. His left foot was polishing its boot against his right calf. 'Mr Moody?'

'Me what?' said Christopher Moody, looking up at the lieutenant from trying to match eyes with Williams.

'The *King Solomon*,' sighed Fanshaw. 'Captain Trahern has testified that you were very profligate, swearing and cursing. That you, piratically and feloniously, put the crew in fear of their lives, and, piratically and feloniously, did steal, take and attempt to burn the said sloop.'

'I don't follow much of that,' said Moody, shaking his head.

'Captain Trahern has identified you as one upon it.'

'Yes, sir,' said Moody, 'that would be right. I was upon it. Up and down it sir. But . . . I'd smack calves' skin that I was forced into the boat as rowed to her.'

'And saying,' said Fanshaw, turning his back on the prisoners and addressing the table of commissioners, 'in our mood of generosity, we see fit to believe you, the acts are still by your own hands, since, according to Mr Glasby, they are done by orders of officers of your own election. Why would men honestly disposed give their votes for such a captain and such a quartermaster as were every day commanding them on distasteful services?'

469

Moody shrugged, exhaled, and then pursed his lips in flatulence. He remained the only man amused.

'Thank you, Captain Trahern,' said Fanshaw, 'I fear that we shall have need of your services over the coming days. Mr Glasby, if you please.' Trahern released his arms from the chair and withdrew from the hall to whispers that seemed almost choral under the high stone ceilings.

Harry Glasby did not look at the prisoners as he entered. He studied his feet carefully all the way to his chair, and then nodded at every single member of the commission. Respectfully, they all returned his acknowledgement, and the row of bobbing heads seemed like keys struck upon a church's organ.

'Good morning, Mr Glasby,' said Lieutenant Fanshaw.

'G-G-Morning, sir,' replied Glasby.

Sympson got to his feet. 'With due respect, your honours, I would rather be hanged this very morning than sit through a single hour of this man's words. There is true pain in it.'

'Sit down,' said Heardman evenly, and the prisoner sank to his seat.

Glasby had not missed much. Without keeping a single written note, he recounted the acts of evil he himself had witnessed, and went on to describe various other offences that he had heard reported, despite his imprisoned state during any engagement. To Glasby's credit, he turned no evidence against Ashplant, his saviour at Hispaniola, but he often scratched at his back, as if to remind his shipmates of the scars that marked him. The whiter he painted himself, the darker the men before him became.

The prisoners were all described as the most active and brisk of the entire crew. Though each, when his turn to speak came, declared himself a forced man, they were still joined by a communal belief in their innocence. They suspected that they were guilty in the eyes of the law, but their business had been their own for so long, and their lives so orderly and independent wherein, that they had ceased to believe in the jurisdiction of the British government.

'What,' asked Magnes, 'gives a country the right to ply its laws upon the seas? Don't belong to no man does it now? This ain't ne'er an English coast, so why's as we suffering under English laws. Turn me over to Dutch, and French, loose me on the Spaniards, hand me to the blackies, but don't try me under English law.'

'An excellent point,' said Fanshaw quickly, 'and one that would hold some substance, had you not plied your own trade upon English shipping, and fired upon His Majesty's vessel.'

'It is,' concurred Heardman, 'a poor time to cry *pro patria*. Lieutenant Fanshaw, you may be seated.'

'Sit down,' shouted Hardy at the lieutenant. The loud voice made the officer wince to the prisoners' amusement. It was the last moment that Williams ever saw Sympson smile.

Heardman stood before the hall. Bowing briefly before the court, he turned to address the prisoners. He held his hands before him as he spoke, his fingers interlocked, his thumbs forming a sturdy cross.

'The crimes of which all of ye have been justly convicted is of all other robberies the most aggravating and inhuman, in that being removed from the fears of surprise in remote and distant parts, you do in wantonness of power often add cruelty to theft.'

Moody, spotting Williams at the back of the hall, smirked.

'Your kind,' continued Heardman, 'unmoved at distress or poverty, not only spoil and rob, but do it from men needy, and who are purchasing their livelihoods through hazards and difficulties which ought rather to move compassion. Still worse do often by persuasion or force engage the inconsiderate part of them to their own and families' ruin, removing them from their wives and children and by that from the means that should support them from misery and want.'

'I's not married,' said Moody, and seemed surprised that none joined his smile. He was ignored by Heardman.

'To a trading nation nothing can be so destructive as piracy, or call for more exemplary punishment, besides the national reflection it infers. It cuts off the returns of industry and those plentiful importations that alone can make an island flourish, and it is your aggravation that you have been the chiefs and rulers in these licentious and lawless practices.

'However, contrary to the measures ye have dealt, ye have been heard with patience and though little has or possibly could have been said in excuse or extenuation of your crimes, yet charity makes us hope that true and sincere repentance – which we heartily recommend – may entitle you to mercy and forgiveness, after the sentence of the law has taken place which now remains upon me to pronounce.'

Moody still searched for Williams's eyes, but he, along with the other Fortunes, was concentrating on the captain's lips.

'You, David Sympson, William Magnes, Richard Hardy, Christopher Moody and Valentine Ashplant. Ye and each of you are adjudged and sentenced to be carried back to the place from whence you came, from thence to the place of execution without the gates of this castle, and there within the flood marks to be hanged by the neck, till you are dead, dead, dead. And the Lord have mercy upon your souls. After this, ye, and each of you shall be taken down and your bodies hung in chains.'

The prisoners were escorted from the hall. None looked at Williams as they were paraded past him, except Moody, who winked as if he were being marched to the Grand Turk's seraglio. The fiddler stared ahead, at the point where the commission remained seated. His perjury now seemed a vain device, that he presumed might only count against him when the true judgement came.

The tavernkeeper accompanied Williams out through the gates of the castle, though they did not speak. Williams walked half a pace upwind, so that he would not have to suffer the malodour of the man's breath. By the time they reached the tavern, a light rain began to fall, and his host bid Williams pause before he entered the establishment, and a small Ibo child wiped the red mud from their boots with a rag.

There, in the room that he and Bunch had shared the previous night with six others of the acquitted, sat his seachest. It was a familiar sight, and it comforted him. The latch had been broken by His Majesty's sailors when they had searched every cranny of the *Fortune* for gold dust or coinage. He knew, without looking, that his bag of moidores, that gave out a sweet muffled clink against their velvet pouch, had been removed. Sitting on top of his remaining clothes was a piece of paper, folded neatly as an envelope.

It was a poor imitation of his own script, hardly fine workmanship, but the considerable efforts of a poor penman striving for mediocrity. It was a hand that might have belonged to any number of men within the castle walls, but the language was singular. It was his own invention of inverted

Latin, sprinkled with meaningless symbols that he had so painstakingly taught Bunch off the shores of Hispaniola. He squinted in the demi-light and muttered as he read the hand out loud.

Williams,

I write this to wish you goodbyes. I am gone on a Dutchman, headed up to Whydah, and I hope to find passage to England from there. Back through the Indies if I must, but away from here. You have been no friend to me, but you are what taught me this trick, so that I can speak now, though I am away. I consider you an arrogant man, and you shall get no further help from me. It is not right to use a man as scribe, and then release him. You think little of me. Men have called each other out over less. But since you taught me this, and my words are as fine as yours, I will tell you – clever coves travel fast. In Corso to save oneself is hard enough. Stay and you'll only see hanging.
Your erstwhile friend,
Phineas Bunch

He read it again. After his third digestion. Williams had memorized the piece, descended to the front of the tavern, and, in exchange for a small coil of brocade that had been sitting towards the top of his sea-chest, he received credit enough to eat, drink and board.

To lose Bunch did not bother him at all. Their temporary brotherhood had been forged by the

475

orders of their captain, and yesterday's conversation had been nothing more than a blessing shared. They had never been fond of one another. Bunch, with his scarlet skin, uneven mop of greasy black hair and unfounded arrogance, was not a man whose absence would be rued. Williams's only regret was to have given him the gift of the written word. He laughed once. Decided it was uncommonly amusing. He had not thought on it before. William Williams was the only man in the world who might decipher the words of Phineas Bunch.

This thought, harbinger of many chuckles, prompted Williams to unfold the precious sheet of paper that he had begged in the courtroom, earlier that day. He made brief notes of the trial, omitting his own testimony and continued:

To have no Bunch is a blessing, though I wish I were by his side the first time he shows his fine hand to some poxed purser. It is a rare laugh along this trail of misery. And yet, amid this pain, I play the part of audience while my friends are on stage. Aged Q dead, Moody, Sympson, Magnes condemned. The doctor, so taken with his fate he can not speak. Cannot speak. It was Roberts who could not speak and it is his blood that haunts me, more so than Catrin's, more so than the doctor's. I have thought long about this. In his last moments, was he incapable of speech or did he deny me of his words? Did he wish to tell me the truth of the

Juliette, *to tell me he had received his silent wish to meet King George in combat? I would guess it takes a strong man to be dispatched in such a manner and to keep hold of the silent reins when the body wishes to howl. The bile of terror and anguish must rise high in a man's throat, and yet he denied it. I think perhaps, that a man's life may unravel at his death, and so it is vital to die well, for it is not only your final action, but the audience's last memory of you.*

Only when Williams's mind, in deepest slumber, smiled at Bunch and the coded trickery did he wake with a start. The fiddler and the cabin boy were the only two men in the world who might read portions of the manuscript. Naked, he rushed to his sea-chest. He searched once, then again, then turned the chest upside down, and shook it till he woke the sailors around him.

His panicked state gathered thin lines of sweat over his eyebrows, the falling beads splashed against Bunch's letter, until it swam in a river of ink. After a minute, where tears welled up in his eyes, he remembered to breathe. Letting air course in and out through his lungs, Williams remembered that his was the gift of life and that all other matters were secondary. It could not be Bunch that had taken it. It was the Admiralty. Perhaps they had seen rough maps and thought it was transcribed in Spanish and held clues to the currents and reefs of the Caribbean. Even if they had taken a close look at it, and divined that it was encoded, there was little chance that any man had deciphered it so soon.

It was not impossible to retrieve it. The captain of the *Weymouth* had been impressed with his ability to write so well. He would pause long enough in Cape Corso. He might temporarily enlist as a member of the Company, where he might have access to the evidence stripped from the *Fortune* and the *Ranger*. It would not be an easy job. He would have to replace the manuscript. There was hope. His manuscript was his dowry, but it was not his life. It was the key to the door of wealth, behind which lurked the bright glory of cities and land, of society and law.

He lay awake until dawn, until his fellow sailors roused one another with their calls for drink. Brattle, acquitted at the same time as Williams, brought his fiddle over to his fellow musician, and the two men provided the tavern with her first tune of the day, 'Hanging John', a slow, wailing tune written for a man on execution day.

When Williams folded his fiddle under his arm, and made to leave, Brattle stepped forward and asked, 'Where would you be going, when your fellows will move together?'

'I need words with Bunch,' said Williams, turning from Brattle. 'I fear I must catch him, less he has sailed already.'

'We shall meet you out the castle walls.'

'And why would that be needed?'

478

'You would not see your own shipmates die hard?'

'Tis today?' said Williams in surprise. 'Why when did justice ever fetch wings so swift?'

'Ne'er in Newgate,' said Brattle.

There was no trace of Phineas Bunch. Corso was subject to the sort of traffic that Williams had not seen in all his travels. He had been crimped some miles from London, never seen the forest of masts that gathered on her shore, and in all his travels in Africa and the Americas, there had been no harbours as crazed as Corso's. Mainly she was stocked with pettiaugers, manned by both whites and blacks, but there must have been some fifteen slavers, and another dozen merchantmen, and there, anchored under the guns of the castle, was the memorable shape of the *Swallow*, her sister ship the *Weymouth*, and their so-called prizes, including the two-masted *Fortune*. It brought a slight smile to the fiddler's face to reconjure the faith that he had had in the *Juliette*, and to briefly imagine her ghostly beauty at Corso.

Williams must have asked over a hundred men whether or not they had met with a cove called Phineas Bunch. He described him, his red skin, his uneven clumps of greased black hair, his thin frame and lack of teeth. No man had seen such a rogue about the harbour. Four ships had sailed on the last tide of the previous day, and Williams could only presume that one held the *Fortune*'s cabin boy. It was no matter. He barely knew why he searched

479

so for him. To box him about the ears, call him unreasonable and tell him how pleased he was to have lost their association? Like him or not, he was the only acquitted man whom Williams had good knowledge of. Without him, he felt a trifle lost.

By the toll of the nine bells, Williams joined the crew of a Liverpool slaver as they walked towards the castle, where the tide rose to meet her walls. These men with whom he walked talked freely with him, as if he were some friend, but Williams could not respond. He knew well enough that had they met upon the sea they would have had few words for one another, and that the sight of the *Fortune* would have made their hearts sink.

The gallows had been erected against the sides of the castle's walls, so that the executioner was silhouetted by the morning sun. It was a simple structure: two upright posts, one crossbeam and six nooses that hung like cherry stalks. There were several chaises, their legs resting on carpet, reserved for the great white ladies of the coast. The remainder of the ground was already occupied by traders, fisherman, soldiers, sailors, children, slaves and slavers. Word of the capture of Roberts's men had spread up and down the coast, and many had travelled to see if the indomitable robber had truly fallen.

The prisoners were marched up to the gallows, their white-gloved hands tied behind their backs. Williams had found a spot towards the front of the crowd. Ten yards to his left, he spied the wild hair of Crackers. He was leaning heavily upon his spear. The fiddler watched as his friend Christopher Moody begged a soldier for his cap, lest he should faint from heat and be thought to have died poorly. The remainder of the prisoners sipped at water. Hardy looked about him. Only their quartermaster, squinting against the sun, continued to perform for the spectators.

'Mr Williams,' shouted Sympson at the fiddler. 'Go find my wife down Cheapside. Bounce her once for me.'

Williams nodded, and watched the six men ascend the scaffold. Despite the heat, enough moisture had gathered beneath the scaffold so that there was a small puddle of dark red mud. Black flies danced between the sentenced and their executioners.

'There's Lizzy,' said Sympson, his voice rising in anxiety. 'I thrice wapped that fusty luggs and she comes to see necks snap.'

One of the lieutenants of the *Weymouth* clambered up to the scaffold to check that every man was confined properly by their noose.

'Does any man have last words to speak before God?' asked the ordinary.

Moody shook his head. Hardy straightened his back.

'We are poor rogues,' cried Sympson, and his voice cracked slightly, 'and so we are hanged. There are others,' and here he cast his eyes about him as if he wished to implicate the very stones of the castle, 'who are no less guilty, and yet they escape.' He coughed, as if he meant to say more, but could not find the moisture to produce the words.

'May God have mercy on your souls,' said the lieutenant, and the six men were pushed forward simultaneously. They kicked madly. Several stepped forward from the crowd and pulled on their legs to hasten death. When the bodies hung still, and even the slow spinning of the corpses had ceased, Williams looked closely at the backs arched, the eyes bloodied and inflated with pain, the fierce angle of the necks. He breathed softly. He did not wish to be heard.

According to the regulations of the court, the bodies remained where they hung until they had been covered and uncovered by three tides. Williams had not moved, not when Lizzy had passed him by and wished him a good morning, and not when Nicholas Brattle had seized him by the hand and asked him to come play a song in honour of the dead. He watched the bodies. Finally, when the clouds of flies had become so dense about him that he could barely keep his eyes open, he turned away from the scaffold, toward the gates of the castle.

'William Williams?' asked a man behind him. The fiddler turned to see a member of the Company standing behind him, a bloody back on either side.

'Aye,' he said.

'Captain Heardman of His Majesty's ship the *Weymouth* wishes for your company.'

'Indeed,' huffed Williams. He flapped his arms once, as if he were ready to fly upon the captain's orders. Obediently, he followed the men.

'Be seated,' said Heardman. Williams swung his arms in time to the beat of his feet, and marched towards the chair in the most military of manners. The captain stared at him. The fiddler's hands, which had been crossed before him, became slick with sweat. Beads seemed to gather on his finger-tips. He let his arms hang loose at his side, then refolded them.

'I have three questions for you, Williams,' said Heardman. He pushed a piece of paper across the desk, and then turned it, so that the fiddler might read it. On it were the words, *May God have mercy on your soul.* It was the same scrap that he had signed before Heardman during yesterday's procedures.

'Is this your hand?' asked the captain.

'Aye,' said Williams.

Heardman withdrew the piece of paper, and then replaced it with another. Williams did not permit a flicker of surprise to cross his face when he was presented with a page of his own manuscript.

'Is this your hand?' asked the captain again.

'It is.'

'Would you care to translate it for me.'

'It would be my honour,' said the fiddler, and

allowed himself the slightest of smiles, 'but, forgive me, I cannot. Unless the man who discovered this also discovered the code of Roberts's devising.'

Heardman nodded in understanding, and withdrew the single sheet of paper. He paused, then pushed a small seal-skin wallet across the table.

'Is this your hand?' asked Heardman for the third time.

Williams unfolded the four corners of the folder. He examined the twenty sheets with great care, running his fingers over every page. His own proud hand of flourishes stood against him, the manner in which the loop of his letter P ended, trailing in on itself like a coiled serpent, the hilt of the letter T, which rose from the page as if it could be grasped. He neatened the stack of receipts, tapped their edges on the desk, put them back in their folder, and pushed them back to the captain. He believed he had signed every receipt with his own name in genipa ink and yet here they were before him, all clearly visible.

'You were not merely the fiddler, were you now?' asked Heardman. 'You were most brisk, I would wager.'

Williams finally addressed Heardman's gaze.

'I was forced,' said Williams. 'Roberts forced me.'

'You have been testified against.'

'I am acquitted,' said Williams softly.

'You do not deserve to be tried again.'

'Might I know who stands against me?'

'If I were you,' said the captain, 'I would think of making my peace with the Almighty, for the time for grudges is now gone. This page,' Heardman held up before him the page of the manuscript, 'was gifted to me by Phineas Bunch. Who, with our assistance, has long since sailed.'

It hit Williams squarely. The genipa ink, so easily substituted by Bunch before Williams signed the receipts. The receipts he had issued to the plundered vessels may have found their way into Heardman's hands one by one, but only the first page of the manuscript was present on the governor's desk. Bunch was the only man who might have delivered it to the governor, so Bunch must still hold the remaining pages. An awful hollow invaded the fiddler's torso.

'Mr Williams,' said the judge, 'I do believe that you are the most offensive example that I try before me.'

'Me, sir?' managed Williams.

'Yes, you sir. The rest are simple noddies. I may be captain, but once I was also midshipman. There is no land between order and mutiny, and I have seen things that would turn a man rogue twice times over.' Heardman's voice hummed in low, deliberate octaves. 'It is only the certainty of the end that keeps most men from it. But you, sir, you are the lowest form. A man who plays at fiddle, who keeps a clear hand, and speaks more tongues than Babel. Gainful employment, sir, would not have been hard to find.'

The fiddler listened to his own voice, though he did not think he could remember how to form a word.

'You do not intend to pardon me, sir?' said Williams softly, the idea so new and shiny that it blinded him. His stomach forced its way up to the rear of his throat, and would have leaped from his mouth had he opened it.

'Pardon you? As you were apart in talent in life, so you shall be in death. You are the most despicable of all these wretches, who thinks himself able to skate above the law and is sunk by his own presumption. Do you leave a father behind?'

'Yes, sir,' said Williams.

'Let us hope that he neither writes nor reads as well as his spawn, for would be awful knowledge to find the low end of his son.'

'You do not intend to pardon me, sir?' asked Williams again.

'According to the law, *Infra fluxum et reflexum maris*.'

'Within the floodmarks . . .' echoed Williams in a whispered translation.

'Tide, three times over. Enough,' said Heardman, and rapped on his desk. The door opened and four seamen marched in. Williams was prodded and beaten back to the depths of the castle. He did not feel a blow, no matter how hard it fell.

CHAPTER 47

When Scudamore raised his head from the Bible and looked across to see the fiddler returned to the dungeon, his mouth stretched in amazement. He pushed himself upright and, pulling against the chains, reached his hand out to touch the fiddler's skin. Feeling the awful flow of pity from Scudamore's fingers, Williams wept.

'I do not understand,' said the doctor. 'You have been tried and released.'

Williams related his betrayal and subsequent undoing in halting breaths.

'Tis bad faith,' said Scudamore. 'We shall share.' He offered Williams his Bible.

'I cannot,' replied Williams.

'More are to be hanged tomorrow,' said Scudamore. 'Armstrong was raised on the deck of the *Weymouth* a day before. Tis said he sang psalms, "I will sing unto the Lord as long as I live."' It almost raised a smile from Williams, had he not understood what Armstrong had meant. The years and days that had passed were of little meaning. But every minute, then every second was of importance.

487

He treasured the dirt that he lay in, even the artisan who had forged his bonds.

'Find your peace with me,' continued Scudamore. 'The Ordinary is a kindly man. We have few hours to prepare.'

'I cannot,' said Williams, shaking his head, refusing to meet the eyes of the doctor.

'I am near to readiness,' insisted Scudamore. 'Join me.'

His request met with silence.

After some moments, Williams confessed, 'I do not wish to be tarred.'

''Tis a poor form of immortality, is it not?' asked Scudamore, with a gentle smile.

'Doctor . . .' moaned Williams. 'Everything, everything is lost . . . it is not my role. I sit with pen and ink . . . I have no crimes.' Tears overcame him and he wept in the doctor's arms.

The following morning, 9 April, Phillips, the mate of the *King Solomon*, his shipmate De Vine and Blake were freed from their chains and handed the white gloves of condemned men. The gaoler carried an extra pair and, walking towards where the doctor and the fiddler sat opposite one another, deposited the gloves in Williams's lap.

The air smelled fresh. Williams breathed in and out, ignoring the masses gathered before him. There was a sharp smell of ladies' perfume. Others exchanged looks of sympathy. They were asked for their last words. He did not hear his fellow prisoners, nor had he any words of his own, but kept hold of his silence. Each breath was glorious. Even the rope, tight around his neck, was alive with a thousand fibres. The hand that pushed his shoulder seemed to pause in mercy.

Innocent marched at the head of the column of negroes captured on the *Fortune* and the *Ranger*. He had spent a second week in the slave pens. It was 13 April. His head remained upright, as if this was his army, but the men he had known, his preacher, the members of the crew he had led up river, had been buried. And though there were no men who might pluck him from the rabble, he remained secure in the knowledge that he was intended for different things. Christ had suffered, Christ had surrendered, and Christ had risen again and was not denied His kingdom. But it was his third year of wandering, and he knew that it was an arduous task and it demanded patience. He had returned to his home with strangers. They were not his equals and had fallen around him.

He only waited for a moment. Strung from high palm poles were the tarred and chained bodies of his shipmates. Where the rope had cut into their necks, the tar had gathered thickly. They had been blackened. Even the birds would not touch them now. Their hides had been ruined, and yet preserved. The vast carcass of Hardy. Magnes's beard rigid and cracked. Sympson's arms tucked around his body, as if he were cold.

Innocent was struck across the back by a long

switch. He resumed his walk but did not take his eyes off the last body on this avenue of blackened souls. William Williams hung higher than the others, raised above them, as if he were a single step further from hell than the rest. His cage was encased by droplets of tar long dried. His fingers were curled upwards against his iron encasement, and his mouth, wide open, was black with pitch. It was as if he had not been hung, but dipped alive in boiling tar, drowned and burned, and raised above the hill. Innocent bowed his head in a respectful nod, but could not understand how he had misjudged the man and falsely presumed him a friend of Christ.

He walked with twenty of the Yorubans to the auction, just outside the gates of the castle. Standing high upon the block, surrounded by the traders of many nations, and those dressed in the colours of the Royal Africa Company, Innocent paid no heed to the slaver who was guessing aloud his age. He brought back the Dogon's teeth to reveal his gums, then licked a finger and ran it across the early growth of his beard. 'No more than thirty, gentleman. An oath and a promise before God.'

Innocent did not listen to the vendor of his flesh. From his promontory he could descry the body of the surgeon still swinging from the morning's hanging. Scudamore had been forgotten when men had turned from the execution to the sale. Only Innocent faced him, watching the first of the birds descend to disturb the thick cloud of insects that swarmed about the dead flesh. He seemed at peace, a gentle pendulum through which time might be kept.

CHAPTER 48

Epilogue
England, 1724

L ondon, five miles in width and riven by a shallow and icy Thames, had been captured by a cruel winter. The deepest of its dirt had been frozen, safeguarded for the spring. Smoke from the chimneys obscured the spires of churches, as great clouds of isolated warmth billowed forth from hospitals, public prisons, pesthouses and the palaces of church and state. The three-masted ships, so familiar to Bunch, formed a thick forest beneath London Bridge. He made his way along the riverside, up Bishopsgate and eventually to Moorfields, tripping between hackney coaches, wagons and carts. Remembering the bilge-infested stink of the fo'c'sle with homely affection, Bunch turned his nose against the pervasive stench of the Thames that seemed to hang about the city in the freezing mist. Only the mud, sombre in its blackness, maintained a liquidity. It sucked at his boots.

There was much movement about the streets: carts filled with herrings and oysters, shops advertising the sale of chocolate, traders' barrows, cattle being driven towards Smithfields, and a thousand men and women, either selling or buying, but all moving with a purpose. It reminded Bunch of the deck of the *Fortune*. Apparent chaos, but each with an objective and the knowledge to execute it. Kennels, running down the centre of the streets, were clogged with dirt and ice, and the street pumps were abandoned. A covered sedan chair moved past him down Shoreditch.

Bunch could not grasp the meanings of the signs that hung above the shopfronts, despite his supposed thorough understanding of the English language. As a sailor, he did not wish to rely on a landsman for direction, but soon weariness overcame his pride. He passed an oyster seller, begged a shell from him, and asked him the way to Grub Street. He was informed he had already found it.

'And where would I find a publisher of words?'

'Sneeze and you may find one, drop a coin in mud, and you shall find a dozen swimming for it.' Phineas Bunch merely walked up the first steps that he came across. Though he could not read the board heralding *Robinson, Publisher of Small Histories, Dictionaries, and Temporary Poems*, he recognized the painting of a quill upon the sign.

Mr Robinson's secretary opened the door and proclaimed Mr Robinson too much engaged to spare a moment of his time. At first Bunch laid siege to the doorway but, realizing that the men of London were every bit as stubborn as himself, he removed a page of the manuscript and slid it under the door. Five minutes later, the door was opened, and Phineas Bunch was ushered into the inner sanctum of the offices.

The office was a dreary affair. Bunch had imagined wealth, small children toting bags of gold from publisher to writer. Instead, all was covered in paper. Piles and loose sheets, books and news-sheets, envelopes opened and closed. Robinson sat in between two towers of paper, looking as if he had been imprisoned by his own profession.

The publisher peered down upon the red face, and would have presumed the young man drunk had not the redness continued about the back of his neck and extended to his hands. This sailor was one of the ugliest fellows he had ever set eyes upon.

'And what is your name?' asked Robinson. He sneezed loudly into a cream silk kerchief.

'Phineas Bunch,' said the cabin boy, standing before him.

'A sailor?' Robinson then used the kerchief to mop sweat from his fevered head.

'Aye.'

'And what is it you have beneath your wings, Mr Bunch?'

'A most valuable thing that I shall not part with for less than a hundred pound.'

Mr Robinson guffawed. 'A hundred pounds, sir?

This is a house of print. You are not so far from a bank.'

'I have a journal here, sir,' said Bunch, levelling his features to promote a solemnity he did not possess. 'Kept not by me, but by the hand of a great man, wise. Recording the tales of sea.'

Robinson naturally recoiled at the sight of such concentrated grotesqueness. He shifted his vast bottom in his chair and, leaning forwards, pointed his dripping nose at the sailor and said, 'Then let us have at it.'

Bunch crossed the floor, and eased himself into the narrow space alongside the great leather chair. Undoing the dirty silk ties of the sealskin wallet for the first time since he had grabbed the papers at Corso, he took a page of Williams's manuscript and placed it directly before the publisher.

The publisher looked hard at the script, then smiled a wide and knowing smile and, without looking up, said, 'Were you sent by Beame? Some Saint's Day prank?'

'Prank, sir?' questioned Bunch. 'You have before you the journal of Bartholomew Roberts.'

'Mr Bunch, I may have the fifth book of the gospels before me, but tis encoded. So unless you hold the key, we may use this to blot copy.'

Bunch looked down. 'I can read sir. I shall read it line by line.'

Mr Robinson offered him the page. Bunch studied William Williams's variations of encrypted Spanish. He saw not the language that was known to him, but a mass of letters that seemed to swirl before him.

'Indeed?' asked Robinson, seeing Bunch stare terrified at the page. 'And what does this say?' asked Robinson, pointing to a Newgate news-sheet that he held before him. Across the top were written the words *The most notorious robber*.

'I cannot say,' said Bunch. ''Tis a foreign tongue.'

''Tis the King's English, you bubby,' shouted Robinson. 'Enough, enough, take your scraps and leave me be. What the devil do you take me for?'

Bunch raised his arm to strike the man, but the door to his office opened and his concerned secretary edged into the room. Quickly gathering his papers and tying them with a slip knot, Bunch stormed from the room, leaving a gob of greasy spit upon the secretary's polished shoes. With a gnawing hunger, he trudged through the mud of Grub Street.

Phineas Bunch, showing the nature of a character so obdurate that it had survived calm and storm, battle and betrayal, forced his way into the chambers of five publishers on a single day. He received an identical response from each of the men. They looked upon him once and knew him for a poor sailor. He would counter by crowing that he could read. Their secretaries would soon eject him. It did not take long for Bunch to perceive the problem. He knew already that Williams had played a trick upon him, but he did not see his position as hopeless. What he needed was a fellow brother of the quill with a touch of patience. This man would obviously not be found in the business of publishing. And that was how, on the following afternoon, Phineas Bunch happened to disturb John Meredith.

St Alphage's of Greenwich was not an old church, though the new building stood above seven hundred years of history. It was, however, a beautiful sight, even to a half-starved Bunch as he entered through her gates. He forgot the long day's walk. Above him hung a suspended oval ceiling. It was the largest building Bunch had ever entered, and its simple majesty overpowered him. When he looked upwards he found himself dizzy from the stillness.

Meredith squinted under the lights of the church's candles, and watched the youth approach him. A scarlet-faced lad, with hands to match, and he would have thought it was the cold, had not there been such a completeness in his discolouring. He had the bow-legged, uncomfortable walk of a sailor. The stranger stared at the wooden carvings on the walls.

'From the hand of Grinling Gibbons,' said the vicar, following his eyes.

Bunch started from his reverie. 'Father,' he said, approaching, 'I have need of you.'

'What is it?' replied Meredith, consciously displaying a kindness in his tones.

'We may talk?'

'We may,' agreed Meredith. 'We may also break bread, if you so wish.'

Bunch smiled for the first time that day. 'It would be some honour,' he bowed before the vicar. 'My name is Phineas Bunch.'

In the vestry, Meredith poured them each a glass of wine, and put bread and cold mutton before Bunch. The cabin boy ate, grunting and nodding in response to the vicar's questions, until he had devoured the entire loaf.

'Do you have paper and ink, Father?' asked Bunch.

When Meredith returned, Bunch put down the mutton.

'A man schooled me in our tongue. I can read and write,' said Bunch. 'Talk and I shall transcribe.'

The vicar began to dictate. After he had dictated two sentences he peered at what the young man had written.

''Tis English?' asked Bunch, with a final desperation.

'I fear,' said Father Meredith, 'that it is not. You have been sorely duped in your education.'

Bunch sat under a new cloud of disbelief. He poured himself a second glass of wine.

'What does this script hold?' asked the vicar. 'What tale does it hold?'

Bunch contemplated his answer. To tell the man that it was an account of robberies committed across the oceans would be to jeopardize his assistance. He should intrigue the man, bait him into the role of selfless assistant.

'Tis unsure,' said Bunch, and then leaned across so that they were close enough to smell the wine on one another's breath. 'Was a holy man who taught me. Said they were the tongues of prophets past . . . scriptures, was what he said. I believe they are scriptures.'

'Where did you find this man?'

'Drifting,' said Bunch, 'upon the Sargasso Sea.'

'In God's name?' asked the vicar.

'Upon God and his blessed son,' swore Bunch.

Meredith sat for a moment. 'There is but one way in which you may unravel these documents that you hold,' said the Reverend, and ran his fingers over the thousand pages of manuscript.

'What is it?' asked Bunch eagerly, and sipped the wine. 'Tell me how it can be done.'

'We shall form a dictionary of sorts. I shall start by showing the truth of the language. Teach you a command of English. When you know this, you shall be able to translate pages yourself.'

'But not all,' said Bunch, 'not all.' He flipped to the beginning of the manuscript, 'This is of no tongue to either.'

The vicar nodded wearily. 'And the author of the tract?'

'A dead man. After he teach me, he expires. His fingers black with poison.'

'Then so dies his tongue,' explained the vicar. 'But of what is written in your own hand, we shall save. It would be of use to you?'

'Indeed it would.'

'Then be of cheer. It shall be done,' said Father Meredith, believing the translation of the mysterious text might be of use to both of them. The sailor was so beaten by life, and yet unbowed, unconscious of his own plainness, that the priest wagered the holy man had spotted some hidden worth in the youth.

'We shall start come the morning,' said Meredith. 'You may rest here, if it pleases you.'

'You are a gentle soul,' breathed Bunch. 'And if you might spare a coin for a thirsty sailor, would be gentler still.'

When Bunch had first walked into his church, Meredith had presumed it was a poor sailor come begging for a drink, and now the vicar revealed the small coins that he carried. Bunch thanked him kindly, then motioned to wrap the manuscript up within its sealskin wallet.

'There is no need for that,' said the vicar. ''Tis safer in the House of God than upon the streets of London. You may return whenever you wish. It shall come to no harm.'

'A priest's word?' smiled Bunch, and they shook hands. Father John Meredith closed the door of the church behind him.

Bunch sat alone in the Frig and Firkin. He was surrounded by sailors, colliers and porters. First, he was examined, then he was ignored. The masts of a thousand ships could be seen from her rooms on the second floor. But Bunch did not need a place to stay. He was welcome within a priest's house, and would live there free until they had translated enough of his own writings so that a portion might be sold and his reputation made. The coinage the priest had given him might be spent upon a second meal and rum. Hunched over his stew, shovelling the glutinous concoction into his mouth off the dull edge of his knife, Bunch talked to no man.

Only after his glass had been refilled by the landlord for the seventh time did Phineas Bunch give up his bowl. Laying his head upon the table, he fell into the deepest sleep of his short life. He did not hear the slap of coin upon the table, did not see the landlord's finger point in his direction, nor even feel the rough hands as four members of the press lifted him on their shoulders. Those who watched from the shadows spied the unconscious body of the sailor being rowed under a half moon, unwilling conscript for His Majesty's Navy, bound at dawn for eastern seas.

GLOSSARY

Bluecoat	A priest or reverend
Bloody flux	Dysentery
Box one's Jesuit	A sea term for masturbation. A crime, it was said, much practised by the reverend fathers of that society
Bube	Any venereal disease
Caboceer	Originally, the headman of a Guinea Coast village. Soon loosely applied to any African with whom trade for slaves was effected
Callet	A whore
Calomel	A mercurous chloride often used as a cathartic
Careen	The process of bringing a ship over on to one side for caulking, cleaning or general repair
Caulk	To seal the seams of a ship by driving in oakum and then covering it with melted pitch
Channels	A broad, thick plank that extends from the ship's sides, extending the base for the shrouds and therefore increasing the support for the mast
Chanty	A sailor's song usually sung during strenuous work to coordinate the

	efforts of a crew. Also sung to pass the time. Almost always in the technique of call and response
Chit	A baby, or small child
Crimp	A man who procures sailors. Also, as a verb, the act of being pressed
Cursitor	A struggling solicitor
Daddles	The hands
Ducks	A strong linen used for small sails and especially men's trousers
Fizzgig	A small harpoon
Gleet	Gonorrhea. Or the discharge from a penis infected by the disease
Guineaman	Ship bound to or from Guinea Coast. Synonymous with slaver
Gut foundered	Exceedingly hungry
Havy cavy	Wavering or doubtful
Hedge whore	An itinerant whore, a beggarly prostitute
Holy stones	A bible-sized piece of sandstone used to scour the deck of a ship
Huff	A bully
Kedge	A small anchor used in mooring
Ken cracker	A house breaker
Lanyard	A short piece of rope used to secure anything that might be in need of securing
Larboard	As opposed to starboard. Later changed to port to avoid confusion
Leeward	Downwind
Linstock	A staff with one end forked, used to fire a cannon

503

Lubber hole	The hole in the ship's top by the mast. The easiest way to climb or descend and generally spurned by seasoned sailors
Marlinespike	An iron spike used in the process of splicing rope
Moidore	A piece of gold, valued at twenty-seven shillings
Nocky boy	A simple fellow
Noddy	A simpleton or fool
Oakum	Strands and sections of old rope that will be tarred for use in caulking
Pettiauger	Originally two canoes attached side by side. Soon came to mean any flat-bottomed boat, open in the middle, propelled by either oars or sail
Pinnace	A ship's boat, especially one used as a tender. Generally ranges from eight oars and down
Press (the)	A group of men, commanded by an officer, who impress men for service
Quadrant	The instrument used to measure the altitude of the sun or other celestial bodies to calculate the latitude of a place or ship
Sennight	A shortening of 'seven nights'. One week
Sharper	A thief
Shrouds	Part of a ship's standing rigging, large ropes stretching from the

	mastheads to either side of the ship, giving the ship enough lateral support to carry sail
Sloop	A small, one-masted vessel
Sounding line	The lead line and lead. By looking at marks on a lead line the leadsman could calculate the depth at which the ship sailed
Sporting blubber	Said of a large coarse woman, who exposes her bosom
Straw booters	In the vicinity of law courts, a man would place a straw in his boot to signal that he was available for perjury, at a price
Teague	An Irishman
Toredo worm	A salt-water worn, extremely destructive to a ship's hull. Common in warmer waters
Under bare poles	With no sails set
Vardy	A verdict or opinion
Waist	The area of the ship between fo'c'sle and quarterdeck
Warp	To move a ship by dropping the kedge anchor and pulling on the hawser
Weather Deck	The upper deck exposed to the elements
Yard	A long wooden spar
Yardarm	Either end of a yard

AUTHOR'S NOTE

Bartholomew Roberts (born 1682, died 1722) was the most successful captain in the history of piracy, capturing over four hundred ships in less than four years. *The Requiem Shark*, for obvious reasons, does not attempt to catalogue each incident. While many of the characters, including Roberts, Williams and Scudamore, sailed on the *Fortune*, there is no record of a surviving manuscript of their voyage. Similar documents, such as Lionel Wafer's account of Henry Morgan's exploits, do exist. An account of the trial of the Fortunes can be found at the Public Record Office at Kew, including the remark by a naval surgeon that a certain William Williams was 'speechless at execution'.